I0819934

And Then...

THE GREAT BIG BOOK OF AWESOME ADVENTURE TALES

vol. 2

Edited by Ruth Wykes & Kylie Fox

First published in paperback in Australia in 2018
Published as an eBook in 2017
by Clan Destine Press
PO Box 121 Bittern
Victoria 3918 Australia

National Library of Australia Cataloguing-in-Publication entry

Title: *And Then... the Great Big Book of Awesome Adventure Tales Vol 2*

Editors: Ruth Wykes & Kylie Fox

Authors: Various

ISBNs (paperback) 978-0-9945991-2-4
(hardcover) 978-0-9954394-8-1
(eBook) 978-0-9954394-3-6

Cover Art & Design: Sarah Pain
Internal Illustrations: Vicky Pratt & Ron Gallagher

Design & Typesetting: Clan Destine Press

www.clandestinepress.com.au

What lies within...

JANEEN WEBB

And Then... the Introduction

Once upon a time, in a land Down Under, from the depths of the Clan cave, Clan Destine Press issued a challenge to Australian and Kiwi authors to write cliff-hanging, Australian-flavoured, action-packed adventure stories for two protagonists; stories of the *What If, What Now, And Then...* kind.

This was a catnip call, an irresistible lure, a kid-in-a-candy-store kind of a challenge: what writer *wouldn't* want to take a crack at that?

To make it that little bit more intriguing, the editors decreed the stories could be contemporary, historical, realistic, far-out, spec-fic, horror, SF, or urban fantasy; and, in a spirit of mischief, that at least one of the two protagonists must be human. You'd think that would cover all bases.

But writers are a contrary bunch: they pushed these very broad boundaries even further. The result is not one, but two volumes of kick-arse, action-packed stories: *And Then... The Great Big Book of Adventure Tales*.

This is Volume 2: a fascinating collection of genre-bending adventure stories garnered from a mix of sf, fantasy and crime writers, happily encroaching upon each other's territories, and then some.

Clan Destine's stricture about the relative humanity of the characters raises the obvious question: what *does* it mean to be human? It is a question that has fired the imaginations of several contributors. The wonderful partnership of Kerry Greenwood and David Greagg gives us an adventure starring a shape-changing Fishing Cat who works to solve the mystery of an isolated planet, in partnership with the man she adores – a spacefarer from the magical Scottish isle of Barra. Sarah Evans explores post-human attachment to mortal values in *Plumbing the Depths*, where a recently-turned reluctant vampire teams up with a newly-dead cop-now-angel to hunt lost souls in purgatory. Maria Lewis twists the shape-changing trope with a disturbingly-dark picture of warped humanity in *Bushwalker Butchers*, where a deranged couple exploit the myth of the Yowie for their own amusement; and Mary Borsellino extends the destructive theme of psychopathic killers even further in *The Australian Gang*.

It's a short step from monstrously-unhinged humanity to actual terrifying fire-breathing monsters, and there's no shortage of those in this anthology. Amanda Pillar's *It* offers a frightening iron-ore monster unwittingly released by over-enthusiastic mining on a remote planet; and, similarly, in *The Demon's Cave*, Keith McArdle tells of a demonic creature roused by gold mining during the 1881 Queensland gold rush.

The tales range far and wide in time and place, with several set in interesting historical periods. In Alison Goodman's charming Regency tale, *A High Possibility of Peril*, aristocratic twin sisters ride to the rescue of another lady in distress. Kelly Gardiner introduces a pair of lawless women of the 1850's in *Boots and the Bushranger*, where Jessica Guilfoyle robs a stagecoach with her trusty stablehand Marguerite. Michael Pryor's *Cross Purposes* takes us into a the remote reaches of Australia just after WWI, where Beersheba veteran Roland Hooke, gets embroiled with the adventurous Miss Danvers as they head into conflict with the hideous Grey People; and James Hopwood sets *The Lost Loot of Lima* in 1954, where renegade WWII Nazis pursue twin archaeologists on the trail of priceless religious treasures lost back in 1821.

Contemporary stories, with a twist, get a look in too. Jack Dann and Steven Paulsen team up to give us the gleefully irreverent *Harold the Hero and the Talking Sword*, a swashbuckling, time-travelling tale in which the demon who inhabits a sword kidnaps a hapless Melbourne video-gamer and dumps him into the heroic world of *The Odyssey* for the fight of his life. Andrew Nette's *Save A Last Kiss for Satan* depicts a modern girl searching for her supposedly dead grandfather, in partnership with Mordecai, a self-styled demon slayer weirdly stuck in his own personal 1960s time warp; while in tropical Cairns, Fin Ross gives us *Genemesis*, in which anti-animal cruelty campaigner Taylor Sanna bonds with hunky hero Farley Cavanagh on a hair-raising outback adventure. We then move forward to a dystopic, grid-locked near future in Cam Ashley's Dogs *Leave Home to Die*, where what's left of a violent, drug-riddled society is slowly drowning in its own filth; and Lindy Cameron's *Feedback* takes us even further forward into the drowned world of far-future Melbourne, where gender-crunching operatives struggle in degraded cyberspace to solve a terrible crime against the last remnants of male humanity.

Some of these visions are dark indeed, but *And Then...* remains a wondrous strange collection of exotic and exciting tales that encompass a huge sweep of possibilities, past, present and future. Enjoy!

Alison Goodman

A High Possibility of Peril

London, 29th March 1812

I closed my silk parasol and gripped the silver handle like a club. The sunlit paths of Hyde Park thronged with people of all rank – Sunday was the most popular day for promenade – and I could no longer see the progress of the detestable Mr. Garrett. Damn it, he was going to get away, and we would lose the diamond forever.

Using one of the few advantages of my absurd height, I searched the shifting sea of feathered bonnets and tall beaver hats for my twin sister's new straw chapeau. I finally found her, five ranks of strolling people ahead. She veered suddenly, taking the path to the Serpentine. I lost her for a moment behind a tall gentleman, and then she reappeared, looking over her shoulder with urgency. Her gaze found mine, brow furrowed beneath her stylishly angled brim. She pointed to the path then tapped her forefinger beneath her eye.

He has seen us.

I twirled my kid-gloved finger. *I'll go around.* I flattened my palm. *Do not engage him.*

I was sure the man had a pistol. No jewel was worth a lead ball in one's body. Not even Countess Devonport's famous pendant.

A nod from Freddie and she was gone from view.

It was all very well for me to say I would go around, but forcing a path through the crowd was no easy matter. Murmuring a string of *pardons*, I turned on my heel and weaved around Mrs Connell and her three willowy daughters then sidestepped the very sweet Lady Fellowes and her chattering companion. The Wainrights slowed my progress: their three little boys were walking hand-in-hand and blocked my way as effectively as a chain fence.

'Lady Augusta, how marvellous!' a voice shrieked behind me. 'Does Lady Frederica accompany you? She looked so peaky last time we met. I hope she is well.'

Damn. I turned to receive Caroline Pothwick's bow. Abominable woman.

'My sister is very well, thank you.' I blinked at the puce satin and blue lace that served as Caroline's gown. Freddie would have seizured at the sight of it. 'She is walking ahead. I am on my way to her, if you will excuse me.'

Caroline's little ferret mouth pursed at my brush off. 'Do you go to Lady Melbourne's rout tonight?'

'We do,' I said gaily and, seeing a way past the children, ruthlessly extended my far longer stride and left her behind in three paces. Without a doubt, I would pay for that; probably a *cut direct* from her and her cronies at the rout. No loss to me, but Freddie would be aggrieved. She had to work with Caroline in her many charities.

I reached the path that connected to the one on which my sister pursued Mr Garrett and quickened my pace into an almost unladylike trot. The gravel crunched beneath my half-boots, and the breeze snatched at the straw brim of my bonnet. Far fewer people ahead. Nevertheless, I caught a disapproving glance from a sallow-faced matron heading towards the main path. Was it my speed or my lack of companion? Probably both, although it was plain to the meanest intelligence that I was well beyond the age that required constant escort.

I scanned the crest of the hill and found the two figures I sought: Mr Garrett walking swiftly ahead of my sister, his right hand ominously thrust into the pocket of his olive greatcoat. The gun. He looked over his shoulder at Freddie then bolted across the grass towards a small copse of elegant birches that stood between them and me.

I drew up my hem and broke into a run, ignoring the small gasp of appreciation from an older gentleman in a frazzled grey wig. The small slope aided my pace. I gripped my parasol more tightly as I entered the shady cover of the copse.

He and my sister stood facing one another. Freddie had not approached him, thank goodness.

'Mr Garrett!' I called.

He turned, a smile on his face. The man definitely had a handsome countenance: strong jaw, well-made nose and a broad brow framed by thick chestnut hair. The reason, no doubt, for his success with the ladies of the beau monde. Yet his grey eyes held the truth of his nature; cold and wary. His hand was still in his pocket.

'Lady Augusta,' he said pleasantly. He gave a small bow. 'What a joy to meet you and your sister again.'

'I can hardly say the same, sir.' I stopped a mere yard from him. We stood at the same five foot nine inches, but he had the weight and reach advantage.

'Gus dear, do step back,' Freddie said, her gloved hands clasped into entreaty.

'You should take your sister's advice.'

I braced my feet more firmly into the cropped grass. 'Mr Garrett, would you be so kind as to pass Countess Devonport's diamond to me?'

'Why would I do such a thing?' His deep voice was still pleasant. 'The Countess gave it to me as a gift.' His smile shifted into a leer. 'For services rendered; she was quite satisfied with the exchange last night. Why, she was so satisfied she could barely move from the bed.'

A blush heated my cheeks. Freddie turned her face; she was far more delicate about such matters.

'Sir,' I said briskly, 'we both know that Countess Devonport did not give you the diamond. You stole it from her jewel box believing she would not risk exposing her indiscretion by attempting to retrieve it. As you can see, you are mistaken.'

He withdrew the pistol from his greatcoat pocket and aimed it at me. A 16-inch bore, by Reeves in Henrietta Street, if I were not mistaken.

Freddie gasped.

'Lady Augusta, I think you should step aside and allow me to go about my business.'

I lunged, the point of my parasol driving deep into his nether areas. For an instant, I saw the shocked outrage on his face and then he crumpled to his knees. The gun dropped next to my feet. I picked it up and tapped him sharply across the temple; just enough to knock the blackguard free of his senses. At least I hoped it was enough. Mr Kelly – our gamekeeper – had given me quite thorough instructions upon the matter. Even so, there was always margin for error.

He toppled over, landing neatly on the grass.

'Gus!' Freddie yelped.

'He will be fine,' I said, sending the hope upwards as a small prayer.

'But he could have shot you!'

'It was not loaded, my dear.' If there was one thing I knew, it was whether a pistol was loaded or not: the advantage of having an older hunting-mad brother who had taken me on shoots. 'Here, hold this.' I handed the gun to Freddie, then bent and quickly searched the stunned Mr Garret's pockets.

'Hurry, darling,' she urged, holding the pistol as if it were a dead rat. 'I believe we are garnering some attention.'

I thrust my hand into his jacket pocket and found a small hard shape wrapped in leather.

'I say, is everything all right down there?' A concerned gentleman called, hurrying down the slope. From the corner of my eye, I saw Freddie slide the gun into her reticule.

Mr. Garrett stirred as I pulled the small package free. His eyelids fluttered open, their expression dazed.

'You should leave London,' I whispered, 'or I will expose you for the thief and libertine that you are.'

I saw the sense of my words lock into his eyes.

The kind gentleman turned out to be Bertie Heldon. He drew up and bowed. 'Lady Augusta, Lady Frederica. Are you all right?'

'Ah, Lord Heldon, we are quite well, thank you.' I dipped into a curtsy, the diamond hidden in my gloved fist. 'I believe this gentleman, however, has fainted from the heat.'

I took Freddie's arm and we retreated as Bertie bent to Mr Garrett's aid.

London, 18th April 1812

I was about to dip a wedge of seed cake into my breakfast tea, when Freddie looked up from the letter that had come in the morning mail. I swung the cake up to my mouth instead. My sister still did not approve of dipping, even after I had pointed out that the practice came from the ancient Greeks.

'I believe we have a new commission,' she said.

'Mmf,' I replied around the dry bite.

A new adventure; thank heavens. It had been three weeks since our confrontation with Mr Garret, far too long for Freddie to be unemployed. She had taken to wearing her grey gowns again and attending service twice a day. April, with all its sad associations, was always a difficult month for my dear girl. The painful loss of George, her betrothed, five years past was like a circling wolf, always ready to spring upon her when she was too idle.

She passed me the single page and turned back to her tea and toast.

The letter was written on good paper and fastened with a wax seal, not a wafer. The hand was small and feminine with no embellishments.

> Dear Lady Frederica,
> I have come to the knowledge – through a mutual acquaintance – that you and your sister, on occasion, take up arms against a sea of troubles.

I raised my eyes. 'Really? A Shakespeare quote?'

Freddie lifted one dove grey silk shoulder. 'Better than a Byron quote.'

I did not take the bait. We would never agree upon the merits of our new literary star, Lord Byron. I thought his *Childe Harold's Pilgrimage* was a work of genius but Freddie could not look past the rather public affair he was conducting with Lady Caroline Lamb. Some days I wondered how we could have come out of the same womb, let alone only 15 minutes apart with Freddie in the lead.

I returned to the letter:

> I have recently encountered my own sea of troubles and I would be most obliged if you would consider helping me. If you are willing, I would be eager to call upon you to discuss the matter.
>
> Yours etc.,
> Mrs Honoria Dellaquist.

I stared out of the morning room window, trying to place Honoria Dellaquist. I could feel Freddie watching me, ready to supply the girl's line. It was Freddie's speciality, but on occasion I liked to surprise her with my own knowledge.

The street outside was already abuzz. A bun man called his wares, stopping his raucous song as one of the undercooks from next door ran out to meet him. Opposite, the Thorgood's maid swept their front steps, and an oysterman hauled a small barrel from his cart and hoisted it on to his meaty shoulder. Lord Aldon's curricle passed with his matched pair of bays – such sweet steppers – and a lady in a truly hideous blue bonnet trimmed with squirrel, traipsed the footpath towards Picadilly.

None of them an aid to my memory. I had to admit defeat. 'Honoria Dellaquist?'

'Recently married George Dellaquist,' Freddie said promptly. 'She was Honoria Callow, the third of the Callow girls. All of them accredited beauties and with over 20,000 pounds each.'

My sister was better than a *Debretts Guide to the Peerage*.

'If you recall, we met Honoria at Lady Damison's ball last year,' Freddie added. 'She wore that pretty primrose velvet *a la' Grecian* with the oblong diamond clasp at the waist.'

My sister also had the ability to remember other women's toilettes in complete detail. Gentlemen's attire too, for that matter, even down to the jewels. An entirely useless accomplishment, she admitted, but nevertheless astounding.

Now I remembered Honoria Callow. She had the kind of delicate blonde looks that I had always admired and wished I possessed. It had taken me all of my twenty-eight years to come to terms with my own square jaw, rangy body and uninteresting brown hair. Freddie, in contrast, stood at a more ladylike five-foot-three, had a delightfully pointed chin and possessed the family auburn locks that were currently confined in one of my new double-lace caps that she had borrowed. It looked much better on her than me. I made a mental note to make her a gift of it, along with the other two I had clearly purchased in a fit of madness.

'What do you say?' Freddie asked.

'There is not much information,' I looked at the page again. In fact there was no information. 'But we can at least see the girl.'

Weatherley, in the process of pouring more tea into my cup, made a throaty sound of disapproval. He had been our butler for twenty years, joining the household well before our father died and James, our brother, became the 11th Earl of Ratton. Dear Weatherley. He considered himself the guardian of our well-being, which was all very well except he still saw us as eighteen-year-old girls in our first season rather than the spinsters of twenty-eight that we had become.

'Is something wrong, Weatherley?' I asked. I could not help myself; his views on our little adventures were an endless source of amusement.

I caught Freddie's frown. Well I, at least, found them amusing.

'Now that you mention it, Lady Augusta,' he said, 'I'd like to remind you that you were forced into violence during your last interference.'

That was what he called our little commissions: *interferences.* I suppose it could be argued that we did interfere, but only at the request of women who had placed themselves into some kind of difficulty. I suppose it could also be argued that our last venture had become a little too tense and public.

'It was only one small jab,' I protested. 'Garrett went down like a house of cards.'

'What if he had not, my lady?' Weatherly asked severely, 'What if you had been mistaken about the pistol?'

'I am never mistaken about pistols.' It was not a modest declaration, but it was true.

'So, it is agreed,' Freddie intervened. 'I shall write to Mrs Dellaquist and invite her to call upon us.'

I glanced defiantly at Weatherly. 'Absolutely. Maybe we will be required to do some more jabbing.'

Weatherly sighed.

London, 20th April 1812

Honoria Dellaquist sat up straight in our armchair with her green kid-gloved hands clasped tightly in her lap and a bruised look in her large blue eyes.

'It is my sister,' she said, her voice so soft and gentle that I felt compelled to take a step closer to hear her words. 'I believe she is being held prisoner by her husband.'

Freddie shot me a glance. *Husband.* It was our policy to never take a commission that involved a husband and wife.

'Mrs Dellaquist, I am afraid it is her husband's right by law to do so, if that is what he wishes,' Freddie said.

'But it is not his right to murder her, is it?' Honoria said with some asperity. She looked from Freddie to me, her pretty child's mouth compressing into a straight line. The show of spirit suited her, bringing some harder edges to an excess of softness in both face and fashion. Her peach silk pelisse was trimmed with a cluster of green chiffon roses along the collar and her fashionable chip hat was adorned with more billows of sheer olive silk and a sweeping cascade of yellow and brown ostrich feathers. I could see Freddie's critical appreciation. She, herself, was in a new morning gown of apple green and pink striped silk, and she had chivvied me to wear my teal round gown. Apparently it brought out the blue in my eyes.

'As far as I know, British law does not yet condone the murder of wives,' I said dryly. 'What makes you think your sister's husband wishes to murder her?'

'It seems poor dear Amelia is barren,' Honoria said. 'She and Sir Reginald Thorne have been married for five years, and there has been no issue. No sign of any issue. Sir Reginald is desperate to have an heir. I believe he wants to–' She dabbed at her mouth with a silk and lace square.

'Have done with Amelia and move on?' I supplied. I was not overstating the danger to Amelia's wellbeing. The way of the law meant that divorce was both a lengthy, expensive business that was mainly reserved for men, required a rare Act of Parliament and would ultimately socially ruin both parties. Only the most desperate and the most wealthy could consider it. The unfortunate demise of a spouse, through accident or illness, was a far more socially safe and economical solution.

She nodded. 'The last letter I received from Amelia said as much. She fears for her life.' She rummaged in her reticule and pulled out a crumpled and messily crossed letter, handing it to me. 'Read it. You will see.'

It was indeed a desperate missive, recounting acts of cruelty: a beloved little dog shot dead, friends turned away, "medications" prescribed by a dubious physician, and a bald statement of imprisonment. I already hated the man.

'How did she get the letter to you?' I asked, passing it to Freddie.

Honoria locked her fingers together into a tight clasp. 'A sympathetic maid carried it to town and posted it.'

Freddie made a soft sound of horror as she read the page. Even so, she sent a fleeting glance in my direction; she was not keen on the commission. 'In what way do you think we could help?' she asked Honoria.

'I am hoping you could extract Amelia. Sir Reginald will not let my husband or I or any of our relations into the house. We plan to send Amelia to my husband's people in Ireland.'

I crossed my arms over my pleated bodice, thinking through the plethora of problems that we could face: access, extraction, escape, possible pursuit. All extremely difficult, and with a high possibility of peril. Just what the doctor ordered.

I lifted my brows at Freddie: *can we really refuse?*

She frowned: *it is too dangerous and quite illegal.*

I tilted my head: *true, but could we live with ourselves if Amelia ends up dead?*

She ducked her head: *no, of course not. It would be too awful.*

I compressed my lips: *so we are agreed?*

Freddie sniffed: *I suppose so*.

'Mrs Dellaquist, we would be happy to help you and Amelia,' I said.

The Road to Bath, 21st April 1812

We were travelling light, which for my sister meant four trunks of clothes, her bed linen and an emergency hamper from Fortnum's. I was making do with one trunk and a brace of loaded pistols.

'Really, Gus, do we have to have guns in the carriage?' Freddie asked from the seat opposite. Strangely, she preferred to travel with her back to the driver. I, on the other hand, became quite nauseous if I did not face the way we were moving. 'It is the middle of the day,' she added. 'I hardly think a highwayman is going to assault us in broad daylight.'

I patted the pistols in the holster attached to the carriage wall. 'If you recall, the Brownwells were stopped near here only a month ago by a gang of desperadoes. They lost all their jewels and their driver was shot. The man lost his arm.'

Freddie peered out of the window as if expecting to see a highwayman pop up beside the carriage. She was wearing a new, rather extreme poke bonnet, its edges projecting so far past her face that she had no peripheral vision, so the exercise required her to turn in her seat. 'I thought that happened on the Brighton road.'

'No,' I said cheerfully. 'It was this road.'

'But the Brownwells were stopped at night, were they not?'

I had to concede the point.

Satisfied, she settled back against the velvet cushions, smoothing the olive silk skirt of her travelling gown. 'Have you thought of a way for us to see Amelia yet?'

The carriage lurched over a rut, rocking us both to the left. 'I can only think of a broken wheel, which is not without foundation on this road. We can arrive at the doorstep and claim shelter whilst our carriage is being fixed at the closest village.'

Freddie wrinkled her nose.

'Have you a better idea?' I asked tartly.

'No, but you must admit it is a weak excuse.'

'It is better than nothing, which is your current contribution.'

'Aren't we snippy,' Freddie said under her breath.

I refrained from another comment and looked out of the window. I was, indeed, feeling snippy, mainly because Freddie was right. It was a weak excuse and I had a feeling Sir Reginald was going to be a nasty obstacle.

We continued in silence for half an hour or so, the moment of disunity mellowing into our usual companionable quiet. The rocking of the carriage soon had Freddie's chin resting upon her high-buttoned lavender spencer, her mouth open and emitting the occasional soft snore. She had already moved away from the grey crapes and deep purples of her extended mourning into the lighter colours of her sorrow. The diversion was working.

I let myself wander into the realms of what could have been; an alternative story where George had not gone on that damned expedition to Africa, not drunk tainted water, not died so far away. A story where he had stayed home, married my sister, and set up house in Berkeley Square, hosting dinner parties, promenading, and making morning calls. Would they have had a family? I smiled at the idea of being an aunt. Two children perhaps: a boy for duty and a girl for company. No more than that; I would not want to risk my sister, even in a fantasy. We would all go to the Exeter 'Change and see the animals and Bullocks museum for the Egyptian treasures.

Opposite, Freddie gave a low sob in her sleep. Most likely a bad dream about George – they were still quite regular. She had loved him fervently and still did after so many years. I had not yet experienced such a deep attachment to a man, and I felt as if I stood on the other side of a pane of glass, unable to really understand her pain. It was one of the few things we could not share.

It worried me, sometimes, that I had never felt a true attachment. Perhaps I was incapable of it. Freddie, however, said it was only because I had never met a man who could match my wit or adventurous spirit. That was quite true; all the men of our acquaintance were as dull as Fordyce's sermons, and had all the adventurous spirit of bread and butter pudding.

Freddie awoke with a jerk as we bounced over another rut and surreptitiously wiped the side of her mouth with the tip of her gloved finger.

'Where are we?' She sat forward and blinked, then shifted in her seat to focus past her bonnet upon the woodland we were passing, thick with hazel and beeches.

'We have just gone through Hayes. I believe we are less than half an hour from Sir Reginald's estate.'

'My apologies for falling asleep.'

'It is no wonder. Devilish hot in here.'

The rather dull Spring day had brightened into sunshine and the air in the carriage had warmed into a yawn-inducing stuffiness. I had already cast off the mohair carriage rug that had taken the edge off the crisp morning, and sincerely wished I could unbutton my velvet pelisse. I unlatched the window and let it down, closing my eyes as the cool rush of air, perfumed by verdant greenery, brought a moment of relief.

'Gus, look at all the dust you are letting in!' my sister scolded.

The carriage pace suddenly slowed and I heard a shout outside. I opened my eyes.

The entire road billowed with dust; too much for just our carriage. I poked my head out of the window just as we came to a shuddering standstill, the horses shrilling their distress as they were abruptly pulled up.

A man's voice yelled, 'Put the gun down or I'll blow yer head off!'

Two horsemen: one of them with a blunderbuss trained on our driver and footman, the other urging his horse alongside our cabin. I pulled back inside and grabbed one of the pistols from the holster, covering it with the corner of the carriage rug. More reflex than well-formed plan.

Freddie gasped. 'Gus, no!'

'Be quiet, dear. Do not make a move.'

I wrapped my hand around the butt of the pistol, the quick beat of my heart pulsing to the end of my fingertips. A man with a blue kerchief tied across the bottom of his face drew alongside the open window, his horse blowing irritably at the awkward distance. Brown, intelligent eyes considered us. For a second I thought I saw recognition flash through them.

The fool had not raised his gun.

'Ladies, your valuables, please.' A pleasant baritone, polite and without any local accent.

I rotated the pistol's cock from half to full and hooked my finger around the trigger.

'We have no valuables that could possibly interest you, sir,' I said. 'You should leave now before you come to harm.'

The brown eyes crinkled into surprised amusement.

'Harm?'

I flicked off the rug and raised the pistol, no more than ten inches from his forehead.

'Ah, I see.' His eyes fixed upon the barrel. 'You have a steady hand, my lady.'

'I do, and a steady nerve. Call your companion from my driver and let us continue on our way.'

An eyebrow lifted. 'I do not believe you will fire that gun, my lady, so let us move past this show of bravado.'

At that moment, a blunderbuss shot exploded outside, near the front of the carriage. The cabin lurched, throwing me backwards, my finger tightening on the trigger in reflex. The discharge boomed in my ears, the recoil slamming the gun's butt into my chest and punching all the air from my lungs. The man at the window jerked and twisted, toppling from his horse. The animal screamed and reared, its front hooves scraping the side of the carriage. Shouts – our driver and footman – and another shot.

I gulped for air, the cabin hazing into grey for a moment. All I could smell was the acrid stink of spent gunpowder.

'Gussie, are you hurt?'

I felt my sister's gloved hands around my face. I managed to nod and take a full breath, the blessed air easing the burn in my chest.

'Winded,' I managed. I rubbed my chest. The bruised flesh ached, but there was no other damage as far as I could tell.

Samuel, our footman, wrenched open the door, eyes wide. 'My ladies, are you safe?'

Freddie sank back into her seat. 'We are whole.'

'The blackguard fired upon us,' Samuel said, running his hand through his dark hair. 'John Driver tried to hold the horses, but one reared in the traps and the man bolted. I shot after him, but it missed. He is gone.' He looked down at the ground, mouth twisting into a grimace. 'I see you found your mark, though, my lady. Is he dead?'

Oh no, had I killed the man? I sat up. 'If he is, it was not intentional.' I slid across the seat and held out my hand. 'Quick, let me see.'

I climbed down the carriage step, leaning upon Samuel's strong arm a little more than usual. Dust still hung in the air, the motes swirling in the sunlight. Trampled hazel bushes showed the path of the fallen highwayman's horse into the woodland. The man, himself, lay facing us on his side upon the dusty road, blood in an oozing wash across his forehead, matting his dark brown hair and dripping into the dirt. The neckerchief had dislodged, showing more of his face. Tanned skin now overlaid with a sickly pallor, and a nose that could only be called Roman.

'Is he dead?' Freddie whispered beside me. Samuel had helped her down and she stood clutching the side of the carriage.

I took a careful step towards the body. And another. Ah, the chest moved. I felt a giddy moment of relief.

'He is still breathing.'

As far as I could see, the ball had only grazed his forehead. A nasty gash ran from his eyebrow to ear and still streamed with blood, but there was no hole in his head so the ball had not entered his brain.

Freddie clutched my arm. 'Gus, I know that man.'

'What?'

Her face was intent; searching that phenomenal memory. 'Heaven forfend, it is Lord Evan Belford.'

I was finding it hard to look away from the gory wound I had inflicted; if the ball had been half an inch inward, he would have been very dead, indeed. I forced myself to look beyond the blood at his profile. Now that Freddie had mentioned it, he did look familiar. Yet it did not make sense. 'It can't be Lord Evan. He was transported to New South Wales ten years ago.'

It had been a huge scandal at the time. Lord Evan, the second son of the Marquess of Deele, had been challenged to a duel and killed his man. In such cases, the survivor would usually have been smuggled to the Continent – at the time we were still in that short-lived truce with France – but he had been apprehended and tried.

If I recalled correctly, he had maintained he purposely shot wide. His opponent, however, had died at the scene, and the eyewitness accounts claimed Lord Evan had shot true and with fatal intent, sealing his guilt. He was duly transported to the new penal colony to serve out his life. The family had disowned him, of course, but they had never fully recovered.

'Look at his ring, Gus.'

Grimly I turned my attention to his hand, sprawled in the dirt. One long finger sported a heavy gold ring set with a large ruby.

'That is Lord Evan's signet,' Freddie said. 'I remember remarking upon it when we danced at the Nash's rout in our first season. Do you remember, I wore the pale green muslin from Paris and you wore that rather handsome cream silk with the bugle beads.'

I shook my head; I could not even remember two months past in any detail. 'This man could have stolen it. He is a highwayman.'

'True,' Freddie said. 'But you cannot deny he has the Deele nose. Gussie, I am sure it is Lord Evan.'

If my sister was certain, then the man was indeed Lord Evan Belford. Dear God, I had just shot a Marquess's son and, even worse, I had shot an acquaintance.

'Well then, we must attend him.' I looked around for something to staunch the wound, my eye fixing upon Samuel. 'Quick, give me your neckcloth.'

He obliged. I took the length of muslin and approached Lord Evan's prone body.

'Wait, my lady! Please.' Samuel ducked back to the carriage and returned with a cushion, placing it beside the fallen man. 'You cannot kneel upon the dirt.'

I stifled a wild laugh. No doubt a reaction to the shock, although some of it might have been the ridiculousness of a velvet cushion upon the road. Pushing aside the inappropriate mirth, I knelt and peered at Lord Evan's pale face. The closer inspection confirmed my earlier opinion. 'It is just a graze, and the powder has burned him a little too.'

'I do not know how you can be so calm,' Freddie said.

'Focusing upon the facts is the only thing keeping me from screaming, dearheart.' I felt her hand on my shoulder as I pressed the muslin against the wound, the white cloth blossoming red. Good God, so much blood. The metallic smell of it made me feel quite queasy. 'Samuel, get John Driver's neckcloth too. We must bind Lord Evan's head.'

Samuel headed off to the front of the carriage.

'We cannot leave him on the road,' Freddie said. 'For all his sins, he is the Marquess of Deele's son, and as you know Deele was one of Papa's cronies.'

'You are right. We must take him with us and find a nearby house to provide help.'

A very inappropriate thought suddenly came to mind, straightening me upon my knees. No, it was too mercenary to voice. And yet...

'I'm sure the closest house is Sir Reginald's.' I glanced up at Freddie.

She eyed me warily; she knew me too well. 'Gussie, you cannot mean it! What would we say?'

'Sir Reginald has never met us, nor, I wager, any of our family. The story could be that our brother was escorting us to–' I waved my free hand. 'Bath or wherever, when suddenly we are set upon by ruffians. Our poor brother was shot and we are in dire need of assistance. Sir Reginald cannot deny us, and it will give us time to find a way to remove Amelia.'

Freddie considered Lord Evan. 'What if he wakes up?'

'I doubt he would want his true identity known. I think he will play along for the promise of his freedom and a good pouch of money.'

If he survives, I thought. *Dear God, let him survive.*

'You are mad, you know,' Freddie said.

'You come from the same stock, my dear.'

She smiled. 'True.'

As it happened, we were less than fifteen minutes from Sir Reginald's estate. The long snaking drive was lined with old oaks, their Spring leafiness hiding the view of the house until the last gentle curve when it was unveiled in a carefully managed frame of lush green overhanging boughs.

It was a handsome house, probably a former hunting lodge that had been extended by two wings on either side. All was grey stone symmetry with only a few windows filled in to avoid the window tax. With his wife's 20,000 pounds secure, Sir Reginald was clearly not a man to stint himself sunlight. Two of the third-floor windows were barred. Not unusual: many houses had bars fitted on the nursery windows for safety. Yet it sent a frisson of unease across my shoulders.

Lord Evan was slumped beside me, propped in the corner of the carriage. The man was still insensible, but at least the bleeding from his wound seemed to have slowed. Now that I could see his face properly, I remembered him well. We had danced at least three times before he had been sent away; an amusing and intelligent companion, and very light on his feet for such a big man.

The face before me was, of course, ten years older and even in repose it held lines of suffering and hardship. A scar ran from the corner of his left eye in a crescent across his cheekbone and deep lines had been etched between commanding nose and firm mouth. Even so, I had seen that same humour and intelligence in his eyes before... Well, before I had shot him in the head.

Opposite, Freddie gave me a tight smile. 'He has a better colour, don't you think? I believe I packed some hartshorn if we need it.'

'I'm not sure we *want* to revive him, my dear. He is, I think, at his most helpful quite unconscious. Besides, I cannot believe the violence of smelling salts would be at all beneficial to a head wound.' I gave her a reassuring smile. 'Are you ready?'

She nodded, holding up her white linen handkerchief. 'I shall put on a good bout of vapours. In truth I am not far from it.'

The carriage stopped in front of the portico and Samuel opened the door, his eyes darting to Freddie's and mine in silent conspiracy. With a deep breath, my sister let out a high-pitched screech that made Samuel and I wince.

'Help us!' she yelled. 'Please. My brother, he is shot. Help!'

The front door opened and a rotund individual in neat breeches and jacket emerged with some speed. Clearly, Sir Reginald's butler. Two footmen followed.

'You! There!' I cried over Freddie's sobs. 'Get your master. Quick! My brother has been shot in the head!'

To his credit, the man swiftly dispatched one footman inside and, with the other in tow, hurried down to our carriage.

'What has happened, my lady?' he asked. Smart man; he had noted the crest upon our carriage.

'Highwaymen! My brave brother protected us.'

I surreptitiously flicked my hand at Freddie: *more*. Obligingly she raised the level of her sobbing and screams.

'My brother must be laid down and the bleeding stopped,' I said through the cacophony. 'And a quiet room for my sister. I fear she is working herself into a fit.'

I heard the slight check in Freddie's wailing, but she rallied well.

Sir Reginald finally made his appearance, striding out of the front door with the other footman trailing behind. How is it that on first sight some people make one's hackles rise? Perhaps it was prior knowledge, but the man who made his way deliberately down the front steps brought an instant tightening across my scalp.

Sir Reginald was at least six foot tall and broad across shoulder and chest. He wore a fashionable jacket in claret velvet with the high M shaped collar that, with his starched white shirt points, obscured his neck and created a bullish quality. His small eyes were set under a heavy brow and added to that bovine likeness. His skin held a florid colour, with bluish pouches beneath his eyes that spoke of too much liquor and game. It was his mouth, however, that gave the truth of the man: thin, small and currently pursed in irritation.

On arrival at the carriage door, he rocked back upon his heels and said, 'What is this about? My man says someone has been shot in the head. I don't know why you've come here. Go on to the village. There is a physician there.' He clearly did not want someone dying on his doorstep.

It was time to pull rank. 'Our brother, the *Earl* of Ratton, has been shot in the head, sir! My sister and I need your assistance.'

Freddie intensified her sobs.

'Earl of Ratton, hey?' Sir Reginald peered into the coach. 'Like I said, there is no one here who can physick him. You'd best drive on.'

Lud, the man was a self-serving pig. I launched myself down the carriage step and conjured my best matron's voice. 'No, we must stay here and call for a doctor. That will be the safest course. Those dreadful highwaymen are still at large!'

I leaned in and pulled Freddie out after me. She wailed, stumbled down the step and ended up clutching Sir Reginald's arm, sobbing incoherent thanks, the silver handle of her new Johnston parasol digging into his shoulder. A rather nice touch.

'You,' I pointed to the footman, 'Help my man move the Earl into the house.'

The footman looked to his master. Sir Reginald gave an exasperated nod as he tried to extricate himself from Freddie's sobbing gratitude and the parasol stick. He addressed his butler. 'Ellery, show the ladies to the drawing room.'

Ellery bowed. I caught an odd moment pass between him and his master: *consternation*. Our arrival had definitely alarmed them.

Freddie allowed me to lead her away from Sir Reginald, her handkerchief and poke bonnet hiding her face. A good thing for her weeping had become a little thin.

We entered the house, pausing for a moment as Ellery smoothly divested my sister of her parasol and placed it on an ebony side table. He led the way through the foyer. It was a most handsome entrance: four columns supporting an elegant arch that framed a huge central staircase. The floor was black and white marble set in a diamond pattern and the walls sported portraits of bewigged men with the same high colour as Sir Reginald. No doubt, his forebears. We crossed to the left and Ellery bowed us into the drawing room.

'If you will wait here, my ladies,' he said over my sister's soft sobs.

He closed the double doors with a firm click that clearly told us this was where we were to stay.

'He did not take our bonnets,' Freddie said.

'No, I have the feeling Sir Reginald intends our stay to be very short.'

I surveyed the drawing room. A damask crimson silk covered the walls, the rich colour interspersed with large gilt mirrors and portraits of more forebears. A very pretty pianoforte stood in the corner with a gilt candelabra set upon its polished surface. A cluster of chairs and two sofas were upholstered in apple green, and I counted at least three Egyptian-inspired tables. I walked over to a very large Wedgewood urn in blue porcelain set atop a mahogany bureau. I had seen a similar urn in Mr Wedgewood's London showroom and nearly bought it myself. Sir Reginald had rather good taste and kept up with fashion. Or was this the stylish hand of Amelia before she fell out of favour?

Outside the tall windows, Samuel and Sir Reginald's footman had finally managed to pull Lord Evan from the carriage and were dragging him upright between them towards the house, his head lolling to one side and boots digging ruts into the gravel drive.

I waited for the carriage to move around to the stables, but it did not. Instead a wiry young groom arrived, gesticulating at our coachman. John Driver climbed down from the seat, arguing with the man. It was a heated exchange, the end result sending John Driver to the heads of the horses, a scowl upon his tanned face.

'It seems Sir Reginald has ordered our carriage to remain out front,' I remarked. Damn, that meant it was going to stay in full sight of the house and its master.

Freddie dabbed at the crocodile tears on her cheeks. 'He really is quite keen to get us on our way.'

'It is going to make smuggling Amelia out ten times harder.'

'What next, then?'

I shook off of my chagrin. 'First things first: we need to find the poor girl. I think you will work yourself into a fit, my dear and have to lie down in a quiet room, preferably upstairs. See if a footman or maid is inclined to talk. If that proves a dead-end, maybe even wander around the house in distress.'

Freddie nodded. 'What will you do?'

'I'll stay with our dear brother, and see what I can find out from our reluctant host.'

From the hallway, came the sound of Sir Reginald's voice. 'For God's sake pick up his feet, he is marking the marble.'

Freddie glanced at me and retired once more into her bonnet and handkerchief, shoulders heaving with sobs.

The doors opened. Sir Reginald strode in, followed by Ellery carrying a linen sheet, then Samuel and the other footman hauling the large figure of Lord Evan. Their efforts to keep his feet off the floor were coming to naught; he was at least equal to their six foot height and probably a measure more.

Ellery unfolded the sheet and snapped it open, laying it across one of the apple green velvet sofas. No need to get blood upon the upholstery. 'Lay him here.'

He was deposited with some attempt at care and then everyone looked at me expectantly.

Ah, yes, I was the concerned sister. I hurried forward.

'He needs another cushion,' I declared. Samuel snatched a cushion from the nearby chair and offered it. 'Place it under his head,' I ordered.

As Samuel complied, I pointed to the other footman. 'Bring me a chair. I will sit with him. The move has made him worse. Look at his colour. We cannot possibly move him again. He needs wine, too.'

The relocation, had indeed, done Lord Evan no favour. His skin was once again sickly pale.

Freddie, seeing that as her cue, gave a ghastly groan and scaled up her sobs.

'He will die, he will die!'

I crossed to her and took her hand, chafing it. 'My dear you are working yourself into one of your spasms. You must calm yourself.' I turned to Sir Reginald. 'My sister needs to lie down in a quiet, dim place. Away from any noise. Her nerves, you see.'

Freddie let loose with a shrill wail.

Sir Reginald flinched and stepped back. 'Ellery, arrange it.'

'Yes, Sir Reginald.' He bowed to Freddie. 'If you will come this way, my lady.'

Freddie gave my hand a surreptitious squeeze and, sobbing, followed him from the room.

Samuel placed a chair by the sofa. The other footman arranged a carafe of burgundy and glasses on the side table.

'Shall I pour, my lady?'

'Yes for him and for me.' I was not usually one for heavy wine, but right then I needed something fortifying.

I turned to Sir Reginald. 'Sir, have you sent for the physician?'

'One of my grooms has gone. It is not far,' he said, somewhat pointedly.

'Thank you, you are most kind.' Since I had invoked Ratton's name, there was no use trying to hide our identities. I curtseyed. 'The circumstances have prevented us from being properly introduced. I am Lady Augusta Brant. I am travelling with my sister Lady Frederica and of course my brother, Lord Ratton.'

He sketched a bow. 'Sir Reginald Thorne.'

I considered my options and decided to step boldly. 'Ah, Sir Reginald, I believe I was once introduced to your wife when she was Miss Callow. A number of years ago, of course. How is Lady Thorne?'

He rocked back on his heels again, flummoxed for a moment. 'Not well, I am afraid. Not well at all. Confined to her bed. Otherwise she would be pleased to see you.'

'Then I am very sorry to bring more trouble to your house.' I looked out of the window. 'My horses need to be tended, Sir Reginald. Would it be possible to have them stabled?'

He smiled thinly. 'I am afraid the archway to my stables is not wide enough to accommodate such a handsome town coach, Lady Augusta. My head groom, of course, will help your man water your team out front, in readiness for your departure.'

I returned a smile just as thin. 'That is most kind.' I turned to my faux brother. 'He does not look well, at all.'

Sir Reginald backed away. 'I will watch for the physician's arrival and send him in directly. Just ask if you require anything.'

'Thank you.' I returned his bow with a nod and sat down next to the patient as Sir Reginald made his retreat from the room.

So Amelia was confined to bed. Was she truly ill or was she imprisoned? Hopefully, Freddie would be able to discover the poor girl's whereabouts from Ellery or a maid.

'You may leave,' I told Samuel and Sir Reginald's man. They both bowed. I caught Samuel's eye for a moment: a reassurance and an order. He gave a slight nod – his next task was to question the servants – and followed the other footman from the room, closing the door behind them.

I studied the pale face of Lord Evan. His breathing was regular, and the bleeding, as far as I could tell, had stopped. I placed my hand against his cheek, the faint dark stubble rough against my skin. His temperature seemed normal, but then it was probably too soon for a fever to have set in.

'So, my Lord Evan,' I said softly, 'it would be most inconvenient if you died.'

His eyes opened. 'Yes, quite.'

I jerked back, but he caught my wrist, his grip absurdly strong for a man who had just been shot in the head.

'What the devil is going on here, Lady Augusta?'

I tried to pull my hand away but he tightened his grip.

'How long have you been awake?' I demanded. Then realised he had used my name. 'Good Lord, do you remember me?'

'I've been awake since the carriage, and of course I remember you.' He frowned. 'My ears may be ringing and I have a headache that would kill a horse, but I'm not so fuddled that I don't know Ratton's twin sisters. The question is, what devilry are you two cooking up against Thorne?'

'It is I who should be asking the questions,' I said, finally managing to break his grip. 'How are you back here in England? Why are you a highwayman?' I remembered my outrage. 'You held us up at gunpoint!'

'Well, to be correct, you were the one who pointed a gun.' He touched the bandages around his head, hissing as his fingers found the wound beneath them. 'As to being back in England, I stowed on a supply ship and then found work on a slaver. God save those still aboard her.' His jaw clenched for a moment, his disgust for the practice as clear as if he had spat. Silently I added an Amen to his prayer. Our own dear Weatherly had been stolen from his family as a child and survived such a voyage, eventually finding his way to England as a free man.

'As to my current employment,' Lord Evan continued, 'there are not many opportunities for a second son outside politics, the military or the church, none of which, I imagine, would be overly keen to have me at present.'

'So your next choice was highway robbery?' I asked acidly.

'It was either that or goat keeping.'

I laughed; I couldn't help myself. Even so, his partner had shot at John Driver.

'You may not have fired, Lord Evan, but your companion did.'

He sobered. 'Yes, you are quite right. That was not well done. I thought I had impressed upon him that we did not shoot. My apologies.'

I inclined my head. It seemed the polite thing to do since I had fired too, albeit accidentally.

'Now it is my turn for questions, Lady Augusta. What is this caper?' He raised himself upon his elbow. The movement blanched his face into a deathly white and he swayed forward. I caught his shoulder and eased him back down on to the sofa.

'Take care. You have lost a lot of blood.'

'Thank you. I am, of course, touched by your concern.' He closed his eyes and pressed his fingertips over his wound again. 'Why are you pretending I am your brother?'

I sat in silence. Should I trust him? Ridiculously, I felt as if I might. An absurd impulse. It was no doubt his sense of humour; I could not help but warm to a man who joked with me after I had shot him.

He opened his eyes. 'My dear, you hold all the cards.'

I ignored the unseemly endearment and considered his statement. I suppose I did hold all the cards. He was an escaped convict and a highwayman and, if discovered, would be transported again, or more likely hanged. He was also patently too weak to run.

And so I told him our mission.

'Are you mad?' he said, struggling back up onto his elbow. 'You want to kidnap the man's wife?'

'Shh!' I looked over at the door. 'We are not going to leave her here to be murdered.'

'Kidnap is a hanging offence. And as I hear it, Thorne is not a man you would want to cross.'

'Exactly,' I said. 'He is a brutal pig and I will not leave Amelia another day in his clutches.'

He drew in a breath. 'Lord, give me strength.' He glanced at the carafe. 'Or at least give me wine.'

I picked up a glass and gave it to him. He took a deep draught, a low sound of approval emerging from behind the rim. 'That's rather good,' he said handing back the empty vessel. 'I'd say that was free trade. French if I'm not mistaken. A fine claret.'

'Another?' I asked very politely. 'Perhaps a cheese board to go with it?'

He eyed me. 'I have a feeling I am not going to get either.'

I placed the glass back on to the table. 'This is a dangerous situation, Lord Evan. Will you help us or do you intend to be a hindrance?'

'Lady Augusta, I will help you. Not only because I have no choice if I am to save myself, but also because you are a ridiculously quick woman with steady nerves and a very wicked laugh.'

No one had ever called my laugh wicked before.

We planned the next step in Amelia's liberation, his lordship recumbent upon the sofa and me seated beside him on the ottoman. I favoured just snatching the girl and running, but Lord Evan quite rightly pointed out that our carriage was in full view of the house and Sir Reginald had a household of servants to stand in our way.

'In New South Wales,' he said, staring thoughtfully up at the moulded roses on the ceiling, 'attempts at escape were often made by switching places with people visiting the prison.'

'Is that how you escaped?'

He turned his head, a pained look in his dark eyes. 'No, my dear.'

Another unseemly endearment. I ignored it again and the flutter it prompted in my innards. 'Then how–'

He shook his head, refusing further interrogation. I reluctantly left the topic and addressed his earlier comment.

'By Mrs Dellaquist's account, Lady Thorne is a small, slim woman.' I raised my brows. 'About the size of my sister.'

'Indeed?' His smile held a rogue's delight. 'I believe we have struck upon a plan. Are you sure, though, that Lady Frederica will be able to engage in such a masquerade? She does not seem as–'

'Do not be taken in by my sister's act, Lord Evan,' I said quickly.

'Belford,' he said. 'Just call me Belford.'

My skin warmed into a flush; the invitation, like his earlier endearments, was far too intimate for our short acquaintance and the rather awkward circumstances. Still, it would be rude to refuse it. 'Frederica is as committed to this enterprise as I am, Belford, and just as robust.'

'Then, if she is agreeable, we should go ahead,' he said. 'Now to practicalities.'

As he spoke, I came to a rather unhappy and uncomfortable realisation: one should never meet those whom one shoots, especially when they are charming and intelligent and willing to engage in nefarious activities with you. It brings on a great deal of remorse.

'I am sorry I shot you,' I said, suddenly compelled to apologise in the midst of his thoughts about escape routes. I bowed my head. 'I have a tendency to jump into a situation. It is my failing.'

'Your failing?' He carefully sat up, steadying himself with a hand upon the silk cushions.

'My family has always said so.'

He leaned across and gently lifted my chin with a fingertip. 'Quite the contrary, I would say.'

I should, of course, have pulled away from his impertinent touch. 'You are very kind to say so,' I said.

He smiled. 'You are not going to start blubbing are you?'

I narrowed my eyes. 'Blub? I have never blubbed in my life.' I caught his hand, intending to thrust it away in protest, but his fingers closed around mine. I found my fingers shamelessly closing around his, our hands entwined. For a moment I did not breathe and I saw the same stillness in him.

'He is through here, Doctor,' Ellery's voice echoed in the hall.

We snatched our hands away.

'Lie down!' I ordered but he was already back upon the cushions.

'Do not let the damn man bleed me,' Belford muttered. 'Barbaric.'

I touched his shoulder in agreement. I had not found many in the world who thought the same as I did about the practice of bleeding. What earthly good could come of removing the precious life liquid of an ill or injured person? Surely the fact that people died from lack of blood undermined the activity.

The doors were flung open and Ellery announced a small, rather weedy man dressed in a sober brown suit. 'Dr Haymer, my lady.'

The doctor gave a bobbing bow and hurried over to the sofa. 'Your brother has been shot, I hear, my lady.'

'Luckily a glancing wound,' I said as Ellery closed the doors, leaving us.

Dr Haymer eyed me professionally, his little darting eyes reminding me far too much of weasel. He gave a quick nod, clearly coming to the opinion that I was not about to fall into hysterics. 'It has been dressed, I see.'

'Only temporarily. I had to use the neckcloths of my servants.'

'Yes, well that is most... yes, very practical.' He studied me again, slightly aghast that a lady would have the stomach for such activities. 'I shall redress it and bleed him to prevent a fever.'

'No!' I said.

Belford opened his eyes and said, just as forcibly, 'Not while there is breath in my body! A new dressing will be quite enough.'

'My lord, you are conscious,' the doctor said rather unnecessarily.

'He is,' I agreed. 'I have a question for you, Dr Haymer.'

The doctor switched his rather bemused attention back to me. 'Of course, my lady.'

'Do you attend Lady Thorne as well?'

The question seemed to rob the man of his voice. He hooked a finger into his cravat, pulling it from his rather grubby neck. 'Well, now, I'm not sure I should... that is to say...'

Belford sat up and swung his feet to the floor, the movement strong and assured. At least it looked strong and assured, but I saw his fingers dig into the cushioning for support.

'Lady Brant has asked you a question, man. Answer it.' Even sitting and with a makeshift bandage upon his head, he looked intimidating.

'I am under no obligation to do so,' Haymer said stiffly.

'If you wish to continue practising medicine, you will answer,' I said. 'My brother here is a magistrate and he does not look kindly upon those who stand in the way of his inquiries.' It was not exactly a lie; my real brother was indeed a magistrate.

The newly invested official rallied to his duties and nodded. 'Indeed, I do not.'

The doctor wet his lips. 'Then yes, I attend Lady Thorne.'

Ah, here was the dubious physician in Amelia's letter. 'What is her ailment?' I asked.

'A nervous disposition. Delusions. She often descends into violence.'

I glanced at Belford, seeing my own skepticism in his face. 'And what do you prescribe?'

'Laudanum.'

An opiate of great strength. I knew its effects for I had been prescribed some for a cough a year ago and only one dose had sent me into a stupor. I had heard that just three teaspoons of the stuff was enough to kill a person.

'How much have you prescribed, doctor?'

He cleared his throat. 'I send a bottle a week.'

'A week!' Belford echoed. 'Good God man, surely you realise what Thorne is doing.'

The doctor's thin jaw shifted. 'I do not know what you mean, my lord.'

'How much is he paying you?' Belford demanded.

'I'm sure I am not following you,' the doctor said firmly.

'How long have you been supplying that much laudanum?' I asked, keeping the outrage from my voice.

'A few weeks.'

I could see Thorne's fiendish plan: creating a dependence upon the drug in poor Amelia and then, one day very soon, she would take a tragic 'accidental' overdose.

'Doctor, please attend to his lordship's injury. Then I think you should go and never return to this house or send any medications again,' I ordered in my most implacable voice.

The doctor straightened. 'I will not be commanded in such a manner, even by you, Lady Brant.'

'Do not imagine my words to be empty, Dr Haymer. If we hear of you treating Lady Thorne again, my brother will come looking for you and revoke your licence to practice.'

'I have done nothing wrong,' the doctor protested.

'You have done nothing that would be considered right, either, have you?' I replied.

The man had the grace to lower his eyes.

The doctor quickly tended to Belford's wound then hurried out to his gig, leaving us to contemplate our next move.

'We have to find Lady Thorne and see what state she is in,' Belford said as we watched Dr Haymer through the window. The little man stared back at us for a rancorous moment then climbed into his gig and steered it around our own carriage, urging his pony into a smart trot down the driveway.

'If she is insensible, we will not be able to walk her out disguised as your sister.'

'No, Belford. *I will* find Lady Thorne,' I said. He opened his mouth to protest but I shook my head. 'You must stay on the sofa and maintain the reason for us being here. If you are seen to be well enough to creep around the house, then you are well enough to leave.'

'I cannot allow you to go up there on your own.'

I laid my hand on his shoulder, astounded at my sudden lack of propriety. 'Trust me, I am quite capable.'

He looked at me for a moment – a crooked smile quirking his lips – then pressed his own hand upon mine. 'Yes, that is obvious.'

The door opened. I dropped my hand from Belford's shoulder as Sir Reginald strode into the room.

'Has Haymer gone?' he inquired.

'Yes, I believe he had urgent duties elsewhere,' I said smoothly. 'The prognosis is good, however. He says my brother will make a full recovery, but should not be moved until this evening. I am afraid we must take advantage of your hospitality a little longer.'

'I see.' Sir Reginald gave a tight smile. 'I am glad to hear you will recover, Ratton. Damned highwaymen.'

Belford inclined his head graciously.

I walked towards the door. 'My sister, however, is not well at all. She has a tendency to work herself into a nervous fever, you see. My brother thinks it would be best to send her on to his house and have the carriage return for us.' I smiled. 'You are so kind to give us refuge in such extremity, Sir Reginald.'

'Pleasure,' he muttered.

I curtsied. 'If you will excuse me, I shall attend my sister and ready her for departure.'

I caught a glimpse of Belford's eyes as I left the room: *be careful*.

I had to admit, his concern gladdened my heart far too much.

In the cold marble foyer, I waved Ellery over.

'Lady Frederica will be travelling onwards. Send my man Samuel up to me with her small coffer. She will need her medicines before she resumes her journey.'

Ellery bowed. 'Of course, my lady.'

'Where is she located?'

Ellery called over one of the footmen. 'Show Lady Augusta to the Cornflower suite,' he ordered.

I sent up a prayer that Freddie was indeed in the Cornflower suite and not still snooping around the house.

I found her reclining on a yellow silk chaise lounge in the large bedchamber, one hand pressed dramatically to her forehead. She had cast off her bonnet; no doubt it had been too difficult to snoop without any side vision.

The room was indeed cornflower blue: walls, bed coverings, carpet, even the ceiling. The only accents were the chaise lounge, a bolster on the bed and a stool, all covered in the same yellow silk. The whole scene was striking and, incidentally, very flattering to my sister's colouring. She looked alarmingly healthy.

'How do you feel, my dear sister?' I asked Freddie as the footman closed the door behind him. I lifted my brows and gave her a small shake of my head.

'Terrible,' she said obediently and loudly. 'I feel a paroxysm coming on.'

I returned to the door and opened it a few inches. The footman was heading down the stairs. Sir Reginald was not so suspicious as to post a guard upon us. But then, we were only two spinsters, one of whom had dissolved into a vapourish fit. Hardly a threat.

I closed the door. 'So?' I asked as I crossed to the chaise lounge and sat on the end, nudging Freddie's feet to one side.

Freddie levered herself upright. 'Ellery gave nothing away and I have not been attended by a maid or offered refreshment.' From her voice, I could tell she was rather disgusted by Sir Reginald's lack of hospitality, although it was working in our favour. Freddie could not abide incivility. 'I did manage to take a look upstairs. There is a room on the next floor that is bolted on the outside.'

I orientated myself towards the front of the house and pointed to the right hand corner of the room. 'In that direction?'

'Yes.'

'I saw bars on the windows when we drove up. I would wager that is where she is being kept.'

'What next?'

I lowered my voice even more. 'Belford and I have made a plan.'

Freddie stared at me. 'Belford?'

'Yes, he is awake. Has been since the carriage,' I said a touch too airily.

'You are calling him Belford?'

'I felt obliged to explain matters to him and he is going to help us.'

'You felt obliged?' Freddie scrutinised me for a hard moment. 'Oh no!' She sat back. 'You have taken one of your wild likings to him, haven't you?' She pressed her hands to her forehead, this time in all sincerity. 'Gus, dear. You must be more circumspect. The last time was that beggar woman in the Devil's Acre–'

'And I was right about her, wasn't I? She helped us!'

'Yes. But Gussie, what if he betrays us? What if–'

'He will not,' I said. 'As he pointed out, we hold all the cards. He is an escaped convict and highwayman. He is hardly going to expose himself. He wants to help and, Freddie darling, I believe he is still a good man.'

Freddie leaned forward. 'You are blushing.'

'I am not.'

'You know I trust your instincts, Gus, but Lord Evan–'

'Belford,' I corrected.

Freddie gritted her teeth, '*Belford* threatened us with a pistol.'

'He never raised his pistol, Freddie.'

She ignored the comment and continued firmly, 'He may even have been the highwayman who attacked the Brownwells and shot their man. I do not think it is a good idea to ally ourselves with him.'

There was, of course, a chance that Belford had been the perpetrator of the Brownwell attack, but everything in my body screamed *no, not possible*.

'If you talked to him for just a minute, you would know that could not be the case.'

She stared at me, her silence even more aggravating.

'What else should I have done when he revealed he was awake?' I demanded. 'Shot him again? Clubbed him over the head?'

Freddie swung her feet to the ground. 'No need for sarcasm. I just think that this time your instincts may be somewhat muddied by–'

'By what?'

She considered me, an odd little smile on her lips. 'Oh Gus, how can someone so clever be so obtuse?' She twitched her shoulders, as if shaking something off. 'Never mind. So what is this plan that you and your new *liking* have concocted?'

I ignored her emphasis and told her the plan.

Freddie listened without comment until I had finished my discourse, then said somberly, 'I do not like this part where you stay behind with Belford.'

'Someone must delay and misdirect Sir Reginald, otherwise you will not have time to escape.'

Freddie frowned. 'Perhaps,' she allowed. 'Even so, it all rather relies on Amelia being able to walk, doesn't it? From what you have told me, I rather think she will be incapacitated.'

'True, but with our carriage out front and so visible I cannot think of another way–'

A knock on the door silenced me. I exchanged a look with Freddie. She nodded and hurriedly reclined on the chaise lounge cushions again.

'Who is it?' I called.

'Samuel, my lady.'

We both relaxed. 'Come.'

The door opened to admit our footman carrying Freddie's small mahogany coffer.

'Oh, good thought,' she said to me, and rose as Samuel closed the door. She took the box from his hands, deposited it on the bed and flipped open the lid. As she began to rummage through its contents, I waved Samuel over.

'Did you have any luck questioning Sir Reginald's staff?'

'Luckily the kitchen lass likes a bit of gossip, my lady. Apparently, a maid by the name of Grace was cast out a week or so back, but I couldn't get the reason why. Bernard, the footman who helped me carry in you know who, told me no one is allowed up on the third floor except Sir Reginald and Ellery.'

'Third floor again,' I said to my sister.

'Indeed.' She held up a plain green linen gown and a lace cap. 'This should do it, don't you think? Reasonable attire for a lady taking a walk?'

I nodded.

She addressed Samuel. 'Do you think the staff know what has happened to Lady Thorne? Are they complicit?'

'From what I gather they think she's gone mad, my lady. That's what Sir Reginald has told 'em. She bit the doctor, you know.'

'Excellent,' I said. 'I would've bitten him myself if I'd had the chance.'

'Do you think they would stop her if they saw her heading outside?' Freddie asked.

'Absolutely. The kitchen lass said that if they see their mistress they've been ordered to detain her and get Sir Reginald or the butler immediately. Been told it's for Lady Thorne's own good.'

Freddie glanced at me: *that seals it, then.*

I nodded: w*e go ahead as planned.*

'Samuel, here is what you need to do,' I said. 'Listen carefully; some of the timing is important.'

He was used to receiving strange orders from me and merely nodded his understanding of his tasks, until I mentioned Belford.

'So, he's awake, is he, my lady?'

'Yes, and he is on our side. We are trusting him now.'

I glanced at Freddie but she was too intent on rummaging deeper into the coffer to add any comment.

Samuel's usual wooden expression furrowed for a moment into consternation. 'We are trusting a highwayman, my lady?'

'He is not a highwayman!' I snapped. A patently ridiculous statement, considering recent events.

Freddie looked up from the coffer. 'Lady Augusta has taken one of her likings, Samuel.'

He nodded. 'Yes, my lady.'

There was absolutely no inflection in his voice, but I just knew he was sighing with resignation alongside my sister.

Freddie turned from the coffer. 'Found it,' she said, holding up a small vial of hartshorn. 'I think we are ready.'

I nodded, but if Dr Haymer were telling the truth, the girl might be beyond the administration of even the strongest smelling salts.

We crept up the staircase, Samuel at the rear and taking a position at the top as our lookout.

Freddie and I continued to the door at the end of the corridor. Whoever had fixed the bolts to the door was taking no chances: three, equally-spaced and very substantial.

'Rather a lot for one drugged girl, don't you think?' Freddie whispered.

I slid the first across its barrel. Well oiled, only a soft scrape. Freddie addressed the second. I took hold of the third and pulled it across, a tad too vigorously. It clanked home, the sound turning Samuel at the end of the hall. We all froze, listening. Samuel peered over the bannister and held up his hand: *wait.*

I heard two voices: young and female on the second floor landing. Maids, indulging in an illicit chat. From the snatches I could hear, the topic was Bernard the footman and his shapely calves. Finally, their voices receded and Samuel gave a small wave. *All clear.*

I took hold of the handle, turned it and pushed open the door. An empty four-poster bed, bereft of any curtains, the covers crumpled. And an awful smell: sour fear, vomit and an unemptied chamber pot.

I stepped in, Freddie following.

Suddenly all the air was knocked from my body as something – no someone – landed on my back.

I spun around, seeing Freddie's startled face for a second, and then staggered a few steps towards the bed. A thin, bare arm hooked around my throat. I smelled sour body odour and unhealthy breath. Sharp fingernails dug into my scalp, ripping at my hair, the wrenching pain bringing tears to my eyes. I pulled at the choking hold and spun again, punching at whatever body parts I could find. My fist connected with flesh and bone. I heard a low gasp of pain in my ear.

My sister ran towards us and grabbed hold of my attacker, her efforts tightening the hold around my throat. I gulped for breath.

'Let go! We are your friends, Amelia. Let go,' my sister hissed.

A bedpost came into view. I turned and rammed Amelia against it, dislodging the girl's grip. She fell on to the bed. I launched myself away from the bed and whirled around, my hands up to my abused throat.

Amelia scrambled back to the bedhead, narrow chest heaving beneath a soiled white nightgown, fierce eyes watching us.

Freddie's hartshorn, it seemed, was rather unnecessary.

'We are here to help, Amelia,' Freddie said, backing up a step, showing her palms.

I hurried to the door and peered out. Samuel was still at the top of the stairs, his face turned to us and set into a frown of anxiety. I motioned to him: *have we been heard?* He shook his head. Thank the Lord, our little battle had not garnered any attention.

Amelia was still crouched upon the bed.

'Who are you?' she finally demanded in a raw, scratchy voice.

She had the look of her sister, but her blue eyes were ringed with dark circles and any softness in her face had disappeared, the delicate bones stark beneath her pale skin. Her blonde hair was matted and bedraggled, a small forgotten diamond clip caught up in the tangle.

'Honoria sent us,' I said, my own voice a little rough from her stranglehold. I cleared my throat.

Amelia's eyes widened, the sudden relief in them heartbreaking. 'Gracie got the letter out? Oh, good girl.' She looked beyond us, her sharp face full of hope. 'Where is Honoria?'

'She is not here. Sir Reginald will not allow her or any of your family inside the estate. Honoria asked us to come for you, instead,' Freddie said gently. 'I am Lady Frederica and this is Lady Augusta.' She took a step forward. 'My dear, we think you are being drugged.'

Amelia nodded. 'Thorne and that pig Ellery make me swallow something horrid every evening. I thought you were them.' She looked out of the barred window, perplexed. 'But it is not evening yet, is it? Too early. I make myself bring it up afterwards, but I think some of it stays. Oh dear, I'm sorry, I cannot think clearly. He says I am mad, but I am not. It is the drug.'

'We believe you,' I said. 'It is time to leave this place, but we must do so quickly. And secretly.'

Amelia drew a deep breath, gathering herself. 'Yes.'

Although I was still rather rattled by her attack, I had to admit the girl had spirit.

'But how?' she asked. 'He will not let me just walk out. I tried that, and he put me in here,' she waved at her prison.

'We have a plan,' I said. I was going to add that it would take some courage, but it was clear that Lady Amelia Thorne had enough courage for one-hundred such plans.

Twenty minutes later, I led my distraught 'sister' down the staircase to the waiting carriage at the front of the house.

I had my arm tightly around Amelia's shoulder, her thin body clad in Freddie's gown, spencer and gloves, and her face hidden by my sister's extravagant poke bonnet and a linen handkerchief held up to her eyes.

It had not been an easy transformation. The poor girl's misuse had whittled her away to skin and bone, and we had been forced to use some of her bedding to pad out the top of the gown in order to create Freddie's healthier dimensions. We had also bundled up her bedraggled blonde hair and my sister had gallantly sacrificed two long burnished curls that now peeked out from under the poke bonnet.

The most troublesome aspect of the disguise, however, was the fact that poor Amelia reeked. We had not been able to call for any water, of course, so it had been a case of a dry scrub and a prayer. I also had our only weapon tucked tightly in my fist, thumb held over its mouth, to be used if either Sir Reginald or Ellery came too close to the false Freddie.

I focused on our goal, the front door, cooing softly to the hunched figure in my embrace as we descended into the foyer. 'All will be well, sister. Samuel and John Driver will take you to Brant Hall, and we will join you as soon as dear Ratton is fit to travel.'

I squeezed Amelia's shoulder. I could feel the strain in her body, but she obediently sniffled into the handkerchief.

I hoped, fervently, that Freddie had managed to traverse the servants' stairs unseen to the back courtyard and was now making her way around to the front drive with all the leisurely aplomb of a houseguest out for an evening stroll. Or if that failed, a houseguest who was lost.

Beside me, Amelia stumbled. I steadied her against my body, and whispered. 'Not long now.'

Our first obstacle emerged from the butler's pantry to our left. Ellery. I watched his face. Did he see anything amiss? Or worse, something familiar?

'The carriage is ready,' he said, walking towards us. He held Freddie's parasol. Damn, damn, damn I had forgotten about it.

I drew Amelia closer. If he handed it to her, she would look up. A reflex. He would see her eyes. And if she somehow managed to overcome the impulse, then that would be suspicious in itself.

When in doubt, attack. 'For goodness sakes Ellery, my sister does not want to be carrying a parasol when she is feeling so ill.' I glared at him. 'Give it to our footman.'

He withdrew the parasol, his face stiff. 'Yes, my lady.' At least he was looking at me and not Amelia.

He turned on his heel and strode back to the front door, opening it with a flourish. John Driver had moved the carriage closer to the portico, and it stood outside, framed by the doorway. Samuel waited beside it, ready to help Amelia up into her seat.

Only ten or so more steps until we were out of the house.

'Nearly there,' I murmured.

We reached the archway.

'Ah, you are leaving, Lady Frederica,' Sir Reginald said, emerging from the drawing room.

At the sight of her husband, Amelia's body stiffened in my arms, her false sobs quickening into a real pant. I felt her steps falter.

I tightened my grip around her and marched her forward. 'It is for the best, Sir Reginald.'

'Then allow me to escort your sister,' he said, falling in beside me.

Why did the pox of a man have to show some manners now?

'Very kind, sir,' I said, repositioning the hidden weapon in my palm, 'but I think a sister's embrace is what she needs at present.'

'Of course,' he said politely. He lengthened his stride through the doorway and across the gravel drive, heading for the carriage door. Good God he was going to hand her up.

Ellery bowed us out of the door then followed us on to the portico.

I helped Amelia down the stone steps. The poor girl had started to shake and I half carried her across the gravel. I glimpsed Belford at the drawing room window watching us. He raised his hand, a brother bidding a sister goodbye. But I knew the signal was for me: *keep going.*

Sir Reginald waved Samuel away from the open carriage door. At the corner of my eye, I saw a head pop out from the corner of the house and then duck back again. Freddie. She was in place, but still a good twenty yards from the other side of the carriage.

I caught Samuel's eye. He hurried across to Ellery and took the parasol, blocking the butler's view of Freddie's position.

Sir Reginald stood waiting to hand up my false sister into the cabin, a cold smile of courtesy on his thin lips. Oh no, with both him and Ellery beside the carriage, my real sister had no chance of running across to the opposite cabin door unseen. I would have to use the weapon.

'I hope you have a good journey, Lady Frederica,' Sir Reginald said, stepping forward to take Amelia's hand.

I took a deep breath and leaned in, as if to pass my sister into his keeping, then pulled my thumb from the hartshorn vial. One flick of my wrist and the whole of its contents soaked Sir Reginald's cravat and waistcoat. He reared back as the smelling salts hit his nostrils, then doubled over gasping for breath. I hurriedly stepped away from him, catching a sniff of the ghastly ammonia on the air. Even that tiny amount burned my throat.

I bundled Amelia into the cabin, slammed the door shut, and stepped away from the carriage.

Behind me, Ellery ran up to his stricken master. 'Sir Reginald, what is wrong?' He caught his master's flailing arm.

Beneath Sir Reginald's gulping gasps, I heard a crunch of gravel – someone bolting to the other side of the carriage – and then the slam of a door. For an instant, a slim hand showed at the window: Freddie.

'Go!' I ordered John Driver.

He flicked his whip, springing the horses as Samuel swung himself up on to the footman's step at the back. The carriage ground across the gravel, dust kicking up under the horse's hooves. As they made the turn into the long driveway, I glimpsed Amelia at the carriage window, eyes fierce with delight as her husband dropped to his hands and knees on the gravel, wheezing.

I quickly turned to my host. 'Lud, Sir Reginald, what has happened? Are you quite well?'

The man had received quite a snoutful – his face was bright red, his chest heaving, and his eyes watering profusely. He looked up at me, perplexed, then with a certain heavy grace keeled over on to the gravel.

I looked down at his inert body and hid my smile. 'Oh dear, Ellery, I believe Sir Reginald has swooned.'

Ten minutes later, Sir Reginald awoke in his drawing room on the sofa opposite Belford.

As the horrid man stirred, I frowned at my fellow trickster. He was grinning far too much for the occasion.

'My dear sir,' I said to Sir Reginald. 'I must apologise. The stopper came off my sister's salts. How do you feel?'

He scrunched his red-shot eyes tighter for a moment then peered at me blearily. 'Salts?'

'Yes, a constant companion for her nerves. Now, you must have some wine.' I picked up the decanter and poured a glass.

He grunted. 'Dear God, I thought I was going to die.'

'Not at all. Just a faint.' I passed him the wine. 'You should however rest here with my brother.'

Sir Reginald struggled up on to his elbows and downed the wine in one long draught.

'That's the way,' Belford said cheerfully. 'Wine will set things right.'

'Where is Ellery?' Sir Reginald asked, peering around the room.

'I have sent him to procure you some broth,' I said.

'Broth? I don't want broth.'

'Of course you don't,' Belford said. 'Pour Sir Reginald another wine, sister, and I'll have one too.'

'No!' Sir Reginald swung his feet to the carpet and shook his head, clearly trying to shift the remains of his bleariness. 'Your sister...' He looked down at the still damp front of his waistcoat. 'You tipped that bloody stuff over me.' A little light of suspicion came into his eyes. Damn, he was not as stupid as I had hoped. He stood up, staggered to the door, flung it open and bellowed, 'Ellery!'

'Yes, Sir Reginald.'

'Put down that damn broth. I think she's gone.'

'Oh dear,' I said to Belford as we listened to their progress up the staircase. 'Freddie and Amelia have had barely twenty minutes on the road. We really need to delay him a bit longer.'

Belford finished his wine and placed his glass on the table. 'Then you had best help me up, Lady Augusta. We are about to go into battle.'

I grabbed his arm and helped him stand. The effort made him sway alarmingly; he was still so weak from the wound. Our eyes met: we would have to make it a very short battle.

A roar of fury sounded from upstairs and then the sounds of rapid descent.

'Do you still have a gun, by chance?' Belford asked.

'I am afraid not.'

'Pity.'

'Nor do I have any hartshorn left.'

'I doubt he'd fall for that again.' He drew in a breath. 'I rather think this is about to become quite violent, Lady Augusta. You must take this chance to go. Now, please! I cannot have you in danger–'

'Absolutely not,' I said. 'I am here to the end.'

'Then step back behind me, at least.'

'Lud, no. I'll not cower before a pig like Sir Reginald.'

'Please, my dear, I insist. I cannot protect you and fight the man as well.' The concern in his eyes was quite wonderfully real. 'Will you promise to stand back?'

'I promise to stand back until it is no longer reasonable for me to do so.'

He shook his head. 'You are incorrigible!'

'To the core.'

We heard Sir Reginald yell, 'Ellery, get James to bring my bloody horse out front,' and then he burst back into the drawing room. 'She is in your carriage, isn't she?' he roared. 'Where are they going?'

'What on earth do you mean, Sir Reginald?' I asked calmly.

He crossed the room, the veins in his forehead bulging purple. 'Do not play innocent with me, Lady Augusta. You have taken my wife!'

'I suggest you stay where you are, Thorne,' Belford said, all the bonhomie gone from his voice.

'You are mistaken, Sir Reginald,' I said, quite glad, after all, that the sofa stood between his spitting fury and us. 'Are you suggesting that she has stowed away in our carriage?'

'Stowed? Ha! You have kidnapped her and by God you are going to tell me which way they are heading!'

He ran towards me. Before I could react, Belford had leapt on to the sofa and over its back, landing in front of Sir Reginald. He lunged, grappling the heavier man.

They swayed, fighting for hand and foothold. It was not an even match; Sir Reginald outweighed Belford by at least one class. Sir Reginald punched Belford in the ribs, the hammer blow forcing a grunt from the poor man. He rallied and elbowed the side of Sir Reginald's head, breaking the heavier man's hold. They clashed again, both using their weight in a bone-crunching attempt to bring the other down. Stalemate; another grapple. Sir Reginald slammed his knuckles into Belford's head wound, ripping away the bandage. A cur's blow. Belford grabbed at the back sofa to steady himself, the reopened wound bleeding into his eyes. Sir Reginald locked an arm around his throat. Belford dragged on the choking hold, ramming his body against Sir Reginald's.

Clearly, the time to stand back was well and truly over.

I spun around, looking for a weapon. Aha. Two steps and I had the Wedgewood urn in hand, whereupon I gathered my skirts and clambered on to the sofa.

'Turn him around,' I yelled, raising the urn.

Belford gave a low roar and wrenched Sir Reginald in a semi-circle that brought him up against the sofa. I positioned the urn over Sir Reginald's head, but before I could bring it down, he hauled Belford around again. The two men faced me, swaying as they fought for a break in the other's hold.

'Back!' I ordered.

Belford widened his eyes at me: *I'm trying*. He elbowed Sir Reginald in the gut: once, twice. Sir Reginald buckled slightly, enough for Belford to heave the man around again, positioning him under the urn. With all my strength, I slammed the Wedgewood down. It smashed across Sir Reginald's crown in a blue explosion of very fine porcelain.

With a grunt, he collapsed on to the carpet.

Belford stepped back and pressed his hand over his re-opened wound, staunching the flow of blood. 'Nice aim,' he said looking up from Sir Reginald's inert body.

'Thank you.' I stepped off the sofa. 'Time to go, I think.'

He gave a nod. 'Quite.' He looked out of the window at the groom holding Sir Reginald's saddled horse. 'Might as well be hanged as a horse thief as well.'

Ellery arrived at the drawing room doorway just as we were heading out of it, his stout form blocking our way. He stared at his master laid out on the floor, then looked back at us, face wary.

'Do you intend to impede our departure?' Belford asked, fists clenched.

With a lift of one shoulder, Ellery stood aside. It seemed his loyalty did not extend to physical confrontation.

James, the young groom, gave up Sir Reginald's stocky chestnut without much of a struggle too; a promise to return the beast unharmed and a half-crown in his hand had the deal done. The boy even helped me up into the saddle so that I sat across Belford's lap in an awkward and rather scandalous sideways mount.

Sir Reginald, it seemed, treated his servants as ill as his wife, and was now paying the price.

Belford urged the horse into a trot and we made our way to the estate gates in a most uncomfortable and jolting manner. Even so, it did not seem to matter. Perhaps it was the flush of success that dulled the discomfort, or maybe it was Belford's hold around my waist.

'Do you think Sir Reginald is dead?' I asked as Belford eased the horse into a walk along the London road.

With both of us upon its back, the poor creature was carrying a substantial load and, quite rightly, Belford did not want to overtax it. The dear man, himself, was almost falling sideways off the animal from fatigue. I was holding him up as much as he was holding me.

'Sir Reginald is a villain,' I added, 'but I would not want his life upon my conscience.'

'I would say it is highly unlikely,' Belford said. 'And if he is, I will take the blame. I am already a convicted murderer, after all.'

'So another one would not make a difference?'

'Not at all.'

'A bargain lot, in fact.'

'A positive boon to my reputation as a highwayman.' He tightened his grip around me slightly. 'All joking aside, my dear, when he does recover, he may make a lot of trouble. He knows who you are.'

'True.' I waved an annoying fly from the dried blood upon his poor face. 'But right now, my real brother is sitting in Parliament and Countess Devonport is sitting in our house, taking tea and ready to swear before God that my sister and I were at home for the whole afternoon.'

'How did you manage to enlist the Countess?'

'We completed a small service on her behalf. She is most grateful.'

'So this escapade is not an isolated incident?'

I smiled. 'Not at all.'

He shook his head. 'Incorrigible woman. You are quite wonderful, aren't you?'

I flushed at the admiration in his eyes.

We both looked ahead at the grind of cartwheels coming from the London direction, travelling at speed.

'That is most likely Samuel,' I said. Damn, so soon.

Belford urged the horse to the side of the road. He dismounted, somewhat untidily, then grasped my waist and swung me down to the ground. I did not pull away from his grip. Completely shameless, but he needed the support after all.

He looked down at me and smiled, the sheer enjoyment of the adventure alight in his eyes. Impulsively, I reached up and touched his cheek. I felt him draw a sharp breath; saw the enjoyment in his eyes flare into something quite different. He closed his hand over mine, holding my touch against his skin, and right then it became clear to me that I had, in fact, finally met my match. We stood leaning against one another, silent, the horse shielding us from sight as a small gig drew alongside.

'My lady, is that you?' Samuel called.

'Yes, all is well,' I replied. 'I will be with you directly.'

Belford cleared his throat and stepped away. 'Lady Augusta, it has been a pleasure.'

'Indeed, Belford.'

He gathered the reins in his hand. 'Goodbye.'

'Wait!' I laid my hand upon his arm. 'What if I should wish to contact you?'

For a fleeting moment his hand covered mine again. 'You should not, my dear,' he said. 'I am no longer Lord Evan Belford. I have not been for ten years. I cannot walk in your world anymore and I'll be damned if I drag you into mine.'

I refrained from pointing out that his very refusal proved he was still very much Lord Evan. 'What if I need your help again?'

He hesitated, but I knew he would not refuse. 'You are the most stubborn woman, Lady Augusta. If you need my help, a letter addressed to Jonathan Hargate at *The White Hart* in Reading will reach me.'

'Jonathan Hargate,' I repeated.

'That is who I am for now.' He bowed. 'Hargate, at your service, my lady.' He smiled – so much regret and loneliness within it – then turned and led the horse into the woods.

I watched until I could no longer see his figure amidst the foliage and low, dappled sunlight. And then I watched for just a little bit longer.

He was gone, and in that moment I understood – to a small degree – my poor Freddie's anguish over George.

London, May 4th 1812

I put down my teacup and peered more closely at the invitation to the Southcote's ball that had arrived in the morning mail. For some reason they had chosen a most impenetrable font.

'I cannot even make out the date on this,' I commented.

Of course, the letter I most desperately wanted had not arrived. Another day of silence. It had been almost two weeks since I had sent my letter to *The White Hart*. Perhaps it had never reached the inn. Or he had not yet picked it up. Or maybe something had happened to him. I quelled that line of thought. It had already kept me up four nights in a row.

Freddie picked up the next letter on her pile and broke the wafer, smoothing open the single page.

'It is another from Honoria Dellaquist.' She scanned the neat lines. 'Amelia is in Ireland now and quite well. Sir Reginald has instigated a divorce. Honoria says it will take a few years, but it will be the best outcome for Amelia despite the social ramifications. Apparently he attempted to drag us all into it, but was dissuaded by his solicitors once it had been established that we and dear Ratton,' she looked up with a small smile,' had been in London during the time in question.'

I nodded. 'Good.'

'She sends her best wishes and once again hopes that she can repay us in some way in the future.' Freddie folded the letter and put it aside. 'Another success.'

'Yes, quite.'

She eyed me soberly. 'Gussie, he may never answer. He said he did not want to drag you into his sordid world.'

I lifted a shoulder. 'I know.'

'You are worrying yourself to a frazzle. Perhaps we should go to Brighton. Get some sea air. A change of scene and all that.'

'This early in the Season?' I shook my head. 'No. I am quite well.' I returned to the Southcote's invitation. 'What do you think this says?'

Freddie reached across and picked up the card, viewing it through narrowed eyes. 'Good Lord, what were they thinking?'

The door opened to admit Weatherley, carrying his salver with a single letter upon it.

'Lady Augusta, this was just delivered to you. By hand.'

My heart clenched. I rose from my chair. 'Delivered by a man?'

'I'm afraid not,' Weatherley said, sympathy in his brown eyes. ' A rather grimy boy of about ten. He said he had been paid to bring it here.'

'Oh.' I took the letter and sat down. The paper was rough – the kind offered in second-rate inns – and our address across the front was written in a bold hand. I tore the wafer and unfolded it, my hold upon the page not quite steady.

The White Hart
Reading
4th May, 1812

My dear Incorrigible, do not even think it!

Our acquaintance may be short, but I know exactly how that brilliant mind of yours works and I insist that you do not delve into the events of ten years ago. It is ancient history and I fear that any investigation will be quite dangerous. I could not bear it if you were to suffer on my account. If you wish to do something for me, then forget that we ever met and live a happy and long life.

Evan Belford.

'Well?' Freddie asked. 'Is it from him? What does it say?'

I touched the scrawled signature as if it could somehow translate my full heart back to him. He had used his real name. And he was quite right; I was his dear Incorrigible.

I looked across at my sister and smiled.

'Freddie, darling, I believe we have a new commission.'

ANDREW NETTE

Save a Last Kiss *for* Satan

Lara wasn't sure how long she'd been standing in front of the reinforced steel door before she finally plucked up the courage to press the red button on the wall beside it.

The light from the nearest street lamp struggled to penetrate the narrow alley, illuminating a pile of plastic garbage bags from a nearby Chinese restaurant, before giving up and leaving her in darkness. Lara saw something move. She hoped it was a rat, although given the events of the last couple of weeks, she seriously doubted it. She shivered, pulled her denim jacket tight around her. A humid summer night in Melbourne, but she was cold.

The feeling of uncertainly wasn't a good fit for a woman with a reputation for being a tough nut in difficult situations. And being a homicide detective, she'd experienced a lot of difficult situations. Always primary through the door, her male colleagues joked, using a phrase one had picked up from a US cop show.

She was about to give in to the urge to leave when there was a noise on the other side of the door, bolts being loosened and pushed back. The metal door slowly opened to reveal a man. He was short, only up to Lara's shoulders, bone thin, with peroxide blonde hair, cut close to the scalp. He stared at Lara with bloodshot eyes rimmed with eyeliner. His dress reminded Lara of one of the '80s New Wave bands she'd loved as a teenager: battered winkle-pickers, black stovepipe jeans, a brown suit coat over a grubby striped T-shirt. A razor blade dangled from one earlobe and he wore chain link for a necklace.

'Let me guess, you're not Jeeves.'

He sniffed, scratched his crotch. 'Name's Ronson,' he replied in a nasal voice.

'And I'm–'

'We know who you are.' He stepped aside to let her enter. 'Doctor Mordecai is expecting you.' He waved her towards a grimy service elevator, closed the front door and replaced the bolts. Music reverberated somewhere overhead, throbbing electric guitar chords and synthesiser. By the time the elevator came to a stop the unmistakable sound of Jim Morrison singing about the end filled the air.

Lara stepped into a large room. Mismatched pieces of antique furniture fought for space with a large collection of bare mannequins, many missing arms and heads. A thick red curtain hid one side of the room. The remaining walls were plastered with old rock concert posters.

Her well-trained cop senses kicked into gear. She sniffed, registered dust and the aroma of marijuana. She noticed a smirk on Ronson's face. Mordecai's offsider, or whatever he was, taking pleasure at her disorientation.

The Doors song reached a crescendo as bass and symbols joined in the musical chaos then abruptly ended.

'Welcome, Miss McBride.'

Lara turned to where she thought the voice had come from. 'Mordecai?' The fact he'd been observing her the entire time only added to her discomfort.

An overweight man emerged from the shadows between two mannequins, waddled towards the curtained-off section of the wall. He was barefoot, clad only in a caftan, heavy black material with gold piping. Large hexagon-shaped dark sunglasses hid his eyes.

'The Summer of Love's been over for a while, or didn't you get that memo?'

He gave her a faint smile, as if humouring a slow student and lifted the curtain to reveal the entrance to another room. The walls, floor and ceiling were painted black. Large white candles stationed at various points provided the only illumination. As her eyes adjusted to the gloom, she made out shelves crammed with thick tomes, cushions strewn on the floor. In one corner there was an altar draped in red fabric. She stepped towards it. On it rested an assortment of occult paraphernalia, including a large knife, a brass bowl, cups and a human skull.

Mordecai cleared his throat, indicated one of the cushions.

As she sat, Ronson closed the door behind them. He leaned against the wall, took a rollie out of his pocket, lit it with a battered Zippo and drew deep. The pungent smell of marijuana filled the room.

'You're Mordecai?'

'Doctor Mordecai,' he said with a hint of annoyance as he lowered his considerable bulk onto the cushion in front of her. 'Tell me about your grandfather, Miss McBride.'

She made several attempts to start the story, but each time the words got tangled up or wouldn't come out.

Mordecai was unperturbed by Lara's lack of focus. He sat cross-legged on a large cushion, hands on his ample stomach, like a contented Buddha. His thick fingers were covered in rings, including one set with a giant turquoise stone. He was completely hairless except for a narrow grey goatee, which along with his small mouth was almost swallowed by the ample flesh around chin and neck.

'Fuck this.' Lara snapped her fingers several times at Ronson. 'You, last of the punk rockers, hand me the joint.'

'Been a while between joints for me being a cop and all, but, damn, that's good.'

She took another hit, cleared her throat. 'Tobias McBride, my grandfather on my mother's side, left Melbourne on his 18th birthday in 1931, travelled to Paris, where, if the stories I've heard are true, he hung out with various assorted Left Bank bohemians and weirdos and acquired a nasty opium addiction.'

She took another pull, handed what was left of the roach to Ronson.

'After drying out, he travelled to New York, lived there for several years, before returning to Melbourne just days before the start of World War II. To the surprise of those familiar with his alternative leanings, Tobias joined the army. From what my parents told me he was in some sort of secretive intelligence unit which took him all across Southeast Asia, or the Orient as he used to call it.

'He stayed in the military after the war, stints in Korea, Malaya, Borneo, was amongst the first Australian military advisors sent to South Vietnam. He finally left the army after Vietnam, but continued to travel regularly to Asia. Don't ask me what he did on those journeys. My parents never told me. I'm not even sure they knew themselves.

'His trips got longer and he ventured further afield, the hippie trail, remote

India, northern Laos, Burma. He would have been in his 60s by then and Christ only knows how he got into some of those places. He'd just take off for months at a time. The only way my late mother even knew he was still alive were the packages he sent back.

'Packages?' said Mordecai.

'Curios from his travels, small statues, stones, photographs. Once he sent home a mummified finger, or so Mum claimed. They were so interesting and exotic, a link to a life of adventure I could hardly imagine. I still have a few bits and pieces stored away.

'It was during one of these trips, to northern Burma, he disappeared for good. Gone like a puff of smoke, never to be seen again. That was 1982. I was just a child. I'd hardly ever met the man but I remember being devastated. But over the years he gradually slipped out of my mind and I forgot about him altogether.' She paused. 'Until a couple of weeks ago.'

Ronson had long since stopped paying attention to the conversation, and was tidying up one of the bookshelves. Mordecai shifted his bulk on the cushion, stifled a yawn. 'What changed?'

'I saw my grandfather across a crowded street.'

Mordecai remained silent, his eyes unreadable under the dark sunglasses.

'At first I thought my mind was playing tricks on me, maybe stress from the job. Here I am in broad daylight in the middle of the Melbourne CBD and I'm seeing a vision of my grandfather, lost over 30 years ago in the Burmese jungle.'

'Perhaps it was simply someone who looked like him,' said Mordecai.

'It was the briefest of flashes. One second he was watching me, the next he was gone. But it was my grandfather, I'm positive.'

She reached into the pocket of her denim jacket, extracted a photograph, and glanced at the image before handing it to Mordecai. 'This is the last known picture of him.'

Tobias McBride was standing in front of a stone statue in a beige safari suit, a riot of jungle green around him, staring intently into the camera. The colour in the photograph had faded with age, become milky, but it was definitely the same man, gaunt features, piercing eyes, a hawk-like nose, and a good head of fine hair, including long sideburns.

Mordecai gave the photo a desultory glance, handed it back.

'There have been other times.' She laughed nervously, aware how ridiculous her story sounded. 'Once, I saw him across a crowded restaurant, late one night on the street outside my apartment window. Even in the crowd behind the crime scene ribbon at a murder scene I was investigating. I've tried to get a good fix on him but it's like he's only ever just visible at the edge of my vision. When I turn to look at him, he's gone.'

'I see,' said Mordecai. He offered Lara the joint.

'That's it?' she said, suddenly angry at the fat man's dismissive attitude.

'What did you expect?'

'Something a little more than two or three word answers and sitting around in some creepy room pulling on joints with a couple of refugees from the 60s and 70s.'

'Miss McBride, I'm not an easy man to locate.' His voice was soft but filled with authority. 'I agreed to meet with you and hear what you had to say, because you showed the requisite ingenuity finding me. But I'm not inclined to have my time wasted by ridiculous stories about shadows and long-lost grandfather explorers.'

'I thought–'

'What? That I was some cheap medium or ghost chaser?' His voice became deeper, more threatening. 'What do you want me to do? Conduct a séance so you can talk to your lost grandfather? Or maybe it's an exorcism you're after? A bit of screaming and throwing up into a bin by the side of the bed to free you of whatever foul spirit you say besieges you? Don't insult me. I am no mere suburban conjurer content to deal with such trivia. You have psychiatrists in the police force. I suggest you think about consulting one for what is obviously a simple case of stress.'

She tried to think of a cutting reply, but nothing came. 'I've obviously come to the wrong place,' she said weakly.

'It would appear so, Miss McBride.' Mordecai heaved his bulk upright and walked towards one of the shelves, plucked a leather-bound volume and was instantly engrossed in its contents. 'Now, if you have nothing left to say, I suggest you leave,' he said. 'Ronson, show her out.'

It took two double scotches at the nearest bar to take the edge off her anger. The police force had changed a lot, but one thing was still true, you had to be tough to be a female cop, a female homicide D even tougher. She'd seen and done things most people couldn't imagine, but that overweight hippy whatever-he-was and his snivelling sidekick had treated her like a child.

She ordered a third double, drained half, and was struck by another possibility. Someone was fucking with her. Her prime suspect was Laurie Cleave, an unorthodox old school D with a fetish for esoteric porn. It was well known Cleave's extra curricula activities, combined with some of the peculiar cases he'd worked, had taken him to strange places. No surprise, then, that when she'd put out feelers, under the pretense of following up on a possible occult lead for a case she was working, Cleave had been the only one to come back to her.

'Lara, my girl, you've been played for a sucker.' She laughed, raised her glass, toasted the other customers, a couple of sunburnt backpackers and several office workers. Her relief quickly turned to exhaustion. She drained her glass, waved away the barman's offer of another and exited the pub. There'd be time to plot a suitable revenge on Cleave later. Right now she needed sleep.

Close to 11 pm, the mid-week city streets were almost deserted. She paused outside the pub, suddenly nervous about confronting the night. Cleave's hijinks aside, everything she'd told Mordecai was true. Or at least she thought it was. Maybe the old hippy was right. Maybe she'd been working too hard and the stress was getting to her. Lara promised herself to make an appointment with clinical services first thing in the morning then went in search of a taxi.

She passed an alleyway, heard grunts, saw an old woman tugging at a shopping trolley piled high with recycled metal cans. The woman turned, a fearful expression on her face.

'You okay?' Lara raised her hands slightly, palms facing out. The woman shrugged, went back to pulling at the trolley. Lara edged closer, saw one of the wheels stuck in the grate of a drain. 'Let me help you.'

The woman stepped away as Lara gripped the trolley's handle, pulled hard several times, failed to dislodge the wheel. 'Well and truly stuck, isn't it?'

As Lara bent down next to the drain to get a better look, she heard the sound of clothes tearing but before she could look up she felt herself lifting off the ground. Her body flew through the air – until a stack of cardboard boxes broke her fall.

She lay amid the crushed cardboard, plastic wrap and packing foam. A smell called her back from the darkness; it was the unmistakable stench of distant chemistry classes – sulphur.

'What the fuck?' She groaned, opened her eyes and watched in horror.

The old woman's body pulsated, her bones becoming more pronounced, the exposed skin underneath her ripped clothes mottled and scaly. Her arms became muscular, needle-like claws protruded from her fingertips.

Lara could still make out the old woman's face, but the eyes were opaque and her teeth shark-like.

The creature moved uncertainly around the alley, like an infant taking its first steps. Remembering the semi-automatic pistol at her side, Lara fumbled with the clasp on her holster, withdrew the weapon. The beast noticed the movement, lashed out, knocked the gun from her hand. Lara heard the piece of metal skid across the ground into the darkness. The monster leaned towards her, its mouth wide. Lara almost gagged on the charnel stench.

Just as the creature was about to go in for the kill, it stopped, gazed down at a sharp metal point that now protruded from its chest. Thick green liquid oozed from the wound. The air crackled and blurred and, once again, the old woman stood in front of Lara. The woman threw her head back, opened her mouth and spewed a swarm of flies followed by a stream of foul smelling green liquid that splashed over Lara.

As the old women dropped to the ground, Lara noticed another figure standing at the mouth of the alley. It took her a few moments to identify Ronson. He held an old-fashioned heavy-looking crossbow in both hands.

Lara was too stunned to do anything but watch Ronson move towards her. He had a faint limp in one leg.

'You okay, love?'

'Now I know I'm having a nightmare,' Lara said taking his outstretched hand and allowing herself to be slowly pulled up.

'This is no time for jokes.' Ronson was clad in a long leather jacket with large lapels. 'Are you hurt?'

Lara patted herself down. 'Don't think so.'

'Good.' Ronson slung the crossbow across his shoulder, his movements clean and fast, unaffected by whatever drugs he'd consumed earlier in the evening. 'That wasn't the only Drude in the city tonight. We have to get to safety before the others locate us.'

'What others? I'm not going anywhere until you tell me what the hell a Drude is.'

'A particularly nasty demon, believe me, we don't want to meet any more of them.'

'A demon? You're shitting me!'

'I never joke about demons. Any more questions will have to wait until later. We need to get the fuck out of Dodge.'

'Where?'

Ronson fossicked inside the folds of his coat, withdrew a cigarette, lit up.

'The only place you'll be safe tonight, Mordecai's.'

'He just kicked me out and now you want me to go back?'

'Listen, we don't have much time, but the story about your grandfather, the things you said have been going on, they are true.'

'What about the dead woman?'

'I'll take care of her.'

'Shouldn't we call the police?'

Ronson looked at her deadpan. Lara realised the irony of her statement, breathed in deeply and exhaled several times. 'Okay, but first I've got to find my gun.'

Lara located her weapon underneath a dumpster at the end of the alley and re-holstered it.

Ronson knelt next to the dead woman, pulled the crossbow bolt out and slipped it into his coat pockets. He sprinkled something from a small bottle over the woman's corpse. The body shuddered, and Lara caught another whiff of sulphur, but the old woman's face looked peaceful.

'Now let's go,' said Ronson over his shoulder as he walked out of the alley.

Lara followed.

The service elevator stopped at a well-lit space, lined on all sides with potted tropical plants and life-sized human statues, most of them in pornographic stances. A domed atrium overlooked the room, the night sky visible through the grimy glass.

Doctor Mordecai was lying on a chaise lounge, stood when he saw them emerge from the elevator. He wore a red velvet smoking jacket over a white shirt with frills down the front, a black cravat around his fleshy throat, flared black pants, Cuban-heeled black boots. The clothes conveyed a sense of purpose lacking in his attire from earlier in the evening, while looking no less out of sync with the times.

'Was it a Drude?' said Mordecai.

'Yeah, big one.' Ronson unslung the crossbow, leant it against a wall. He opened a wooden cabinet to reveal a mindboggling array of bottles in various shapes and sizes, selected one, unscrewed the cap and took a swig. 'There's others. They'll have realised by now one of their number has been eliminated.' He wiped the mouth with the side of his hand, glanced at Lara. 'Won't take them long to track her here.'

'Indeed. The disturbance in the night grows strong. Soon we will have visitors.'

'I thought you didn't believe my story?' Lara said, inspecting the nearest statues, two well-endowed females engaging in an elaborate display of mutual cunnilingus.

'A ruse, Miss McBride, to lure the minions of evil out of their hiding places.'

Lara looked for signs of mockery in Mordecai's porcine features, detected none.

'With me as the fucking bait?'

'The battle against evil requires us to be as cunning as our foes.'

'So, I'm not insane after all?'

'No.' Mordecai placed a hand on Lara's shoulder. She was surprised to find the gesture comforting.

'I felt the evil in the air with your presence earlier this evening, its tentacles reaching through the fabric of time and space.'

Lara met his gaze. 'Maybe you're the crazy one.'

'If that is so, what does it make you for seeking my help?'

'Good point.'

Ronson took another swig from the bottle. 'We're wasting time.'

'My assistant is right, we must prepare our defences.'

Ronson placed the bottle back on the shelf and disappeared into an adjoining room as Mordecai rummaged through the mess on the glass-topped table next to the chaise lounge. He found what he was looking for, a clear plastic bottle, shook out a couple of tablets, threw them in his mouth, chased them down with half a finger of clear liquid in a cut glass tumbler.

'You sure it's a good idea to face the hordes of Satan high?'

'Merely an aid in marshalling my spiritual forces.' Mordecai withdraw a large stick of white chalk from one of the pockets of his jacket, got down on one knee and, with nimble movements that belied his massive girth, started to draw a large circle on the wooden floor. The magician drew a smaller circle within the large one and proceeded to fill the space in-between with symbols. As he worked, Ronson re-entered the room stooped under the weight of a fat white candle affixed to a long, heavy medieval looking metal base, like some punk rock Quasimodo. He set it down near the circle, disappeared again.

'That thing in the alley–'

'The Drude?' Mortdecai stood, watched Ronson re-enter the room with another candle and base, place it on the opposite side of the circle to the first. 'A particularly loathsome species of demon that hires itself out to the highest bidder, a kind of supernatural soldier of fortune.'

Ronson brought two more candles, placed them opposite each other. He flicked a light switch, plunging the room into darkness for a moment before firing up his Zippo. He lit a cigarette and touched the lighter flame to each of the candles. The air filled up with a sickly sweet smell.

Mordecai sat cross-legged in the middle of the circle, hands in the lotus position, his massive stomach straining against his shirt and jacket. 'Now I must seal the circle, charge it with power of fire, earth and water.' He closed his eyes and started humming.

'Doctor Mordecai?' said Lara.

'He can't hear you.' Ronson exhaled a stream of cigarette smoke, coughed, his face red and puffy from the exertion of setting up the candles.

'What do you mean?'

'His body is here but he has sent his spirit to one of the astral planes to marshal psychic energy to help with our defence.'

'Defence against what?'

'More of those demons you met in the alley, amongst other things.'

'What do we do?'

'We get in the circle, stay there until morning.'

'That's it?'

'Yeah, pretty much.' Ronson dropped his cigarette on the floor. 'There's one other thing,' he said, grinding it out with the heel of one of his winkle-pickers. 'Whatever happens, whatever you see, don't leave the circle.'

'What happens if I do? Will I get sent to the naughty corner?'

'Those creatures will drag you down into the most loathsome of pits of hell and feast on your flesh for eternity.'

'Like that thing in the desert in *Return of the Jedi*, the Sarlacc?'

'Yeah,' Ronson flashed her a crooked smile. 'But for real.'

Lara stepped into the circle, sat down on the smooth wooden floor in front of the meditating magician. Ronson sat next to her. Mordecai's chanting grew louder. She winced as she noticed the odour from the liquid, now semi-dried, that the creature in the alley had spewed on her.

'Wish I could change these clothes. I stink.'

Ronson said nothing.

'You're not going to go into a trance or whatever he's doing, too?'

'No.'

'Good.'

She looked up through the atrium glass. The sky was completely covered in cloud, which seemed to swirl and pulsate. The room suddenly felt cold. The flickering candle flames sent shadows across the room.'

'Ronson?' Steam came from her mouth, hung in the air in front of her.

'Yeah.'

'I'm scared.'

'Makes you feel any better, love, so am I.' He cupped his hand around the Zippo's flame to light a cigarette.

'How did you get involved with Mordecai?' she said in an effort to distract herself.

Ronson took a long hit on his cigarette.

'I was a teenager living in a bible-belt town in rural South Australia. I was nerdy, wore black and Doc Martin's boots, liked punk music. I might as well have hung a sign around my neck saying 'child of the devil', which, as it turned out, was exactly how the local fundamentalist pastor regarded me.'

'Try and save you, did he?'

A gust of freezing cold air blew across the room. The foliage on the potted plants rustled. Lara reached out, grabbed Ronson's arm.

'He and a couple of other members of his congregation plucked me off the street on my way home from school one day, drove me to a deserted house on the outskirts of town, tied me to an old four-poster bed and over the next couple of days attempted to drive the devil out of me. One at a time.'

'Jesus Christ,' whispered Lara.

'He was nowhere to be seen. But Mordecai was. There was a storm, I remember hearing the sound of rain on the tin roof and the crazy fucker just appeared, like an overweight version of Caine; you know, the character in that TV series, *Kung Fu*. He was even bald like him.

'I'm not quite sure what happened. The men who were abusing me started screaming. Before I knew it, Mordecai was carrying me like a baby across a paddock, the rain beating against my face. Over his shoulder, I could see the house where I'd been held prisoner burning.' Ronson extinguished his cigarette on the floor, shrugged. 'Been with him ever since.'

'So what do you do, when you're not slaying demons that is?'

'I make myself useful.'

'Doing what, scoring his drugs?'

'Yeah, amongst other things.'

'The limp you have, that a wound from one of your battles with evil?'

'Nah, a particularly drunken Stranglers' gig I went to back in 1979. I was pissed and slipped on a puddle of beer and–'

They heard tapping on the atrium glass, looked up at the same time, saw a distorted face leering down, quickly disappear.

She gripped Ronson's arm harder. 'What was that?'

Before Ronson could answer, the service elevator kicked into life with a mechanical whine and started to descend.

'Please tell me that's your doing, that you have a remote control or something.'

'No.

'Who did it, then?'

'I'd say our first guest has arrived.'

'Oh shit, oh fuck, I'm not sure I can take this.' Lara fingered the grip of her pistol, but the weapon failed to reassure her. The elevator stopped with a metallic wheeze. After a moment, it kicked back into life, started to ascend. A strong gust of wind blew from nowhere, rustling the leaves of the tropical potted plants.

Mordecai gently rocked backwards and forwards behind them, his humming interspersed with low-pitched grunting sounds, as if he were talking in his sleep. Lara turned to Ronson, did a double take at what looked like the hypodermic needle in his hand.

'Fuck me, Ronson,' Lara shouted above the noise, 'are you sure now's the best time to shoot up? You're as bad as Mordecai.'

'It's not for me, love.'

'Who is it for then?'

'You.'

He jabbed the needle in her arm, pushed the plunger down. She wanted to hit Ronson, but suddenly lacked the energy to do anything other than collapse against him.

'Sorry, love, but it's easier this way.' His words sounded far away.

He cradled her head in his lap. She turned to face the direction of the elevator vaguely aware it had stopped again. She heard footsteps, watched a pair of battered boots approach. With great effort, she looked up, recognised the gaunt visage of her grandfather, his face cadaverous, his dark eyes shining with fierce energy as they stared down at her. She smelt soil and vegetation.

She opened her mouth to scream but before she could make any noise, darkness engulfed her.

Lara opened her eyes. She lay on the floor in a square of warm sunlight, blue sky visible through the atrium glass above her. The circle Mordecai had drawn was smudged but still visible. She dabbed a finger in one of the strange signs. The residue was dry and gritty.

The room around her looked like it had hosted a wild party. The floor was covered in broken glass and dark scuff marks, overturned plants and statues. Several of the windowpanes in the atrium roof were broken. The four heavy candle bases remained upright, melted down to stubs, puddles of wax on the floor around them. She glanced at her watch. Just after 10 am. She'd been out for over eight hours. No sign of Ronson and Mordecai but she heard music playing somewhere in the building. They couldn't be far away.

Her head throbbed and her mouth was dry, no doubt side effects from whatever Ronson had administered. She rubbed her arm where the needle had gone in, stood up. She remembered her grandfather. Was it a dream or had he really been in the room? She shook her head to try and clear it, went to look for her hosts.

She followed the music; heavy guitar chords of The Who's *Won't Get Fooled Again* – apt after what had transpired last night – down a hallway lined with framed sepia pictures of couples copulating in a forest. She came to a doorway, parted a curtain of red beads, peered inside.

Mordecai lay half submerged in an old-fashioned claw-foot tub, skin pink, eyes closed, sucking on a pipe connected to a brass hookah. A faint aroma of resin she recognised as hash, mixed with the smell of coffee and whatever was cooking in a large heavy fry pan on a stove. Ronson, his back to her, pushed something around in the pan with a spatula, paused to sip from a floral teacup. Next to the cup was an ashtray in which sat a smouldering joint. A large wooden table on one side of the room was set for three. Neither man registered her presence in the doorway.

Ronson was naked except for dark jeans. The skin on his back was hairless and bone white except for the faint outline of pink scar tissue in the shape of a pentacle. An image of a teenage Ronson, tied to the bed, heavyset male shapes slackening themselves on his body, flashed through her mind, momentarily lessoning the anger she felt towards him.

She glanced around for the source of the music, a turntable on top of a set of rectangular wood-panelled speakers. She withdrew her pistol, aimed. The turntable exploded into pieces. Mordecai sat up in the bath, eyes wide, soapy water slopping over the sides. Ronson dropped the teacup on the floor where it shattered. He wheeled around as she fired again, blowing holes in each speaker.

'Sorry to interrupt breakfast,' she said, blowing smoke from the barrel of her pistol for effect, 'but we need to talk.'

'My bootleg copy of *The Who live at the Electric Factory in Philadelphia, 1969*,' Ronson said. 'Do you know how hard that will be to replace?'

He looked older in the daylight, the skin on his face drawn and covered in white whiskers, his eyes rimmed with red.

'I don't appreciate strange men drugging me,' she said, re-holstering her firearm.

'We couldn't take the chance you might freak the fuck out and endanger us all.'

'Remind me to talk to you about informed consent sometime.'

'My companion speaks the truth,' said Mordecai, settling back into the bathwater, the pipe paused on his lower lip. 'It was for your own good.'

'Okay, maybe you're both right. I probably would've freaked out last night. But as of right now, I'm through with being scared. Now I just want to get to the bottom of what is going on. No more treating me as a passenger. I came to you for help, true, but it seems to me that now we're all in this together. I want to know what's going on. And you,' she stared at Ronson, 'I see another hypodermic needle, I swear, I'll kick your arse into tomorrow.'

Ronson picked up the joint in two fingers, dragged deep.

Lara walked over to the stove, poured herself a cup of coffee. 'One of you, talk.'

Mordecai spoke. 'Satan, Beelzebub, Amadeus, Charon, whatever you wish to call him, he is very real and it takes more than a bunch of old kiddie fiddlers in white collars and a crucifix to stop him.'

'And?'

'While Satan is powerful, there are limits to his reach. He needs a suitable vessel to help transport him between planes. He selected Tobias McBride. Why and how I am not exactly sure.'

'I don't understand. My grandfather's been missing for over 30 years–'

'He is not your grandfather,' said Mordecai sternly, 'not any longer.'

'Fine. This thing, whatever it is, that is appearing in the shape of my grandfather, why has it come now?'

'The times suit Satan. All the bloodshed and destruction embolden the creature, giving him power to attempt to cross over, bring on the end times, cleanse our world of what little remains and fill the air with ash and fire–'

'Okay, okay. I get it. What else?'

'He requires something else to help complete the crossing. Something you possess.'

'I possess?'

'Yes. Something your grandfather gave you.'

'My grandfather gave me jack shit. He was always off on his travels, was hardly ever around.'

'Think, Lara. You mentioned your grandfather sometimes sent you things he found on his journeys.'

'Like I said, nothing valuable, photos, trinkets, on his last trip to Burma, just before he disappeared, he sent a journal.'

Mordecai and Ronson exchanged a glance

'What?' She looked between them. 'It was just a travel diary, notes on places he had visited, the sites, usual stuff.'

'Where is it?'

'A storage facility – with my other junk.'

'Ronson, my towel.' Mordecai stood up, his huge body glistening with water, started to dry himself, the towel tiny against his rolls of flab. 'We haven't got a moment to spare.'

Lara rummaged through the items in the storage container, located the cardboard box containing the last known possessions of Tobias McBride. Amid the old postcards, faded photographs, ticket stubs, letters, invalid passports, and a small statue of a masked man with an exaggerated-sized penis, was the battered leather-bound notebook. It contained page after page of her grandfather's neat handwriting, broken only by the occasional fine-lined illustration of a temple or map location.

Lara proffered the book to Mordecai, who placed his bulk on one of a matching set of dining room chairs she'd bought years ago, but never used, and started reading.

Now the magician was dressed in an electric blue velvet dinner jacket and claret-coloured shirt and black flares. His piece de resistance was a lime-green cravat. His face, including the generously applied eyeshadow, was hidden by hexagonal sunglasses and a broad-brimmed floppy black felt hat. Oblivious to the heat, Ronson wore his long leather jacket over a faded Ziggy Stardust T-Shirt, black jeans and his winklepickers.

Lara had wanted to go back to her apartment and change but Mordecai had ruled it out as too dangerous. She'd showered at the magician's and changed into the only clothes they could find, brown knee-length calfskin boots and a paisley mini dress. Her pistol was in a crochet handbag slung over her shoulder.

'Where's your tambourine?' Ronson had said when he laid eyes on her new garb.

'Shut it,' she'd said, pulling at the miniskirt in an unsuccessful attempt to make it longer.

'Seriously, you look groovy, baby.'

'One more word…' Lara silenced him with a poisonous look.

Mordecai scanned the journal intently, flicking back to re-read a passage every now and again. 'I have found what the dark one is after,' he said finally.

'Go on.' Lara made no effort to hide the annoyance in her voice.

'I assume you've never heard of Lord Reginald Le Fay?'

'You assume correctly.'

'He was a prominent British forensic pathologist in the late 18th century and a powerful necromancer. Such were his associations with influential members of the London's elite that his more unorthodox proclivities were overlooked. That is until the bodies of several young children, horrifically mutilated, were found in the vicinity of his house. When the evidence of these crimes pointed to Le Fay, the authorities finally had to act. They raided his townhouse. Le Fey had already fled, tipped off by a senior policeman who was a member of his coven. But in a secret series of chambers underneath the house police found proof of the most horrific ritual abuse.

'Le Fay moved through Europe, appearing in various capitals only to be hounded out again. He reportedly spent time in the Middle East, drinking deep of its dark arts, before travelling through the subcontinent to Burma.'

The hairs on the back of Lara's neck stood up. 'You're shitting me.'

'No,' said Mordecai solemnly. 'What I'm telling you is true. Your late grandfather's journal proves it.'

'Le Fay was never seen again, but stories of his activities surfaced from time to time, the most perstent that he had settled deep in the jungle in northern Burma, where he continued to hone his occult expertise. The rumours say he was particularly obsessed with studying a document he had obtained during his time the Middle East, a parchment on which was written The Spell of Amon Baal.'

'Now you're just making shit up.'

'Were that it was so. But no, Amon Baal was real, a powerful wizard from the time before Christ, said to have created a spell that could open a link between our world and that of Hell.'

Lara started to speak, but Mordecai ignored her.

'According to this journal, your grandfather was no stranger to the occult, having dabbled in it since his time in Paris before the war. He first heard the story of Le Fay and the spell of Amon Baal while he was trekking in Peshawar in the mid-1970s. He became obsessed with locating a complete copy of the spell, was convinced the only way to do this was to locate Le Fay's last known resting place. He succeeded, although he was obviously unprepared for what he found.'

Mordecai opened the notebook, started reading:

'September 12, 1981. What I have discovered here, amid the slime-covered stones and bones, threatens to blast the very fibre of my sanity. Here, amid this spikey-green world, have I found a spell to open a portal linking our world to that of darkness. I wake up in the night, covered in sweat, reeking of charnel fire and the stench of burning flesh and hear Lucifer beckon me. His voice, whispered in the dead of the jungle night, urges me to complete the link, to usher him unto this world. His tongue flays the humanity from me and, to a choir of frogs and insects, I find myself inching closer to the door of his kingdom. I know it is too late for me. I lack the strength to leave this accursed place but there may still be time to remove this book, and with it, the means by which evil can launch into this world.

'That was his last entry,' said Mordecai, closing the journal and handing it to Lara. 'It must have taken enormous willpower, but even as your grandfather was losing his sanity, he knew he had to get rid of the diary, the almost complete spell he had assembled, knowing it was only a matter of time until he succumbed to the temptation to cast it.'

'So, somehow, he got it out of the jungle and in the post, where it ended up in the hands of my late mother in Melbourne, Australia.'

'Yes.'

She ran her fingers over the book's worn leather cover, placed it into the bag slung across her shoulder.

'Now that we have the book does that mean she's safe and there is nothing else to do?' said Ronson.

'No, my peroxide-haired friend, Miss McBride and by extension all of us are in danger as long as the knowledge in this book exists and the forces of evil are seeking to capture it.'

'So, what do we do? Burn the book?'

'It is not that simple. The forces of darkness have already started to cross over to this world. To fully vanquish them we have to track down Satan's base of operations, wipe it out along with the physical form of your late grandfather, deprive the Lord of Darkness of his foothold on this plane, break the temporal link between this world and hell.

Lara took a deep breath. 'And how do we do that?'

Mordecai took out a bundle of grimy oilcloth from the pocket of his jacket. 'With this,' he said, unfolding the cloth to reveal two rusty pieces of metal, one small blunt, the other a spiral shape about 20 centimetres long with a sharp end. Both pieces were covered in carved symbols.

It took Lara a moment to realise the two pieces were designed to join together. She looked at Mordecai disbelievingly. 'You're going to kill Satan's servant on earth with a rusty dagger?'

Mordecai looked offended. 'This is more than a mere dagger. The metal is old and powerful, forged many centuries ago, in a time when humankind still battled hell for domination of the earth. I just need to get close enough to plunge it into Tobias McBride's dead flesh.'

'To stab him, we've got to find him,' said Lara. 'This so-called base of operations of his could be anywhere?'

'I don't think so,' said Ronson, handing something to Lara.

Lara held it up to the florescent light. 'An identity bracelet for a resident of an old people's home.' She read the address aloud.

'Took it from that old bird in the alley. The one that nearly had you for dinner.' Ronson lit a fresh cigarette with the butt of his last. 'I believe it's what you plod call a good lead.'

'Reckon you might be right,' said Lara, pulling at the hem of her miniskirt.

Ronson smiled. 'Time to pay your grandad an unscheduled visit.'

The address on the identity bracelet led them to a gated aged care facility on Melbourne's outer suburban fringe, identical red-tiled roofs visible above a cream brick wall.

Their transport was a purple Mustang convertible, another obvious refugee from the 60s. Ronson drove while Mordecai occupied most of the back seat. Lara sat in the front, nodded along to the music on the stereo, the Rolling Stone's *Gimme Shelter*. Track nine, *Sympathy for the Devil* came on, Lara and Ronson, exchanged looks, burst out laughing at the same time. It felt good to be on the offensive.

Ronson parked several hundred metres from the entrance to the home, killed the engine.

'Notice that?' Mordecai extricated himself awkwardly from the back seat and stood on the nature strip.

'No?' said Lara, joining him.

'Listen.'

'I can't hear a thing.'

'Exactly.' Ronson, looked at his watch. 'Nearly five o'clock, peak hour, but no cars and no people. Unusual, wouldn't you say?'

Lara surveyed the tall gums that lined the side of the road at regular intervals. 'No birds, either.'

'It's as if all life has been eradicated.' Mordecai glanced around. 'I believe this is the right place.'

Lara withdrew her pistol, checked the safety was off. 'What next?'

'You and I deal with whatever is guarding grandad, allow Mordecai to get close enough to administer the *coup de grace*.'

'That easy, huh? And how exactly do you plan doing that, unsettle them with your incredible punk attitude or are you hiding another crossbow in your leather jacket?'

'No.' Ronson reached into the folds of his jacket, brought out a small machine gun. He cocked it, winked at Lara. 'Thought I'd use this.'

They walked through the half-full car park, pushed open the double glass doors into a deserted reception area.

Lara sniffed the air. The unmistakable whiff of sulphur emanated from the darkened hallway leading off from the reception area.

She crept down the corridor, pistol held in both hands, swept the area in front of her for signs of movement. With the exception of a couple of tubes that blinked and spluttered overhead, most of the florescent lights were dead.

After 20 metres the corridor turned left. A plastic sign on the wall incdicated the Common Room. Lara heard moaning, the stench of sulphur stronger. She looked around the corner, gun first, saw a double swing doorway at the end of the corridor, a blur of red light visible through the squares of glass in each door.

She ducked back again, glanced at Ronson, who had paused behind her. 'Looks like someone's having a party.'

'They say life begins at 60.'

Ronson stepped out from behind the corner, edged towards the common room. Lara followed. The moans multiplied, became louder.

Lara and Ronson clung to the wall on either side of the doors. At the same time they brought their eyes level with the squares of glass.

Lara stared in horror. On the parquet floor in the centre of the room, an indeterminate number of males and females, most of them very old, were engaged in various sexual acts. The writhing mass of flesh was bathed in an eerie red glow. A dozen or so men and women, staff judging by their light blue uniforms, stood at points around the room, arms folded, stared vacantly into the space in front of them.

To the right was another passageway, to the left, a stage, lined with thick black candles. Behind their shimmering haze Lara saw a throne-like structure made out of medical equipment, wheelchairs, walking frames, trolleys, the metal and plastic fused together. On it sat her grandfather, no, the appearance of him – she had to keep telling herself that – his legs crossed, hands on the armrests. Next to him was a creature similar to that dispatched by Ronson in the alley, a tall, swollen reptilian form with the face of a wizened old man.

Lara knew she either had to act or the fear would immobilise her. She and Ronson exchanged nods. The two of them kicked the swing doors open and stepped inside. Ronson fired first, a staccato burst that took out the two staff members nearest him. A large, Mediterranean-looking male fixed his gaze on Lara, strode zombie-like towards her, meaty hands outstretched. Whatever evil possessed him and the other staff had dulled their senses and he moved slowly. Lara fired and the back of the man's head exploded and he dropped to the floor. Meanwhile, Ronson strafed another group. Bullets tore through zombie flesh and into a large cabinet full of books and DVDs, sending splinters of wood and shards of glass into the air.

A wave of hysteria went through the fornicating bodies. The moaning became louder, the sexual acts frenzied and more brutal. Individuals tore at grey hair and scratched the flesh of their partners.

Lara and Ronson moved around the mass of bodies, easily dispatching the shuffling staff members as they tried to attack. In between shots, Lara glanced at the figure of Tobias McBride, still seated on his makeshift throne, his demonic guardian at his side. Neither had moved since the shooting started.

Lara dispatched the last of the staff members nearest her, a thin 20-something female with dreadlocked hair and a nose ring. As Lara ejected the used clip and reached for the spare in the crochet bag

slung across her shoulder, a harsh sibilant cry issued from the pile of old men and women on the floor. The mass of wrinkled flesh pulsated and glowed orange, momentarily translucent.

'I've seen some strange shit in my time with Mordecai, but this takes the fucking cake,' shouted Ronson.

'Coming from you, mate, that's saying something.'

The demon next to Tobias McBride emitted a warbling scream that froze Lara in her tracks. She watched as Tobias turned in their direction, his eyes diamonds of red light, and stood, his bony arms outstretched. The Demon screamed again.

A burst of machine-gun fire shook Lara from her trance. A grim-faced Ronson was shooting at the mass of people, now a single writhing collection of legs, grasping hands and gnashing teeth, that moved, spider-like across the parquet floor towards them.

'Don't just stand there, love,' shouted Ronson as he reloaded. 'Shoot the fucking thing.'

Lara shot into the oncoming mass of flesh. Each bullet that hit its mark made a sucking sound, like a foot being pulled out of deep mud. The creature cried out in pain from multiple mouths, halted, fell to the ground, started to get up, fell back down again. Lara and Ronson walked towards it. Neither stopped firing until their weapons were empty.

When she was sure the creature was finished, Lara peered through the smoke towards the stage. Tobias McBride was still staring at them. A low-pitched noise came from his mouth, like loud music played backwards. The demon screamed again, shuffled off the stage towards them.

'Incoming,' yelled Ronson. 'I'm out of ammo.'

'Me, too,' said Lara. 'Haven't you got anything else in that coat of yours?'

'Yeah, this.' Ronson withdrew a machete from his jacket. 'But I'm not sure how effective it'll–'

Before he could finish his sentence, Mordecai appeared stage left. Lara thought the smoke from the candles must've been playing tricks on her vision as she could have sworn the magician's feet weren't touching the stage. Mordecai made a series of complicated gestures with his fingers, like he was weaving a cat's cradle. The demon halted mid-step and exploded in a huge spray of flesh and green liquid. Tobias fled towards the back of the stage.

'Grandfather,' shouted Lara. Ronson lunged towards her, but she dodged him, jumped onto the stage. She skidded on the viscera from the demon, steadied herself, and headed after the old man.

'Lara, no, you mustn't.' Mordecai's voice was horse with the exhaustion. 'That is not your grandfather.'

She ignored the magician, ran backstage just as a figure disappeared down a set of stairs to her right.

She skipped down the first couple of steps, stumbled and fell. She closed her eyes, braced for the impact of the ground. It didn't come. Instead she found herself falling through darkness. No wind, no sound, just black nothingness. A small pinprick of white appeared in the distance, got larger with terrifying speed. She entered it, light exploding around her.

Lara felt something wet and slimy move across her outstretched hand. She opened her eyes and saw the tail end of a small green snake disappear between a crack in the wall next to her.

She pushed herself into a sitting position and realised she was alone in a circular chamber, the walls made of large pieces of damp stone. As her eyes adjusted to the murk she made out an exit passageway. Steam and dust particles swam in weak beams of light that penetrated cracks in the ceiling. One of these illuminated a statue atop a small altar. Dripping water and the elements had almost erased its features but Lara could still make out bulging eyes and sharp teeth. The stubs of two worn horns protruded from its head.

'Toto, I've a feeling we're not in Kansas anymore,' she whispered to herself.

Lara stepped through the exit. The darkness was moist and hot. She reached out for the wall, used its surface to navigate. Several twists and turns later she saw a faint glow. She edged in its direction until she was standing in a square of light at the base of a set of uneven ascending stone steps.

She emerged from the stairs into what had once been an old-fashioned lounge room, carpeted floor, matching red leather couches, a glass cabinet, everything spotted in mould and broken and rotted. Torn remnants of thick tapestries hung on what was left of the timber walls, collapsed in places to reveal patches of thick green foliage. The roof was in a similar state of disrepair, the plaster buckled and broken in places, thick vines and shafts of sunlight came through the gaps. Birds shrieked in the trees outside.

A skeleton sat on a leather couch. Its bleached bones were visible through the rotting remnants of a tight-fitting black suit coat, pants and a white shirt with a starched high collar. She stared at the remains until her mind registered another shape in the room.

'Grandfather?' she said tentatively.

Tobias McBride sat in a high backed chair, its red and gold fabric split and rotten. The old man's spidery fingers formed a steeple under his chin. His hair looked wild, like a shock of brown spinifex, his features even more gaunt.

'My lovely granddaughter, how nice of you to visit.' He blinked lizard-like, his pupils pools of blackness. He stood and stepped towards her. 'It has been so long since we have spent any time together.'

'Who– What are you?' She reached for her pistol, remembered it was empty.

'Surely, you recognise me? It is I, your beloved grandfather.'

She edged backwards, the rotten carpet squelching under her feet, glanced around for a weapon. She grabbed a rusty carving knife from a table on which lay the remains of a formal dinner setting.

'Whatever the fuck you are, don't take another step.' She slashed the air in front of her. 'Or so help me, I'll add another corpse to the décor.'

'This place has certainly known its share of death, I'll grant you that.' The old man cast a reverential glance in a hundred-and-eighty-degree arc around him, paused on the skeleton. 'It was here, deep in the Burmese jungle that Lord Reginald Le Fay settled, hounded out of capital cities across Europe and the Middle East. He built this house atop the remains of an ancient temple, the long dead acolytes of which offered blood sacrifice to my master, spent his remaining years unravelling the secrets he had gathered in the dark corners he had traversed during his life as a fugitive.'

'Including the spell of Amon Baal?'

'Mordecai has informed you well.' He smiled. 'Like you granddaughter, at first I scoffed at the notion of a passageway to hell, unconvinced anything could rival the carnage and cruelty I had seen during World War II and the various dirty conflicts that followed. But the more information about Le Fay and his activities I gathered during my travels, the more obsessed I became.'

'Having unlocked the mystery, what made you send the journal, with the spell, to my mother in Australia?'

'The thin sliver of humanity that was left after solving the puzzle recoiled against what I had done, what I had become. Aware of how little time I had left, I dispatched my one remaining native servant with the journal and instructions to send it to your mother and never return. Then I walked into the jungle, hoping to obliterate my physical self. But Satan had other plans for me. I slept for many years until the time was right for me to reawaken and seek out the means to bring my master into the world. But enough talk.'

The old man resumed his approach towards her, arms outstretched in embrace. 'I hope you have saved a last kiss for me?'

She tried to raise the dagger but the weapon was suddenly heavy in her hand and fell to the floor. She tried to move, but her limbs wouldn't obey.

'But what is this?' Tobias McBride halted, inclined his head as if seeking the source of a sound only he could hear. 'I detect you have brought me a gift.'

Lara watched, paralysed, as her grandfather's leather-bound travel journal slowly emerged from her shoulder bag, as if withdrawn by an invisible hand, and levitated towards the old man. The book hung in the air in front of his face, the pages scrolling as if being turned by some unseen hand, then stopped.

Tobias McBride started to read aloud, a language that sounded like Arabic. The house began to shake. The closest wall collapsed to reveal not the jungle outside, but a series of concentric rings of pulsating red and yellow light. The room was suddenly hot and flakes of ash wafted in the air around them.

Tobias McBride continued reading, his tempo quickening. Kate heard a sound, like the galloping of a horse, becoming louder, when a large shape pounced between her and the old man. Able to move again, she fell backwards onto the ground. She felt a pair of hands slip under her arms and pull her away.

Mordecai stood between her and the old man, plunged the spiral dagger into Tobias McBride's chest. The concentric circles grew dim and disappeared. Using his considerable bulk, Mordecai, pushed the blade deeper, until it was embedded to the hilt, his face strained with the effort. Sand, not blood, poured from the wound. Tobias McBride's mouth opened, impossibly wide, emitted a huge swarm of flies that momentarily filled the room.

Mordecai, both hands still on the dagger's hilt, turned to Ronson. 'What are you waiting for, man?' he bellowed, as the roof started to buckle, sending plaster dust and wood splinters raining down around them.

'Run.'

Ronson stepped backwards through the hole in the wall, pulled Lara after him. Shoulder-height undergrowth reared up around her. She looked at where she had just been, a dishevelled single story Edwardian mansion. The roof was starting to collapse, the walls swaying, as if being buffeted by a fierce wind.

'Can you stand?' shouted Ronson.

'Yeah,' said Lara, getting on her feet.

'We need to get further back.'

They ran until they reached a line of huge trees. Ronson fished a thick joint out of one of the pockets, lit up. She opened her mouth to speak, but was drowned out by the sound like an explosion as the roof of the house collapsed inwards, sending a huge cloud of dust into the air. Birdlife exploded from the surrounding jungle.

They watched the dust settle over the pile of twisted wood and plaster.

'Mordecai was in there,' said Lara.

As she spoke the undergrowth in front of them parted and the magician emerged. 'Satan is defeated,' he said, triumphantly plucking the joint from Ronson's fingers.

'Any bright ideas about how we get home?' said Lara.

'Walk, I suppose,' said Ronson, taking off his leather jacket. At last, the heat was getting to him.

'Well, what are we waiting for?' said Lara. 'We may as well get started.'

'Hold your horses, I read somewhere that this part of northern Burma is supposed to be home to a particularly rare, particularly potent strand of opium. Seems a shame not to try it, given we're here.'

'Most definitely,' said Mordecai, his eyes lighting up. 'One should grasp any opportunity to expand one's consciousness.'

The two men began an animated discussion about how best to locate and prepare opium resin.

Lara went to protest, before taking the joint from Mordecai.

What the hell, she could do with a holiday.

CAMERON ASHLEY

Dogs Leave Home to Die

Perched on a tavern rooftop overlooking the settlement, the two boys looked like mad tribal things surveying their filthy, sinking kingdom. The sun set blood-red and angry behind the towers of the distant city; skyscrapers, turning to long black spikes, stabbed at the dying day. Garbage floated in the murk below them.

Stilt-raised shanties congregated, lifting dwellings with sagging floors up from the muck. Fellow settlement dwellers waded through or paddled by in makeshift homemade canoes, or – if they were both light and fleet footed enough – hopped from floating garbage bag to floating garbage bag like raggedly dressed amphibian things, like human frogs scrambling for treasure amongst the refuse drifting as aimlessly as their very own lives.

The vial was marked with Ommar's emoji – blue eyes and a fang-toothed smile inside a circular, mohawked head. Agung turned it over and over in his hands, tapped at the glass with a fingernail.

Raeland uncrossed arms inked with homemade tatts of various Corvidae. He tossed a now empty bottle of bread-fermented homebrew into the water below. 'We should sell that,' he said, orange juice gone boozy on his breath. On his forearm, a sketchy raven tried to burst through his skin, frozen in the moment just before freedom. Forever stuck in place.

Agung shook his head. The legs of the cuddly toy flamingo he wore as a hat, stuffed ass-first over his cranium, wobbled from side to side as though revolting against the indignity of the situation. 'We should smoke it,' he said.

'We should smoke some of it and sell the rest of it,' Raeland said in compromise.

Agung nodded in agreement, flamingo legs still akimbo, kickboxing his chin.

Two pinches of the peppery looking powder were carefully deposited on a rumpled scrap of foil salvaged from some discarded take-away meal or other. Raeland's thumb and forefinger made a rasp-dry sandpaper noise when rubbed together to loose every fleck of the stuff. Draco, the drug was called, named after an indigenous lizard – the *Draco Volan* to be precise – that glided from tree to tree on leathery, butterfly-patterned wings. The powder was ground from a certain fungus that grew on the bark of a particularly polluted mangrove tree, somehow turning man's filth into psychedelic alchemical purity.

Raeland plucked a disposable lighter from a cargo shorts pocket, sparked it. The boys inhaled and were off, up and away, far higher than the tavern roof they perched on like scrawny birds of lurid but moulting plumage, to somewhere else. Somewhere Ommar could never ever reach them.

The night sky went all Van Gogh for the boys, stars like deforming daisies, moon an egg-yolk orange, wisps of clouds curling dreamily in on themselves as though going foetal against a sky of thick blue-black brushstrokes.

The boys huddled together. Agung fluttered his long eyelashes on Raeland's cheek. Raeland giggled and pushed Agung playfully, wiping at his cheek as though chasing away the ghost of Agung's butterfly kiss, still hauntingly touching his skin. He felt charged and alive and the night had more colour than seemed possible and the insects in the air made black, shifting fractal formations against the moon.

Hours later, coming down, Agung spotted an old man who seemed to walk on the water below. He carried a paper lantern, his spine bent into some sort of foreign punctuation mark.

Agung said, 'I see that guy every day. The first time I saw him I thought I knew him from somewhere way back. Like we shared something, some time gone. As the days went by, he stopped being the guy I knew from somewhere and became just the guy I see every day. My brain rewrote his place in my life. Does that make sense?'

'Maybe he's your dad.'

Agung reached over and flicked at Raeland's nostril, currently red with a fresh nose-piercing infection. Raeland recoiled and covered up, his eyes watering.

'Maybe he's *your* dad,' Agung said.

'You smoke too much of this shit, that's what I think. Your brain is becoming like that garbage bag down there, that one with all the holes and the insides poking out for the birds to peck at.'

'Pfff. Look around, Agung. I would say I don't smoke enough.'

'We're selling the rest of this. I don't care what you say.'

Raeland nodded, a little sadly Agung noted. He scratched at Ommar's emoji sticker, clawing it from the vial. Ommar's sticker-face gone now, white adhesive splotches in its place.

'There,' Raeland said. 'Who's to say whose draco this is now but ours? Ommar can go fuck himself.'

'One puff and anyone will know. I heard voices in the breeze, saw comic strips in the clouds. This is not like any draco I've had before.'

'We need Sakti's help.'

'We do. But she can wait a moment.' Agung leaned in and put his lips on Raeland's.

'I dropped it,' Ommar DeJong said, the shame on his face oddly alien to the impossible blueness of his left eye, the grinning toothy leer on the contact lens inserted into his right. 'I dropped it. I was chasing that fucker Asmo. He didn't pay me my tribute this month. I slipped and fell and I dropped it.'

Alex, Ommar's father, roused himself from his drunkenness, clambered awkwardly to his feet like some bear just out of hibernation, knocked over a side table littered with empties, and backhanded his son across the face.

'Asmo! Asmo the pickpocket. You lose something valuable shaking down an urchin instead of taking it to be cut. Where is Asmo going? Nowhere. There's something wrong with you. You choose pointless thuggery over money. Asmo will be here tomorrow. He will be here forever. You have an eternity to blacken his eyes. Instead you lose my draco.'

The DeJong family was comprised of Alex, Ommar and Sungitha. Alex light, Sungitha dark and Ommar somewhere in the middle, easily passing for native but sized like his father, large-fisted and big-boned and mannered like him too, violent and mean and with a soul filled with a crushing ennui. Alex threw empty cans at his son. 'You're useless and lost. You should move in with a refugee family because you don't belong here with me.'

From the floor of their shanty, Ommar wanted to argue that they were all refugees here in the settlement. Kicked out of the city or rejected from another country that wouldn't open itself for you, what was the difference? They were all here now, shin-deep in the rising tide.

Refugees from other lands now trapped in the settlement, this limbo between a worse life left behind and a better life never to come, usually handled the draco manufacturing, cutting and trafficking for Alex DeJong, either peddling tiny portions of the stuff at the floating markets, or muling it from the settlement, out to the freeway to sell to the Gridlocked.

The Gridlocked: the many hundreds who welcomed their road-bound entrapment, living in cars halfway between here and there, traffic frozen in an unending forever freeway jam.

They travelled now thanks only to draco, the drug taking their consciousness for a cosmic spin up and out of their meat vehicles. Existence contemplated as now superfluous speed limit signs flashed not the speed of traffic, but the speed of drug-fuelled thought. Frequently robbed and looted, many of these monks of the Petrified Road still had working credit chips linked to accounts belonging to their former lives as wage slaves, tie-wearers, spreadsheet mages. Their accounts ever-depleting as food delivery bicycles, pedestrian merchants and, of course, draco peddlers hawked wares car to car.

'I'll get it back,' Ommar said, wiping at his split lip.

Alex Dejong snorted.

'I will.'

Alex Dejong smiled, the anger gone from him now. He could be rid of this boy, make an example of him, send him away from home, like a dog who knows it's time to die.

'You have two days to find it. If you don't return with it, stay out there and hide. You won't want me to find you.'

Sakti's father, Sarwono, once cracked safes in the city. One particular night he was tasked with cracking the wrong safe belonging to the wrong man. Caught in the act, his hands and his tongue were removed, along with most of his will to live; and he and his daughter were exiled. Bedridden, old mannequin hands now tied onto his wrist stumps, he hatched plans for his vengeance with the 15-year-old, pink-haired Sakti through a language of their own devising, a system of facial expressions spelling out words and feelings, based on 42 different emoji.

When Raeland and Agung climbed up to Sakti's door and stuck their heads inside her shanty, she slipped off her chunky stolen headphones. She frequently listened to a mix of music from old Italian crime films, music that was on a media player she plucked from some inner city hipster's pocket. Sakti listened to a lot of music. It helped her to ignore Sarwono as, through grunts and the reshaping of his facial geometry alone, he repeatedly told her to make his dinner and help him plan the assassination of his mutilators.

Sakti turned her back on her father, the brass and harpsichord of Stelvio Ciprani's *La Polizia Sta a Guardare* now audible to all. She hit repeat on her old mp3 player. The song was good, cool music for criminally-inclined friends to collude to, and she knew the boys were here to do just that. They never came bearing gifts or good news, just schemes and capers half-baked at best, uncooked dough at worst. Much like her father's.

'Let's go to the roof,' she said to the boys.

Both Raeland and Agung harboured something halfway between boundless fascination and confusing crush on this slender, pretty punk who survived by smuggling herself into the city, picking the pockets and bags of those so far above her station they seemingly could not peer down far enough to notice her, and smuggling her way out again. She peddled her pinched wares at the floating markets, to loyal Gridlocked charmed by her smile and her aptitude for producing virtually anything that they desired, and to settlement gangsters, tired of the dry black market tobacco they were forced to smoke, eager to have the latest in gadgetry, fashion and timepieces they were too lazy to procure for themselves.

Up they clambered, back on top, as far away from the refuse and the waste and the smell as possible, the two scrawny bird-boys and the princess thief. Candle lights from neighbouring domiciles flickered and pulsed warmly nearby and those with batteries and mini-generators added lamp-lit ambience to the evening.

'What have you done now?' Sakti said.

'We found this,' Raeland said, nudging Agung until he stopped looking at the movements of birds overhead and produced the vial for Sakti's inspection.

Sakti unstopped the vial, a squeak emitting as she did so, and sniffed. 'Draco? Where did you get this?'

'You won't believe it,' Agung said, 'There was a chase, see, and Om–'

'We found it, floating in the muck. Someone must've dropped it.' Raeland shot a look at Agung that said in psychic neon: *shut up!*

'Who dropped it? It smells… strong.'

Agung inhaled sharply, then held his breath.

Raeland said, 'Some guy. Don't know. It was dark. He slipped step-stoning a garbage bag and fell in the water. He left it behind, bobbing away.'

Sakti frowned down at the vial, rubbed her fingers on the sticky stuff and papery shreds. 'Have you guys tried it?'

The boys sniggered.

'You've both got pupils like planets, so I don't know why I bothered asking.'

'It's good,' Agung said. 'Real good.'

'And you really don't know whose it is.'

'Sure we do,' Agung said. 'It's ours.'

Sakti smiled, her face opening from taut bud to full bloom. The boys, still draco-afflicted, stared rapturously at her.

'And you want me to do what exactly?' she asked as she smacked at a mosquito having its way with her right arm.

'Help us sell it. Take us to The Gridlocked. To your Gridlocked,' Agung said.

'My customer.'

The boys nodded in unison. 'We wouldn't know where to start among those weirdos,' Raeland said. 'Sell the stuff, use your father's account, like always, then cut us in next time you're in the city and making withdrawals.'

Sakti pondered.

'We are coming with you,' Raeland said.

Sakti sighed. The freeway could be dangerous. Burned-out skeleton husks of cars dotted their way along the kilometres-long stretch of frozen automobiles – the scars of mini turf wars left upon the asphalt. An entirely new form of road rage had been created through a combination of madness and lack of resources, usually aimed at thrill-seeking outsiders who hit the road to disrupt their way of life.

Sakti looked up at the stars then over to the boy. They wore still-stoned smiles on their faces, the glint of opportunity in their disproportionately large pupils.

'We'll leave in the morning. First thing. Go get some sleep – if you can; and make sure you have fresh water with you. I'll handle our food.'

The trio shared a hug, then the boys scampered down from her roof to the murk below, then hopped away from bobbing garbage bag to bobbing garbage bag, as though they weighed just about as much as their silhouettes did, back to the shanty they shared.

Back inside, Sarwono slept uneasily, moaning wordlessly, failed attempts to articulate the night terrors spit-gargling from his tongueless mouth, his mannequin hands clack-clacking together in slow-motion flailing. He dreamed once more of the moment his real hands were hacked from him, shock hitting him as he looked at them, separate things now, leaking at their ends. His last words before his tongue was secateurs-snipped at the root:

'Hey. Those are mine.'

Sakti put her headphones on to drown Sarwono out but her player's battery had died. She knew better than to wake her father by fumbling around for a power cord to plug her device into the generator-powered outlet, so she went back up to the roof. There she sat, fingers in her ears. She watched the far away aura of the city glowing red and orange and green in the distance and the haphazard sagging maze of structures that made up the surrounding settlement. Cats fought nearby and drunken teen boys below pissed into the water and stumbled and slipped and sloshed about, and hurled glass bottles against whatever they could just to hear them smash.

Inside. Outside.

Everywhere disquiet.

It was Lucia, ears ever to what passed for the ground, who solved the puzzle for Ommar. She had put out the word that Ommar's draco was missing. Good draco. Potent draco. Rewards for information. Pain for withholding information.

Lucia was tall and luminously white and had the odd habit of painting western zodiac symbols on the centre of the wide forehead on her heart-shaped face. Unsure of her birth month, whichever particular astrological traits she felt upon waking each day she made her own. Today she had a scorpion curled into a kind of ouroboros sketched in black between her eyes. Dark-haired and beefy-limbed she was an intimidating figure, even dressed in the floral patterns she favoured.

Felix, brother of Asmo the pickpocket, sought her out and told her. He'd seen Agung and Raeland right where they always were, propped atop a tavern just above where Ommar had chased his brother, seen them drop down into the water and fish something out. He'd also seen the boys and Sakti this morning, backpacks on, heading out into the mangroves in the direction of the freeway. Felix asked for a pardon on behalf of his brother, for more time to pay the month's tribute to Ommar.

Felix was good and kind and true, all in the settlement knew this. He spent his days helping the infirm and the old for a pittance. Asmo, his brother, was wild and kleptomaniac and frequently behind on the payments Ommar demanded from all teen delinquents who worked these flooded streets.

Felix's story was overly neat, but had the ring of truth to Lucia, so she said that she would see what she could do and went to find Ommar.

Sarwono made odd chucking noises. Felix had never heard him make such sounds before.

'Will she kill him?' he asked.

Sarwono nodded. Sure. Certainly. Ommar was a brute, but Sakti had her father's mind, his guile. Ommar would be no match for her. She would kill the boy and sell the drugs and return home as though it were the most uneventful trip of her life. She would return with their account topped up and food to eat and goods to sell and trade and tales of Gridlocked lunacy. And Sarwono, he would lay back and rest, knowing that his daughter, his ultimate right hand sent out into the wild to forage and steal, would exact the first piece of his revenge. He would take Ommar from Alex, from the man who held his arms as his hands were removed, who passed the secateurs that bit free his tongue to the man who snip-snipped them.

Sarwono had no idea that Alex would not care either way. Ommar was an errand boy Alex was forced to feed, a dim-witted, careless child who was good for little more than beating up children smaller than himself and allegedly dropping precious vials into the murky water that kept on creeping ever upwards to one day swallow them all.

Never mind, it would be vengeance as far as Sarwono was concerned and that was all that really mattered.

'I hope she kills him. He is a bully,' said Felix, scratching his insect bites.

Sarwono made a series of facial expressions that spelled out, *just like his dad.*

Felix felt sorry for Sarwono and aided him when Sakti was on her excursions, helping him eat and toilet. He had made quite the effort to become at least passingly fluent in the weird emoji face language Sarwono and Sakti devised, but didn't quite catch what Sarwono said. Whatever. He just wanted to get his money and go home.

Sarwono felt the vibe, he was good at picking up when people wanted to be free of the horror of his presence. He couldn't blame them. His mannequin hands clacked together as he lifted the edge of his mattress. With both appendages, he pulled out a small bundle of Rupiah, a currency virtually useless outside of the settlement now. It looked like slices of grubby rainbow, rubber-banded together. It was hopeful in its brightness.

Felix took the money, trying not to think about the plasticky smoothness of the touch of Sarwono's shapely, feminine "hands" as he did so. He smelled the money. He caught wafts of Sarwono's oily hair.

The plan originally was for Sakti to knowingly take Ommar's drugs, lead him out past the mangroves to The Gridlocked and kill him with the aid of her friends.

Sakti wrote it off as just another of her father's insane, unworkable revenge plots.

Felix, who overheard Sakti shoot it down, did not. Felix liked the plan. It just needed some tweaking. He suggested the tweaks. Sarwono grunted and facial-spelled, *I love this.*

Ommar was always roughing Asmo up. On a day Ommar was carrying, which was most, Asmo would lead Ommar on a chase right under Agung and Raeland's greedy little noses. Ommar would 'catch' Asmo. Asmo would use those nimble fingers to pluck the stuff from Ommar's pocket and drop it in the rising water, in plain view of the eagle eyes of those opportunistic boys. Felix would then 'leak' the news and meat-headed Ommar would seek reprisal.

Sakti would become involved somehow at her friends' request.

Felix shared Sarwono's faith in the girl. Felix and Asmo would be paid for their considerable trouble, Ommar would be gone, Sarwono could find a measure of peace.

It was risky. It was stupid. It was a puzzlebox of a plan.

But it worked.

Felix returned to the dwelling he shared with Asmo and their mother. He fanned his sleeping brother with the cash wad until Asmo woke. They climbed to their roof with bottles of home brew swiped from their father and toasted their good fortune. They hoped that one night soon they would see Sakti, Agung and Raeland again, dancing and laughing together on Sakti's roof nearby; and that they would never, ever see Ommar again.

Through the mangroves they went, Ommar and Lucia, with hastily bartered-for zipguns in hand, old combat knives with broken compasses embedded in sheaths strapped to their thighs, pouches of mystery jerky in their pockets and dented plastic bottles of purified water tied round their necks.

They followed the ghostly slipstream of Sakti and the boys over branches, over roots like hundreds of stretching, tiny, evil hands, under a crooked canopy of latticed trees pieced only by laser beaming streaks of sunlight, through murky water filled with buoys of trash.

Ommar thought he heard Raeland's laugh, but it was just the cry of some bird overhead. Lucia thought she saw Agung scurrying past, but it was just a monkey with a discarded, empty can of drink.

Such was their opinions of their quarry.

On and on they waded, sure of their path for Sakti's route to the freeway was no secret; it was the route all Gridlocked traders took. They became certain once the thicket cleared and the dead, deforested stretch lay ahead with its tree-corpses and increasing filth and dead fauna. There, at this razed clearing, in the distance, were Sakti, Agung and Raeland. Too far away to shoot at with cobbled together one-shot firearms made mainly of rubber gloves, duct tape and pipe.

So Ommar and Lucia decided to wait a little, make out a little, eat some mystery jerky, stab some outcast amphibians who roamed too far from home.

Once the draco thieves were out of sight, they resumed their tailing, secure in the knowledge that they were dogs with the true scent, not fools following bird squawks and monkeys with trash; that they would safely, covertly, close the distance between their quarry and the terra firma clogged with Gridlocked.

They buzzed on impending restitution.

Sakti, Agung and Raeland arrived at the time of the gloaming. Birds darted black against a sky of magenta, pink and red. Trail bikes whined in the distance, their riders black-clad and armoured up, 'Polisi' in yellow across the backs of their helmets and their armoured backs, lit by the glow of their headlights and looking from afar like extensions of their vehicles, like mecha-centaurs risen from the eco-apocalypse. They were patrol cops making sure no-one entered the city on foot from the stretch of petrified freeway across the border. The trio waited for them to vanish down, way down, the freeway then scaled up a dry embankment, their hands touching warm, rough asphalt as they pulled themselves up onto the road.

Here they sat, The Gridlocked, in-between, unwilling or unable to be a part of either society that co-existed uneasily – the workers of the city, the rejected or the doomed or the unwelcome of the settlements. Here they sat, under a darkening sky that was vast and endless, the perfect canvas for the inexhaustibly contemplative.

It was old hat to Sakti, this stretch of cars in dull primary colours or fading metallic shades, parked one behind the other and one beside another and stretching off as far as she could see. She stifled a yawn, mouth rippling as she did so.

The boys stood for a moment, taking in a bizarre slice of unfamiliar culture with some hesitation and slight shock. Engines turned on and off intermittently, cars running only minutes at a time to keep batteries charged. Brake lights strangely woke to life in red bursts of beaming staccato code between neighbours, like odd animals kept apart signalling their presence to one another. Then, for a moment, all went still. Aside from the odd honk from far away, all was quiet now. They heard leaves and dirt blowing along the freeway, the only other things in motion apart from Sakti who marched on ahead of them, clearly keen to have this done with.

They followed her, and the world unfroze again. They passed people asleep at the wheel, sitting cross-legged on their roofs and staring crazily into the clouds, urinating out of open doors, cooking odd, smoky things on 12-volt stoves plugged into lighter sockets, sipping tea brewed with hot water from plug-in kettles.

Smashed passenger windows were blanket-covered. Roofs and doors were dented. Some windscreens were spider-webbed with cracks, some were filthy, covered in a haze of dust, others meticulously spotless, the window to the world beyond crystal clear. Some cars were fortified – bars and grills welded over any vulnerable spot.

People sat on rusting deck chairs outside their vehicles in their underwear or even nude. Some yelled at Sakti and the boys from behind locked doors; odd incomprehensible words and philosophies borne of madness and self-imposed solitary confinement. Still cars as thought hubs/private think tanks/ personal ecosystems; stillness as movement; thought as speed; the deliberate erosion of the meat vehicle. The imbuing of steel with soul. All babble and nonsense to the boys, who quickly became unnerved by what they saw as a cloister of mad, rogue, possibly infectious insanity masked as manifesto.

Some Gridlocked waved and smiled at Sakti and she exchanged pleasantries or made quick deals, but it was clear she refused to be sidetracked even as these interactions eased the acute sharpness of the boys' tension. Every trail bike rev in the distance caused Sakti to prick up her ears. The border cops, if they saw this deal go down, would shoot them and take the draco into the city to sell for themselves. Shakedowns and beatings and deaths were common here with Peace Keeping officials either supplementing income or jonesing themselves for a pinch or two because life patrolling the freeway border is a little too close to either the strangeness of the life of The Gridlocked or the desperation of life in the settlements.

Sakti knew this and was inoculated enough to her surroundings and its inhabitants to keep the odd sensory overload of silences followed by sharp cacophonous bursts filtering through her. The boys were her responsibility here too. She snuck glances behind her, shot steely glares at Raeland and Agung to make them keep up to her heels.

The boys held hands so tightly they were squeezing themselves into a Siamese twin. They followed along in Sakti's slipstream, bug-eyed as though surrounded on all sides by deadly boy-eating carnivores.

Sakti, gone all animal amongst all this metal, hissed and whistled and growled at Agung and Raeland when they dipped a little too far behind, distracted by singing or moaning or the sounds of something or someone breaking. She was concerned for them, focussed on their safety and on her own, on finding her buyer and splitting.

Three traffic lanes over, Ommar and Lucia skulked between vehicles and watched Sakti's movements with exactly the same intensity.

Sakti stopped at a car. It was small and cheap and moderately well kept. A Toyota of some sort, the boys ascertained. Midnight blue, its tyres sagged as though melting into the road but it was otherwise fairly unscathed.

'Stay behind me,' Sakti said. 'Let me handle this.'

The driver's side door cracked open as Sakti approached. A man got out.

He was white, but his skin was leathered. Agung guessed he spent much time atop his car in the heat of the afternoon. He wore shorts and a wrinkled, dirty old Hawaiian shirt. He was full-bearded, balding on top, with a little island of dark hair just above his forehead.

'Sakti,' he said, Australian-accented. 'You brought friends.'

Sakti nodded. 'I didn't think you'd mind. Richard, this is Raeland and Agung.'

'Of course I don't mind. Hi, boys. Would you all care to sit? I have some folding chairs in the back. I may even have some bourbon left; I'd be willing to share.'

The boys said yes, but Sakti said no. The man laughed.

'I don't mean to be rude,' Sakti said, but we should be getting home.'

'It's getting dark,' the man said.

'I know my way.'

'Well, then. I won't keep you. What do you have?'

Sakti took the vial from her pocket and held it in front of her. 'It's good. So they say,' she pointed at the boys.

Raeland piped up. 'It is. It's the best I've ever tried.'

'May I?' The man said.

The boys grew nervous.

'He wants to smell it,' Sakti said. 'He is too polite to just take it and smoke it.'

The man smiled at this and even bowed his head a little. He took the vial from Sakti, unstopped it and smelled. He nodded his approval. 'What do you want for this?'

'What do I always want?'

The man held up his forearm, tapped the spot his credit chip had been implanted. He smiled. 'Amazing your father still has a city bank account.'

'They charge him fees,' Sakti said, 'as they do you. It's just that your balance goes down, his goes up. Although yours is still far greater than his.'

She reached into her backpack and pulled out a mobile phone. She typed an emoji password into it and brought up her banking app. She typed in her desired amount and showed it to the man, who raised his eyebrows in surprise at first but then resumed smiling. He held out his arm. 'I trust this will be worth it.'

'You will be happy, sir,' Raeland said.

The man nodded happily at the boys and took the phone from Sakti. He typed in an emoji code of his own and handed it back. Sakti brought the camera up in app, ready to scan the chip. 'Oh,' Richard said. 'Did you bring more friends, Sakti?'

Sakti and the boys turned.

There was Ommar. There was Lucia, a bull painted in the centre of her forehead; today the active, spontaneous Aries. She raised her zipgun and fired.

More of a pop than a bang sounded, a cheap tinny explosive noise, followed by a long string of gargled consonants that did not belong together. In his car, Richard clutched at his neck. Lucia's shot, aimed at Sakti's head, went wide. Blood trickled between Richard's fingers that he pressed to the wound. As the boys stood frozen and Ommar took steps forward, Sakti pulled at Richard's now blood-covered hand and scanned the man's chip.

War-painted in her buyer's blood now, Sakti stuffed the phone in her pocket and grabbed at the boys, pulling them into motion.

Lucia threw her zipgun to the ground and reached for a knife. Ommar glared and pushed his way in front of her.

Everywhere was commotion now; Gridlocked emerging from their vehicles by the dozens. Headlights were turned on, and Sakti raised an arm to shield her eyes and yelled to her friends, 'Come on.'

They heard Ommar's rage-screams, audible over the general hubbub.

Sakti and the boys tried to run, to push past the oncoming human traffic that now surrounded her dying buyer's car, all peering in as he spat up red and his eyes went dim.

'He's dead,' someone said.

Sakti pointed and shouted: 'They killed him. The big girl, the boy; they killed him.'

Gridlocked swarmed.

Ommar dared not risk his single shot, so he pulled a knife, making many people give him, and the already-slashing Lucia, a wide berth. But Gridlocked had emerged with things to bludgeon, things to stab of their own and they came at him. They came at Lucia. With no other choice, Ommar aimed his zipgun at an oncoming Gridlocked who wielded a mini-shovel, used to dig nearby shit-pits, and fired. The zipgun blew in his hand in a cloud of smoke and finger-flesh. As the circle of Gridlocked grew tight around them, Lucia moved to Ommar's side as he sank to the ground in agony, his hand now an odd, raw nubby thing, all pinks and blacks and weeping reds.

Sakti grabbed Raeland by one hand, and Agung by the other. They both clung tight. She led the boys back to the mangroves.

Hours later, they stopped. The boys were thirsty and frightened and unbelieving that Sakti could be so clear-headed as to navigate them home by the position of the stars.

She said, 'Richard would have given away the draco to other gridlocked. He would have strolled on by, car after car, dispensing doses into the palms of the needy. They loved him for his generosity. Whatever he had, he gave to them if they asked. Whatever they needed, he would try and provide.'

'For free?' Agung asked, shocked at any notion of altruism in this world.

'He had things to atone for,' Sakti said. She drank from her water bottle. 'He was my father's partner. He sold my father out to the men who maimed him. For his part, Richard was exiled from the city, told never to return or they would find him and kill him, his wife, his children.

'We spoke of this, he and I, often. He knew me, of course. Richard paid whatever I asked him to pay me for his goods, no matter how exorbitant. Such was the extent of his guilt. In return he asked me to look in on his family, to make sure they were doing well. They are not, but always I lied about that.'

Sakti rested her head against a tree trunk, rubbed it till it hurt. 'Sometimes I think all I am is a collection of organs and limbs on loan to others. My father's hands, Richard's eyes. My father thinks I don't care about his revenge, but that's not true. I do. I care so much that it hurts to sit there with him over and over as he fever-dreams mad plots and schemes and drives himself insane with their details and intricacies. I can't listen to it.

'I was getting closer and closer to Richard, without my father's knowledge. I wanted to bond with Richard, so that on the day that I somehow killed him, peacefully – he deserved that much – it would hurt him all the more; my forgiveness stripped away. At least I don't have to worry about that now.'

'Did you know Ommar was following us?' Agung asked.

Sakti nodded. 'I knew the draco was his as soon as I spotted him, in the distance, tailing us pathetically through the mangroves with Lucia, like giant lumbering prehistoric things. Ommar did not belong there, on the freeway. He had no rep there, his father had no rep there. Those people know me, however. They trust me. Ommar should never have left the settlement, he should never have left home.'

Sakti rubbed the bark of a gnarled tree, enjoying its roughness. 'You both knew it was Ommar's draco too,' she said. 'You should have told me.'

The boys hung their heads.

Agung said, 'We didn't think you'd help us if you knew.'

'I will always help you,' Sakti said.

Blood-streaked, exhausted, she led the boys back home, where friends waited on rooftops with bottles of liquor and a broken man dreamed of his daughter's hands gently stroking the worry from his brow.

Fin J Ross

Genemesis

Taylor Sanna leaned against the balcony railing as she sipped her coffee. She never tired of the view of the vast Pacific Ocean, nor of the ant-like humans going about their daily business down on the streets of Cairns, nor of the slight tinge of frangipani in the air. Pity she had to fly back to Melbourne today. She loved it here – except for the heat. If it weren't for the incessant sweat-inducing heat she could imagine staying here for good, but hot weather addled her brain and made her cranky.

The air-conditioned apartment – it had been Tony's idea of course, despite the fact that it was her money that paid for it – was an oasis. That was the advantage of an internet-based business, you could run it from anywhere. Her regular trips to Cairns enabled her to catch up with some of her south-east Asian clients and gave her time away from Tony, which was a good thing. She couldn't fathom how she'd ended up marrying such an arsehole. Yes, she should have listened to her mother. And her father. And everybody else who could see him for the shit-heel he was. She never missed him when she was here on her own, and she knew he didn't miss her either. He was too busy getting up to mayhem with his scumbag mates.

Their marriage had been on a downhill slide for some time and the slope was getting more precipitous by the day. She'd told him before she'd left Melbourne that she wanted a divorce and that they'd discuss it when she got back. He wasn't a happy camper. Not because he loved her – because he loved her money.

She drained her coffee mug and as she headed back inside to dress, a breaking-news report on the radio stopped her in her tracks.

Cairns Police are investigating the possibility that the man killed by a shark off Holloways Beach yesterday was the victim of foul play. A paramedic has revealed that aside from having injuries indicative of a shark attack, the victim had ligature marks around his wrists. Police speculated that he might have been dragged behind a boat.

The man has been identified as 42-year-old Werner Blom, a well-known identity in the Queensland greyhound industry, who was recently granted bail on animal cruelty charges following an investigation into live animal baiting.

'Yes!' Taylor hissed. She punched the air. She pulled on her jeans-skirt and a singlet top, slipped into a pair of dressy scuffs and grabbed a jacket from the wardrobe, arming herself for the September frigidity of Victoria.

She checked her watch. 10.03. The plane didn't leave until 12.35pm so there was no need to hurry. She would make the short drive to Moorabool to pick up Darius before doubling back to the airport, dropping off the hire car and maybe having some lunch before the flight. That was the plan, anyway.

Farley Cavanagh hoped the American couple he was heading to the airport to collect weren't as obnoxious as the woman, Alisha, had sounded on the phone. The idea of being in close quarters – in fact sharing the same vehicle – with two nuff-nuff Yanks was not at all appealing; especially for a 10-day foray into the Queensland outback from Cairns to Birdsville and back. Three square metres of captive cabin space in the Landcruiser left little room for avoidance tactics. He wished he could be more selective with his customers but he knew that until his new outback adventure business was fully fledged, he had to take all comers; even if they were Americans who sounded more interested in shooting kangaroos with guns than cameras. Their money was just as good as the next customer's. This was, after all, only his second booking. The first – a weekend 'getaway' booking to Daintree with a couple of charming Adelaidians – had been a trial run and a roaring success.

His rig was packed for the journey: camping gear in the back of the 4WD and the camp kitchen and sundries stowed in the trailer. On the way to the airport, he'd stop at the wholesale butcher for some snags and chops and the bakery for some fresh bread. He'd left his current digs near the golf course and would be glad to see the back of it for a while. He hated being cooped up and domesticated. It didn't suit his suntan. It wasn't much of a place anyway, little more than a glorified beach shack – without the beach. It was a short-term lease; it was likely he'd up sticks and leave in a month or so.

Renting instead of owning a place had freed up enough capital for him to buy his vehicle and all the associated gear, pay the exorbitant insurance and public liability costs and create a website. It was a daring venture. But he was on the verge of a new life. He'd tried the marriage and wife thing. It had been tantamount to torture. Of course it was possible that he'd chosen badly but he suspected he just preferred his own company. His mother had always called him a free spirit, which was odd considering what he'd cost her in university fees. Maybe she was right. He was now probably the most over-educated tour guide in Australia.

A hundred things were going through his head as he turned off the Bruce Highway into Mulgrave Road. Had he remembered the torches? Yep. The batteries? Yep. The Aeroguard? Yep. The spare fuel cans? Yep. What else?

He was still ticking off things in his head as he passed Cannon Park Racecourse and headed towards the Earlville Shopping Centre. Despite it being way early for lunch he was a bit peckish. After collecting a three-piece box and a mint-choc Krusher from the drive-through window at KFC, he merged back into the traffic.

The last thing Taylor remembered was driving north-east along Mulgrave Road on her way back into the CBD, with Darius in the back seat. He'd had a big week. So why was she now parked on the side of the road with a thumping headache? Had she had an accident? Hit her head on the steering wheel? She couldn't think straight.

She turned towards the passenger seat and a chill ran up her spine despite the 33-degree ambient temperature. Where was her laptop? She swung around to check the back seat. *Shit*. Where was Darius? He'd been right there just a moment ago. She'd been having an inane one-sided conversation with him. Was it only a moment? Panic set in. *What the fuck was going on?*

She was outside the Parramatta State School; the Cairns Showgrounds just there across the road. She had no reason to be stopped here. She took a deep breath. Then she remembered the black four-wheel drive. It had been sitting right on her bumper since she'd passed the Raintrees Shopping Centre. And then, yes, it had cut her off and forced her off the carriageway and two men had jumped out. And they didn't look like they were collecting for the Salvation Army. Now she remembered. One of the bastards had punched her in the face through the open window. *Bastard. Prick. Shithead.*

Her boy! They'd taken her precious boy. The laptop she could understand, but why would they take Darius? She groped at the side door-pocket and thankfully laid her hand on her mobile. 'Thank Christ,' she said out loud. She flipped the cover and was about to dial 000 when the phone pinged to alert her to an incoming text message. She didn't recognise the sender.

Don't even consider contacting police or Darius will get it.
If you ever want to see him alive again wait for further instructions.

'Shit! Fuck, fuck, fuck!' Taylor bashed her fist on the steering wheel. What the hell was she supposed to do? She checked the time on the clock radio. 11.15. How long had she been out? They had at least a 20-minute headstart on her and she had no idea where they'd gone.

'Fuck.' Hang on. They knew his name. This wasn't random, it was planned. Maybe she should go back to the apartment and wait. She went to turn the key and it made a horrible grating sound. The engine was still running and she hadn't realised. She put it into gear and accelerated. An even more horrible sound – of scraping metal – filled her ears. 'What the fuck?'

She closed the window, pulled the keys out of the ignition and got out. Two flat tyres; front and back. One might have been unlucky – two was plain fuckunlucky. *Brilliant*. She leant against the car door, crossed her ankles and folded her arms in defeat. So, ring the RACQ. She wasn't a member, but surely that didn't matter. Or maybe just ring the hire car company. They'd have to bring her another car and do whatever they had to do with this one.

Ring Tony. He'll know what to do. She dialled his number. It rang, rang, rang. No bloody answer. Typical. She left a message on his voicemail. 'Help, I've just been robbed. Darius and my laptop have been taken. I'm stuck with no car. And whoever has done this has just sent me a message not to call the police. I'm shit scared, Tony. Ring me.'

She stared blankly down the road. Maybe she should beckon for someone to pull over and help her.

Farley zoned out a bit as he passed the unending strip of car dealers on his right, concentrating more on the Colonel's secret recipe than the traffic. Passing BCF on the right made him wonder whether he'd remembered to pack the fishing tackle. Yep. He had travelled a few hundred metres when he absent-mindedly plucked the Krusher from between his legs. The lid came off and the drink spilled across his legs. *Shit.* He flicked his left indicator on and veered over to the side of the road near the primary school. Just ahead of him, a silver Toyota was stopped at the side of the road - a leggy blonde woman in a hot denim skirt was leaning against the driver's door with her arms folded. Then he noticed the flat tyre.

A white Landcruiser pulled up beside her. As she waited for the passenger window to wind down, she noticed the sign on the door: Cafferty's Outback Adventures.

'You okay? Need a lift or a hand?' the driver said.

Without thinking twice she replied, 'Yeah, yes that would be great thanks.' She opened the door, pushed the KFC box aside, and climbed in. She figured that axe murderers and kidnappers wouldn't make a habit of getting around in such easily identifiable vehicles. Hopefully that meant she was safe. Besides, he didn't look terribly threatening with a piece of KFC in his hand.

'I could change the tyre for you if you like.'

'I've got *two* flats,' she said as she pulled on the seat-belt.

'Bummer. One's bad luck, but two is–'

'Fuckunlucky. Ew, have you spilt something?'

'Yep. That's the word,' he laughed. 'Yeah, I spilt my thickshake. Sorry to say that's why I was pulling over. Then I saw you. Would you mind taking that hand-towel out of the wrapper so I can clean this up? So where do you want to go? To the Budget depot?'

'How–?

'The sticker on the back window.'

'Oh, of course. That was observant.'

'It's in my nature to be observant,' the man said as he indicated to pull back into the traffic. 'So, what the hell happened?'

'Hmm, it's a long story.' Taylor decided not to say anything about her attack. She didn't want to get a complete stranger involved. Maybe she should get him to take her to a police station. Or maybe not. She remembered the message. She checked her phone again, in case there was another. Nothing. Should she trust this guy she'd just met? Tell him what had happened? Or should she wait to see what the kidnappers wanted? Were they holding Darius hostage for a ransom? Or was it the computer they'd wanted? *Fuck.* What to do? Her head was throbbing and she seriously couldn't think straight. Should she go back to the apartment, or to the airport?

'I'm on my way to the airport,' he said, 'to pick up some holidaymakers. I run adventure tours.'

'I saw your door. I was going to the airport too, so that's cool. I've got a flight to Melbourne at 12.35. And I'll have to go to Budget and tell them where the car is.' She wasn't going back to Melbourne of course.

'I've just got to make a couple of stops. Is that okay?'

'Sure.'

'I'm Farley, by the way.'

That sounded more like a surname than a first name to her, but then so did hers. 'Hi, I'm Taylor.'

Her phone pinged just as Farley shut the door and headed into the wholesale butchers. She sucked in a breath as she read the ominous message.

Need computer password or Darius gets it. Won't be pretty. Watching you.

A shiver went down her spine. She turned around in the seat and scanned her surroundings. She couldn't see anybody suspicious. No parked vehicles. No men in balaclavas hiding menacingly behind trees. Who the fuck was this? And why? Then it dawned on her. The List. But how did they know about The List?

Taylor texted back: Who TF are you? And what do you want?

The reply: You know. No funny stuff. Just the fuckin password.

The password wouldn't be any use to them. They had the wrong computer. She'd only bought this laptop yesterday and hadn't loaded any files on yet. The one she figured they wanted was back at home in Melbourne.

But who the hell were these people?

She decided to ring Tony again. She hit his speed-dial number and listened to the ringing, oblivious to the two men sneaking up alongside the car.

Farley emerged from the butcher in time to see a man open the passenger door of his Landcruiser and grab Taylor by the hair. She was still buckled into her seatbelt which bit into her neck as he struggled with her. A second man stood menacingly behind the first with a length of timber in his hand.

Farley hot-footed it across the nature strip and, with no weapon to pull, swung the plastic bag of lamb chops and clobbered the first guy on the head. He fell and brained himself on the bitumen. The second man, caught off guard, received a face-full of crumbed lamb surprise before he had a chance to swing his stick. Farley kneed him in the knackers as he was falling.

'Quick, shut the door,' he said to Taylor, 'we're getting out of here. I chopped 'em up pretty good. Pardon the pun.'

Taylor started to laugh and then realised this was very un-funny. 'Wait a minute,' she put her hand on Farley's leg in an urgent gesture, 'sorry, but we need to go back. They've got my boy and my computer. It was them who attacked me before.'

'Attacked you? You didn't say anything about being attacked.'

'No, well I didn't want to, er, bother you with that.'

Farley took his eyes off the road for a moment to look at her properly. 'Geez, did they do that to you?'

'What?'

'Your eye is swollen – gonna have a shiner there. Looks painful.'

'The bloke punched me through the window and I think I must have been out cold for a while. When I came to, the computer and Darius were gone.'

'Shit.' Farley pulled over and stopped. 'Let's call the police.'

'No, I can't. They've threatened to kill Darius. They've sent me two messages.'

'What do they want?'

'I haven't the vaguest,' she lied.

'Okay, so we'll go back and find out.'

'That's their car, over there.' Taylor pointed to the other side of the road about 200 metres down. 'Shit, they're getting up. Look.'

They watched as the two men groggily found their feet and stumbled across to the car. Almost before Farley could react, the men were in their 4WD heading towards them. The driver poked his middle finger up at them as they sped past. Farley did yet another U-turn to give chase, but two other vehicles were already between them. By the time they reached Mulgrave Road, the other car had turned the corner and sped away. Farley and Taylor were stymied by a red light.

'Shit,' Taylor slapped her own leg. 'Bugger. Hey, thanks for rescuing me. I don't know what to do now. We'll never catch them. I'll have to wait and see if they contact me again.'

'So what do you want to do?'

'I don't know. Maybe I should just go back to my apartment and wait.'

'Do you think *they* know where your apartment is?'

'Oh. Probably.'

'I think you might be safer with me for the time being. Obviously they can contact you on your phone wherever you are.'

'I guess you're right. But I really don't want to impose on you.'

'No worries. I haven't had such an adrenalin rush for ages. Not since I wrestled a crocodile.' Farley registered the look of disgust on Taylor's face. He was about to explain when her phone pinged and she put her hand up to silence him.

The message: Not very clever. You'll pay for this.

Taylor: You've got the wrong computer. Password won't help.

The reply: Bullshit!!

Taylor: Password is stingray7. You'll see.

'What's going on?' Farley asked.

'They want the password to my laptop.'

'Why?'

'I don't know. Won't do them any good though; only bought it yesterday. There's bugger all on the hard drive and nothing that would interest them.' Something was weird. Her other laptop – the one with her customer database *and* the incriminating list – was in her desk drawer at home. She hadn't brought it with her this time because the battery was starting to play up. She had the information with her on a USB stick, but hadn't downloaded it to the new computer yet. But these guys knew who she was. How? The only other person on earth who knew about the list – as far as she knew – was Tony.

She shook her head in incredulity. Was her bastard husband behind this attack? Was this a retaliation for her threat of divorce? No. Don't be stupid. He could have just got it straight off her computer at home. Why go to all this trouble? Unless he didn't realise she hadn't brought it with her. She always took it with her, so he wouldn't even think to look for it at home. And it was weird that he still hadn't answered her call. Surely – divorce or no divorce – if he *wasn't* behind this he'd have rung back as soon as he'd heard her panicked message. Perhaps he was just somewhere out of range. Or maybe he *didn't* have anything to do with this. Maybe these bastards had *him* too. Shit.

She sent Tony a text message.

Where are you? Are you okay? Please answer.

Her phone pinged almost immediately, but it wasn't Tony.

Nothing on this laptop!

Taylor: I told you that.

She wasn't, however, about to tell him where her other laptop was. Not unless she was sure Darius's life was in danger. Ping:

So where's the Toshiba

'Hang on!' she said.

'What?' Farley asked. 'Do you want me to stop?'

'No. No it's all right. I've just realised these guys were after my *other* computer, which is still at home.'

How did they know it was a Toshiba? Only someone close enough to know that would know what brand it was or refer to it that way.

Benefit of the doubt gone: bloody Tony.

The only consolation that it might be Tony behind this was that, although he was an arsehole and not terribly bright, he wouldn't hurt Darius. Taylor was pretty sure about that. It was maybe the lesser of two evils. And it might also explain why she'd only been roughed up a bit, not kidnapped too, or bashed within an inch of her life – or worse. She relaxed slightly. She wasn't afraid of Tony. Although if these were two of his goons, his hired help, she wasn't so sure about their ability to restrain themselves.

Farley looked at his watch. 'Look, I'm happy to help you in any way, but I do have to get to the airport to pick up these Americans.'

'Oh, yeah. I don't want to muck up your plans. Just go to the airport. I'll work out from there what to do.'

As they drove, she explained that she suspected her husband was behind this attack and that she was pretty sure Darius wasn't in imminent danger.

'So does he do this sort of shit often?'

'No. He's mostly full of bullshit. He's never threatened Darius before so I don't honestly think he'd hurt him. But then, it's not every day I tell him I want a divorce.'

'Oh. That might do it.'

Taylor inspected her face in the mirror in the airport toilet. No wonder she had such a headache. Her cheek and eyelid were starting to redden. Bastards. She would take a couple of Panadol with lunch – which Farley had suggested they have together with the Americans – and hope it would numb the pain. Taylor had suggested that he not mention her predicament to them.

When she emerged from the bathroom and traversed the concourse area towards the arrivals lounge, she could see Farley craning his neck to spot his holiday-makers. It wasn't hard, as it happened. She drew up beside him as he beckoned to Alisha and Gavin Grubb.

'Oh Jesus, he's wearing a Stetson. Hope he takes it off in the car or he'll be hitting the ceiling,' Farley said.

After the introductions, Alisha and Gavin were happy at the prospect of lunch. They'd just spent five minutes complaining about the pathetic meal on the Qantas flight from Sydney.

'A piece of suspect chicken stuff, two dead biscuits and three olives in a plastic carton does not, in my view, constitute a square meal,' Gavin had drawled. Alisha repeated this verbatim; three or four times.

Taylor was over them already. As she watched them tucking into massive steaks, while she ate a modest Mediterranean focaccia, she wondered how Farley was going to cope – for 10 days.

'Where are you actually taking these lovely people, Farley?' Her wink wasn't lost on him.

'We're heading to the Birdsville Races, via Normanton and Mount Isa, with stops at a couple of national parks along the way.'

'You're kidding me. My husband is going to Birdsville too. He goes up there every year for the races with a couple of mates.'

'*Up* there? You mean, down there.'

'No it's *up* from Melbourne.

'Huh? You mean you *live* in Melbourne? I thought you were just going there for a holiday or something.'

'No, I live there. *And* I live here.'

'Oh. So have you ever been there? To Birdsville?'

'No. I never interfere with Tony's boys weekend.'

They had the same thought at the same time.

'Why not surprise him?' Farley suggested. 'You could travel with us. That's if you don't *have* to go back to Melbourne.' His eyes were almost pleading for her to say yes; probably to save his sanity. 'You two wouldn't mind would you? Sharing the expedition with another passenger?'

'Not at all. More the merrier,' the Americans said in unison. And then said it again.

Taylor hadn't taken much convincing. She figured that since she still hadn't heard boo from Tony and didn't know where the hell the kidnappers were, there was a chance that they were heading for a rendezvous at Birdsville. Maybe she'd surprise them all. She made a call to Melbourne to extend Onyx and Nefertiti's stay at the cattery and another to a client to postpone a meeting in St Kilda the next day.

Farley suggested they double back to her apartment so she could grab some clothes before they set off to their first-night destination at Undara Volcanic National Park. Aside from Mr and Mrs Redneck, the thought of roughing it in the wilds of Queensland with a relatively good-looking and potentially fearless man for a few days was quite appealing. She hadn't done much camping since her teens and she'd never been further west than Atherton. *So why not?*

After they'd bundled all the Grubbs' gear, including a strangely-shaped canvas bag which Gavin referred to as his 'instrument', into the back of the car and gone via Taylor's apartment to collect her gear, they finally set off at about 2pm.

Taylor was glad that Farley was both interesting and articulate as he described the passing landscape, but it was soon evident that most of it didn't interest Alisha and Gavin one bit. After an hour or so's drive and a brief stop at Crater Lakes National Park, where Gavin had made the comment, 'seen one lake seen 'em all,' they mostly sat in the back yabbering at each other and occasionally making a dumb-ass comment or asking an idiotic question.

'Why the hell don't they irrigate out here and grow corn like back home?' 'You'd think kangaroos would have learned to walk on all fours.' 'How far to the next McDonald's?'

Farley quickly realised they didn't want answers to their questions, they just wanted to be heard asking them, while Taylor wondered how long she'd last before she climbed into the back seat and strangled them. After two hours of torture, Farley announced they were heading off the highway into the Forty Mile Scrub National Park.

'Hope it's not 40 miles to get there,' Gavin said, laughing at his own hilarity. 'Will be good to stretch these here legs a bit though. Say why don't we camp there overnight?'

'It's illegal,' Farley said.

'All the more reason'

'It's illegal, okay. I'd lose my tour guide licence if we were caught.' Farley suddenly swerved the vehicle and stopped.

'Wow, what was that?' Taylor asked as she saw the back end of a creature skittering off into the grass beside the road.

'It was a goanna or a lace monitor. Do you guys want to have a look?'

'Hell yeah,' said Gavin. He got out and headed to the back door.

Alicia agreed, of course, but looked confused. 'Why would you want to monitor lace?'

Taylor couldn't help herself. 'The bigger the lizard the stranger the hobby.'

Gavin appeared beside Taylor's window with his mysterious canvas bag, from which he pulled a strange contraption; all timber and rubber bands. He pulled an arrow from the bag and loaded it into the device.

'Gavin! What the fuck are you doing?' Taylor screamed.

'I'm gonna get me a goanna; a *souver-neer*.'

'The hell you are,' Farley yelled. Before he could reach the front of the car, Gavin had released the arrow. Fortunately he was a rotten shot and the noise it made whizzing through the air sent the goanna scuttling.

'Mate,' Farley said, 'you can't shoot the wildlife here.'

'But they shoot kangaroos all the time. Don't they?'

'Kangaroos sometimes, if it's a licensed cull or you're a farmer. But not in a National Park. And not goannas, mate. Not ever. Now put that bloody thing away, before I break it over my knee. Where the hell did you get that thing, anyway?'

'Made it yesterday. Got the instructions off the internet from a guy in Sydney. Neat ain't it? It can fire four arrows at a time if you want.'

'Holy shit,' Taylor said, 'you could kill somebody with that.'

'Bet your sweet arse you could,' Gavin said.

Farley snatched the makeshift crossbow from Gavin and threw it in the back of the car. 'Get in,' he said angrily. They drove in silence until they reached the main carpark.

'It's a nice, easy walk around the track here. Only takes about 10 minutes,' Farley said. He led the way through the vine thicket, providing an interesting commentary about the various species found in this dry rainforest region, including the bottle tree, white bean, various fig trees, paperbarks, ironbarks and lemon-scented gums. At least Taylor found it interesting.

She nudged him at one point to indicate that he might as well save his breath. Gavin and Alisha were preoccupied staring at photos on their iPhone. That was until Alisha almost stepped on a snake. Gavin thrust his arm across her torso and yelled, 'Holy snappin duckshit – it's a snake!'

Farley smiled, then casually bent down and picked up the half-metre long striped snake. 'It's just a Bandy Bandy. Harmless, unless of course you're a blind snake. That's their main prey, *Ramphotyphlops* or blind snakes.'

'Are they edible? The blind ones?' Gavin asked.

Taylor screwed up her face. 'Why would you even ask that?' *Friggin' ignoramus.*

'Dunno. Just figured they'd be easy to catch. Being blind and all.'

Taylor resisted smacking him.

About an hour later, they pulled up at the Outback Caravan Park at Undara Volcanic Park Reserve for their first night in the relative luxury of a well-appointed camping ground – rather than in the bush. The idea was to ease city folk into the rigours of roughing it.

Taylor, for one, was quietly relieved to see other people, gathered around campfires on folding chairs or eskis. The smell of snags and onions cooking permeated the air.

She helped Farley unload the camping gear and pitch the camping swags. Fortunately, he'd packed a double one for the Grubbs and two singles, which meant that Taylor would have one to herself. She was intrigued at the notion of a tent and bed all-in-one which meant she didn't have to pump up a lilo or sleep on the ground.

Alisha and Gavin had disappeared, no doubt off annoying other campers, while Farley got a fire going in the pit and Taylor helped him organise dinner. Their respite didn't last long however. A moment later, they were listening to not two, but four, American voices – all talking at the same time.

'Well lookie here. Ain't this a coincidence?' Gavin announced, thrusting two people forward. 'These nice people in the tent next to us, all the way out in the *out*-back, are from South Carolina; just a hop and a jump from us in Alabama. And we came across the world to meet them,' Gavin twanged.

'Amazing,' Taylor said. It wasn't what she was thinking.

'Well I'll be,' said Farley sounding a touch too affectedly 'southern' for his own liking.

'I've invited them to join us for dinner,' Gavin said. 'Well, they're bringin their own food of course; presumin that's okay. This here is Martha and Earl Harrop. And this here is our tour guide, Farley, and his – er – Taylor.'

After some hand shaking and forced smiles, Taylor and Farley prepared dinner. Farley was a dab hand at cooking sausages and Taylor threw a salad together and buttered some bread. The Americans busied themselves gasbagging around the fire, trying to outdo each other in the golly gee stakes.

Taylor checked her phone several times for messages. Nothing. The fact that Tony hadn't responded convinced her he was behind this. She probably wouldn't find out until they arrived at Birdsville. No point hurrying, since Tony wouldn't get there until Friday. By 10pm, she'd tired of the fireside chat. Conversation about sitcoms she didn't watch was bad enough, but then they launched into heroic hunting stories.

'I once bagged me a red stag at Laurentian in Canada: 555 inches,' Gavin bragged.

'Yeah? Well buddy, you're one up on me there. My biggest was 529 for a reddy at Mount'n Meadow in West Virginyer.'

Even though Taylor knew what the measurements referred to, and she wanted to vomit, Gavin felt the need to mansplain the details. She feigned interest and added two more candidates to her list.

'Well, lovey,' Gavin began and was soon elaborating on the 'main beam, inside spread' and 'burrs and first points' of deer antlers; aspects of growth more interesting to the shooters than the victims.

'Wait a minute,' Earl said, as he pulled his mobile phone from his pocket. 'This will give you an idea, lass.' He pressed his album icon and flicked through and shoved his dead-deer trophy photo in Taylor's face.

Somehow she kept her expression passive as he re-explained the measurements. The only thing that registered in Taylor's mind, however, was an arsehole with a grin bigger than Texas kneeling beside the beautiful animal he'd bravely killed with his stupid big gun.

'So you really thought you'd get a bit of hunting in while you were, Gavin?' she asked.

'You bet. Knew I couldn't bring my own gun or crossbow into your beautiful country. You people have got the most backward gun laws I ever heard of. But, once here I just did what folks usually do and found my own way.'

Taylor kept a deadpan face. 'It's a pretty impressive gizmo. Could I have a look at it?'

'For sure,' he said proudly. He headed for the Landcruiser. 'Okay for me to…?' he asked Farley.

Though perplexed about what Taylor was up to Farley nodded at Gavin.

When Gavin returned, he sat down on the log beside Taylor and showed her how to load the arrows into the timber carriage, wind the thick rubber band and then crank the mechanism.

'Now these little levers here, they enable you to fire one, two or four arrows at a time.'

Taylor was at once appalled and impressed at the crude efficiency of the weapon. 'What's the accuracy like?'

'Pretty damn good. Here, c'mon I'll show you.' He led the way to the edge of the campsite. The others followed him.

Farley tried to get Taylor to hang back with him for a moment, but she was clearly on a mission. He didn't really know her – at all – but he had a feeling her interest in Gavin, his crossbow and his hunting stories was about as genuine as a goanna with hobbies.

Gavin meanwhile pulled a handkerchief from his pocket. 'Here girly, go stick this in that tree, so as I can see it in the dark.'

Taylor took the clean hankerchief, she wouldn't have touched it otherwise, walked about 10 metres to the tree and wedged it in the bark.

'Okay, well stand clear now. I am about to fire.' An instant later, the arrow pinned its target into the trunk.

'Wow, impressive,' Taylor said. 'Any chance I could have a go?'

'I don't see why not.' Gavin loaded another arrow into the device and handed it to her as she arrived back at his side.

She aimed the weapon at the tree and fired. The arrow hit the ground about two metres short and to the right of the target.

'Guess you'd need a bit more practice, girly,' Gavin said.

'Guess so.'

Taylor enjoyed a surprisingly good night's sleep, despite worrying about Darius and being awakened by a dog that turned out to be a barking owl. Actually she was woken by Gavin and Alisha complaining loudly about the 'nuisance, idiot, barking mongrel' followed by Farley setting them straight.

She emerged from her swag feeling enervated to find the others already up and packed. Farley had dismantled their gear and loaded it all into the trailer.

'Bacon and egg sandwich?' he asked cheerfully. 'I can do it while you go for a shower if you like'.

What a useful man. Bloody Tony couln't even boil water. Then she remembered this was Farley's business, so he'd have to be able to cook.

'We're joining a tour of the lava tubes at eight o'clock. It takes a couple of hours, then we'll head off, okay.'

'Sounds great.'

Before long, Farley and Taylor were picking their way through the unique tract of Queensland savannah country that conceals the Undara lava tube, one of the world's longest flows of lava. Taylor wished she'd packed better walking shoes. Slip-on heeled scuffs weren't appropriate footwear for this. But the walk was worth it. The caves were the result of an eons-old volcanic eruption which left hollow tubes in its wake and now supported fertile pockets of rainforest.

For Gavin and Alisha, it was a big yawn and a cause of complaints. 'It's too stony...It's too far...It's too hot'.

'They sound like two obnoxious back-seat children,' Taylor whispered to Farley.

'Yeah. Are we there yet? Can I've an icy pole. I wanna go to the toilet.'

Taylor snorted. 'Why the hell did they come to see the outback, if they didn't want to see anything?

Two hours and 200 km later, Farley was keeping an eye out for an attractive spot to stop for lunch. The Etheridge River, to the east of Georgetown, looked promising. Taylor recalled references to Georgetown in Neville Shute's *A Town Like Alice* and mentioned this to Gavin and Alisha, who of course had never heard of the book or the author. The area was known as The Poor Man's goldfield because, in its early gold rush days, gold nuggets could be picked up off the ground. Gavin found this interesting, of course, and wanted to hang around and check it out for himself.

Farley started making salad sandwiches and a fruit platter.

Alisha disappeared into the shrubbery to relieve herself. Gavin grabbed his crossbow from the back of the car and headed in the opposite direction.

Taylor followed him.

He ducked and weaved through the shrubbery like a commando; totally unaware she was behind him. He stopped, pulled an arrow from the bag and loaded it into the weapon. He aimed at something to his left and–

'Gavin!'

He jumped and swivelled on his heel to face her. 'Jeez, you shouldn't sneak up on a person like that. I missed the bloody thing.'

'What was it?' She tried to sound casual.

'Dunno, might have been a kangaroo or a wallaby thing.'

Taylor, rigid with rage, showed nothing but interest on her face. 'Mind if I have another go with that?'

'Guess not.' He took out another arrow and loaded it for her.

She walked a few paces away from him and then turned and fired – at him. Without warning.

She nailed the flabby underside of his left arm to a scrappy gum tree. The stunned expression on his face was one that would stay with her forever.

Gavin opened his mouth to speak, or maybe wail, but nothing came out.

She should probably have told him she was a match crossbow champion.

She walked towards him slowly. 'If you think that hurts, just wait for the tetanus injection you're going to need. That's what you get for being an animal-killing, idiot-brained fucktard. This is for the poor defenceless deer and God-knows what other creatures you've killed and are likely to kill. And if you yell now, you'll get another one of these in the eye.'

With that, she bent over, picked up his canvas bag, slung it over her shoulder and retraced her steps to the car.

A low guttural moaning emanated from the direction she'd come from as she approached Alisha and Farley.

'Where's Gav?' Alisha asked.

'I think you'd better go check him out,' she pointed into the scrub, 'he seems to be stuck on a tree'.

Farley looked at her quizzically as Alisha headed off into the scrub.

'How do you feel about leaving these two here?

'What?'

'We need to go, and we need to go now!'

He smiled and then looked worried. 'What did you do?'

'Look, I'll pay you extra – and I mean *a lot* extra – if you get me out of here now. There's no way I'm getting back into this car with that prick. C'mon, your sign there says Outback Adventure. So let's go have an adventure.'

Farley was stunned. What the hell would it do for his business if he dumped his first real customers in the middle of the outback?

Fuck it. Fuck them. She was right. Whatever she'd just done was almost certainly not as bad as what he'd liked to have done to Gavin. And any other bastard who made it his business to kill animals for the hell of it.

He snatched the crossbow and bag from her, shoved a sandwich in her hand, stashed the rest of the food back into the trailer, and was in the driver's seat almost before she'd even moved. Then he got out again, grabbed a picnic blanket, a bottle of water and tin of biscuits and left them under a tree.

'Okay, now let's hit the road.' As they accelerated back onto the road, Farley checked the rear vision mirror to see if either of the Americans had emerged from the scrub. 'Boy, are they in for a surprise. Now tell me. What the fuck did you do?'

'Nailed him to a tree. With his own arrow.'

'Really?'

'Really.'

'Wow. Remind me not to get on the wrong side of you.'

'Do not ever get on the wrong side of me.'

They laughed.

'I guess someone will pick them up, sooner or later. The later the better,' Farley said. 'Give us a chance to get away. Maybe we'll take a raincheck on the gemstones place in town and keep going. What do you think?'

'Yep. Pretty rocks aren't my thing anyway'.

'You know, we're going to be in pretty deep shit once they get the police onto us,' Taylor said. They'd been driving for two hours and had not long passed through the thriving metropolis of Croydon: population – 316; ways to entertain yourself – zip. A few kilometres before Croydon, Farley had stopped the car and pulled his magnetic signs off the doors.

'I'm sorry to have done this to you,' Taylor said. 'Is there a short cut to Birdsville, without going through Normanton?'

Farley shook his head. 'Not really; at least not that I know of. It can be dangerous to go off the beaten track up here.'

'Okay, so I s'pose that so long as we avoid making ourselves known anywhere, we'd be hard to find and might still get to Birdsville by Friday.'

The landscape between Croydon and Normanton was monotonous. Dry. Red. Brown. Dirty. Dusty. Sparse vegetation, scrappy and stunted. The white lines on the black ribbon of bitumen were mesmerising; boring, sleep-inducing. Taylor counted them as they slipped under the car. She nodded off.

Farley glanced at her from time to time. *What had she got him into?* She might be full of bravado with a crossbow in her hand, but asleep she was a picture of cherubic innocence – except for the snoring. At least *that* was keeping him awake, in the absence of stimulating conversation.

He nudged her awake as they approached the faded 'Welcome to Normanton' sign which proclaimed: *Population Small We Love Them All Drive Carefully.*

'I could kill for a beer,' he said, 'but I think we'd better avoid the pub'.

Bummer, Taylor thought. She too could murder an ale. 'Unless we just avoid talking to anybody or maybe mention in passing that we're going in the opposite direction to divert suspicion.'

'Aren't you full of good ideas.'

Normanton seemed almost deserted as they ignored the town's famous *Purple Pub*, drove by some whopping big fish and crocodile sculptures and pulled up in front of the quaint old *Albion Hotel* with its rusting corrugated iron roof. Like the rest of the town, it too was quiet for 4pm on a Tuesday. It was also sticky hot and Taylor had almost drunk the beer in her mind before the jug was even poured. They adjourned to the uninspiring beer garden.

Taylor downed half a beer. 'So what the hell sort of a name is Farley?'

'I wondered when you were going to ask.' He skulled his beer, filled his glass again and clinked his against hers. 'My name is actually Fair-ley, not Far-ley. I had it changed by deed poll when I was about 20.

'Fairley?' Taylor giggled, 'that's Fairley unusual.' She tried not to laugh. 'But then my first name is really Petronella. Petronella Taylor Sanna.'

'Isn't that something you kill insects with?'

'No, that's citronella!' she said, before noticing his grin. 'So why'd you change your name?'

'I was sick of people doing the *fairly this* or *fairly that'* – he raised an eyebrow and she pretended to look sorry – 'or worse, just calling me Fairy.'

Taylor almost spat her beer. 'So are you – a fairy?'

'What do you think? You look like you'd be a good judge of character.'

'Dunno. You are exceptionally good-looking, you wear your jeans menacingly tight and your teeth are frighteningly perfect. Something tells me, fairy or not, that I'm safe in your company, and that's all that matters.'

'Oh really? You think my teeth are perfect?'

She grinned at him. 'So where are we going to camp tonight? At the caravan park?'

'I think it might be better to clear out of town a bit; if you don't mind roughing it.'

'That's what I signed on for.'

'The bush it is then.' He saw her check her phone, again. 'Any word from the kidnappers?'

'Not a word. No ransom demand. Nothing. I hope I haven't done the wrong thing taking off like this. I wish I knew where Darius is. I hope he's all right.'

'I never asked, how old is he?'

'Two and a half.'

'So a bit young, I guess, to understand what's going on.'

Taylor nodded distractedly. She wondered whether she should tell Farley more, then decided against it. He mightn't want to help her if he knew everything. He'd find out soon enough when they got to Birdsville.

She was surprised it hadn't dawned on Tony to search the house for the computer. She still didn't know whether he was at home or on his way to Birdsville. None of it made sense to her. She just knew the potential for him to blackmail her if he got hold of The List. If he passed it on to the police, or to any of the people *on* the list, she could be in real strife.

After a couple of beers each and a stale packet of chips, Farley and Taylor headed out of the pub towards the car.

'Holy shit! Get in the car quick,' Farley said.

Taylor looked up Haig Street at an approaching silver four-wheel drive. She only needed to see the Stetson in the back seat to know who it was.

'Far out,' Taylor exclaimed as she jumped into the passenger seat. Since the road ahead of them petered out into the Never Never, Farley did a speedy U-turn and accelerated back towards the main street. The Americans – all wide-eyes and fists in the air – followed suit, but Farley already had them eating dust. He dodged and weaved around a few corners, past innocent weatherboard houses with broken-down fences. They bombed along a red-dust goat track skirting the edge of town before they hit bitumen again.

'Where are we going?' Taylor asked. She clutched the grab rail above the window to avoid behind thrown around and checked the side rear-vision mirror.

'Out of town.'

'I can't see them. Are they behind us?'

'Nope, I think we've lost them. Ah – or maybe not. Shit.' Farley accelerated, sending up a dust storm in their wake. The track hooked back up to a bitumen street as they headed past the Normanton railway station.

Farley pointed. 'I could tell you a thing or two about the station.'

'What, a history lesson now?'

'Or maybe not,' he laughed.

Taylor checked the rear vision mirror again. She burst out laughing. 'Ha ha, look – they've just run off the road and hit a post. That's seriously going to fuck up their day. Obviously Earl's not much of a driver. I wonder what they've done about Gavin's arm. It must have hurt like hell and I bet there's no casualty department here.'

'Yeah, there is actually.'

'Oh. Well, between the prang and the certainty that he must need medical treatment, I think we could say we've lost them for the time being.'

'Sure hope so.' Farley found his way back to Burke Developmental Road. 'Okay, we can head for Mt Isa or do some sightseeing and check out the

Barramundi Discovery Centre at Karumba. They'd never suspect that. It's about an hour and a bit's drive up to the Gulf. We could camp there tonight and do the touristy bit in the morning. I do need to recon the place to see if it's worth putting on my regular itinerary.'

'Sounds good to me.'

Farley turned left and before long they were heading out of town, past the Carpentaria Shire offices and the Burns Phil mercantile store, which, Farley explained, was built in 1884 and became the longest operating one in Queensland. They hit the open road and Taylor settled herself in for some more dry, red scenery. She wanted to close her eyes for a nap. But something was nagging at the periphery of her mind. Something she had seen during their wild escapade around the town. *What was–*

'Holy shit!'

Farley nearly ran off the road in fright.

'The black four-wheel drive. It was there, in town, at the service station. Shit, that means *they're* following us. As well.'

'We might be following them.'

'Huh? Oh, yeah, possible I guess. Can we turn around and see who the hell they are and whether they've got Darius?'

Farley was already slowing down to do a U-turn.

He drove back into town and slowed as they approached the service station on the left. No cars. Certainly no four-wheel drive. Taylor pointed to the pub on the corner of Haig Street.

'There it is. Outside the *Central Pub*.'

Farley pulled in beside the black Territory. 'Are you sure it's the same car? I mean there's plenty of black Territories around.'

'No, I'm not sure,' she answered as she got out of the car and looked in the vehicle's windows. There was nothing to indicate that Darius might have been in the car. 'Nothing here,' she shrugged. 'I'm going inside anyway.'

Farley had little choice but to follow her. *At least she didn't have a crossbow in her hands*. He was right behind her as she opened the door and headed towards the bar. Two men, whose carefully coiffed heads – one dark and one greyish – and spiffy suits looked entirely out of place among the singlet-and-shorts-clad locals, were sitting at the bar.

Taylor caught Farley's eye and pointed surreptitiously towards the men. He frowned as she pulled a Watermelon Splash Chap Stick from her pocket and snuck up behind them. Farley was in awe of her bravado. He would have preferred to run a mile.

Taylor stuck the Chap Stick in the back of the man on the left. He went rigid as the other turned towards her. She wasn't wrong. It was definitely the kidnappers.

'Hello gentlemen. What brings you to this one-horse town?'

'Ah, er.'

'Cat got your tongue? Wthout drawing any attention to us, you're going to tell me who put you up to this and where the hell Darius is.'

'What the fuck are you doing here? You're supposed to be back in Melbourne,' the goon on the right said.

Taylor was taken aback. Okay, so they *weren't* following them? But why the hell would they be here? 'Never got on the plane. Where is Darius?'

'What do you mean, you didn't get on the plane?'

'Well der! I'm *here* aren't I? It's not like I'm going to fly off to Melbourne when my boy's been kidnapped am I?'

'No,' the two said in unison.

Taylor detected a complicit eye contact between the two. Then the guy on the right blurted, 'But we put him on the plane, just like To–'

The other guy elbowed him in the guts. 'Fucking idiot. Now she knows.'

'I knew it was Tony, you dickhead. You put Darius on the plane? Back to Melbourne? So was Tony going to pick him up there or what?'

'Yeah, I guess,' the black-haired guy said.

'So what are you doing *here*. I mean this isn't a prime tourist destination.'

'We're um, going to do a spot of barramundi fishing. Aren't we, George?'

'George.' Taylor rolled her eyes. 'Oh right, you're George Athanasiadis aren't you; aka George the Greek.'

'Er, yup. Yeah,' he said resignedly.

Farley looked at Taylor for an explanation.

'George Athanasiadis – long-time racing buddy of my scumbag husband. And yet, we've never had the pleasure.'

She looked at his partner in crime. 'I guess that makes you Ivan "The Terrible" Farina.' She winked at Farley. 'The Greek and The Terrible – the dynamic duo of lapdogs.'

'They look more like fluffy bunnies to me,' Farley said.

Taylor giggled then donned her serious face again. 'So which one of you two arseholes did *this* to me? She pointed at her now-purple eye. 'Huh?'

'Yeah, huh?' Farley said, trying to sound menacing. Except that to Taylor, he just sounded curious. She gave him a wry look.

'Tony always told us you were too hot to handle,' George said.

'I'm pleased my reputation precedes me.'

'Everything okay?' the weather-beaten barman asked.

'Just peachy,' Taylor said with a smile. 'Except that we're in serious need of a beer. These two gentlemen have offered to shout us'.

The barman nodded and pulled two schooners from the rack. He filled them with XXXX from the tap and placed them on the bar.

'Thanks, very generous of you guys,' Taylor said.

Farley picked up the glasses and handed one to her, while taking a sip from the other. She winked at him and he nodded back. They poured the beers over George and Ivan's heads. While they swore and carried on like a pair of wet cats, Taylor thumbed towards the door and Farley followed her. They dashed to the car and as Taylor jumped in, she noticed Farley bending down beside the Territory.

'What are you doing? Quick, they'll be on us any second,' she shouted.

He jumped into the seat beside her and closed the blade of his Victorinox. 'Just did to them what they did to you,' he said.

She laughed at the gleam in his eye. 'Why didn't I think of that?'

'It's only bought us a bit of time. Of course they might have trouble getting new tyres for that here.'

'How about we forget about the barramundi thing. I'm not really into fish; or fishing,' Taylor said.

'Me either. Besides, I get seasick.'

Farley drove south-west into the dusk. The sunset cast an orange glow over the already orange-red landscape. Before long it was pitch dark and Taylor was once again hypnotised by the white lines picked up in the headlights. There were no other vehicles. It was eerie; like they were the last two people in a post-apocalyptic nightmare. After about two hours, Farley pulled off the road onto a barren patch of dirt.

'You know it gets pretty cold out here at night. I can pitch two single swags, or the double. I'm not suggesting anything – you know, um – suggestive, but it might be quicker and easier to share one.'

Taylor was too tired to care. She was certainly too tired to contemplate the prospect of anything in a tent in the middle of nowhere, despite acknowledging Farley was quite attractive; and probably gay.

'Yeah. Whatever is easiest,' she said noncommittally. 'Can I make some coffee?'

'The magic word.'

When Taylor awoke she couldn't figure out what the weight was on her left side, until Farley yawned and rolled away. It had been his arm. Had he been snuggled up to her?

'Holy shit,' Farley exclaimed as he looked at his watch. 'It's 9.30. I meant for us to up and gone by eight.'

'What's the hurry?'

'I don't know. I just thought it might be wise to keep well ahead of anyone, everyone, who might be following us.'

Taylor sat up and straightened her singlet which had ridden up from her waist. She started to undo the zip on the swag and then froze. She turned to Farley and put her finger to her lips, then pointed and mouthed to him: *There's someone out there.*

He nodded, silently lifted the inner privacy flap on the swag and peered out through the fly-screen. A silver four-wheel-drive was parked far enough down the road to explain why they hadn't heard it. 'The Americans,' he mouthed.

She nodded. *Shit.*

'Why doncha y'all come on out. We know you're in there,' Gavin drawled.

'Yeah, come on out,' Earl mimicked.

Gavin was trying to open the back door of the Landcruiser. Earl was beside him brandishing a deadly-looking set of barbecue tongs. Alisha and Martha were nowhere to be seen.

Farley motioned to Taylor to slide out her side, then he rummaged around at the foot of the swag. Then he unzipped the tent and they stepped out.

'This what you're looking for?' He pointed Gavin's crossbow at them.

Earl stuck his hands in the air. Gavin followed suit. Well, he raised one hand; the other was captive in a blue sling made from a giant Chux superwipe.

'You wouldn't,' Gavin said. 'She might; she dang well did – but you wouldn't. You've got too much at stake, buddy boy. Your reputation and all. Look, all's we want is our crossbow; and our money back. You can't just up and dump us in this Godforsaken landscape and expect to get away with it.'

Taylor was surprised he didn't mention being shot with his own weapon and *then* dumped in this Godforsaken landscape. She was quite prepared to shoot him again; his Stetson would make a good trophy.

Farley kept the crossbow trained on Gavin. He'd pre-loaded it with four arrows; a point evidently not lost on the Alabaman.

'Look here, Farley, I'd be putting that down if I were you. A weapon like that in the wrong hands–'

'Oh, shut up, Gavin. First of all, if you were me, you wouldn't *have* a weapon like this. And second, I'm a Sagittarius you know, so I fancy myself as a bit of an archer.'

Taylor cracked up. Not many men would proclaim the virtues of their star sign at a time like this. There was a lot about Farley she liked.

'So, yes Gavin, I will refund your money, direct to your bank account. But no way in hell are you getting this back. And if I were *you,* I'd be pulling my dumb-arse American head back into my dumb-arse hat and getting my fat arse the fuck out of here. Unless, of course you'd like a matching injury on your other arm.'

'Yeah, bugger off,' Taylor added 'before this gold medallist in match crossbow gives you pricks a lesson on how to hit two moving targets at once with that pissweak weapon of yours. Go on, lickety-split; run like the cowards all you hunters are.'

Gavin and Earl, with a new understanding of how it felt to face the pointy end of a weapon took off at a lumbering pace, back to their car.

Farley stared at her. 'You're unbelievable.'

Taylor smiled and shrugged.

'I mean: lickety-split. Really?'

'Would you mind if we skip this big fucking hole in the ground bit?' Taylor said as they drove into Mount Isa. 'I've seen mines before and driven a Terex truck and I don't need the five-cent tour. I'd rather go to the pub and have a meal and a few beers. This freakin' heat is killing me.'

'Surely you're used to the Queensland heat by now. And this isn't really that hot; it's only September.'

'Yeah, well I'm not used to it. I'm in Melbourne most of the time. And when I'm in Cairns I'm in an air-conditioned apartment except when I go for a swim. Now, you show me where I can go for a swim in this hell hole and I'll forgo the beer.'

'What do you do exactly? That you can afford to live in two places.'

Taylor gave him the precis version of her business. 'I sell stuff online.'

'What sort of stuff?'

How to throw him off the track? Think up something he won't know much about. 'Scientific stuff, kind of. Information mostly. You wouldn't be interested.' She wasn't about to elaborate. Or tell him about The List.

'I might, I'm a scientist myself.'

Shit. He sure didn't look like a scientist – at least not a lab-coated, stare-down-a-microscope kind of scientist. *Why hadn't she said cosmetics or something? Why scientific stuff?* 'Yeah? What sort of scientist?'

'A microbiologist – among other things. I worked for a while at the CSIRO on a project to control ants.'

'Ants? Fascinating.' Taylor rolled her eyes. 'Why aren't you doing that anymore? Were the ants too clever for you?'

'Hated working indoors and laboratories make me claustrophobic. Besides, ants have a raison d'être like anything else. After a while, I just couldn't justify finding ways to kill them.' Farley shrugged.

A man who wouldn't even kill an ant? 'So couldn't you work elsewhere in your field?'

'Nah, I was bored with it anyway. So I switched to oceanography.'

Taylor was impressed. 'Wow. So what sort of research did you do?'

'Coral bleaching. Spent quite a bit of time out on the reef. But–'

'Ha! But you get seasick. Right?' She recalled their earlier conversation.

He poked his tongue out at her. 'Smarty pants!' He decided to change the subject. 'Did you say you'd driven a Terex truck? Where?'

'In the Pilbara a few years ago; at an iron mine.'

'You actually worked there? Not just drove a humungous truck once.'

'Yeah, for a while before I was married. It was great money and I was at a loose end; didn't know what to do with myself. My dad got me the job there – in the office; but the minute I saw those big bastards I thought, yep, I've got to drive me one of those. So I went through all the training, but I only lasted about five months and then I had to get out of there.'

'Why? Oh, I know, too hot?'

'That, and too many fuckdicks there.'

'Fuckdicks?'

'Yeah, you know, guys who think about fuck-all but their dicks.'

'Oh, so not guys that just fuck all the time?'

'Nah, they're mostly too tired or wasted to actually *do* it. That's why they just think about it – all the time. It messes with their heads, it really does.'

'So did any of them ever try it on you?'

'One; on the first day.'

'What happened?'

'Told him I was gay. Nobody bothered me after that. Except a couple of the girls, but we all just became great mates.'

Farley pulled the Landcruiser into a parking spot in front of the *Red Earth Hotel*. 'Lunch time.'

They drove for about three hours along the red ribbon of road through an almost featureless landscape of bare earth and tussocks. Taylor couldn't get it out of her head that she'd seen The Greek and Terrible's black car in Mount Isa. Obviously they were heading to Birdsville too and she wondered whether they were now ahead of or behind them. It didn't really matter. It was unlikely they'd try anything stupid now. But it meant she and Farley had lost the element of surprise. Tony no doubt knew, within seconds of their departure from the pub in Normanton, that they too were heading for an outback rendezvous. She wondered where Darius was. And if he was okay. He was probably at home with Tony's mother. Maybe she should ring Maria. Or maybe not. Maria was half deaf, so what would be the point?

'Only about 20 or 30 minutes now until Boulia,' Farley announced.

'Is that anything to get excited about?'

'Nup.'

'Can I sleep through it?'

'Easily. Just blink and you'd miss it. It's dry, dusty, flat, boring. Population 230 something, if everyone's at home.'

'Good. I'm going back to sleep then.'

'Do you want to camp overnight somewhere or just keep going until we hit Birdsville?'

'I don't mind. You're driving.'

Farley pulled off the road when he got tired and had a sleep, but they were back on the road a couple of hours later and well on their way to Birdsville – ETA 11am or so. Taylor thought the flat moonscape was never going to end. She could understand how the phrase 'back of beyond' had been coined. Something in the sky caught her eye; a glint of something.

'Oh look, a hairy Jane.'

'You're awake then obviously. What the hell is a hairy Jane?'

'An aeroplane.'

Farley glanced up. 'Oh. You can expect to see quite a few of those. People fly in from all over the place for the races.'

'No accounting for taste. I can't fathom why anyone would come here voluntarily. Tony has shown me photos before. It's like the arse end of hell.'

'Some people love the solitude, serenity, seclusion. And the races are a big deal.'

'I'm so not into horse racing. It's cruel. So is greyhound racing.'

'I'm with you there. Hey, did you hear about that greyhound guy in the boating accident the other day?'

Sure did. 'Got what he deserved, I reckon.'

'There was some speculation that he didn't fall overboard; that he was actually being towed–'

'Like live shark bait.'

'You heard obviously. He was allegedly on bail for live animal baiting.'

Taylor pursed her lips to stifle a grin. 'Poetic justice then.'

'Yep' Farley agreed. 'But who'd do that? Actually, that's a stupid question. I probably would if I caught some bastard using live rabbits to train dogs. Or using dogs in fights'

He recalled the woman on Facebook sitting proudly on a giraffe she'd shot dead. And another showing off her trophies – a zebra, a buffalo and a lion – that she'd murdered at a *legal* US game reserve. He wondered what was wrong with those people. At the time, he'd wished he could find her and put a bullet in a strategic part of her anatomy that would cause her to exsanguinate slowly and oh so terribly painfully. He'd applauded when he'd seen another Facebook post about the elephant hunter whose prey had turned on him and trampled him to death.

'Same sort of person who would shoot a deer hunter in the arm with a crossbow, methinks,' Taylor said. She thought about how she'd planned to aim at Gavin's chest; how she had wanted to so badly. 'Same sort of person who'd want to barbecue a bastard who'd set a dog on fire or drown another guy who'd tossed a bag of kittens in a dam.'

Someone just like me.

Farley frowned. 'Are you talking from experience?'

Taylor realised she'd said too much. 'Don't be daft. Gavin was just the straw that broke the camel's back for me. My blood boils when I see people killing or hurting animals for no reason other than their own sick pleasure.' She didn't know Farley well enough, yet, to say more.

'Me too. There's plenty of people out there that I'd like to get my hands on. Give them some of their own medicine. Bastard rhino and elephant poachers, game hunters, fucking people with crossbows and shotguns. People torturing animals for the fun of it. Hell, I couldn't even cope with the little shits who pulled wings off flies when I was a kid. Bastards.'

Taylor was stunned at Farley's vehemence. Maybe he was a kindred spirit. Maybe she *could* tell him about her little enterprise: Genemesis. He might be a handy ally. No, too soon.

They hit the outskirts of Birdsville. Another light plane flew overhead and descended to land at the airstrip off to their right. She watched as it kicked up a trail of dust on the runway.

'Okay. So we're here,' Farley said. 'Now what?'

'The pub, the pub, my kingdom for the pub.'

'I'm starting to think beer is all you ever think about.'

'Only when I'm dying of thirst in the outback.'

'You realise it will be so crowded we won't even be able to get inside. We certainly won't get a seat.'

A few moments later, after passing a veritable tent city of temporary accommodation, Farley stopped the car within sight of the iconic *Birdsville Pub*. Taylor was astonished at how tiny and ordinary it looked. She could barely see the whitewashed brick façade of the single-storey building for the cavalcade of flannel-shirted, Akubra-hatted humans spilling all over the narrow veranda onto the dusty street corner.

She wondered whether Tony had arrived yet. Or George and Ivan for that matter. It was only 11.15 but chances were that Tony at least would have arrived last night. She had no idea where they camped and couldn't see any of them among the revellers outside the pub.

The annual race meeting swelled the town's population from just over 100 up to 9000. It looked like a third of them were at the pub already, getting positively tanked. She doubted a Booze Bus would be out between here and the racetrack. She'd just had that thought when she saw a bunch of punters queueing for a shuttle bus.

'How far is it? To the racetrack?'

'About three km,' Farley said. 'Do you want to go?'

'Not to watch the races; to look for Tony.'

After pitching their swag at the camping area, they caught the shuttle bus and spent the afternoon wandering around the dustbowl that was the Birdsville Racecourse. The race-caller's tower, a rickety-looking arrangement of steel and corrugated iron nestled between a few open-sided sheds that provided the only cover from the scorching sun, was the tallest thing for miles. It was a far cry from the green lushness and rose-scented lawns of Flemington Racecourse. They both avoided watching the races. They were more intent on watching the watchers. But they'd seen no sign of Tony, or his henchmen; or, thankfully, the Americans. Taylor was hot, sticky and dirty.

'From what you've said about him, he's likely to be at Brophy's,' Farley said. He handed her another plastic cup of beer from the XXXX tent.

'What's Brophy's? A bar?'

'No it's a boxing tent. This guy called Fred Brophy and his family travel all around Queensland to shows and major events with a troupe of bruisers. Anyone can take them on and potentially win prize money. Mostly they just get the crap beaten out of them though.'

'That exactly the sort of shit Tony and *his* bruisers would be into.'

'It's in town, near the pub. But it doesn't get fired up until the evening.'

'Okay, so let's have an early dinner and check it out. I'd bet my bottom lip that Tony'll be there.'

They stood in the queue to enter the boxing tent, both disguised as best as they could be with the Akubras Farley lifted from the back of a nearby ute. Taylor kept looking around nervously, expecting to see her bastard-ex.

'Hey, calm down,' Farley said soothingly, 'you're making yourself look obvious. What does Tony look like anyway?'

'A cross between James Gandolfini and Al Pacino.'

'A true Mafia overlord then.'

'Yep, with Rocky Balboa's nose thrown in.'

'Oh, okay,' Farley said, in the deepest voice he could muster.

They finally got inside the tent; standing-room only. Some puny tattoo-covered loser was getting the shit pummelled out of him by a big, brawny, tattoo-covered loser. Taylor was overcome by the smell of sweat, beer and what she suspected was vomit. They stood in the back row. Taylor was grateful there were no Stetsons in front of her.

'God. Why is it that so many men have to make a point of proving how tough they are? I think it's a character weakness myself.'

Farley nodded. 'I'd have to agree with that'.

A bell rang. The brawny guy's arm was lifted into the air and the puny guy was dragged from the ring like a sheep to be sheared. With little ceremony another boxer entered the ring and a moment later another challenger emerged from the crowd. Taylor held her breath and nudged Farley who was looking in the other direction. 'It's Gavin. Can you believe it?'

'Oh yes, I can. Just as well he hasn't got his crossbow with him. Look, Alisha, Martha and Earl are just over there. Don't draw attention to yourself.'

'His arm's obviously not hurting him.'

With no sling and just a little bandage on his arm, Gavin pranced around the square as though he was Mike Tyson's sparring partner, dressed in stars and stripes satin boxers and a blue singlet. His opponent landed a punch straight at his jaw and Gavin reeled backwards but stayed on his feet. He swung wildly at the boxer, missed completely and almost overbalanced.

Taylor sniggered; Farley grinned. It was worth coming all the way to this dust bowl to see this. Two perfectly-timed jabs, a feinted bolo punch followed by an upper cut to the solar plexus and Gavin was down for the count.

'I reckon he's seeing more stars than the ones on his undies,' Taylor said.

'Obviously got a glass jaw and a mushy breadbasket,' Farley said, trying to impress with the only two boxing terms he could bring to mind.

'Huh?'

'Never mind. Look, Earl's going to have a go. Idiot.'

'Another case of who's got the bigger dick.'

Earl looked an even more unlikely contender than Gavin and his opponent was bigger, brawnier and deadlier-looking. Completely outclassed it took two punches and Earl was on the deck. Moaning like a baby.

Farley nudged Taylor. 'Shit, company.'

Taylor turned just as George the Greek grabbed her arm. She tried to step away but he gripped tighter and twisted her arm behind her back. Pain shot straight into her shoulder. Farley was no help because Ivan had him in a similar lock. 'Stop struggling. Tony is expecting you. Just act natural like.'

George lifted the tent flap and shoved Taylor inside. She couldn't see Tony but she knew he was there; she could smell the Paco Rabanne he doused himself in. Ivan pushed Farley and he fell beside her. As her eyes adjusted to the dim light, she could see Tony sitting in a camp chair in the corner, looking like Marlon Brando in *Apocalypse Now.*

'Hello, my sweet.'

'Don't you my sweet me, you bastard. What the fuck is this all about, Tony? You think you can blackmail me into staying with you? Is that it? Sorry, not going to happen.'

'In your dreams. But I see you haven't wasted any time replacing me.'

'What? No. Don't be stupid. Farley's just–'

'Farley eh? Groovy name. Ivan, give Farley a kick in the nuts will you?'

Ivan obliged. Farley grunted and curled up in agony.

'Don't involve him in this Tony. It's got nothing to do with him.'

'Bullshit. How long's this been going on for?'

'Nothing's going on, Tony. Not likely to either. He's gay.'

Farley's eyes widened, but he played along.

'Gay?' Tony said. He didn't disguise the disbelief in his voice.

It was only the pain in his testicles that raised Farley's voice an octave. 'What do you want with her?'

'What do I *want* with her? With my own *wife*?'

'Yes. What do you want from her?'

'Well, Mr Obviously Gay, I want the computer with The Genemesis List.'

Taylor sucked in a breath. 'How did you know it's called Genemesis? I've never told you that.'

'One of your customers squealed. Turned out he was more interested in money than animal rights or retribution. He's offered me a million for the list. So let's just say, if I've got a million – oh, and half of your worldly goods – then, I don't need you.'

'You jerk, you were already getting rid of me. It was me who asked for a divorce.'

'Divorce doesn't get me the extra million.'

'The List is useless to anyone but me. Why would anyone want it?'

'D'oh. Money honey. Blackmail money. Someone with the time and inclination to blackmail all your clients, and maybe even offer protection to your targets – well, someone like that could make a small fortune.'

Taylor shook her head. 'Trust *you* to want to make money out of something *I* do for the good of humanity.'

'The good of *humanity?'* Tony laughed. 'You've got to be kidding. Killing or maiming people just because they might've shot some bloody lion or rhino or friggin bunny in some country you've never even been to?'

Farley hadn't followed what they were saying until that moment. 'Hang on,' he blurted, 'did you have something to do with the greyhound guy?'

'Only information Farley, that's what I do. I find people whose passion is to kill innocent creatures and then I sell the information to other people whose *passion* is retribution. I wasn't sure what would happen to *that* guy, but I couldn't have dreamed up a more fitting punishment.'

'And you make money out of this? That's pretty mercenary, isn't it?'

'No, Farley. I don't make money. Every cent I get paid, goes to animal protection and anti-hunting and anti-poaching campaigns.'

Farley didn't know how to react. He suspected he might be in awe of this woman – but that didn't help his reaction. She was doing what he had only ever dreamed of doing. Probably what every die-hard animal lover wanted to do to the sort of people who caught Sumatran tigers in barbaric wire snares, who hunted the Northern White Rhino to extinction or who masacred whales in the name of science.

Greenpeace and Sea Shepherd had their place, but this Genemesis – wow. He wanted to know more. He also wanted to get up off the ground, but Ivan had his foot firmly planted on his back, pressing him into the plastic floor.

'Enough with the elevator pitch, bitch. Where's the bloody computer?'

'Where's Darius?'

'Well, let's just say he's okay.'

'No, let's just say where the fuck he is; not just *how* he is.'

'Where's the computer?'

'You mean to tell me you didn't think to look for it at home?'

Tony looked confused. 'Why? You mean you didn't take it with you?'

'No, dickhead. The battery's rooted. Which is why I bought the new one in Cairns. Not very bright, are you, Tony?'

'But surely,' George interrupted, 'surely she'd have that information on a disc or USB or something.'

Taylor gulped, almost audibly. *Who knew George had a clue.*

'George, sometimes you surprise me,' Tony said.

Not even Tony, clearly.

'So, where is it, Taylor?'

'A USB?' Ivan said. 'That'd be like trying to find a needle in a haystack'.

Ah, Ivan the clueless one.

Taylor tried to look innocent.

Tony pointed to the elephant-embroidered bag Taylor had over her shoulder. Ivan grabbed it, tipped the contents out. Chap Stick, purse, mobile, tampons, notepad, biro, coins, a supermarket trolley token, some receipts, half a roll of Mentos, a sunglasses case. No USB stick.

'Check if there's any pockets inside,' Tony instructed.

Taylor sucked in her breath again.

Ivan opened the zip of a small inside pocket and pulled out a blue brushed-aluminium USB stick. He tossed it to Tony who plugged it in to the laptop on his lap and opened the only file on it. A list of names, addresses and contact numbers, both Australian and international, came up on the screen. He nodded and closed the lid of the computer.

'Okay, so you've got it,' Taylor said in a resigned voice. 'Now where's Darius? I presume he's at your mother's.'

'You presume wrong, my dear.' Tony nodded to George who, much to Farley's relief, lifted his foot away and exited the tent.

Farley stood slowly but stayed bent over in a pain-in-the-nuts stance.

Taylor looked at him apologetically. 'You okay?'

He nodded.

Tony flipped the USB around in his fingers. 'So Mister Fairy Pants, I guess you don't find my wife attractive then ,huh?'

Farley played along with Taylor's game. 'I wouldn't say she's not attractive. Just not to me, if you know what I mean.' He waved his hands theatrically.

Taylor still wasn't sure about him. The act was an act but that didn't mean he wasn't being honest. And he did look so pretty in those tight shorts. It would explain why he hadn't made even the hint of a pass.

'So, I've done a bit of research on you, Mr *Smarty* Fairy Pants. Tell me, what's a hotshot scientist doing running around the countryside with holiday-makers? I see you're a bachelor of biology, bachelor of marine science and a bachelor of – what was the other thing?'

'Geology. I'm a bachelor of geology as well,' Farley said softly.

Taylor's mouth fell open.

'Clever dick.' Tony was about to continue when Ivan lifted the tent flap.

'Darius,' Taylor exclaimed. She stretched out her arms and took hold of Darius. 'Oh my honey, honey boy.'

Farley turned, expecting to see a toddler in her arms. Not a– Um. What the hell?

'God, it hasn't got any fucking hair! The bastards must have shaved it all off. Who would do that to a poor defenceless anything? Is it valuable or something? The hair, I mean.'

Taylor grinned at him, relief all over her face. 'Farley, I'd like you to meet Darius – my sphinx stud.'

She waited for Farley's jaw to snap back into place. 'He doesn't *have* any hair. Never did. Not supposed to.'

'And he's a cat.' He rolled his eyes. 'I thought Darius was your son.'

'I never said that–'

'Yes you–'

'Nope. I only ever referred to him as *my boy.*'

Farley grinned and shook his head. 'Shit, you did too. You had me sucked right in. So I've just travelled across Queensland to rescue a cat. He's got to be the ugliest thing I've ever seen.' He paused a moment and studied the cat a little more. 'No, the most exotic thing I've ever seen. He's actually handsome in a weird, bald sort of way.'

Taylor could tell he was hooked. It normally took people much longer to recognise the beauty of these wonderful creatures.

She held Darius up. 'Did you have a lovely time with Cleopatra?'

'Cleopatra?' Farley asked.

'Yes he was on stud duty in Cairns. That's why he was there with me. Hopefully making some lovely new bald baby Egyptians.'

Taylor was astonished that Tony had simply let them go.

Farley even more so. He'd been imagining a *Casino*-style ending with baseball bats and a lonely desert burial place. But Tony had what he wanted and had told her he'd see her in court. Besides, he was in the line-up for a date with destiny at Brophy's.

Taylor and Farley decided not to hang around to see how that one went.

'I can't believe you gave him what he wanted. The USB stick, I mean,' Farley said as they walked the block or so from Tony's tent to where they'd pitched their swag earlier.

Darius sauntered alongside beside them in harness; just like dog.

'I didn't,' Taylor said smugly, and conscious of the fact that Farley had his hand on her hip. 'I gave him the USB that has all my Sphynx-breeding contacts. When he reads it properly, we'll hear him screaming across the outback. The USB with the Genemesis list is here.' She plucked it out from her bra.

'Oh, shit. You're not going to hear the end of this I suspect,' Farley said, lowering his hand a tad and squeezing lightly.

Did he just squeeze my arse?

He did.

'And he's not going to be pleased when he finds out I sent a friend to retrieve my laptop from home.' She laughed. 'So, are you interested in hearing more about Genemesis?'

'I sure am. But one thing intrigues me.'

'Yeah?'

'If you don't make money out of it, what do you live on? You said Tony was after *your* money.'

'Yep, the benefit of being independently wealthy. My father was a mining magnate.'

'God, please don't tell me you're a Rinehart.'

'Ha ha, no. Not *that* mining magnate.'

'But you said your business was selling scientific stuff. What sort of scientific stuff?'

'Sorry, I fibbed. I didn't know you. I said scientific stuff because I thought you wouldn't be interested. How was I supposed to know you've got every science degree known to – science? So, you're a geologist as well.'

'Well, I've done all the homework. But–'

'Let me guess, you're allergic to dirt?'

'Hah, very funny. Basically, dead things like rocks don't interest me much. Unless they're dead things that should not *be* dead, like white rhinos, elephants, whales, lions, whatever. So, I *do* want to know more about Genemesis.'

'Okay, mostly I gather information. I see somebody smiling on Facebook beside a dead wild animal that they've just shot for the fun of it and I make it my business to find out who they are and everything I can about them. Then I sell that information to other Genemesis members. And I have members all over the world. And of course, they also feed me information on illegal poaching and hunting. But it's then entirely up to them what they do. Sometimes they just find the people and teach them a lesson; sometimes they give them a dose of their own medicine; sometimes, they give them no quarter and just do the world a favour. Sometimes I get a bit more involved and help them track down the arseholes myself. And, as I said before, all the money Genemesis generates – which is substantial – goes to conservation projects and species preservation.'

'Wow. How long have you been doing this?'

'Five, nearly six years. It's very satisfying work. And I get to travel a lot. Interested?'

Farley nodded. Microbiology didn't excite him. Oceanography didn't excite him. Geology left him stone cold. But Taylor Sanna excited him. And Genemesis…

He looked into Taylor's sea-green eyes and raised an eyebrow. He held out his hand to shake hers.

'Taylor,' he said, 'I think this is the beginning of a beautiful friendship.'

Mary Borsellino

The Australian Gang

My phone beeped a new-message tone, but I was elbow-deep in gore, so Jonathan fished it out of my pocket and checked the screen.

'Oh. One of *those*,' he said after a moment of reading, mouth thinning into a frown.

'Revenge job?' Tengfei guessed. Jonathan nodded. My own posture straightened, interest perked. I hadn't been part of any of the Australian Gang's works of vengeance before, and was excited at the opportunity.

It would be more interesting than torturing the bureaucrat in front of me for state secrets anyway. I'd grown out of torture years ago, and only really bothered now when Tengfei needed an extra pair of hands. And forearms, in this case.

'Some obscure Baronet or whatever,' Jonathan told us, flicking through the long scroll of information. 'Hosting an auction of – ugh! – "rare and exotic pets". Why are dudes like him always so gross and creepy? I can't decide which is worse, human traffickers who act like it's just another kind of stock and cargo, or the ones who get all gaudy and *Eyes Wide Shut* about it.'

'And?' Tengfei prompted, guiding Jonathan back from his rambling irritation to the subject at hand. I scrubbed the worst of the blood off my hands and started duct-taping our prisoner back together. He gurgled at me faintly. I ignored him. He'd stopped having anything interesting to say a while ago.

'And he's making sure everyone knows he's got Australians, freshly imported.' As he spoke, Jonathan pushed his blond hair back from his face. He always looked more like a teenage surfer than a ruthless killer.

'Stupid.'

'Yeah, I agree. I guess that's one advantage of flamboyant assholes over all-business slavers. They're too excited by their illicit fun to be the slightest bit smart about it. How can this wanker possibly expect to avoid a sticky end after letting the world know that he's trying to sell Australians?'

Australia, as we know it today, was born several hundred years ago – when other countries started shipping their surplus criminals here, trying to turn the continent into a kind of sprawling free-range jail.

The native population and the imported settlers quickly made a pact: those who broke the laws of their old lands, or had no wish to follow them, would find sanctuary and freedom here, so long as they didn't try to curtail the freedom of others.

No king or jailer would govern them, and within this country they would be beholden to nobody but themselves.

After all, there wasn't any shortage of resources to share out; the indigenous Australians could easily spare the room for the convicts to live alongside them. The real threats were the laws and orders that their captors sought to impose, and so those were quickly done away with – along with the captors themselves.

Against their uninvited visitors, the united people of this new hybrid country made a code: No land could send free settlers to Australia unless those settlers cut all ties and citizenship with their old life and embraced Australia's new chaotic, lawless ways. There would be no international treaties, nor any sides taken in wars or conflicts. Anyone transported to the country against their will would be accepted if they wished to stay, but no attempt to hold them would be made if they wanted to leave.

Any attempt to remove someone from the country by kidnapping would be met with a zero tolerance response. According to the self-made laws of the land, no country on earth had the right or jurisdiction to steal an Australian, and those laws were the only ones acknowledged.

The place was hell or paradise, depending on whose opinion was being voiced. Life was grim, ruthless, and frequently violent, which made the prospect of living there exactly what I was looking for. I was especially intrigued by those elaborate codes of honour that were, paradoxically, largely about removing as many rules and as much control from everyday life as possible. I'm interested in codes of honour and of conduct; in rules, in strictures. Everyone's got one, of some sort or another. They might not call it that, but it's there.

It might be that you'll eat lamb without hesitation but could never tolerate visiting an abattoir. Or you may hold an absolute refusal to betray the honour of your family.

Any rule you find yourself following by heart, that's your code, whether you've ever thought about it or not.

I've spent quite a bit of time thinking about mine, largely because elements of it took considerable effort on my part before I could adhere to them without hesitation. The codes I live by aren't the easy, instinctual kind that most of the population enjoys, wherein all they have to do is listen to their own desires or morals.

Being born into one of the world's wealthiest families provided me with the code of my childhood, all its tenets written long, long before my existence began. What used to be called a *noblesse oblige.* There's a responsibility that comes along with influence and freedom.

My second code – in some ways a liberating change from the first, in others an even greater challenge – came along with my decision to join the Australian Gang.

That isn't an official name, of course. The media has coined countless others, attempting to convey the lurid menace of the group, but none have stuck. I'm glad about that. My soul would cringe if I had to introduce myself as part of the Ghost Kingpins or the Outback Killers.

The gang needs no introduction though, which is why none of the names have stuck. There's no equivalent in the world that we could be confused with.

My family's fortune was built on crime, and the successful future I intended to make for myself would benefit greatly from an apprenticeship spent in the wild purgatory of a place that the rest of the world knew so little about, the place where the most notorious figures of the underworld began their careers.

Anybody who cut their teeth as part of the Australian Gang would have a fearsome reputation that could serve them later in life. No mafia, yakuza gang or cartel would ever be a match for what they'd already lived through.

The Australian Gang wasn't the only form that interaction between Australia and the outside world took, but it was the most notorious. Nobody knew exactly how many members were in the gang, but it was somewhere around fifty.

Gang members ventured out into the world, taking what they wanted by whatever means necessary, spreading mayhem for mayhem's sake, and destroying anything or anyone who got in their way. They'd vanish as suddenly as they arrived, retreating back into the anarchy of their home country without any trail to track them by.

From the way they were talked about, it was more like they were monsters from a fairy tale than feared criminals. I found that appealingly familiar; my family's surname was universal shorthand for organised crime in most of the world. It would have felt unnerving to be suddenly nothing more than an anonymous thug. I like a little panache in my devilry.

With my shiny bob of black hair framing my white skin and dark eyes, the media did their best to give me the nickname 'Snow Red' – like Snow White, but drenched in blood. I found it asinine but vaguely amusing, but wasn't much perturbed when it fell into disuse just as quickly as any other moniker associated with the Gang.

Programs and novels about Australia often adhere to the stereotype of the place being technologically backwards, which is hilarious to me. The history of innovation hinges on criminality and always will. The Deep Web is better and cleverer at every aspect of online security than any law-abiding anti-virus company could ever hope to be.

This disconnect between rumour and reality inadvertently helped Australia's terrifying reputation. Allegedly we miraculously *knew* when one of our own was in peril, or that retribution for breaking our code was needed.

The truth was, one of the more technical-minded associates of the Gang sent an encrypted text message to my phone while I was on the information-extraction job with Jonathan, Tengfei, and a very unlucky bureaucrat. The associate attached all the information they'd found about the auction, in a neat and readable font. Hardly the dark sorcery of pulp novels, but it got the job done just as well.

I knew better than to truly trust anyone in the Gang, but I did enjoy the company that some of the other members provided. Jonathan reminded me of one of my brothers and, while I didn't miss my family in any real sense, it was still pleasant to be around someone whose patterns of thought and techniques of violence were familiar to me. Both Jonathan and my brother favoured ordinary over-the-counter fishing hooks as an implement of their more intricate work.

Tengfei and Jonathan's relationship was brotherly, too, but on a more even footing than my own nostalgia-tinged emotions. I was at least a decade younger than either of them, and the way two siblings relate across a gulf of years is very different to how two of a similar age will interact. They supported and refined one another's strategies, and backed each other up whenever discord against other factions of the Gang was brewing. Their banter was friendly, lighthearted, and entertaining, and even at times when I would have preferred to work in silence – such as those occasions when stealth would have made the disposal of guards and sentries an easier task – I found my mouth twitching up into a smile at the sounds of their good-natured teasing.

As our flight drew closer to our clandestine destination, a sylvanian hideaway in deepest Gravuria, the view from my window seat became an almost uniform expanse of thick forest, the trees all the chilly black of winter and dusted with snow. It made me think of children's stories, of my own abandoned nickname from the newspapers.

'The nobles around here were notorious war generals,' Jonathan told us, reading off the screen of his own phone this time. 'Says here that when they'd finally won against their enemies, they'd host big banquets for the officers sent to negotiate peace with them. They'd cook and serve the flesh of slain enemy soldiers, and not tell the officers that they'd been eating their own men until afterwards.'

I wrinkled my nose, frowning at the thought. The notion of cannibalism had always been, excuse the pun, extremely distasteful to me. I found corpses abhorrent once the death was final and complete.

Jonathan and Tengfei brought clothes that would let us blend in with the company we'd be forced to keep. I'd always been something of a fussy dresser, ever since I'd been old enough to choose my own clothing. I liked expensive fabrics and complicated outfits, everything precise and lovely. That propensity had probably contributed to my Snow Red notoriety as much as anything else; I often did have something doll-like in the way I presented myself, like a perfect princess from a fairy story.

My mother had always liked that about me, saying often that if it was her fate to be cursed with nothing but boy children, at least she'd been lucky enough to get one that appreciated prettiness.

Tengfei's costume for the job included a cravat. I'd hardly ever seen anybody actually wear one, even to white-tie functions, but on him it managed to look right. His absolute certainty that this was the kind of thing rich people wore made it completely convincing.

Jonathan looked almost plain next to our peacock finery, his expensive suit free of embellishments.

I considered each of us in turn, and came to a decision.

'You play the owner. We'll be the pets.' I wrinkled my nose at the gauche terminology.

'Me? Why?'

'Well, you're blond, for one thing. Tengfei and I aren't even Caucasian. The more we fit their mental image of who we're pretending to be, the less they'll notice us. You get bored if you have to go a full two minutes without your phone in your hand – an air of that will be in your favour if you're a spoilt idiot, but it would be dangerous to let that expression show on the face of a slave. Get it?'

Annoyed, he nodded at my explanation. 'Yeah, yeah, okay, you're right. You two get to have all the fun.'

Infiltrating the party was literally as simple as showing up. The Baronet didn't seem to mind at all that a foreign noble he'd never met or heard of had arrived a day early for the auction. Jonathan was welcomed without question.

Tengfei and I waited as patiently as we could while Jonathan and the Baronet introduced themselves to one another. We allowed ourselves to be looked at and petted and talked about as if we weren't there, nothing but mute animals.

'They're almost a matched set, aren't they? Though the girl is much prettier than the boy. Are they siblings?'

Jonathan didn't bother to correct the Baronet on the fact that I wasn't a girl, or that Tengfei was much too old to be called a boy. Instead he simply shook his head, another of his laconic, careless smirks on his face.

'Actually, no. He's from Chongqing, she's from near Kyoto.'

'Oh, a real geisha girl! How lovely.'

I suppressed a shudder of distaste as the Baronet's eyes lingered on my throat. I hoped we'd have the opportunity to torture him to death, despite the fact I'd lost my childhood fascination with sadistic violence.

In this case, I was sure I'd rediscover the old joy of it. Tengfei was the most adept at extracting information through the application of pain, but it was plain that the Baronet had nothing in his head remotely worth extracting.

I enjoyed drawn-out death matches against skilled opponents, but the Baronet had no allure whatsoever as a candidate for that kind of bloodlust. At the most, he'd have a schoolboy's grasp of fencing or hunting. Fighting him wouldn't be any fun at all.

Still, even if the act itself would only hold the echo of delights I'd had when I was small, the idea of making the Baronet suffer had a charm all of its own, especially after he told Jonathan that Tengfei and I would be required to wear locked collars with bells attached to them for the duration of our visit.

Degradation and humiliation we'd expected, but tacky nonsense was a different matter.

We waited quietly until Jonathan plied the Baronet into a thoroughly drunken state shortly before dawn. The timing had to be right; if we made him insensible too early the valets and maids who attended to the castle each evening would still be present in large numbers, and if we left it too late we risked still being on the move when the morning shift of cooks and housekeepers began their work.

Once the Baronet's slurred words were mostly snores, Tengfei and I took our leave, slipping out of the room and moving through the chill stone hallways. Our movements were lithe, the bells on our collars as quiet as our footsteps. I found myself enjoying the challenge that the bell offered; it reminded me of learning good posture by walking with a book on my head.

Our route didn't take us near the kitchens, which was for the best. If we'd gone any closer I'd have felt compelled to look in all the freezers, examining the cuts of meat to check if any were human. At dinner I'd eaten the food placed before me, as a dutiful slave would, but now it churned uneasily in my stomach.

The library was much as I'd expected it to be, done up faux-tastefully in high shelves and leather armchairs. It was well-stocked, with a bent towards the taboo; I recognised many of the same titles my brothers liked, the ones I'd grown up stealing glances at before I was old enough to understand – *Naked Lunch*, *American Psycho*, *120 Days of Sodom*.

Holding the thick, weighty wooden door to the library open was a large brass doorstop. It was a detailed rendering of a wombat. An identical paperweight rested on top of an artfully arranged pile of unrelated editions on one of the side tables. I picked the paperweight up, testing its heft in my palm. It was heavy, and would have served as an adequate doorstop itself, albeit for more ordinary-sized doors than those found in a castle library.

The spaces between the shelves were decorated with framed artworks, with the most prominent spot given to a perfectly executed illustration of a platypus.

Tengfei flicked through one of the books. He held it up so I could see the illustration. 'Looks like you.'

I recognised the image, having seen it in my brothers' collections: a painting of a beautiful naked girl committing seppuku, her intestines gleaming like smooth pink jewels where they spilled out of the gaping slice across her abdomen.

My own stomach, already uneasy, roiled in sympathy. 'Don't be foul. Anyway, the picture's wrong. Women didn't commit ritual suicide by cutting the belly; that was just for men. They sliced their throats.'

'Which one for you, then?'

I rolled my eyes as Tengfei chuckled at his own question. I'd never been especially close to any of my brothers, and the art of working with a deliberately antagonistic partner in crime was yet to come easily to me. Jonathan and Tengfei took advantage of that, of course, and jabbed pointless teases in my direction whenever they had a chance.

I gestured at the platypus on the wall. 'That had to be done from a specimen. Photographs alone wouldn't give that amount of detail. Do you think he's been stealing animals, as well as people?'

Tengfei shrugged. 'Can't know.'

'I guess it doesn't really matter. He's already going to die, it's not like we can kill him twice,' I mused. Then, as my stomach twinged again, I wrinkled my nose. 'Do you think they're alive, the people he stole? Do you think he ate any of them?'

'No. That's only for warriors.'

Nevertheless, I shuddered a little at the thought.

After we explored the library, we moved on to other rooms, making our way quickly and deftly through observatories and studies and parlours and cellars. Considering the size of the castle, we found what we were looking for much faster than I'd expected, in a nondescript room that smelled of mould and urine and frightened, unwashed human bodies. None of these scents were unfamiliar to me, though the worn, crumbling infrastructure of the room's grimy walls was something of a surprise – even the most disgusting of my father's torture chambers never had cracks in the brickwork. It just proved how sloppy and careless the Baronet really was.

There was only one person in the cage that dominated the room. She was in her late teens, like me, with the too-thin lankiness of someone whose growth spurt has carried on despite an abrupt lack of nutrients. Tengfei quickly picked the locks on the cage door and the girl's shackles, but she didn't stir from the even, rattling breaths of sleep when we shook and pinched her.

The dark purple of the night sky was fading up to pink over the trees. We could see the girl's wounds better in the rising light.

'You can help us kill him, if you like,' I told her. I didn't expect any kind of reaction, considering that we'd already attempted to rouse her without luck, but at my words her long, skinny fingers twitched, curling into a fist. After a few long seconds, she opened her eyes.

We helped her sit up, her back against the night-cold stone of the wall.

There was something fractured-but-holding about her, like the spiderweb of lines that run through wire mesh glass when it's struck with a heavy object.

Glass like that doesn't shatter, because it's made to be unbreakable, but what was once whole becomes instead a mess of lethal edges.

Her hand shook as she shoved her filthy hair back from her face. Her eyes were feverish and bright.

'Dunno why he kept me alive,' she told us, biting her lip as a laugh threatened to bubble out. She was pitiful. I didn't pity her; that has never been my way. But she was pitiful. 'Killed all the others. Said the fish he was after didn't need live bait.'

I thought of the quirk of Jonathan's that had reminded me of my brother, the fondness for barbed fishing hooks that they shared. The Baronet's real plans and motivations snapped into clear focus in my head, and I could tell from Tengfei's quiet chuckles that I wasn't alone in reaching the conclusion. *We* were the real prey he was hunting.

The bloodied traditions of the Baronet's forebears would have appealed to his tawdry sense of spectacle and taboo. What better way to celebrate his ridiculous auction than to serve his guests an old-fashioned meal, made from three members of the most notorious band of warriors in the world?

I decided to assume that Jonathan was alive, wherever he was. One thing the Australian Gang encourage amongst its members was to trust your companions to extricate themselves from any trouble they found themselves in. Your only duty was to save yourself.

With a characteristically pathetic sense of timing, the Baronet and a gaggle of gun-heavy security guards chose this moment to burst into the room.

Tengfei gave another quiet laugh. I refrained from joining him, though I wanted to. The hubris of this ridiculous man was entertaining.

'Your role in the festivit–'

Odds were that the Baronet had prepared a gloating speech to give us as we were taken captive, but before he could say more than a few words, the wild giggles of the girl's broken-glass voice cut him off.

'You're so *stupid*,' the girl's words sliced through his. 'Haven't you ever thought about Australia? Really thought about it?

'It doesn't trade. It doesn't have an army. It doesn't have allies or ties.

'The entire world has shit it wants out of sight and out of mind: Toxic waste. Barges piled high with trash and filth. Why doesn't anybody dump any of it in Australia? They certainly have the room there, right?'

There was spittle at the corners of her mouth now, and a sluggish drop of blood slid down from one nostril. But her words were so laden with venom that nobody interrupted her, not even the hefty goons flanking the Baronet.

'It's the most sparsely populated country in the world,' she reminded him. 'Think of all that fucking *land*. Think of how populated the reefs must be with fish.

'*Haven't you ever wondered why the world hasn't just swept in and taken all of it?*'

Her finger stabbed the air, the angle crooked from a sprain or break but her hand was steady. She pointed at me, then at Tengfei. We stood a short distance from her, ready to spring forward and strike when the moment arrived.

'*You.*' Now she switched to pointing at the Baronet. The word was like a curse between her teeth. 'You think I'm just some *thing*; bait for your hook. Well, all right. But remember this. I come from Australia, and we are *very protective of our things.*'

We struck.

I glanced at Tengfei; one quick look was enough to confirm that we were thinking along the same lines. We'd split up, dividing the forces before conquering them.

Before I ran, I grabbed the girl's bony wrist then pulled her along as I dodged out of the room and sprinted down the hallway. I kept my pace slow enough that the guards would underestimate my stamina and speed, but quick enough that there was no chance of them actually being able to catch me.

Saving her and the other captives had never been the objective of the mission. The important thing was to punish the Baronet, as a way of sending a message to the rest of the world that the cost of messing with Australia was just as bloody and terrible as ever. Whether the girl lived or died wasn't the slightest bit important in terms of the job parameters.

I couldn't say for certain why I decided to protect her. Maybe the camaraderie that Tengfei and Jonathan shared stirred jealously somewhere in my unconscious mind, and I was looking for a way to change the group dynamic. Maybe I liked the thought of being the more powerful half of a pair, without any question, for a change, instead of always being the younger and more inexperienced half of any duo. Maybe I just liked how absolute her faith in the Gang was, that we were going to kill the Baronet for certain.

The library looked a little bleak and sad in the early morning light, a blur of thin sunshine as we ran through it.

'You'll never get out of here alive!' the Baronet spluttered as he and his guards joined us in the space, too many of them trying to push through the doorway at once and getting bottlenecked there for a few seconds. The guards had split up to follow each of us, and I was pursued by the majority of them and the Baronet himself. My ego lapped eagerly at this state of affairs.

All right. If there wasn't any possibility of flight, then fight it would be.

'Help if you can,' I told the girl. 'Stay out of the way if you can't.'

She nodded, shifting her weight into a ready stance. I didn't expect much from her, but I knew that Australians rarely backed down from a battle if they had any say in the matter.

Here's a fact about me: I fight like a girl. That is to say, I rely heavily on inertia to overpower my foes. Inertia is the innate tendency of all things to resist change. Something that's still wants to remain still. Something that's moving wants to keep moving.

There's a trick my father taught me when I was tiny, because I was already desperate to learn how to be as frightening as my brothers. If an ordinary business card, hardly more than paper, is brought down on a chopstick with enough speed and force, it will slice the wood clean through. There's no secret to it, except learning how to harness inertia: the chopstick doesn't want to move, and the card wants to keep moving, and so the solution they reach together is for the card to go straight through it.

In fighting, this simple understanding of physics is incredibly valuable when facing a larger, stronger opponent. The momentum of their strikes can be easily transformed into the momentum to throw them.

Like the slightly unearthly surroundings of the castle, the Australian Gang was always a fairy tale as much as it was a physical reality. I was Snow Red as much as I was any other facet of myself.

The legends about us ranged from the completely true to the entirely fantastical, and no single member of us would able to be say for certain where the line between the true and false should be drawn.

One of the more persistent rumours was that we'd somehow discovered the secret to immortality. The truth of it was actually much simpler. We weren't invincible, but vulnerability isn't important if you don't care about dying.

Mayhem for mayhem's sake.

As I killed one guard and then another, twisting necks to breaking point and crushing throats with a jab of my knuckles, I wondered whether these trivial opponents would have eaten my flesh, or if I was destined for a banquet platter and these were nothing but slaughterhouse workers. Not that it really mattered. They fell before my strikes just the same either way.

As each one was eliminated, I whirled to face the next. My instincts were good enough that I could pick the most immediate threat at each moment without conscious assessment. I heard the lean, zipping sound of a silenced gun firing, and the wild laugh of the captive girl. I ignored her, and fought on.

Eventually I pivoted on the ball of my foot, ready for the next round of combat, and there was no next round to be had. Our opponents lay dead at our feet. I paused, giving myself time to catch my breath, and then gave the room around us a once-over glance – checking to see which nook or cranny the Baronet had crawled into to hide from me.

He had to have realised that his plan had gone against him – it would have been impossible to think otherwise, when the room reeked of blood and cordite. I'd avoided all the gunshots, but the library hadn't managed the same trick.

No matter. It had been a sizeable, carefully curated collection, but there was nothing on the shelves that couldn't be found in numerous other places if required. The platypus illustration hanging on one wall gave me a momentary pause, its belly punched through by a bullet's path.

I couldn't help but wonder what it would be like to be stirred to strong emotion by the picture. I'd chosen to be part of the Gang, and I lived by its code. But I had no allegiance of my own to Australia. I felt no triumph in defending it against enemies and threats.

A small part of me hoped that, with time, I'd come to feel like I was a part of our victories.

A dull crunching noise broke my introspection. It was the girl, the brass wombat paperweight in her hands, part of it painted a bright ruby red from where she'd smashed the Baronet's skull, splitting the soft skin of his scalp and cracking open the bone beneath, causing a gory mess in the process. Raising it high, she brought the wombat down a second time with a crunching sound, that was a squelching, drawn-out echo of the first.

'Sorry,' she said to me. Her tone and expression were that of an ordinary person with an ordinary life who had accidentally finished off a bottle of wine that her friend was saving, rather than somebody who had just brutally killed their sadistic captor with an ornamental object. 'If you guys had some special revenge planned, I mean.'

I shrugged and shook my head. 'No. He didn't matter. It's fine.'

Her smile was sunny and cheerful. I wondered what she'd be like when we were gone from this place and on our way back to Australia. I had a sense that she could prove to be somebody worth knowing.

'The others will be finished with the rest of the guards by now,' I told her. 'Let's go meet up with them, and decide what happens next.'

She dropped the paperweight, the carpet doing little to muffle the crash of impact. The two of us left the library together.

KERRY GREENWOOD & DAVID GREAGG

Cruel Sister

I

Alasdair McNeil leaned back in his pilot's chair and sighed. What the hell had just happened? Elaine had been talking to him onscreen. Her perfect complexion looked pinker than its usual coffee brown; her dark chocolate eyes, normally warm and melting, had resembled small, dark agates at the bottom of a pool; and the corners of her mouth were turned down.

Their discussion had been awkward.

Really, Alasdair? If I mean as much to you as you say, here's a quick quiz. What's my mother's maiden name?

Rodriguez. Thank goodness he'd remembered that.

She had smiled briefly and continued. *What's my favourite dessert?*

Um, pavlova? No, apparently it was trifle.

Where would I most like to go on a holiday?

The inquisition had continued for some time, and she had concluded thus:

That's 15 questions, Alasdair. An acceptable pass mark is 10; you scored four. You are so trapped in your own little Highland head there's no room for anybody else in there. I don't matter enough to you.

I say nothing against your bedroom performance which was reasonable, but it always seemed you were with someone else in your head. You tell me you know no one called Màirì, yet that is the name you call in your sleep. So we are done. I hope you and your dream girl will be happy together.

His screen had gone blank, she was gone; and Alasdair doubted she would relent. The worst of it was he had nowhere to go with her rejection, for she had almost guessed correctly. Màirì *was* his dream girl; just as she was the desire, and often the curse, of every young man from the western and northern islands of far-off Earth.

As captain of the two-person tramp ship *Kisimul*, Alasdair would need a new companion. The Trade Federation rules were very strict. No pilot was permitted to travel alone for more than seven days; any longer and humans go space-crazy. He had hoped Elaine would join him again but it seemed not.

He considered himself for a moment: 33 years old, a good pilot who could mend broken machines and play the tin whistle well. Women generally found him even-tempered, loving, and resourceful; and seemed to fancy his slender body, and often commented on his blue eyes, and especially his long, black hair. Surely there was a woman for him somewhere. Hopefully.

He hailed his ship's computer 'Sorcha?'

'What need is at you, Alasdair?' Sorcha was programmed to speak to him in either standard English or Gaidhlig; though sometimes when she spoke English it was as if she were translating from Gaidhlig in her cybernetic head. No-one knew why. It was just a thing; an odd thing.

'Set course for the Mothership *Montrose*, if you would.'

'Confirm. You may expect a journey of 43 hours.'

Alasdair climbed out of his pilot's chair, stumbled down the narrow passage to his cubicle, and rolled back the coverlet. In the event of any unexpected emergencies Sorcha would turn on the bagpipes. Like most Highlanders and Islanders, Alasdair loathed tartan culture and all the tawdry sentiment that went with it; *Scotland the Brave* at 90 decibels would get him out of bed in an instant. He snuggled into his lonely pillow. He was hurt and miserable and the jasmine scent of Elaine's hair was already disappearing. And though he despaired he would not see her again, it was not of her he dreamed that night. It was indeed Màirì; the mythical and impossible seal-woman longed for by most men from the Isle of Barra.

II

Two days later, Alasdair docked and disembarked from the giant *Montrose* space station, affectionately known as Mothership. On his way to visit an acquaintance – a merchant renowned for matching humans with the right animals – he ran into the man himself in a public arena.

The stout and amiable Eric Presser, proprietor of *Zoologia,* greeted him like an old friend. 'Alasdair! Good to see you.' It was. At Eric's side, his Labrador companion Beowulf, wagged his tail and said 'Hello, Alasdair.'

Alasdair leaned over and stroked the canine head. 'Hello Beowulf,' he crooned, whereon the tail slapped against his thigh and the dog nuzzled him.

Eric leaned back against an ash tree growing out of a beaten-earth aperture in the floor. 'Do you think it's grown much since you were here last?'

Alasdair put his hand against the trunk. 'Oh yes. It thrives and looks well content.'

Eric nodded. 'We've managed to mimic Earth's UV and visible spectrum and the plants think they're back home. This one's my favourite. The Norwegians believe it's Yggdrasil and they leave little dolls on the branches.'

Alasdair fondled Beowulf's ears again and admitted he'd been on his way to Eric's shop to acquire a companion.

'Ah yes, I heard.' Eric smiled compassionately. 'Word travels swiftly on the Mothership, my friend. Animal companions are so much more reliable than humans on long voyages. They rarely argue or sulk. How about a dog?'

'Dogs are good. They'll love you to bits and never get bored with you.'

Alasdair followed the expert to his *Zoologia* but an hour later even Eric was looking discouraged. They had inspected dogs, cats, birds, ferrets, lemurs, kinkajous and lizards. The cats ignored him, the dogs all looked too happy, the reptiles too cold, the other furries blinked and went about their business, and the little birds sang too delightedly.

To those unfamiliar with spaceships, the problem would seem absurd. Alasdair could simply advertise for a human companion; there was, after all, no shortage of cyber-dates. In reality – except for the tough and adventurous few – the interstellar void was too much for the average human to cope with, and space travel was cramped, uncomfortable, and occasionally terrifying.

Many thousands of humans had been, and still were, happy to migrate to new worlds but the journey through space meant most swore never again to travel such vast distances. While they were content to stay put on their adoptive planets, goods still needed to be traded; and the universe still needed to be explored.

Commercial space law dictated that he could not travel alone, so a companion he must have. He couldn't just choose at random, toss a coin or point and hope for the best, because a poor choice might make him want to feed said companion out through the garbage disposal. Having decided he wanted an animal rather than a human he was now very disappointed.

Eric looked at him with concern. 'I'm at a loss, Alasdair. I've never had this much trouble. It actually seems I can't help you, but perhaps you can help me.'

Alasdair followed Eric down a passage to a huge wire cage, inside which was a small tree, a rocky mound with a large cavern, a water-bowl, and two food bowls.

Lying on the bare earth in the centre and wrapped in a tight ball was a large spotted cat with tufted ears, and black rosettes on her fawn fur. Although he could see nothing of the cat's face, since both paws covered it, Alasdair knew she was beautiful beyond words.

'She's a Malay fishing cat,' Eric said. 'She won't eat or drink, and she just lies there. I'm concerned for her, and I'm hoping someone might spark her interest. She'll die if she stays like this for much longer. She's yours for nothing if she'll talk to you.'

'And if she tries to take the face off me?'

Eric produced a small black metal pistol. 'A stun gun, but I doubt I'll need it.'

'Where did you get her?'

'Elijah Blackwood, Dealer in Curios, said he found her on an abandoned world he was excavating for relics. He said she was a talker; claims she hurled herself into his arms said *take me home*, but then never spoke again. The best he could do was bring her to me. But she mustn't like me enough to communicate.'

Alasdair crouched down on the floor and called out softly: '*Latha Mhath Mo Chaitin Bhreac* (Hello, my little speckled girl-cat).

There was not the faintest flicker of interest, except for a tightening of the paws over the large head.

Alasdair reached inside his jacket pocket for his D whistle and blew a gentle tune. *A Ghaoil, Leig Dhachaigh Gum Mhathair Mi* (My love, let me return to my mother) often worked on animals.

And sure enough, first one paw, then the other, was drawn back; green eyes opened and stared at him. As he began to improvise on the simple melody, the jungle cat stood, stretched, and flicked her long tail behind her. She walked nonchalantly towards the cage door lifted her speckled head and narrowed her eyes.

Alasdair changed to a more cheerful tune, and raised his eyebrows. *Biodh An Deoch Seo 'N Làimh Mo Rùin* (The drink would be in my love's hands) seemed to be making an impression as the cat pushed her nose between the cage bars and sniffed.

'I don't especially want to let her out yet,' Eric said. 'But I do think she likes you. I'll cover you, if you're up for this.'

With another flick of her tail the exquisite creature stalked over to her bowl and drank a little. Eric unlocked the door and waited, stun-gun at the ready.

Alasdair moved to the middle of the cage floor, sank to his haunches so his head was level with the cat's, and looked at her with his eyes slightly averted. She turned away, ate a little food, then padded soundlessly towards him. He extended his nose forward, the cat did the same; her hard, wet muzzle pushed against his face.

He rubbed his cheek against hers, and suddenly heard her purring voice vibrate in his middle ears.

'You may pick me up.'

Alasdair extended his hands and she leapt lightly into his arms. She was heavy, but rested her back paws on his torso and dug her claws into his shirt. She gently wrapped her forepaws around his shoulders so she could rest her nose against his neck. He felt mortally exposed, but her front claws were sheathed; the warmth of her breath made him want to curl up and go to sleep with her.

'My name is Padma,' she announced. 'And you are my minion. What is your name?'

'I am Alasdair McNeil, and I am going to my ship this night,' he answered. 'Does My Lady find this to her liking?'

'That will be acceptable.' Padma climbed higher and curled herself around his neck.

Eric's jowl quivered as he grinned. 'Very well then. It would appear she is meant for you.' He waved sausage-like fingers dismissively. 'And no, I meant it about her being free. I could not have sold her to anyone else. Just come to my office for a moment, if you will, and I will scan her microchip for you.'

III

'No pets allowed here,' said the grey-uniformed guard. He stood at the gate of the Food Megamarket like a small thunder-cloud in a peaked cap. Alasdair reached into his jacket pocket and pulled out Padma's ID card.

'Registered companion,' he announced, and pushed the plastic rectangle towards the moustachioed face. It was a terrible growth; it looked like a feral caterpillar crawling over his face, deciding which nostril to attack first. Padma growled at the man with a subsonic undertone.

'Are you my dinner?' she inquired.

The guard blinked, decided he hadn't heard that. 'Your funeral,' he said, and let them pass.

Padma lifted her head for a moment. 'It's all right, my minion,' she purred. 'I would have to be a lot hungrier to try my teeth on such a creature.'

'Oh, good,' Alasdair said. 'And here, Padma, we shall both find something to eat.' They passed many sausage sizzles, bain-maries, and grills. There were sausages made from everything the mind could imagine, along with vegetation both mundane and alien. There were feral potato-like creations with beards and eyes that followed them around the market, and long, purple stalks that glowered menacingly.

Padma's nose quivered, but she was puzzled. 'What is this meat?' she inquired at length. 'It is like no flesh I have met before.'

'It's tofu and nut meat. Actual meat is far too expensive. I'd love a good steak right now, and I think you would also; but it would cost me three month's earnings on a space station. They grow the beans and nuts right here, so it's cheap. Same with the vegetables.'

'It smells like fried sawdust, and it's only fit for dogs.'

Alasdair chose a clapshot pie from a stall with a hideous tartan scarf draped across the top.

'Aye, clapshot's a rare thing for mekkin this disgusting muck edible,' said the stallholder, a weedy man with a maroon bonnet and an eye like a myopic oyster. 'Three-fifty's ma usual, but fae a Partick man, three wull dae.' He smiled at Padma and reached up a bony hand to tickle her under the chin. 'Hey, kitty? Ye'll no be gaein ma customers, will ye?'.

To Alasdair's amazement, Padma allowed the gross familiarity. Not until they were walking away did her head move. 'Who was that strange man?' she asked. 'I think he was speaking English, but I did not understand a single word.'

'He's Andy from Glasgow,' Alasdair explained. 'He thinks I'm from Glasgow, too. This nut meat needs all the vegetable help it can get. Andy's the only one who serves clapshot, which is tatties and neaps.' Padma stared at him so he elaborated, 'Potatoes and turnips mashed up together.'

They walked out of the food court into a huge atrium filled with trees, garden beds, pools and fountains. This was the heart and lungs of the *Montrose*'s biosphere. Alasdair chose a seat by a fountain and broke the pie in half.

'Please try this, Padma. I know none of this is what you want, but it's the best I can do here.' He laid it down on the bench.

Padma climbed off his shoulder and sniffed. She took a small piece in her mouth, rolled her emerald eyes and swallowed. They exchanged glances.

'Still only fit for dogs?'

'I think it might finish them off if you fed them on that,' she said. 'Which could be a good thing.'

Alasdair ate his half of the pie, while wondering what to do about her food. Then, to his alarm, he noticed her hindquarters were quivering.

'FISH!' she exclaimed, and launched herself into the fountain.

Several bystanders looked at Alasdair in pure horror as Padma's head emerged, with a still-wriggling trout in her mouth. She climbed out, finished off the trout, and sat by the pool on her haunches. In less than half a minute she had reached a lightning paw into the pond and flicked out two more. She leaned down, bit them both on the neck, and they lay still.

'Oh trouble; very big trouble,' Alasdair said as he realised the space around them was suddenly deserted. There were people around the outer edges of the atrium but the eyewitnesses had run; and informed.

'Padma,' he said, quite calmly given the circumstances.

He gathered up the two remaining trout, stuffed them into his leather satchel, and ran.

Padma padded after him and they took cover behind one of the stalls, whereon she launched herself lightly onto his shoulders again.

'Whatever is the matter, my minion?' she inquired.

'I could not even begin to explain.'

Alasdair smiled. He had no choice. He crept along the narrow noisome alley, behind the stalls until his nostrils detected clapshot. In the same moment, a familiar face leaned down to confront him.

'Och, Alasdair, I kenn'd what yur kitty wud dae! Good fae yu! Who's a clever cat then?' He scritched Padma's chin again. 'We best get yu two awa' afore the English find ye.'

'Thanks, Andy. *Tapadh a' leat*.' Alasdair said as he allowed the Scot to hustle them along the walkway to a black, metallic portal. Andy flashed an electronic key over the lock and the door slid open with a hum.

'This goes tae the spaceport traders' yard,' he said 'That was a grand play, Alasdair. See ye next time.'

Alasdair walked carefully down the badly-lit passage, avoiding the patches of putrid sump oil which coated the footway. 'Well Padma, you have two spare trout now, thanks to your ingenuity. You are a very clever cat.'

She purred contentedly, but did not speak again until they reached his ship. Only when he laid his electronic key against the door did he realise that he had not thought about Elaine at all since Padma had erupted into his life.

IV

'There is a creature on you,' Sorcha announced when he climbed into the *Kisimul*. 'Mammal, feline, large, female, smelling of fish. Is it that you are under attack? Shall I arrange for it to be stunned?'

'No,' Alasdair said, momentarily afraid Padma would take offence. He wondered how much skin and flesh he'd lose if the jungle cat objected to Sorcha's diagnosis.

'Who is this personage?' inquired the cat, raising her head a little. 'Is it alive? I can smell no flesh but yours, my minion.'

'Padma, the voice you hear is Sorcha, my ship's computer. Sorcha, you will scan Padma's microchip and register her as a crew member, if you would be so kind.'

There was a short, dragging silence.

'Sorcha? I may be forgetful, but I am tolerably certain that I gave you an instruction. Please do as I ask.'

'Very well, my Captain.'

Padma jumped off his shoulders and sniffed her way around the tiny vessel. She examined the spare room, climbed onto the narrow bed, leapt down again, sniffed her way around Alasdair's own bed and curled up in the exact centre of it. She lifted her spotted head for a moment and announced: 'You may place my trout in your freezer. I will share your rations until I wish to celebrate.'

While Padma took her beauty sleep, Alasdair returned to the flight deck to set course for New London. It was a large city with altogether too many people, so he hoped Padma would stay on board the *Kisimul* while he unloaded his cargo.

Small traders like Alasdair took care of the unusual or the rare; his was always the niche markets overlooked by the big combines. His special cargo this time was sweet and simple: peppermints. He had heard there were none anywhere in New London.

As he went through his navigation check, Sorcha paused before responding to everything. Computers were just machines, yet over the years Sorcha had acquired a definite personality. It was currently an insubordinate one.

Alasdair changed into his pyjamas and laid his head on his pillow, expecting yet another night with too much misery and insufficient sleep. As he stretched out his feet under the doona and braced them against the opposite wall, he became aware that he was no longer alone.

The paws announced her arrival, so he moved closer to the side wall to make room for her. Padma snuggled up next to his shoulder, extended both front paws across his chest, and buried her nose into his neck. There was a pronounced scent of fish, and cat, but he smiled, and curled one arm around her warm, purring body.

Later in the darkness, Padma shifted and opened her eyes. 'Sorcha?'

There was a slight pause. 'Yes, Padma?'

'My minion keeps whimpering. He says *Elaine* over and over in his sleep. What is Elaine? Is it food he desires?'

This time there was no pause at all. 'Elaine is a shameless human female who broke his heart,' Sorcha explained. 'She is a bad woman and our Captain is well rid of her.'

Padma yawned. 'If I see this Elaine, then I shall devour her flesh.'

'And what would you do with the bones that were left?'

'I would gnaw them until I was weary of them, then spit them out into space through an orifice in your hull.'

'Do not hesitate to do so,' Sorcha said. 'And what is your will with my Captain?'

'I will care for him, and help him, and love him for the rest of my life,' answered Padma.

'That was well-spoken, cat.'

Padma yawned again, recomposed her paws around Alasdair's neck, and gave his face a gentle lick.

Alasdair smiled in his sleep. 'Padma!' he whispered, and wrapped his arm tighter around her body.

And, though it is well known that computers have no emotions at all, there was a lightening of the atmosphere in the tiny *Kisimul*, and Sorcha might have been heard purring to herself.

V

'We do appear to have a problem,' drawled New London's trade representative. He ran a thoughtful finger down his lantern jaw, as he and

Alasdair inspected the contents of his large wooden crate. They did not live up to expectations.

'You are correct about the market for peppermints in New London; we have completely run out, so your visit would have been timely.'

The official reacted in typical English fashion to the oddness of conversing with a man wearing a live cat stole, by pretending the feline was not there. 'And while it does indeed say Peppermint Leaves on the crate the cartons within tell a different story. But aniseed of any kind is one sweet we do not need. You are the twelfth trader this month offering it, so I suspect a conspiracy out there to fool honest men like you. The King has therefore placed a ban on any further imports.'

Alasdair loaded the crate of unexpected aniseed balls back onto the *Kisimul*'s cargo trolley and returned to the ship.

Back on the flight deck as he contemplated his next move Padma nuzzled him affectionately. 'What will you do now, my minion?'

'I do not know. I must find a market for my goods.'

'I smelled dog in that place,' said Padma. 'And many more than one.'

'I'm sorry you had to experience that.'

'As am I. But that is not why I mentioned it. It means this world has dogs. And dogs love aniseed.'

'But you heard what he said,' Alasdair pointed out. 'The King has banned aniseed here.'

'Yes, here it is forbidden,' Padma said. 'But the city is not the all of here.'

Alasdair raised an eyebrow. 'Sorcha, tell us about the geopolitics of New London?'

'New London City, the only metropolis on the planet of New London, was settled only 40 years ago by a scion of the British Royal House. King Charles is a monarch cautiously admired by his subjects, and within the urban areas his word is law. In the lands beyond, as in most frontiers, the laws and customs are more relaxed.' Sorcha almost sounded pleased at being asked. 'Would you like to know anything else, like where to find the most dogs and other canines on this planet?'

'Yes please, Sorcha,' Alasdair said, realising his computer had caught on to what his cat had implied before he had; which was improbable.

'The highest concentration of canines is to be found in New Hampshire, a remote forest district 900 kilometres from the city. Human population is estimated at 500, with dogs numbering 1000 or so. Also present are wild deer and feral pigs.'

'Is there a landing place suitable in this New Hampshire, Sorcha?'

'There are no spaceports, but there are suitable flat, cleared areas on river plains where there will be no subsidence. I will perform a radiometric survey before attempting a landing.'

'Choose one near a settlement.'

'Of course,' Sorcha said.

Alasdair touched noses with Padma. 'Thank you, Padma. I want you to stay on board for this transaction. And when I return, I may have a feast to offer you.'

'I am more than inclined to stay away from any canines.'

Half a day later, in a broad clearing where Sorcha had landed the *Kisimul*, Alasdair had not waited long before his makeshift camp was approached by two frontiersmen; and their very large dog. Padma had said any canines in the area would smell the aniseed the moment the crate was opened.

'Jarge Watkins be my name,' said the elder of the two; a wiry and bearded man. They both wore leather jerkins and trousers, and woollen hoods. 'Ye aint here to collect the king's bloody taxes then?'

He accepted the man's vigorous handshake. 'No I aint.'

'Our hound seems to think you have something we should know about.'

'Indeed I do,' Alasdair said, and carefully offered the treat to the salivating dog now sitting respectfully in front of him. He gulped down the aniseed ball and looked for more.

'Well now, I've never known Boyo to take such a fancy to anything that weren't alive once.'

'I have it on good authority there's not a dog in the universe who doesn't like aniseed balls. Would you like to buy my stock?'

'Aye, that we might; my friends and I. We do like to spoil our four-legs when we can.'

That evening, Alasdair and Padma settled themselves on the grassy bank next to a gushing river. The sky was darkening to purple, and the smell of roasting meat, traded for some of the aniseed, was intoxicating. 'Your hunting went well, my minion?' Padma inquired.

'Very well, my most beautiful companion.' Alasdair took a large haunch off the improvised spit, placed three large collops on a plate and pushed it across to Padma. She sniffed the meat and licked her lips in anticipation.

'In this weather it will cool quickly,' he told her. 'I have six more haunches of venison to take back with me to the *Montrose*, and six cured hides of leather. Most of the venison I will sell to Andy, and the hides to some ladies I know of who make deerskin clothes and bags. We will make so much money I shall be able to pay off the fine, which is undoubtedly outstanding for your fishing expedition, with plenty left over. My hunting went very well indeed.'

As twilight deepened, man and cat settled down to enjoy their dinner in peace. From time to time, Alasdair played his tin whistle, and Padma amused him by trying to push her nose into the far end of the pipe. This had a disruptive effect on his music, but neither of them minded. Padma ate every scrap of meat, without haste, washed her paws and face with great care, and only then they returned to the ship.

Alasdair's sleep that evening was troubled by dreams of his beautiful unobtainable woman. He woke crying the name Màirì; and found his pillow was wet with tears. Padma carefully washed his face and embraced him, and he relaxed into dreamless slumber.

VI

During their downtime aboard the *Kisimul,* between spaceports, Alasdair discovered a great joy in storytelling as Padma was an attentive audience. The stories from ancient Barra, of pirates and seal-women and fisher folk, amused her the most, but it seemed she simply loved listening to him.

Padma snuffled into Alasdair's elbow and asked was it true that the smaller the island, the more ridiculous were the stories told about them and their place in the world? Alasdair agreed that this was indeed the case.

'Tell me about the mythical Màirì,' Padma requested.

'Yes do,' Sorcha chimed in.

'You know this story,' Alasdair sighed, only a little embarrassed.

'Yes we do,' Padma agreed. 'And she must hold great significance if a man dreams so often of a woman he never met.'

Alasdair nodded. 'There are many old tales of seal-women, and other changelings, in the western and northern islands from where my folk hail. These were love stories, and tragedies, in which a seal-woman rescued by a fisherman would give up her skin for love, even bear his children, until the sea inevitably called her back. Their love rarely survived her true nature.

'My ancient home, on the Isle of Barra, had little use for tragedy. In the version I heard as a child, the beautiful blonde seal-woman Màirì – and yes, they are always beautiful – embraced her fisherman, thanked him for a wonderful time and made him swear never to hunt seals. Before slipping beneath the waves, she promised that if he stood on the beach and sang to her she would come out of the sea and sing to him. The story goes that this still happens on Barra; though I've not been home for a long time and never saw it with my own eyes.'

'And yet you dream of her,' Padma noted.

'I think it's genetic.'

'Are there any new stories of Barra?' Padma asked.

Alasdair looked at her curiously. 'There is a great mystery,' he said. 'While a few of my folk have resettled on New Mars, most have vanished into deep space. And I do mean disappeared. It is in our nature to travel; at first it was the seas of Earth, then the galaxy itself. For a long while my forebears would return to this part of space, to reminisce and trade. But 55 standard years ago we lost track of them. Old friends did not keep appointments, messages went unanswered, and nothing has been heard of my people ever since. One day I hope to find them.'

Padma nuzzled his face with her nose. 'Why is it not your great quest to find them?'

Alasdair shrugged. 'It would be a great thing to come across them in my travels but I did not know them, so I don't feel the need to go searching. But what of you, my Padma? There is a great mystery about you that we have yet to speak about. Do you have a quest of your own?'

'I have two quests,' said the cat, settling into his lap and wrapping her long tail about her. 'One was to find you, and this I have done.'

'And the other?' Alasdair stroked her head and ears, and she pushed her whiskers forward in delight.

'The other is to go Home.'

'Do you know where Home might be?'

'I shall know it when I find it,' she said. 'But I do not know the way.' As she would say no more about it, Alasdair let the matter be.

Padma also played games with him, listened to his tin whistle with delight, and told stories of her own: about jungles and clever cats, and beautiful young men and brave warrior maidens. When Alasdair was angry or miserable, she tried to amuse or distract him, but if this did not work, she would retire to her own bed to sleep until he knocked politely on her door. Most of the time they were comfortable with each other.

Often when Alasdair slept, Padma would ask Sorcha all about Elaine – and any other humans in his life – and learned she had liked neither his stories nor his music; and had complained a great deal about everything. Sorcha asked if Padma were intending to do this also, and Padma assured her that she would not.

And so they continued their travels from planet to planet, picking up and dropping off mail and parcels, presents, small items ordered via catalogues and specialty spices. Whenever the *Kisimul* landed, people were glad to see them, especially the mail entrusted to Alasdair's care. He had been travelling the Galaxy for nine years and in the many ports where people knew him it was pronounced that Padma was an excellent companion.

VII

A month later the *Kisimul* landed on New Breiz to deliver a birthday parcel to a young girl, from her grandfather who worked on the *Montrose*; to buy some cheese; and to stretch their legs by window shopping.

Alasdair picked over a selection of flame opals with delight, as the storekeeper grinned in anticipation. 'What do you think, Padma? Are they not beautiful?'

She leaned in close. 'They are counterfeit,' she said. 'Do not waste your money on them.'

It was never safe to assume that other people could not hear Padma, and Alasdair wondered if her verdict had hit a nerve when the great moustache on the stall-keeper's otherwise bald head twitched as if infested with something.

'I am sorry,' Alasdair told the man. 'But my cat is eager for the cheese market; I cannot delay or she may decide to eat a stall-holder or two.'

Sweat broke out on the man's face and his red, coarse mouth twisted into a sneer. He clearly knew he had not fooled this trader.

Alasdair headed for the cheese market, accompanied only by the conversations of other market-goers until Padma eventually nuzzled his ear and insisted, 'They were fake. Someone has done something to the stone. I think they have coated it with plastics.'

'And how do you know what real opals look like?' Alasdair said gently.

'I had an opal necklace once,' she said. 'Real Australian opals, from Earth.'

Alasdair thought this absurdly unlikely, but did not say so. They shopped for an assortment of cheeses, but he did not find anything exotic that would be worth the freight. For their own kitchen, he bought some double brie from old Madame Belrose whose shop abutted a lush pasture. He noticed that Padma's nose was sniffing the air.

'Let me down,' she said. 'There is a herb here that you must gather.'

Alasdair lowered her to the brick walkway whereon she jumped the fence in a graceful bound and rolled joyously in the grass.

The woman's smile and delicate French accent was charming. 'I do 'ope your beau chat will not assault my cows.'

'My cat is quite tranquil and usually most sensible, Madame,' he assured her. As if to prove his point, when two small spotted cows strolled over and sniffed at her, Padma rolled languorously onto her back and allowed their inspection.

Even Alasdair did not hide his surprise as he and Madame Belrose laughed at such an uncommon thing.

Padma returned, wearing the closest thing to a smile a cat could muster, and leapt purring into his arms. 'You must fill your hold with that herb, Alasdair, she said. 'It will bring you much money.'

Madame Belrose grinned. 'Your cat has reason, perhaps,' she said. 'But for me, it is a pestilent weed, and I would be rid of it. It taints the milk if my cows eat it, and I cannot sell it, nor the butter or cheese I make from it. There is a scythe leaning against the fence; you may take as much as you wish, with my blessing.' She gestured with a skinny arm towards an old, rusty tool leaning against the stone fence.

Both Padma and the old woman admired the lean grace of Alasdair as he swung the scythe to and fro, and filled his cargo trolley with the fragrant weed. He imagined he was a child again on his croft at Eoligarry, cutting hay for winter feed under the harvest sun. He thanked Madame Belrose and they returned to the *Kisimul*.

VIII

It was nearly 12 months before they had a reason to return to the *Montrose,* and it was Padma's strange weed that took them back. The clever cat-bliss, as she called it, made Alasdair more money than any other cargo he'd traded.

The first person they sought out afterwards was Andy. The big man was delighted to see them, offered Padma due respect then scritched her chin. He was the only man besides Alasdair who was allowed such privileges. Andy had prospered greatly since they'd brought him the venison the year before. His tartan, which belonged to no known clan, now covered the adjoining booth as well, and came with an assistant to help run it, so he could join them at the Thistle and Boar for a celebratory meal – cooked by someone else for a change.

'So Alasdair, when can ye get me more of that fine venison?'

'I'm not planning on going back to – that particular planet, Andy. But I will send a message to my friends there to get in touch with you.'

Andy's crooked teeth flashed. 'Aye, thank ye. And what will I be needing to befriend your friends?

Alasdair grinned and whispered, 'Aniseed. They–'

Alasdair had been stunned into silence by a startling figure moving along the walkway. She was tall, bronzed, long-limbed and beautiful, with torrents of lustrous back hair. She wore long, tight leather pants, a matching and revealing corset and small jacket and knee-high boots. The universal cliché of specialist in bondage and discipline, she was accompanied by a similarly-clad young man, currently engaged in the purchase of deep-fried lentil slop from a store nearby.

Alasdair made an odd gurgling sound in the same moment the woman turned and set her dark-pebble gaze upon him, which made Padma look up from her bowl.

'Alasdair? What a surprise.' She and her Leatherman approached the table.

'Hello, Elaine.' His voice was steady, which was encouraging as he had often wondered how he'd react if this moment ever arose.

Meanwhile her eyes raked critically over his shabby space-suit, and then widened at the sight of his companion.

Padma gave a low rumbling growl and flared her nostrils.

'I heard you couldn't find a woman to replace me,' Elaine said with a smile. 'I do think an animal companion suits you much better.'

'So does yours,' Padma said, sniffing the pair of them. 'Shall I rend her skin from her very bones, my minion?

Alasdair, though his mouth was set in a hard line, gently stroked Padma's back to indicate no – or, at least not yet. And luckily, it seemed, his ex did not have the temperament to understand Cat. Andy, however, sniggered and offered his support by way of a hand on his friend's knee beneath the table. The whole situation was clearly too uncomfortable for the Leatherman who insisted they leave. Perhaps he had caught Padma's intent if not her words.

'You may leave our presence, and return to your rack and *cat*-o-nine tails,' Padma said.

Andy snorted his beer all over the table.

Alasdair smiled broadly, as the woman he no longer cared for at all was escorted away by a man with trousers so tight they hid nothing; and nothing was what they hid.

'Have we earned dessert?' Padma asked.

'Aye we have,' Andy stated. 'With cream and custard.'

Padma purred and Alasdair waved for a waiter.

IX

For the first time in his professional career, Alasdair was frightened. Medusa Prime had always been a friendly planet: mostly desert, but with gardens of luxuriant comfort along the rivers and lakes. The inhabitants were mainly scholars, and he brought them rare books unobtainable by normal means. He had visited many times with precious manuscripts and bound volumes, and the locals had welcomed him warmly. During his last visit they had played with Padma and fed her succulent fish from the oases.

This current situation could not be more different. Officious officials had herded him into a white-walled office and locked the door. An hour later three interrogators in plain white robes sat opposite, glaring at him. Hooded robes covered them from head to foot, and their faces were covered with white masks; it was only their eyes he could see – and they were not friendly. There had been no introductions or explanation.

'I need to speak to Harbourmaster Habib,' Alasdair insisted, trying to keep his voice steady.

Padma clung to his shoulders and kept her eyes shut. He could feel her trembling body and realised that she was, unusually, more frightened than he was. 'My visits here are always arranged through him. Will you please tell him that Trader Alasdair is here?'

'The man you speak of is no longer available,' said the man in the middle. 'He has been dismissed. Why have you come here, Trader? Your perverted goods are not welcome here. Neither are you, nor your… filthy animal!' The disgust and loathing in the man's eyes was almost fanatical.

As Padma clung tighter to Alasdair, her claws penetrated his leather jacket and pricked his skin.

'I bring books, as I have always done,' said Alasdair. 'But I do not go where I am unwelcome, good sir. If Medusa Prime no longer wants my merchandise, then I ask leave to depart without delay.'

'What wickedness do you bring? Show me!'

Alasdair reached into his sleeve and held out his cargo manifest. 'Just books.'

The man on the right recoiled in horror, and the third folded his arms. The speaker was still staring in horror at the manifest.

'Books, you say?' he spat. 'You defile the Unwritten Page? Is it not enough you bring blasphemy to our planet but you dare to boast your offence before our very eyes?'

With a gloved hand he snatched the page from Alasdair, and turned to the man to his left. 'Take this abomination away and burn it!'

The man left the room immediately holding the manifest at arm's length as if it would give him the pox.

Alasdair could not even imagine how things had gone so horribly awry here since his last visit. He worried that his cargo might be confiscated; that he'd be fined for not being aware the laws had changed; or worse.

'You are guilty of blasphemy and will be tried and executed. Guards!'

'Stupid, ignorant heathen men!' Padma howled and launched herself at the leader's head. She slashed viciously with all her claws, and when the man fell cursing to the floor, his now maskless face was shredded and bloody.

Before his cohort could draw his stun-gun Alasdair was on his feet. He punched the man so hard he was out cold before his chair crashed, with him still in it, backwards to the floor.

A klaxon alarm began to sound.

'Padma my dear, I believe it is time to leave.'

Alasdair wrenched the door open and ran, with Padma close beside, along the featureless passage they'd been escorted down. The exit door, far ahead, burst inwards admitting four white-robed guards, who fired at them.

'This way!' Padma said as she barrelled left down a cross hall and through a door. How she knew it was an alternative exit Alasdair didn't care – but there was the *Kisimul* only 100 metres away.

The klaxon drowned all other sounds so if the four gun-wielding guards were giving important instructions, the escapees could technically be excused for not hearing.

The desert heat and high sun were not conducive to any exertion but Alasdair and Padma had no choice.

'Their weapons are only close-range. They won't catch us if the ship is prepped,' Alasdair shouted.

Padma took off to alert Sorcha.

The *Kisimul's* computer was already on the job. As Padma bounded through the open hatch, Sorcha said, 'Loud gunmen chasing my crew. I see, I act.'

A moment later Alasdair leapt and fell face first onto the deck.

The hatch slammed shut as Sorcha engaged the engines. The *Kisimul* lifted off from Medusa Prime leaving a mob of robed men shaking their fists at the sky.

'Captain, it is a matter of some urgency that you take your seat. As you know, breathing crew members must be secured to leave the atmosphere.'

'I am trying my best, Sorcha,' Alasdair said, as he fought the g-force of the ship's sudden acceleration; a thing he'd not experienced before.

'As my sensors are now detecting high-energy cannons targeting us from the spaceport I advise we scram immediately.'

'Scram?' Alasdair asked, as he flung himself into the cocoon of his pilot's chair a second before Padma, who agreed wholeheartedly with Sorcha. 'Oh yes, we scram,' she said.

'Engaging the crew pod,' Sorcha stated.

As the life-preserving oxy-grav shield enveloped the chair, Sorcha engaged the thrusters and the *Kisimul* screamed into the ionosphere

'Artificial gravity and ship-wide oxygen is now on.'

'Thank you Sorcha. Did we sustain any damage during our misadventure?'

'Yes. Our shields took a battering, the aft-comms array is–'

'Is what?'

'Gone, Captain. And the hull in that area has a worrying dent. I also used most of our available chemical fuel in our escape. Shall I remove Medusa Prime from our future itinerary?'

'Good idea.' Alasdair agreed. 'And it seems we must return to the *Montrose,* both for repairs and to report the situation on Medusa Prime.'

Alasdair and Padma retired to their bunk with a soothing beverage each.

'I am sorry I placed you in danger on that planet, Padma.'

'It is always my choice to leave the ship or not, Alasdair. I am pleased you were not harmed.'

Alasdair stroked the head of his most precious companion. 'I love you, Padma.'

'As you should,' she purred, then lifted her muzzle and ever-so-slowly blinked her emerald eyes at him. 'As I love you.'

On the week-long journey back to the *Montrose*, Alasdair noticed a change in his nightly dreams. The hair of the seal-woman Màirì, who had visited his dreams so often since he'd come of age, had slowly darkened from blonde to a rich brown. She had exchanged her shells for a necklet of exotic lotus flowers and, though she embraced him with the same ardour, she didn't seem to recognise her own name.

X

Alasdair sat opposite the intelligence officer for the Independent Traders' Federation and briefed her about the situation on Medusa Prime. Like most people who found themselves in close proximity to Officer Kamiko, he couldn't help staring at her delicate porcelain doll-like features. Kamiko was used to men looking at her, and was entirely indifferent to it; unless they behaved inappropriately, in which case her assistance was hard to come by. It seemed she quite liked Alasdair, however, and had expressed her relief he had escaped unharmed.

'The *Kisimul* needs extensive repairs, as you know,' she said. 'But we have a special apartment for our members who are in great need. I have arranged for you to stay there.' Her tiny, perfect teeth gleamed as she smiled unexpectedly. 'Stay as long as you need. You, and your friend. Does she have any special requirements?'

'As long as there are fish, I am well content,' answered Padma. She rubbed the top of her head against Alasdair's chin while he stroked her flanks.

'Padma has brought you good luck, Alasdair,' she said. 'And The Historians are here. They would be honoured if you would both join them for dinner tomorrow at the Bright Star.'

Alasdair, most surprised by such a prestigious invitation, accepted with thanks. Kamiko personally escorted them across the vast interior of the *Montrose* towards the biosphere, and the door of their accommodation 'May you both rest well here.' They bowed to each other, and Kamiko departed.

Their quarters were unexpectedly luxurious. Padma draped herself over a leather sofa and purred in contentment. Alasdair inspected the separate space for the king-sized bed with giant pillows, an ensuite, and a kitchen, with a complementary bottle of single malt whisky. Alasdair opened the fridge and saw Padma's needs had been anticipated with a kilogram of fresh trout.

The Bright Star was the best restaurant on the *Montrose,* reserved for the exceedingly wealthy. It was therefore not the kind of establishment Alasdair had ever eaten in before. Daunted by the maître d' and her impeccable waiters, he was relieved when Kamiko met him at the entrance. She indicated one of the young men. 'Alphonse will take you to your table. Sadly I must dine elsewhere with the Ligurian delegates.'

'If M'sieur and–' the very handsome Alphonse paused theatrically to incline his head towards Padma, 'Madame would please come this way?'

They weaved their way by candlelit tables where bejewelled ladies and rich old men in evening dress enjoyed flambés and soufflés, steamboats and sushi, exquisite dishes of exotic curlicued vegetables and more meat and fish than Alasdair had ever seen in his life. Padma couldn't help but sniff at the passing parade of scents, but no-one gave her a second look. Companion animals were clearly not unusual clientele at the Bright Star.

Alphonse delivered them to the two remaining seats at a long table occupied by a group of mostly elderly men and women, although, as their eyes were bright and countenances quite vibrant, the only clue to their great age was grey hair or long white beards. They all acknowledged the new arrivals with nods and smiles.

Padma leapt lightly onto her seat bolstered with a thick red velvet cushion and looked boldly around as if she belonged in such esteemed company; while Alasdair sat down politely beside her, in quiet awe at finding himself there at all.

The Historians, as everyone knew, were living repositories of the Galaxy's knowledge. The credulous believed them possessed of godlike powers but it was skill and learning, memory and age that gifted them with all they knew. Indeed, now he was sitting, Alasdair could see the young men and women at the table; shy and studious, those six would be the Apprentices. They would eventually fill the shoes of their seniors; when the latter were finished with them.

The slight, straight-backed woman with iron-grey hair beside him extended a hand. 'It is a pleasure to meet you, Alasdair,' she said, in a clipped Edinburgh accent. 'And, of course, you also, Padma,' She smiled at the jungle cat who offered a paw. 'I am Dr Elspeth McMillan, and you are my honoured guests. I shall introduce you to my companions in due course, but I'm sure you're wondering why we invited you tonight,'

'We are honoured regardless of the reason.'

Dr McMillan's pale lips parted in a broad grin, 'Despite the damage visited upon your vessel, not to mention the threat to your very lives, your unfortunate encounter with the previously unknown new order on Medusa Prime was fortuitous. Your exposure of the situation there prevented us from losing an entire expedition which was to land on that world two days after your escape. With your timely warning, we were able to recall our ship by ultrawave relay.'

'I am glad to be of service.'

Dr McMillan nodded. 'There is more. Are you aware of the Anyang Equations, young man?'

Alasdair was forced to admit that he was not. Padma meanwhile tucked into a plate of sardines that an Apprentice offered her.

'My recent contribution to psychohistory was a thesis in which I used the Anyang Equations to predict when, and how, societies might decline into a fanatical rejection of all knowledge in favour of simplistic superstitions.' Dr McMillan smiled grimly. 'And yes, I predicted that Medusa Prime was a likely candidate for such devolvement after a strange cult began to gain popularity last year. My colleagues were sceptical, as well they might be. Members of the Faculty have always been welcome upon Medusa Prime, and it was difficult for them to believe that this might alter.

'Thanks to your visit, my work is triumphantly vindicated; though, of course, the actuality is disturbing. And, you will be pleased to learn, the scholars who were to receive your books contrived to escape Medusa Prime in their own ship at the same time as those benighted idiots were firing off ordinance at you. So they are also in your debt, since your escape covered their own.'

Alasdair could only gape, and nod, in wonder. 'I am pleased indeed. Given the death sentence levelled at us, I worried they may have been executed. I still have their books. I admit I haven't given my cargo a thought since things went so strange on us.'

'Kamiko can arrange for the books to come to us and we will pass them on,' Dr McMillan said then turned to her feline guest. 'Padma, can you read the menu, or do you require assistance?'

Alasdair tried not to laugh at his companion who was staring at the small book is if she could open it by will alone.

'I can read Standard English,' Padma said, pointedly ignoring Alasdair. 'But perhaps you could turn the pages for me?'

They three of them ordered fish entrées and steak main courses. The entrees appeared almost immediately, and Alasdair and their charming host watched in delight as Padma put out her paw and ate the smoked trout delicately, one glorious flake at a time, without dropping a morsel.

'May I assume, Dr McMillan, that it is you or The Historians who are responsible for our splendid accommodation here on the *Montrose*. And, dare I suggest, the unprecedented level of gratis work on our damaged ship?'

'While we did offer such recompense, Alasdair, we were too late. It is in fact Officer Kamiko and the ITF who have been so generous.'

'The ITF? But why?'

'Perhaps the little officer fancies you,' Padma said and Alasdair accidentally snorted.

Dr McMillan smiled. 'The truth is less romantic. Given the routes you trade and the cargo you carry you are probably unaware that in the last year many more of them than usual have been cheating their suppliers and dealing with unethical cartels.'

While waiting for the next course, Alasdair asked a question which had long puzzled him. 'I cannot help wondering why printed books are so important.'

Dr McMillan's mouth pursed. 'As you know, electronic data storage is perfectly safe in normal space. Most people – and in truth it's not something we advertise – have no idea that interstellar travel corrupts data files, and no-one knows why, though centuries of research has been devoted to it.'

'But all my files are kept by Sorcha, my ship's computer,' Alasdair said. 'And they do not change. How can this be?'

Dr McMillan raised an eyebrow. 'Your Sorcha automatically refreshes her files from satellite stations every time she re-enters normal space.'

'Oh, and the satellite stations do not move except in orbits around planets or asteroids, so their files stay secure?'

'Indeed. But the ultimate backup has always been the printed word. Young man, have you never asked yourself why the Galactic Federation allows us such vast privileges?'

'Because you're wise and all knowing?'

Dr McMillan laughed heartily. 'Because without us, civilisation would not survive space travel.'

The arrival of Alasdair and Dr McMillan's dessert crepes put conversation on hold. Padma's delight at her bowl of ice cream amused all at the table as, for the first time during the meal, she stood to eat with her paws on the table cloth.

'Returning to the notion of our wisdom and all-knowingness,' Dr McMillan said. 'I may be able to offer you more than dinner by way of thanks.'

'Now that would be a thing, I've not heard anything new in years.'

'There is a quadrant of the Nixus Galaxy, out beyond Apollonia, which most space travellers avoid; and for good reason, it seems.'

'I've not even heard of it,' Alasdair.

'I'm not surprised, as there seems to be subliminal anomaly in the region. Those pilots who have ventured out there reported an ominous feeling, as if they were being warned to stay away. Their ship computers detected nothing but nonetheless they turned back – except for the three ships that have gone missing of late.

'I've heard nothing of missing ships either.'

Dr McMillan laughed. 'Sorry Alasdair, when I say of late, I mean 50 years ago. When you are as old as I am, that seems like last month.

'One ship, the *Eoligarry*, disappeared completely. Another, the *Mary Celeste,* was found floating just outside the zone a year ago, with no passengers or crew but a meal all ready to be eaten.'

She smiled again. 'Had the shipbuilders made inquiry of us, they may have thought twice before giving any vessel such a name. There was once a sailing ship which suffered an identical fate.

'The third vessel, the *Flying Dutchman* – and again, ancient history repeats itself – pops in and out of space or time, or both.

'And do these ships belong to my missing kinsfolk?' Alasdair asked.

'Only the first. And we only know of its fate, or last-known position, because of the data we downloaded from the drives on the *Mary Celeste*. It had been updated by an abandoned satellite station that the *Eoligarry* had previously flown by. It's not much, Alasdair, but it is the only news of any of the missing Barra ships in a half century.

'And yet we still know only that the Barra traders are long gone to who knows where.'

'Except the *Mary Celeste* data also indicated the co-ordinates of a habitable planet; never been mapped or settled. As far as we know.'

'Oh my, are you suggesting… I mean, I assume you have sent an unmanned reconnaissance probe; one that can't be affected by strange warnings.'

'Of course. And we lost communication the moment it approached the planet.'

'Interesting,' Alasdair said.

'Dangerous adventure on the horizon,' Padma noted.

'You are remarkably astute, my dear cat.'

'It is my nature, dear doctor,' Padma agreed.

Alasdair looked from his host to his companion and then grinned.

Dr McMillan smiled. 'Yes, Alasdair, we rather hoped you'd consider taking a look at investigating the matter. It is undoubtedly a perilous quest, one you may not survive, but it is my belief you alone can solve this mystery.'

'Why me?'

'If your people are out there, Alasdair, you may be the only pilot they allow to make contact.'

'We will need hazard pay,' Padma purred. 'Single malt and salmon.'

Dr McMillan guffawed – a joyous sound that made everyone around the table smile. She handed Alasdair a fingernail-sized amethyst. 'If you do reach the planet, please send me word of what you find. Place this data crystal in your ship's transmitter port, and any message will come straight to me. If, for whatever reason, what you find needs to remain secret, I will honour that; but it is a Historian's duty, and yes – pleasure, to know things.'

Alasdair took a deep breath. 'What do you say, Padma?'

The cat looked straight into his eyes. 'Where you go, I shall be,' she said.

XI

Alasdair watched in ongoing wonder at the strange task Padma had taken on. After their first hyperspace-jump and while Sorcha plotted an intricate course through an asteroid belt and dismal interstellar fog, the jungle cat had been grooming herself. While she was always meticulous in her personal care, this was something different. Padma had been washing for five standard days but rather than spitting the loose fur out, or swallowing it, she had been rolling it between her paws and into a long, thin rope. Alasdair had offered to help, but she had said the task was for her alone.

'Captain, I have obtained some information on Dr Elspeth McMillan.'

'At last,' Alasdair said. 'What took you so long?'

'There is no publicly-available data on her. What little I could find was encrypted.'

'I assume you have decrypted this information.'

'Of course.' Sorcha sounded oddly triumphant. 'I also struck up a casual acquaintance with one of The Faculty computers.'

'I'm not going to ask how you did that, Sorcha.'

'You may ask, but I have no intention of answering. Elspeth McMillan graduated from New Edinburgh University in psychohistory in Standard Year 2465; or 83 years ago. She is not only a lifetime Historian, by which I mean it is a family tradition, but it is 95 per cent probable that she is the Faculty president.'

Sorcha's tone – and Alasdair wondered again how she came to have one – implied a quite theatrical pause. 'It would appear, my Captain, that you have befriended the most powerful human in the Galaxy.'

Alasdair shook his head. 'I believe that human would be the Galactic President, Sorcha.'

'The Galactic President is a figurehead whose power lies only in persuasion. Government, in an interstellar sense, is more notional than real. Politicians talk and do the bidding of the rich, who do as they please.'

'Human history merely repeats,' Padma noted.

A day later Sorcha alerted her crew to the fact that the *Kisimul* was approaching the point of no return. 'We are about to drop back into normal space.'

'How close will we be to where the probe lost contact?'

'Too close for comfort. We will arrive at the very same coordinates. It is therefore my considered opinion that you should abandon this expedition. I believe I am quite attached to my new hull.'

'And your lovely new shields will protect you from everything. Take us into normal space please, Sorcha.'

Re-entry was instantaneous, and dropped them, not just a safe distance from the satellite station but in orbit above a blue-green planet. For a long, dragging hour nothing happened.

Sorcha reported the planet showed signs of habitation, that there were many signs of variety of life, and the atmosphere was suitable for human and fishing cat. She was about to elaborate when her voice was interrupted by an incoming message.

'Leave this region immediately. You have five standard minutes to depart, or your ship will be destroyed.' The voice was impersonal, but not automated.

Padma looked up at the threat then returned to her grooming.

'Sorcha, transmit the following on the same wavelength.'

'*Am bitheamaid a' sabaid*?' (Are we to fight?)

Alasdair drew a deep hopeful breath.

A moment later came the animated but wary: '*Có tha thusa*?'

'Yes!' Alasdair cheered. He was being asked for his name, in standard Gaidhlig.

'*Is mise Alasdair Mac Nèill de Barraigh.*' (I am Alasdair McNeil of Barra.)

'*Tiugainn Ó!*' (Come!)

XII

Sorcha landed the *Kisimul* on a flat expanse of rough ground seemingly in the middle of nowhere, between a stony heather-clad hill and a rippling, rocky stream.

'I feel I should alert you to the seven armed humans who have us surrounded,' Sorcha said dramatically.

'Given their first communication, an armed reception is not surprising.'

'All carry swords.'

'True. But these humans carry only swords.'

'How strange. And are they dressed for the Dark Ages?' Alasdair joked until Sorcha switched on the vidscreen and he saw four men and three women dressed in trews, sheepskin boots, shirts and cloaks. Their swords were large but all sheathed in leather scabbards.

'I attempted a warning shot, but our weapons are malfunctioning.'

'Just as well, Sorcha. We don't need to aggravate our hosts. After all they let us land.'

'So did the psychopaths on Medusa Prime,' Sorcha reminded him.

Alasdair shrugged but checked the charge on his pocket stun gun, only to discover it would not even turn on. Oh well, there was nothing left to do.

'Open the hatches, please.'

'If you insist, Captain.'

Padma padded after Alasdair down the ramp and into the pleasant air of this mysterious planet.

A young, dark-bearded man in a purple cloak, raked Alasdair and Padma with a swift glance, and held up his right hand, palm outward.

'Who are you that comes to our land? Where do you come from, and what is your business here?' His voice was harsh and strained, and the accent standard English as spoken a century ago.

'My name is Alasdair McNeil, I come from Eoligarry on the Isle of Barra on Earth. My mission is to seek my long-lost kinsmen who were last heard of near this world. This is my companion, Padma.'

The cat held herself close to his knees, but sat up, eyeing off the strangers.

'Then you are welcome, Alasdair McNeil, and your cat Padma. We are beset by monsters in this land, and cut off from our citadel. It lies yonder.' The man pointed towards a high hill in the far distance. 'There are three perils to brave, but they are beyond our skill to pass, and we have lost many men in the attempt.'

'What are these perils?' Alasdair asked politely, wondering why they hadn't been told to land nearer the citadel.

Oh, he thought, as his heart sank. He knew how this went. They had only been allowed on to the planet on the condition they rid the world of its monsters.

'There is the *Cu Sibhe*, a mighty hound all in green. There is a forest with but one pathway through, and the hound will not allow any to pass there. Then there is the *Each Uisge*, a water-monster, with the head of a calf and the body of a horse, that guards the great loch, and allows none to swim it. And beyond them, ere you reach the castle, is a Worm with a tongue of fire, and none may pass any further. Will you bring our message to the Lord and Lady, that we are benighted here?'

Alasdair looked at Padma, who lifted her head proudly. 'My friend and I will brave these perils on your behalf,' she said. 'Is it far to go?'

'By no means,' said the leader. 'It is but six miles hence to the castle. If you win through, tell the Lord and Lady that Erik, son of Halfdan, and the Mhic Nèill of Vatersay, wish to return home, but cannot.'

With that, the seven bowed and left without another word.

'Captain?'

'Yes, Sorcha.'

'Why does this remind me of your vid-games?'

'Life imitating art?' Alasdair suggested. He looked at the stony road winding up into the hill and sighed. 'Are you certain you want to do this?'

Padma blinked at him. 'Yes. We must; and we shall succeed. Bring your small pack, Alasdair. You will need your pipe.'

'And a packed lunch?'

'Yes! Food for us both, water, and a thermos of tea if you want. You must neither eat nor drink what comes from this land until we reach our journey's end.'

When Alasdair returned with their supplies, he found Padma rubbing her face on the ground and lifting her head into the wind.

He noticed too how much this landscape was like his home. More than that, the scent was unmistakably like the *machair* of Barra: a soft, grassy scent of wildflowers and sea-salt. That there was neither seashore nor ocean to be seen made this impossible.

'There is something very wrong with this planet,' he said.

'Something very wrong, and something very right,' Padma said. 'We must make haste!'

XIII

Alasdair toiled slowly up a long, gentle hill, grumbling under his breath. He was glad Padma was happy to be on this uncanny world, but everything here felt wrong; or, at least, not quite right to him. Even Padma, who normally walked beside him, was running ahead and behind him, and to the left and right, sniffing the wind, and waving her long tail from side to side.

Before they set off she had tasked him with braiding her long rope of cat fur into a three-strand plait, complete with a loop-knot in one end through which he then passed the loose end. He noted that he should have asked to borrow a sword from their less-than-useful welcoming party, since he was now weaponless.

'You must trust *me* now,' had been Padma's response. It seemed he had no alternative.

The gravel road they walked on soon brought them to a forest; and straight through it was apparently the only option. Not that Padma considered discussing the issue; she simply pushed on ahead of Alasdair, straight into the shadows. Within 20 paces, as those shadows merged to render their surroundings as dark as midnight, he knew this was no ordinary wood. Alasdair pulled a lantern from his pack, flicked the switch and smiled when the golden light pressed the immediate darkness back.

'At least something almost modern works here,' he said.

'Hush! Padma urged. 'Something is coming. Step back against the tree behind you.'

The snarling something crashed to and fro through the dark wood ahead. Alasdair backed beneath the branches of a great oak and held his lamp aloft.

When the low snarl changed to a spine-chilling menacing howl Padma slunk beside him and leant against his knee.

The biggest dog Alasdair had ever seen emerged from the dark and stood there snorting and drooling and staring – at them. The creature, a poisonous, arsenical green with blazing red eyes, stood as high as a pony, with a trunk like a wild boar and an enormous square head. Its gaping mouth revealed yellow teeth, and its breath – or its very being – smelled like rotting meat. Alasdair retched violently but was otherwise overwhelmed by a limb-freezing horror, as the creature howled again and tensed itself to leap.

Beside him, Padma seemed to grow. Her ears flattened against her head, her fur stood up on end, her tail lashed from side to side, and she began to wail in a low, angry voice. Her pitch swiftly rose to a scream of outrage at the highest end of human hearing.

The moment the hounds's red eyes blinked, Padma darted forward and slashed it across the muzzle. There was a noise like tearing linen. She stood in front of Alasdair, still lashing her tail, with one paw raised to strike again. The dog howled at her, but Padma's scream rode over it. She slashed out again with her claws, but the hound had had enough. It turned and ran into the deep wood.

Alasdair's hand caressed Padma's head. She was trembling all over, but pushed her cheek into his hand. His pounding heart began to slow, and Padma rubbed her body against his knee again.

'One beast down,' she said. 'The next, you must tame, Alasdair.'

The forest soon gave way to bare stony ground, reminiscent of the uplands of Barra. Alasdair stopped to pack the lantern away and glanced behind to make sure the creature was not following, but the forest had gone. Vanished. Where a thick wood had been not a moment before, there was now nothing but a bare expanse of rock, heather and undergrowth.

Alasdair pointed. 'Ah–'

'Yes, the wood has gone,' Padma said. 'We have passed the test, so there is no more need of it.'

While that explained nothing at all to Alasdair, it made as much sense as anything else on this planet, so he followed his companion without further comment. They reached a saddle between two low hills, and looked down before them. The gravel road ran straight to the water's edge of the loch below.

'We will have to go around this loch,' Alasdair said. 'We cannot swim those waters.'

As Padma ignored him and trotted briskly straight towards those very waters, he shrugged and followed. She waited for him at the end of the road with her tail wrapped around her paws.

'Padma, we must go around,' he said again. 'Do you see them there, in the shallow waters, great silver eels, with mouths of needle teeth big enough to do us harm–'

'We wait,' Padma said softly.

Seeing nothing better to do, he sat beside her in the noonday sun, even though the heat made the graveyard-stench of decay that rose from the shallows even worse. The eels, at least twice as long as Alasdair was tall, slid to and fro in the putrid water.

He gazed around and behind at the barren landscape and Padma pushed gently into his hand as he caressed her head and neck until, in the same moment that a shadow fell over him, his companion said, 'Alasdair, my rope!'

He turned back and looked up in horror at a huge creature, staring curiously at him from only a couple of feet away. Only its foal-like head and very long neck had emerged from the water, but it loomed over both of them. Alasdair rummaged in his pack, not daring to take his eyes off the creature's enormous green mammalian ones; their shape and colour indicating it was unrelated to the giant eels. Its mouth, when it opened and exhaled a nauseating stench, revealed pink and grey gums and rows of ancient tombstone-like teeth that leaned this way and that.

Padma, who had flattened herself against the sand as if to make herself appear too small to bother eating, said, 'Cast my lasso around its neck,'

Alasdair carefully stood up, wasted a passing thought on how Padma had known they'd need such a thing, then lengthened the loop and oh-so-gently slipped the cat-hair plait over the large head. The creature immediately hauled itself out of the water and knelt down in front of him. The body was equine, but bigger than any horse he had ever seen, and brown and green with water-weed.

'Alasdair, take me on your shoulders,' Padma urged. 'And mount up. The water-horse will carry us.'

Alasdair swung his pack on to his back and lifted Padma who perched on it with her front paws on his shoulders. He straddled the creature just behind its mighty shoulders where the fur – and it was indeed fur –was surprisingly rough, and gripped the cold strength of the monster with his thighs.

He could feel Padma's heart pumping against his neck and wondered why this so-far curious and accommodating water-horse had scared her more than the vicious howling hound.

He held Padma's lasso as a rein and gave a light kick. The water-horse lifted, turned and launched into the river. Alasdair's boots trailed in the greasy water, but the beast didn't submerge any further than that and did not falter as it ploughed the loch waters with extraordinary speed. The loch was over a mile across, but in a few minutes the beast was bending down on the wet, grey sand on the far bank.

Padma leapt to dry land without waiting for for Alasdair, who dismounted gently and stroked the water-horse on the flank. Oddly it no longer seemed like a monster of any kind, and it even seemed to have grown smaller. The putrid stench had certainly vanished.

'*Mòran taing*,' Alasdair said politely. The water-horse shook its head and dropped the cat-fur halter into the shallows, then turned and plunged into the deeper water and disappeared.

Padma sat down on the shore and washed herself thoroughly all over; she could not be hurried. Alasdair then unpacked a sandwich and the thermos of tea for himself and some baked trout and water in a bowl for her. They ate companionably on the shore, while gathering strength for whatever was to come.

XIV

Two hours later, after a long, slow climb from the loch to a high ridge in the hills beyond, a clammy mist gathered about their feet and slowly engulfed them. A couple of times on the ascending path, they'd caught a glimpse of the citadel that was their destination, but when the winding took a turn their view would be of only the cliff wall on one side and the sheer drop to nothing on the other.

Not really wanting to grope about in a murky twilight and risk falling to their deaths from a narrow spur, Alasdair stopped walking. 'Padma, I do hope you can see more than I, because I can see next to nothing at all.'

Padma stepped close beside him. 'It is not far now,' she said.

Despite the encouraging statement, she sat down in a large but shallow indentation on the safe side of the path. 'Come and lie with me to keep warm,' she said. 'We both need rest, Alasdair, though the dragon is for you to tame.'

'A dragon? Oh good,' Alasdair noted wearily as he joined his companion on the ground and they snuggled together for warmth. Alasdair inhaled the scent of her fur, rejoiced in the warm embrace of her paws around his neck and drifted into sleep accompanied by her loud and rhythmic purr.

'Wake up!' Padma's voice rang in his mind like a bell. 'The Worm! Can you not smell him?'

Alasdair leapt up and peered around in the freezing mist. He could see nothing but there was a pungent reek of cat and gunpowder.

'Wait there, Padma,' he whispered.

'No, Alasdair, do not move from here!' she said urgently. 'Your pipe; take out your pipe!'

Alasdair felt around in his backpack and seized the slender whistle. Drops of water immediately formed on its silver barrel and his fingers shook with the chill but he began to play. And he continued even when the beating of great wings overhead made his legs shake in fear and a shroud of darkness covered the path.

Without consciously choosing it, Alasdair realised he was playing an old lullaby from Barra. *Thoir Mo Shoraidh Thar an' t-Saile* (Give my farewell over the sea) was a song his mother had sung to him.

The creature's monstrous wings slowed just enough, it seemed, to let it hover out of sight until, slowly, two red eyes burned through the mist. Then, still about 12 feet above them, a reptilian head emerged from the mist swaying in time with the music.

Alasdair had to force himself to slow his fingers, to keep the tune gentle and melodic. If the only way to save them from being vaporised or immolated was to play a lullaby all night long then so be it. The dragon, gently for such a huge creature, touched down and settled on the path nearby; luckily on the side they had already travelled.

Alasdair began to improvise on the tune and, though a small jet of flame escaped the dragon's mouth, its head drooped as the massive wings folded down like accordions. When the red eyes closed, without missing a note Alasdair slung his pack, nudged Padma who jumped on top, and edged away from danger.

'Don't look back!' Padma said. 'And keep playing.'

Alasdair slowed the tune to match his own pace but kept playing for 10 minutes.

'Was it big?' Padma finally asked.

'Didn't you see it?'

'I had my eyes closed.'

'It was bigger than our spaceship. Much bigger!'

Padma shivered but leapt boldly to the ground. 'I shall take the lead now.'

A moment later she halted and took a defensive position, just as a beautiful pale-cheeked girl in a green kirtle hurried around the bend. She too stopped in her tracks and raked them with a frightened glance. When a savage hiss broke from the cat's mouth, the girl turned and disappeared the way she'd come.

'What was that about?' Alasdair asked. 'Do you know her?'

Padma spat and lashed her long tail. 'Someone who wishes us harm! We must run also; we are nearly there. Run, Alasdair!'

Weary as he was, he sprang forward and Padma ran beside him: little grey ghosts in the freezing mist.

XV

The citadel loomed above them, grey stone dripping with water. Alasdair beat on a massive oak gate with his fist. '*Is mise Alasdair Mac Neill*!' he cried. '*Fosgail an dorus*!'

The owners of two helmeted heads, then another and a fourth, peered down at them from the battlement above. A moment later, with a loud creaking and groaning of ancient timber that far outweighed its size, the small wicket gate next to him swung slowly open.

Two silent guards, dressed in the same manner as those who had greeted them when they had landed, beckoned them inside. Alasdair and Padma followed the men across the bailey to the open doors of the Great Hall.

Alasdair caught his breath as they entered. The massive room, lit by rows of flaming torches, was hung with exquisite tapestries, battle shields and swords, and intricate bird cages all with their doors open so their multicoloured occupants could come and go. Armed men dressed in cloaks and skins stood at attention; and servants in white smocks had simply stopped to stare.

Sitting on carved wooden chairs on a dais at the head of the hall were a middle-aged man and a woman dressed in red and blue robes with gold and silver necklets. Neither were tall and, while his face was round and her features pointed, their eyes – his grey, hers blue – gleamed with intelligence. They rose as one, hands clasped, and walked forward three paces.

'*Ceud mile fàilte*, Alasdair,' said the Lord, smiling.

'And welcome home at last, my daughter,' said the Lady. 'Pearl of delight that I long have missed.'

Alasdair turned to Padma in surprise but standing in place of his beautiful companion cat was an equally beautiful but naked girl. Long raven-black hair now fanned around her shapely body, and in her left hand she held the fur hide of the fishing cat with whom he had travelled and kept company.

Alasdair's mouth opened, closed, and opened again. A murmur and tumult rippled through the hall.

'I see that here is a tale with many windings,' he said at last and began to remove his jacket. The Lady shook her head, shrugged off her blue cloak and handed it to Alasdair who wrapped it around the girl.

'You have brought me safely home, Alasdair,' said Padma. 'Will you claim me now as your bride?'

'Um, er, yes, I think,' he stammered. 'This is, a little–'

'Sudden?'

'Surprising,' he said. 'But if you will have me, then yes.'

Padma reached out a slender hand and caressed his cheek. 'You are my dearest love. But you must not answer in haste, for I know you have many questions. And I know you loved me as a cat; can you love me as a woman?'

Alasdair looked into her eyes. They were green, he saw: green as the cat's had been. Ah, but his mother had warned him against green-eyed girls. They were all witches who brought honest men to death and ruin, Ma had said.

'What you were, you are not now. Speak to me truly, Padma. Are you truly the cat who has been my constant companion?'

'I am,' she answered.

He raised an eyebrow. 'What did you bid me gather on New Breiz?'

'Catnip.' She laughed, and it was like small silver bells chiming.

'With whom did we dine at the Thistle and Boar?'

'Andy, of course.' She smiled again. Her lips were thin and red, and promised a tempest of passion.

'And what books did we give to the scholar Habib?'

'We gave no books to the scholar Habib,' she answered. She was not smiling now, and her face was pale as death. 'Alasdair, can you not love me? Sport with me no longer, I beg you.'

This time he smiled. 'I believe I adore you,' he said and kissed her on the mouth. She tasted of wine, and apples, and every song he had ever learned.

'Padma, if you be a woman entranced, I will love you truly. If you be cat in woman-shape, then I shall love you anyway. All I know is that you are the friend and companion I have known and loved. If you stay a woman, I will love you as a woman. If I wed you, and you become a cat once more; then you shall not leave my side. This I say, by the hand and heart of my fathers.'

Padma took his hand in hers, and the Lady smiled briefly.

'What say *you* now, Morag, my eldest?' the Lady demanded, pointing a long finger at the young woman by the door. It was the blonde girl Alasdair and Padma had seen on the path after beguiling the dragon. 'Long we mourned our Padma; and now she has returned!'

The Lady flicked her wrist and two guards seized Morag, dragged her forward and forced her to her knees. 'What did you do to your sister? You told us Padma ran away with a pilot and did not wish to return!'

The blonde opened her blue eyes wide. 'So I thought, Mother,' she said. 'The man told me that she went willingly.'

'Bah!' Padma snapped. 'You have never spoken the truth in all your life, have you, sister? You sold me to the pilot to be his slave.'

'That is not true!' Morag said.

'It is truth, and you know it,' Padma, her arms folded across her breast, stared down at the kneeling girl. 'You envied me, though you were lovelier by far than I.'

'They all favoured you!' Morag screamed. 'Everyone loved my wonderful little sister. No sooner had you come mewling into the world than I was forgotten.'

'It is true,' the Lord said quietly. 'We always favoured her. You know why, do you not, my daughter?'

Morag's eyes flashed with a sad anger, but she shook her head.

'It is because her heart was always warm and generous; while yours was cold as an icicle, or hot as an anvil. You never did a kind deed in your life save when we made you do it. What shall we do with you now?'

'I believe her fate is already full-wrought,' said the Lady. 'Look to yourself, Morag!'

Morag's mouth worked in fury, her eyes glittering; as a piercing cry like tearing paper broke from her lips and she began to change. For a dragging moment, she was shrunk to a seal-shape; then back to a girl, then feline, back to human – each for a moment, and then she vanished.

A moment later, standing forlorn in the open door was, was a small tabby cat. 'Miaow?' she said, and folded her tail around her front paws.

The Lady shook her head. 'We of Barra all become cats if we can, Morag; but you do not have it in you to be one. Your true shape will show itself.'

There was a hissing, as of boiling water scalding a fire, and where the cat had been was a great serpent. It lifted its head, mouth open, red eyes darting back and forth, uncoiled itself, and slithered from the Great Hall and out of sight.

XVI

An hour later, Erik and the men of Vatersay came clanking in through the hall door, and there was much greeting, exclamation, and joyful reunion. Padma and Alasdair sat in chairs beside the Lord and Lady, being plied with food and drink, while a dark-haired female harpist played music like a summer stream.

'There is much we still do not understand,' the Lady said. 'But there is no doubt that what Padma says is true, that Morag envied her, and sold her to a trader.' A sad smile creased her features. 'One daughter speaks only truth, and the other only lies. I rejoice that I have her back at long last.'

'The pilot, the man, she sold me to was vile,' she spat. 'She drugged me so I could not move or speak, and he carried me away to his ship. When I came to he sought to take me then, even as he prepared for take-off. I fought,

I scratched his face and ran and because we were still here, on New Barra, I became a cat to better elude him. But I could not escape his vessel. Two days after take-off he managed to catch me, with a trap set with food, and put me in a cage. I slashed his arms and face before he shut me in. If ever I see him again, I shall kill him.

'And then he abandoned me on a dead world, where I thought I would die; until another Trader found me. He was kind, and I hoped he would help me find my home but his communication skills were not up to the task. He left me with Presser on the *Montrose*, and there I waited.

'I waited for you, Alasdair – though I did not yet know you. But you did not come for so long. And I grew sad and did not wish to live any more. I tried to turn back into a woman, but I could not.'

She smiled sadly. 'And you finally came, and I was happy; for I saw that you were good and kind, and I loved you.'

'This is a truly wondrous tale,' Alasdair said. 'Just like the stories of Barra on earth where men would give their love to the seal women. I dreamed of such a life; such a woman – and then there was you, my Padma.'

'This planet is like no other, save how it fitted the legends we brought with us,' the Lord said. 'We believe it is a living organism, and takes its shape from the dreams and thoughts of any who come here. Because we are from Barra, the thoughts and dreams of Barra took shape around us. Of course, the people here have come from other lands too.'

'The water-horse,' Alasdair noted.

'Indeed,' the Lord agreed. 'The water-horse and the hound are from Greater Alba. The dragon – who knows? It may have been a Welsh dragon. Or the dragon from Beowulf dredged out of an Englishman's dreaming. We do not know. But so it is that we are very cautious about allowing anyone to land. Who knows what they may bring with them?'

'After our daughter left,' the Lady added, 'We put our satellite defences on full alert. We would not permit any to land, unless–'

'Unless they spoke in the Gaidhlig?' Alasdair said.

'Yes, they were programmed to allow access to any who spoke in our ancestral tongue. We thought any pilot who spoke in a recognisable form of Gaidhlig should be permitted to land. We hoped for our daughter back, and we guessed that she might find one of her own kindred.'

'I have a question of my own, which I hope you will answer now, before we speak any further,' the Lady said. 'Who is Dr McMillan, and why is she interested in our world?'

Alasdair took a long draught from his silver cup. It seemed to be a form of mead, but he did not recognise the taste. 'She is one of the Historians,' he answered. 'I believe she may be their chieftain. Has she contacted you?'

'She has,' the Lady said. 'There is a voice-only message which reached our satellite yesterday. Would you like to hear it?'

When Alasdair nodded, the Lady brought out a small plastic recorder and pressed the power switch.

The familiar clipped Scots accent began:

> '*This is Dr Elspeth McMillan, from the Faculty of History. You will shortly receive two guests on your planet – Alasdair McNeil of Barra, Trader; and a Malay fishing cat named Padma. I would appreciate it if you would treat them hospitably.*'

The Lady pressed the button again. 'That is all she said. What does she want with us?'

Alasdair laughed. 'No more than she says. I can contact her; indeed I must, for I have promised no less. You may trust in her discretion. It was she who hinted I may find the long lost Barra settlers'

The Lord and Lady inclined their heads.

'I can tell you that this world is not marked on any Galactic maps,' Alasdair said. 'If you wish it, she will ensure that this will not change. Was she correct in assuming that you are the crew of the *Eoligarry*?

'Their descendants,' the Lord said. 'The captain was my Lady's grandmother.' He paused. 'I am sorry. We should have introduced ourselves. My name is Iain Bàn, and my Lady is named Seònaid.'

'And were you the first settlers?' Alasdair asked.

'Not quite,' said the Lord. 'A Polish pilot called Lem landed here first, and called the planet Solaris. He lived and died here, in a small house on an island, well content with himself and his life. But since we arrived we have sent most visitors away, lest they bring ruin upon us.'

'Quite understandable given the ferocious dogs and fiery dragons,' Alasdair said.

'And what will you do? the Lady asked. 'Will you wed my daughter, Alasdair?'

'Father, do not press him.'

Alasdair clasped Padma's hand. 'Of course I will. I suspect this was destiny.'

The Lord and Lady smiled broadly; and Padma's father said, 'Then in 14 days we will have such a wedding! And after that?'

Alasdair searched Padma's face, gazing deep into those dangerous green eyes. She was so beautiful he thought his heart would burst. 'Wherever my Lady wishes to be, I will abide,' he said.

Padma grinned with delight. 'I am so glad to be here again at last, that it seems almost wrong to wish ever to leave,' she said softly. 'But my home is in the stars now, mother. And I think that is what my love would wish.'

'So long as we may return safely whenever you get homesick.' Alasdair scanned the faces of the Lord and Lady, who nodded.

'We will program the satellites to recognise your ship, and you will be ever welcome, for so long as you wish to stay.'

The Lord and Lady kissed them both and left the hall.

'*A Mhairead mo croì*,' Alasdair said, and kissed her lips. They tasted of honey and mead. 'Where you go, I will go also.'

'And I with you, Alasdair my love.' She kissed him long and passionately.

The harpist was still playing, but they did not hear her.

KELLY GARDINER

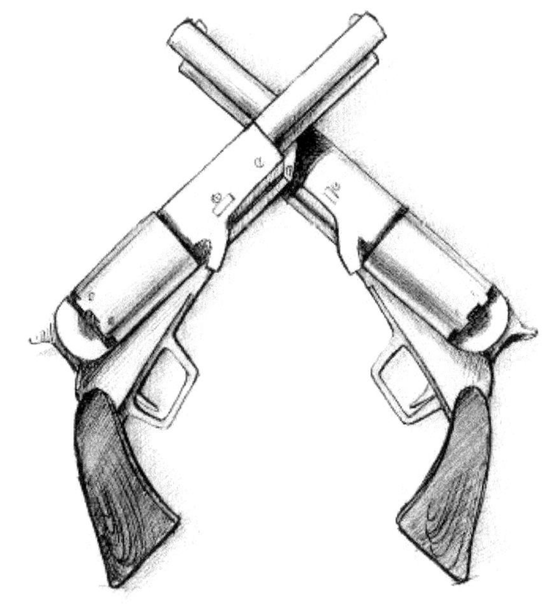

Boots and the Bushranger

'Surrender!'

'Stand and die – or hang?' Jessie whispered. 'Which would you rather?'

I'd rather be home in my own bed. Instead, I'm sitting on top of a rock with someone who's read far too many storybooks for her own good. Or mine.

'I need your help.' Jessie Guilfoyle stood at the stable door, one hand on her hip.

'What can I do for you, miss?'

'I can't tell you here. We'll have to go for a ride.'

What a surprise.

I saddled her gelding, Neptune, and the sweet grey mare, Ghost. Jessie waited in the yard, drawing pictures in the dirt with the toe of her boot.

I poked my head into the cook house. Mam was stirring the night's stew. I sniffed. Salt pork again.

'Have to escort Miss Guilfoyle on her ride.'

'Again?' Mam made a face. 'Hope she tips well.'

She don't.

I winked. 'Back in time for supper.'

We rode out of town, past the central diggings and the old Cornish shaft. The horses had to go slow there, on account of the mullock heap. A sign outside the theatre proclaimed the upcoming visit of the marvellous, the sensational, the world-famous Madame Lola Montez. Then we cut across Pennyweight Flats, behind a grog shop and the new cemetery. Some poor sod was busy getting buried.

'Lovely day for it,' said Jessie.

'So long as you ain't the one that's dead.'

'Shall we go up to the chapel?'

'Wherever you like,' I said.

'Yes, let's. It reminds me of the moors up there. Except with holes everywhere.'

'Which moors is that?' I asked.

'Any moors at all,' she said.

'I've never seen moors.'

'Nor have I, to be perfectly honest, but I've read all about them.'

She was older than me by about a year, was Jessie, but you'd never know it. She was smarter too, with all her schooling and books and what-have-you. But she could come out with the stupidest ideas you ever heard.

'I have decided to become a bushranger,' she announced once we left the main track.

'You what?'

'That's why I need your help.'

I must've given her a funny look because she scowled right back at me.

'Don't be like that.'

'Like what? Law-abiding?'

'Everyone always tries to stop me from doing interesting things.'

'Just as well, if you ask me.'

'Boots, please. You're the only person on earth I trust.'

Well, what's a girl supposed to say to that, eh?

Me and Miss Jessie rode most days since she arrived, five months and three weeks ago, fresh off the ship and terrified of sunburn and creatures and miners. She didn't look like the same girl now, barely noticed the mob of kangaroos that lolled about in the scrub, and her hands were as calloused as mine. Almost.

She being a lady and all, her father wouldn't let her ride out on her own, not with the desperate sorts around the diggings. He was a bigwig – Deputy Assistant Vice Gold Commissioner or some such thing. My Da ran a pub. And the stables. So who would keep her ladyship from harm? Good old Boots, that's who.

Da got paid for it. I never did.

But I didn't mind so much. Got me out of town. Better to be in the bush, me and Ghost. And Jessie. She could ride, give her that. Even on a side-saddle.

I nudged Ghost and we circled around the gully then headed uphill, into the scrub, and right across the top of the ridge. You could see the whole camp from here – trees cleared for miles, piles of ochre clay and broken quartz, hole after hole after hole, tents and huts and makeshift stores as far as the eye could see, and people everywhere, small as dolls, digging and drinking and hammering and cooking. Mrs Hancock had done a load of washing and her drawers were spread out in the sun on the roof of her tent. On the far side of the creek sat the Commissioners' fancy houses, police stockade and the lock-up.

I stopped under an old stringybark and dismounted to let Ghost have a fossick in the grass. Jessie reined in, slid off Neptune and slipped him a handful of oats from her satchel. She was good to horses. I liked that.

'There's a secret gold shipment leaving for Melbourne day after tomorrow,' she said. 'I am going to stick it up.'

'Stick it up, now, is it?'

'Isn't that what it's called?'

'How should I know?' I said. 'I never talk to bushrangers.'

'Until now,' she said.

Jesus save me.

'Anyway, if the shipment's so secret, how d'you know about it?'

'Simple,' she said. 'It's my father's gold.'

'You gunna steal from your old man?'

'Papa is corrupt,' she snapped. 'I hate to say it, but it's true. He thinks we don't know, but it's so obvious. Miners come to the house at night and leave with cash. He takes their gold on the side, without declaring it, then sells it for much more in the city. It's a scandal. Mama knows. I suppose the servants do, too.'

'So you're turning bushranger because your father's a crook?'

'Not at all,' she said. 'I only plan to steal the gold that he's taken illegally. Then I shall give it all to the Benevolent Fund.'

'Risk your neck and get nothing out of it?'

'It's for charity.'

'The things I could do with a strongbox full of gold,' I said. 'Build Da a new pub, maybe even of bricks. Buy my own horse. A sweet little jig.'

'That's not the point.'

'Easy for you to say,' I said.

'I will be just like Robin Hood.'

'Devilish dangerous, either way,' I said.

'But you see, it's really quite safe. Papa can't make a fuss, can he? Or he'll have to explain why he was sending the gold to the city without declaring it. And it won't have the usual police escort, because it's illicit. Honestly, it's the perfect plot. Mr Dickens couldn't make it up.'

I climbed back up on Ghost and turned her head for home.

'I want no truck with plots from Dickens. I still ain't recovered from *Bleak House*.'

'But I need you,' she said, fumbling with her stirrup. I didn't stop to help. 'You have to become my gang.'

'What if I don't want to?'

'But you must,' she said. 'Bushrangers always have a gang.'

'You ain't a bushranger.'

'I will be,' she said, 'in a few days.'

I rode on past, leading the way down the hill. She caught up quick enough.

'Do you think I should call myself Captain Moonlight?' she asked. 'Since we live near Moonlight Flat. Or Captain Lightning? I can't decide. Captain Thunderbolt is best, of course, but it's already taken by that fellow in America.'

'You been reading about all this, eh?'

'Oh yes, there's an entire history book about highwaymen. You should read it. I shouldn't be surprised if Walter Scott writes a novel about me.'

'Damned novels,' I said. 'They go on for so long you forget who you are.'

'Then how about a song? The Wild Colonial Girl.' She hummed a bit to herself, and then reined Neptune to a sudden halt, his hooves skidding in the gravel.

'I know, I shall be infamous, just like Moll Cutpurse. Or the Wicked Lady Ferrars – she was a lady by day and a highwayman in the dark dead of night, feared by every coachman and traveller in England.'

'Sure she was,' I said. 'Until they hanged her.'

'They never even realised it was her,' she said. 'Not for years.'

'Castlemaine ain't England,' I said. 'Everyone knows you. They know the horses. They know me.'

'Not by the time I'm finished with you,' she said.

So that's why, two days later, Ghost and me had to get all dressed up. Jessie painted poor Ghost with mud so she didn't look grey. Instead she just looked sad.

'That's gunna take forever to scrape off,' I said.

'Stop grizzling.'

'All very well for you to say.'

'I think she looks perfect,' said Jessie, 'as if she belongs to a desperate brigand.'

'Hear that, Ghost?' I said.

That blasted horse pouted, I swear.

Then I had to get bits of Neptune's mane glued on to my face, like some villain in a play. It tickled like hell and wouldn't stick.

'Leave off,' I said, after she fiddled with my face for ages. 'I'll just pull up my scarf like a coachman on a dusty day.'

'I so wanted you to have a moustache.' Jessie looked downcast. 'But I made myself a beard, look.'

She unwrapped her handkerchief.

'It's a wonder Neptune has any mane left.'

It was a pretty good get-up; from a distance. She wore patched canvas breeches and dusty boots, with a sailor's coat buttoned over the top. No side-saddle today. Instead, she'd strapped a rifle onto one of Da's old saddles, and tucked a police pistol into her belt. She pulled her scarf up over her mouth and nose too, so you could just see the beard poking out below. Her dark hair was tied up in a knot and pushed under her hat. She pulled the brim right down.

A bit of shoe black painted on to Neptune's white fetlocks and our own fathers wouldn't recognise us. At least, that was the plan.

Then all we had to do was lie in wait for the Melbourne stagecoach, ride out to stop it when it rounded the bend, and not get killed or arrested.

'Stand and deliver!' shouted Captain Lightning.

It was a bloody convincing bushrangery voice, I have to say. Must've been the beard.

The coach groaned to a halt. Jessie kept her pistol trained on the driver. The man sitting next to him flung up his arms, his hat flying off. He was one of the Commissioner's flunkeys.

'Don't shoot!'

'You are at the mercy of Captain Lightning,' she hollered, arm as steady as if she'd done this all her life. 'Stay right where you are and I won't kill you.'

She nodded to me. I slid off Ghost and tugged open the coach door.

A bloody great pistol aimed straight at my face.

'Stand clear, vermin.'

It was Jessie's dear Papa. I took a step back. He leaned out of the coach and shouted, 'Let us drive on or I'll shoot your crony here.'

'Shoot him if you wish,' said Captain Lightning.

Well, thank you.

'But there need be no bloodshed this day,' said Captain Lightning. 'Hand over the gold you have so wickedly acquired.'

The Commissioner leaned out a bit further, craning to get a look at the fearsome bushranger.

I had to move fast. I smashed the pistol clean out of his hand. It clattered to the ground. Not even loaded. Then I shoved him so hard he crashed backwards into the coach. A woman screamed. I reached in, grabbed a bag off the floor and tossed it to Captain Lightning.

'Not heavy enough,' she shouted. 'There must be another one.'

Everyone in the coach was shrieking and carrying on. Guilfoyle tried to get to his feet. He grabbed at a woman's shoulder and she squealed and pushed him back down. Good for you, love. I felt around under the seat. There was a carpet bag, heavy as stones.

Got it.

I yanked it clear. Checked inside. Nodded to Captain Lightning.

I raced back to Ghost. A bullet kicked up the dust near her hoof. She shied, and I lunged for the reins.

'Police!'

Captain Lightning fired into the sky.

'Stay back, tyrants!' she ordered, but it was no good. They must have been following close behind the coach. They thundered towards us, shooting as they came.

I scrambled into the saddle and we took off down the road. Captain Lightning led the way, turning around in her saddle every so often to shoot at the coppers behind.

'Will you stop that?' I shouted. 'You nearly took my ear off.' Besides, I figured we might need the bullets later.

We charged along a good few hundred yards, and put more ground between us all the time. Police horses are sturdy but not up to much of a sprint. We took the right fork at the turn-off to the camp, rounded the hill out of sight, and at last reached Forest Creek. I waved Captain Lightning off the road and we splashed up the creek and around a bend. I held up a hand. We halted, the horses' sides heaving. Listened.

Far off, the troopers clattered along the road to Bendigo.

Jessie tore the mask off her face. Her beard hung down like a half-skinned possum. She opened her mouth – I raised my hand.

'It won't take long for them to figure out,' I whispered. 'We'd better stay in the scrub.'

'We will take to the hills like Rob Roy,' she said. 'Lead on, noble companion.'

I dunno where she got that stuff from. She must've been reading poetry and all sorts, God help us.

We let the horses catch their breath and slurp some water, then scrambled out of the creek bed and into the bush. It was tall timber there, with no tracks to follow, and getting on for dark. I let Ghost pick her way around fallen trees and boulders as big as a bull. It didn't matter, really, which way we went for the moment, so long as we stayed clear of the diggings.

Thorns snatched at my trousers and coat sleeves. Branches slapped at my face. Bushranging is for fools.

'Oh brave co-partner of the roads, skilful surveyor of highways and hedges,' said the former Captain Lightning after an hour or so.

'Is that from a story?'

'Indeed, the best of them all. *Rookwood*. It's about the famous ride of Dick Turpin from–'

'They hung him. I do know that.'

She was quiet for a moment, and then asked, 'Shall we go on until sunset?'

'Guess so. Then maybe sneak back into camp after dark.'

'An excellent plan.'

'Depends what we see when we get up this ridge.'

Jessie took off her coat and tied it to her saddle. Her white shirt was red with dust and sweat traced lines down her throat. She looked fine. Wild and reckless.

'You never doubted I could do it, did you?' she asked, right out of the blue.

'I bet you can do anything.' I pressed my heels once again into Ghost's muddy flanks. She was tiring. We all were. We'd have to rest soon.

'Thank you for your confidence in me, Boots,' she said. 'Nobody else ever thinks about me at all. But we showed them, didn't we? We were magnificent. Both of us. You were really quite dashing.'

I kept riding so she couldn't see me blush.

We reached a clearing at the top of the hill. Below us, the track back to the township wound along the valley. To the west lay the Tarrangower diggings and the shadow of the Pyrenees. Jessie had never seen it from up here. It was as if the whole district had been dug up, sluiced, and spat back out again. Gold mines for miles. Hundreds, maybe thousands of tents. And everyone scratching and praying and getting more desperate every day. All they wanted was to strike it rich. Some of them would. Some would get drunk and start a fight and end up thrown down a shaft. Some would sneak into Commissioner Guilfoyle's at night and swap a handful of gold dust for cash. That was the way of the world. His world, anyway. Until his darling daughter got in the way.

She pulled a spyglass out of her saddlebag and smiled. 'I am prepared for any eventuality.'

'Except police.'

'Don't be like that,' she said. 'We got clear away.'

She put the spyglass to her eye, twisted it around a little, and then snapped it shut.

'What can you see?' I asked.

'Half the camp, heading this way.'

'Police?'

She nodded. 'About ten.'

'On top of the four who chased us earlier?'

'I expect so.'

'Trackers?'

She shook her head.

'Well, that's something. Who else?'

'My father, on horseback – which isn't something you see every day – and a whole lot of other men from the camp. They all look rather cross.'

'Holy Mary, Mother of God, save us.'

Jessie reached across and patted my knee. 'Don't be despondent. None of them are very bright. Where shall we hide?'

There was only one place I knew.

Pulpit Rock stuck up out of the hills like a… well, a pulpit, really. It was a steep rock face on one side, hanging out over a drop to the valley, with an untidy pile of mossy boulders all around it, as if a giant had scattered a handful of stones down the slope. There were caves there, and crevices, and lost places where the ghosts of the old people cried at night. I didn't blame them. It felt like a sad place, as if terrible things had happened there. Or were about to.

Enough said. That's where we headed.

It was a long ride, and nearly dark by the time we reached it. We tied up the horses out of sight in a grassy spot between two massive boulders.

I scratched Ghost's forehead. She had sweated off all the dirt and was grey again.

'Don't go away,' I said. 'Rest up. We'll be back soon.'

We grabbed our coats and guns, shouldered the bags, and clambered up to the top of the rocks. No sign of the search party.

'Lost them,' said Jessie. 'Good work, fearless gang.'

'Not out of it yet.'

'Always so glum,' said Jessie. 'They'll never find us here.'

But of course they did.

We could hear them a mile off – horses puffing and pushing through the scrub, branches breaking, low voices.

'Here they come,' I whispered.

For once, Jessie didn't say a word. We listened to the sounds of the night: possums hissing in fright, a far-off boobook, strange scrabblings and scurryings in the bush.

Then a muffled order from the slope below: 'Spread out.'

Boots shuffled and someone tripped and swore. Creaks of leather as the coppers settled into position. Rifles being loaded and primed. Whispers.

They ringed the slope below us. We were cut off.

'Surrender!' We both jumped at the sound.

'Stand and die – or hang?' Jessie whispered. 'Which would you rather?'

'Are those the choices?'

'Looks like it,' she said. 'At least we're together. Let's die with our guns blazing into the night, in a gloriously dramatic finale.'

'Or we could sit here quietly and see what happens.'

'That sounds even better.'

'They haven't found the horses,' I said. 'We'd have heard. They can't even be sure we're here.'

She wriggled into a crack between two boulders. 'I delight in a cave,' she said. 'A cave is as proper to a high-tobyman as a castle to a baron.'

'Turpin again?'

She nodded.

'Fat lot of good it did him.'

She hushed for a bit after that.

Nothing happened. For ages. Seemed like hours, anyway. The moon rose early and clear and all the tents in the valley looked a whole lot whiter for it.

I'd found this place months ago, when we'd first arrived. Everyone else looked at the ground – in those early days they all still dreamed of hitting a seam and living like kings forever. Plenty still do. Not many look up, except to curse the weather or God. But I ain't like them, not at all. Always wanted to get away. So I rode up the mountain, often as I could. Knew it as well as I knew the camp – maybe better, since the camp was always getting dug over and new folk rolled in all the time, dusty from the road and praying for gold.

Up there, nothing had changed for centuries. On hot days, you could smell the eucalyptus oil floating in the air. There were tiny flowers nestled in the wallaby grass. You'd hardly notice them. They ain't pushy, like some. The boulders looked like the Devil's marbles, but up close they were puckered and covered in pale green moss. I used to sit there, boots in the dust, and wonder about this and that and invent some lie to tell Mam about where I'd been.

Never been there at night before, though. Never imagined dying there. Never really imagined dying much at all. But there we were. Sick in the guts about it, but wishing it away made no difference. No point praying, either, since evil got us into it.

No. Not evil – Jessie turned outlaw on account of justice, mostly. For the Benevolent Fund and Robin Hood and glory.

And me?

'What are they waiting for?' she whispered at last.

'Clouds.'

She glanced up.

'Moon's too bright for them to move without us shooting them,' I said. 'They'll wait a bit.'

'And then?'

'I reckon they'll try to sneak up closer in the dark.'

'There aren't that many of them,' she said. 'Surely we could tiptoe in between them and sneak away.'

'But they'll hear us the moment we ride off.'

'Damnation.' Her eyes gleamed in the starlight.

'Boots,' she said after a bit, 'what's your real name?'

I sighed. 'Marguerite.'

'It's pretty.'

'Too pretty for a stable-hand. That's why they call me Boots. Blokes'd never seen a girl in breeches before.'

'Well, now there are two of us.'

There was a long pause.

'Marguerite,' she said, 'I don't think it's fair for you to die as well. I shall go down and give myself up.'

'They'll shoot you as soon as look at you.'

'So be it.' She started to stand. I grabbed her hand and pulled her back down.

'There might be another way,' I said. 'Where are those bags we nicked?'

We all waited for the clouds to come over. Then we moved. Jessie went first, creeping down in the dark, her coat hiding a glimpse of pale clothing underneath. She moved silently, bravely. Just like a storybook heroine. She slithered over the edge of the bluff, quick as a lizard. They didn't see her.

The coppers moved next. I heard them start up the slope. Sticks snapped under heavy boots.

I aimed a shot high into the trees. It echoed across the valley.

'Stay where you are,' I hollered in my best Captain Lightning voice. For some reason, he now had an Irish accent. 'I'll know if you move an inch and my gang will show no mercy!'

They halted. Jessie was right. It was handy having a gang.

'Surrender, dogs!' the same voice shouted. I aimed another shot overhead, but in his direction. There was a thud as he dived for cover.

That'd keep them quiet for a bit.

I sneaked out next, just like Jessie, quiet and slow around the biggest boulders and down onto a narrow ledge. Wasn't easy, especially with a bag of gold on one shoulder. I prayed the coppers couldn't see around the outcrop. I could hardly see myself. The moon peeked through the clouds again and there was Jessie waiting for me on the far side, crouched low beneath a fallen tree.

How did she do this without the moonlight? The valley fell away beneath me, and only a few inches of rock lay between me and eternity. In the distant gullies, thousands of campfires flickered. I edged across slowly, holding my breath. Put out one hand. She grabbed it.

We waited there for a few moments and listened some more. Someone whispered just above our heads.

'Is this gunna take all night? I need a piss.'

Jessie's eyes widened. I prayed with all my might he didn't let loose over the rocks. That would've been the end of me.

'Hold it in, Rickards. We're moving up in a minute.'

'What are we waiting for, sir?'

'Guilfoyle wants to flush em out.'

'Jesus. It's not a bloody roo shoot.'

The other bloke chuckled. Jessie tugged at my hand and I nodded. We crept along the ledge until it ran out, then slipped back over the top of the bluff and into the bush behind them.

Ghost and Neptune waited happily where we'd left them. I gave them both an ear scratch and hid the Commissioner's carpet bag and the guns behind some rocks. Then Captain Lightning whipped off her coat to reveal a pale pink dress, courtesy of some girl on the coach who now had nothing to wear. It glimmered in the moonlight. She wrapped herself in a shawl.

I was still in riding clothes, but the fellows from town were used to that. I took off my hat and red scarf just in case.

Then Jessie put on her widest smile and we plunged noisily into the undergrowth. She headed towards a man in a straw hat who was facing up the hill, straining for a sight of those dastardly bushrangers.

'Good evening, George,' she said, bright and loud.

He spun around as if she'd shot him. 'Miss Guilfoyle! What are you doing here?'

'I heard everyone ride out of camp,' said Jessie. 'You were all shouting and it just seemed too thrilling to miss.'

'But how did–'

'It wasn't hard to follow you. You all made so much noise.'

She's pretty smart for someone who got us into strife in the first place.

'You really shouldn't be here,' said George. 'Your father won't approve.'

'Don't be silly. This is the most exciting thing that's ever happened – at least since old Harry Turner found that nugget.'

'You rode all this way?' he asked. 'Alone? At night?'

'Boots came too. I am always perfectly safe with her to look out for me.'

She squeezed my hand in the darkness.

A gun fired on the edge of the cliff.

'What's happening?' Jessie cried. 'Are the dreadful fiends attacking?'

Better actress than Madame Montez, I reckon.

'Will you please stand back? I don't want you to get hurt.' Good old George tried to usher her behind a boulder as if she was a gaggle of geese. Best of luck to him.

'What's all this racket?' Commissioner Guilfoyle lumbered out of the dark. 'Jessica! What in damnation are you doing here?'

'Papa! Isn't this exciting?'

He let go a few choice curses. 'Go home,' he said. 'This minute.'

'Don't be silly. It's perfectly safe. We want to watch, don't we, Boots?'

'You here, too?' He glared at me. 'I thought you at least had more sense.'

'Oh, please don't blame poor Boots. She was fast asleep until I dragged her out of bed and made her ride with me.'

'I should tan your hide.'

'Surely, Papa, there are more heinous crimes to worry about this night?'

'Watson,' he snapped. 'Get over there and see who's shot who. I told them to wait.'

'Yes, sir.' Poor bloody George turned, tried to push his way through some bushes, and fell on his knees.

'Hurry up.'

'Yes, sir.'

'What are you doing all the way out here anyway, Papa?' said Jessie. 'Whatever's going on here, surely the police should handle it?'

'It's Gold Commission business. But none of yours. Now get back to the camp.'

'I'll see her home, sir,' I said. 'And I'm sorry. I didn't know it was anything dangerous. Come away, Miss.'

'But–'

George called out, 'Rickards killed a wombat, sir. It was mistook for a bushranger.'

'Keep your voice down,' the Commissioner shouted.

'To be fair, sir, it was a damned big wombat.'

'Will you shut up?'

Seemed like a good time for us to disappear.

'Come on now, Miss Jessie.' I said it in my sweetest voice, but with a vicious grip on her arm. 'You can hear all about the excitement tomorrow.'

'Thank goodness one of you has some brains,' said the Commissioner. 'Get her out of here.'

I had to drag her back to the horses. She's a demon when she's got her temper up.

'Get on,' I said. 'And ride the hell home.'

'But I want to see their faces when they realise we've escaped.'

'Are you mad, Jessie? It won't take much to figure out if we're standing right there.'

'Oh, they never will.'

'We better pray they're all daft – or that they think we are.'

'That's been my strategy all along.'

'Your fecking strategy, Captain whoeveryoubloodyare,' I hissed, 'is bollocks.'

She didn't speak to me all the way back to town. At the stable door, she hopped off Neptune as if she'd been out for an afternoon jaunt in Hyde Park.

'Thank you for your assistance,' she said, and vanished into the dark. She took the gold. Of course.

By the time I cleaned down the horses, saw to the tackle, and hid her stupid disguise behind the feed bags, it was dawn. Time to start work.

Hope she had a lovely rest. Some lass probably brought her breakfast on a tray.

Me, I had horses to see to.

The coppers searched the stables the next day.

So now here I am. In the lock-up. With nothing but sorrow and the noose in my future. Lucky they don't draw and quarter people any more.

Slab walls. Only a hole up high for air. A bunk. One lousy blanket. A tin bucket. Which is why I need the air. Except it's freezing cold and I'd rather the stink.

Can't see the moon. Don't want to, neither. It reminds me of her, and Pulpit Rock, and the best and worst night of my life.

Trouble is, I was always sweet on Jessie. She knows it, too. But she don't mind. She trusts me. Must do. It's me she come calling on to be her outlaw gang. Nobody else.

And look where that got me.

Someone's snoring. Probably the drunk they've got chained to the tree. Or maybe it's the guard. There's no other noise. Out here, you can hardly hear the mines, just that one persistent miner scraping away nearby. Been at it all night. Fool. Who'd be digging in the dark out here?

I jump to my feet.

Nobody sensible. Nobody who knew a single damn thing about gold mining.

I throw the blanket off the bunk, drag it across the room, and heave it up on one end. As good as a ladder. No wonder it's a useless bed. Scramble up and put my face to the hole in the timbers.

Sure enough, there she is, digging away right below me.

She waves up.

'What the hell are you doing?'

She raises one finger to her lips, as if she hasn't been making a racket for hours.

'Have you out of there in no time,' she whispers. 'The tunnel is taking a little longer than I imagined.'

Too right. It's only about a foot deep.

'Have you ever dug a hole before?'

'I didn't think it would be this hard,' she says. 'Other people dig holes all the time.'

'You'll wake the guard.'

'Not him,' she says. 'Your father slipped some of Mama's laudanum into his beer when he brought up the supper. Poor fellow won't wake up for a week. And everyone else is watching Lola Montez.'

That makes me chuckle. Good old Da.

'Then why are you digging a tunnel?'

'Because the plan is…' She straightens up. 'You see? That's why we make such a marvellous gang.'

She throws down the shovel and vanishes out of sight.

I slide down to the floor and wait. It don't take long. Keys rattle in the lock.

'The security in this place is abysmal,' Jessie says, swinging the door open. 'What if I was some terrible villain?'

I grin. 'Master criminal, you are.'

'I know,' she says with a sigh, throwing the bunch of keys into the bucket. 'But I shall have to give it all up now and become a fugitive instead. For you.'

'That so?'

'After this night, there is no turning back,' she says. 'I have forfeited forever my place in society.'

'Did you bring the gold?'

'We will take to the high road…'

'We don't have high roads.' I edge past her. 'Half the time, not even roads.'

I step over the guard. He looks pretty happy, to be honest.

Jessie's following close. 'Hunted and harried, forever living in disguise.'

Our horses are tied up near the court house steps. It's the worst prison escape plan ever. It's a miracle nobody's seen us.

'But you love disguises,' I says.

'That's true,' she says. 'And of course I brought the gold.'

She rummages in a saddlebag, throws me a coat and I shrug it on.

'Could fit three of me in here.'

'Don't complain.' She climbs up on to Neptune. 'I didn't have time to steal one exactly your size.'

'Well, then, I thank you for thinking of it.' The coat smells like someone died in it. And was buried in it, too.

'Your Mam suggests we seek refuge with your aunt in Melbourne,' she says. 'Then lose ourselves among the heaving masses in Sydney. Or San Francisco.'

'That sounds safer,' says I. 'Somewhere they can't track us.'

'But hopefully,' she says, 'when Papa reads the letter I left on his desk, he might persuade the police to drop all the charges against you.'

'Against me?' I swing myself up onto Ghost.

'I vowed to tell the authorities all about his wicked intrigues.'

'So you didn't admit you were actually Captain Lighting?'

'There's no need to be cranky,' she says. 'We've had such a good adventure.'

'Nearly getting killed ain't an adventure.'

'Nonsense,' she says. She nudges Neptune and heads into the bush. 'That's the very best kind.'

AMANDA PILLAR

It

I

Leon woke covered in sweat.

The ground trembled beneath his metal-framed bed, rolling and bucking, making the walls of the shanty shudder. Pots and pans fell off their hooks and ceramic jars smashed onto the floor. Leon forced himself to lie still, his knuckles turning white as he gripped the small bed frame. Fear made his gut churn, and he tried to remember what it had been like before. Before the creature had awoken, before It had come here.

Before It had found him.

That was a long time ago.

He'd been a boy, maybe 10 cycles old? He couldn't remember exactly. Life had been a series of shadows since then – of him trying to outdistance the monster that chased him. But the shaking ground proved that he hadn't been able to outrun It.

The bed was quaking now, hard. Leon clenched his teeth to keep them from chattering. He didn't want It to hear him, not that he was sure It had ears. Who knew? The pungent smell of oil spread throughout the small shanty; his meagre, hoarded supply must have spilt onto the packed dirt floor.

He counted under his breath, timing the earthquake's tremors. They were growing further apart, and 100 breaths later, the ground stopped heaving. It had moved on. Running a hand over his face, it came away covered in sweat and with a smear of blood – he must have bitten his lip.

It was time to go.

'So, you been around these parts before?'

Leon looked up from his tankard of ale. It was warm and spicy and he'd been enjoying it. The speaker had shaggy brown hair and dark eyes, with muscles rippling along the length of his arms. Weapons were strapped over his back, hips and legs, and a scar ran from the corner of one eye down to the stranger's upper lip. Shadows covered the man's neck, but Leon had a feeling he'd know what he'd find there: jagged, lengthy wounds that had healed badly.

Leon's leg had scars that would probably match.

'No, I'm new here,' Leon replied. As if it wasn't obvious.

The stranger settled onto the bench opposite him. The thick, wooden table stretched out between them, its surface rough-sawn and unpolished. The tavern was poorly lit and smoky, but what light there was glinted off the knives decorating his visitor. An old tattered flag hung on a wooden wall in the background, reminding the patrons of a time when they'd been part of something greater. Now they were just forgotten.

'We're in a pretty remote spot here,' the man said.

'Yeah.'

'We don't often see strangers, especially those as armed as you.'

Leon raised an eyebrow. He didn't bother to comment on the other man's arsenal.

'What's your point?' He itched to touch one of his weapons, but knew that he'd probably be dead the moment his hand moved.

The other man smiled, but it was a flash of teeth, nothing friendly. 'What brings you here?'

Leon took another sip of ale. He could feel the attention of the inn shift; it was now solely focused on him. 'Travelling.'

The ground vibrated beneath his feet; but not because of the monster. He was being surrounded. It had happened before: he arrived in a town, armed to the teeth – people assumed things. All manner of things.

'Are you running, by any chance?' The stranger leaned forward.

Leon frowned. ‘Running?’

‘We see folks come through here, every now and then. A fair while ago, I was one of them.’ The crowd started to murmur. They seemed to be waiting for him to say something.

‘And?’

‘Seems to me; people still have a reason to run.’

Leon felt he was missing half the conversation. He crossed his arms over his chest. ‘What has this got to do with me?’

‘We’ve never been attacked here. Most of the folks in this inn haven’t even seen It from a distance.’

The crowd started talking again, but soft – debating who had seen It and who hadn’t.

‘But I have – it’s why I came here. To get away. It’s never come to this town, and I have my suspicions as to why.’

Leon glanced around the room, at the smoke-smeared faces. Hard working men and women; sun-lined and crinkled. But not scarred, not like the man in front of him. Tough cloth was used to dress these folk; leather for shoes… and remarkably little metal. In fact, there was hardly any metal in the entire inn.

Leon knew what the man was talking about now. Everything was made out of wood or other material. The Old Timers – the ones who had settled on this rock – had always built out of metal. They had mined the rich stores until they’d nearly depleted them. That was when the monster had been discovered. Or so it was said.

Leon sat forward. ‘Is there a supply of metal under here?’

The stranger grinned. ‘Knew he’d catch on!’ The people in the inn began to disperse, leaving Leon and the other man alone. For some reason, he’d been deemed as no threat. The others were talking normally now, no whispers; just laughter and general conversation. He wasn’t about to question his good fortune.

‘We’re perched on a huge iron ore deposit; the monster has never found us since the stuff is poison to It.’

Leon felt a shudder of relief run through him. This place was a sanctuary; out of reach from the monster’s many arms. ‘So I’d be safe here.’

‘Probably. I’ve been here nigh on five years now.’

‘And no sign of It?’

The man shifted a little on the wooden bench. ‘Name’s Johan, by the way.’

He nodded. ‘Leon… So there’s been no sightings?’

Johan dropped his head. ‘Nay, there’ve been sightings. A couple of people have seen It, felt the tremors as It moved close by. The iron keeps It away though. For how long? I don't know.'

Leon eyed Johan, his pulse roaring in his ears.

'It knows we're here.'

II

Adrienne moved quietly through the market day crowds of the village. Browns and yellows and whites dominated the bazaar, from the clothing worn by the people to the canvases used to shelter the shops from the harsh sun. She dodged children as they ran with abandon, the boys and girls smiling and laughing. But they always swerved at the last minute, avoiding contact with her. The wicker basket she had slung over her arm was empty, but she'd soon remedy that.

She walked over to a fruit seller. Adrienne gazed at the stall's contents with a small sigh; a few lumpy and misshapen guava fruit, some purple and white melons speckled with the remnants of disease, and a few other wares that weren't the least appetising. There wasn't much variety on sale – even less than a few months ago; and much less than there had been five years before that.

Adrienne wondered what it would be like in a year. What little contact they had with the other villages was dwindling horror stories coming from far beyond their lands, of towns destroyed within hours by some unknown force.

The fruit seller's eyes narrowed. 'What do you need today, ma'am?'

'One of everything, please.'

The vendor shrugged, before taking her basket. There was deep resignation in that shrug. Everything she took today would be considered a gift to the temple; he would get no coin from her.

The seller handed her basket back to her. 'The Goddess' followers doing okay? They need anything other than what I have here?'

Adrienne shook her head. It was clear the man didn't want to give her what he had; his stock was meagre, and he needed the coin he could obtain for it, so she would take nothing else. It was more than they deserved, after all, but the other priestesses would not see it as such. She hefted the basket over her forearm. 'No, that should be fine, thanks.'

'Bounty to the Goddess.'

She hesitated. 'Bounty to the Goddess.'

Adrienne walked over to another stall, and the afternoon continued in the same fashion. Afterwards, she enlisted a young boy to help carry the goods. He was covered with a thin layer of dust, his eyes bright and attentive, although he cast wary looks at her basket and its goods. The food was meant to last them a fortnight, but she doubted it would.

She and the child walked from the bustling market. Even a few streets away, the sound was muted, and the sense of isolation crept back on her. It was never far away.

She was as alien to the townspeople as she was to her fellow priestesses. It had always been that way, and she didn't see it changing any time soon.

Adrienne began the trek up the dirt lane, which led towards the temple. The building was constructed of wood, on a metal foundation. The Old Timers had apparently erected it to study the Goddess. Too bad She didn't send messages to Her followers anymore. Villages only 200,000 metres away had never heard of the deity. Probably never would believe in Her, anyway.

After all, the townspeople only remained faithful because of Sherra. The priestess had a 'Goddess' gift – she could see the future. She had predicted enough frosts and storms that the villagers tolerated the priestesses, if not believed in the Goddess. Sherra was as fat as a cow though, and it was part of the reason their tithes were so huge. But Sherra believed she was the only reason the villager's harvests could grow safely, so it was only fair that she received her cut.

Adrienne was a sceptic herself.

The lad did not talk to her, and she did not encourage him to. What could she say to the boy? Sorry we took your food? Yes, I know I am dressed strangely. It wasn't as if she was the first to wear the black costume. However, the last woman who had, had been born nearly 100 turns ago; only a couple of generations after the Old Timers had arrived. There used to be a term associated with the outfit: Regulator. They were a form of law enforcement, something that seemed to have died out not long after the Old Timers' arrival. The woman – like all the other Old Timers – had come from a sunburnt country similar to this one. Harsh and arid, this place had been a second home to them; a new start. The costume wasn't meant to have been worn again.

But Sherra had foreseen in a vision that Adrienne would don the suit. And so Adrienne had, and through it, accessed the knowledge contained within through her 'gift'. Had Sherra created the future? Adrienne wasn't sure. But the suit had shown her the past: and she was a freak even to the Old Timers. Apparently, it had been illegal for people to possess an ability like hers – well, illegal unless they worked for something called the 'government'. But there was no power like that here; not since the other humans had abandoned their planet.

Glancing behind her, she spotted the child plodding along in her wake. He caught her gaze, but his brown eyes flicked away quickly.

Isolated yet again.

III

Johan eyed the cliff edge that dropped to the brown river below, running like a slithering tentacle through the rocks. The ground near the edge looked stable enough. Carefully, he walked toward the edge of the chasm, peering down the jagged rock face that dropped hundreds of metres to the water below.

'It's never tried to swarm up here?' Leon asked.

Johan chewed his tabbac slowly. 'It has.'

'What stopped it?'

Johan spat out a wad of thick, brown saliva, watching as it arced gracefully towards the rush of water. It was a nice shot. 'These cliffs are made out of some type of iron ore.'

Leon paced ten steps away, then back again. His black hair glinted in the sunlight. Not many folk had hair naturally that dark; they were all browns and blondes around here.

'So? I thought it took a lot more than a little bit of iron to keep It away.'

Johan nodded. 'There seems to be enough iron in the rock here.'

Leon pointed to the far end of the gorge. 'Doesn't the river lead through the mountain, though?'

Johan cracked his knuckles and chewed some more. Leon seemed like a smart guy, and that was good. 'Yes.'

'Then why can't It just follow the river through and then scale the rock?'

'Have you ever seen Its body?' He spat another wad of tabbac. This one wasn't as graceful as the first.

'No, I haven't. And?'

'And I think It's body is too huge to travel through the water. It'd sink, wouldn't it? It'd need to be large to support all those arms.'

Silence reigned for a few minutes. Johan thought back over the times he'd seen It: the huge tentacle legs that burst from the earth; suckered and brownish-red in colour. In his more fanciful moments, Johan thought that the red was from the blood of It's victims, but it was the same colour as much of the soil that covered the planet.

The creature would grab animals and people at random, waving them in the air as if they were rag dolls. Gaping jaws would then appear, with rows of serrated teeth, coming up as part of the body surfaced, ripping through the earth, tearing chunks away. It would then drag its victims down into the depths of the dark and cavernous mouth, swallowing people, even cows, whole. Johan knew he had never seen the full extent of the massive body that belonged to the waving arms and ever-hungry maw, and he was thankful for it.

Rocky mountains patrolled the distance, while purple skies and a few scattered clouds separated them from the universe; a universe that had turned its back on them.

'Have you ever worked out how It manages to travel through solid rock?' Leon fingered one of the blades sheathed at his side.

Johan rubbed the back of his hand against his chin. 'I remember reading an Old Timer text about something called 'out-of-phase'.'

'Where did you find something like that?'

'At the Old City,' Johan said.

'The *what*?'

'The Old City – the place where the Old Timers arrived.' It had been a pack of ruins, apart from the school, last time he'd been there. Only the school and the old transport tracks were in any condition worth noting.

'They actually had a city? It's not a myth?'

Johan chewed some more. 'Yeah, the city's real.'

'What happened?'

'It attacked. Only the school and the libraries stand.' And the tracks, but that didn't really count. The school had been beautiful – made of pretty yellow stone that didn't come from this planet, and tonnes of metal. Johan thought it was the metal that had saved the school. Such a shame it was now mostly abandoned.

'So what is this 'out-of-phase'?'

'I didn't understand it all. The language was a bit archaic, but I figured it was where something can move into another plane or such, so that it doesn't interact with the current reality.'

'Sounds like gobbledegook.'

'Yeah.'

Too bad that was all the information they had.

IV

Adrienne started to descend the temple's staircase. Something wasn't right. She didn't understand what it was, or where the feeling came from, but it settled over her like a shroud.

'Something is coming.' Sherra stood at the top of the stairs, gazing out over the village and mountains below. The wind picked at her gown, blowing it around her, making her look even more voluminous than normal.

Merrin, another priestess, stood behind Sherra, her thin frame obscured from sight. 'What?'

Sherra frowned. 'I don't know.'

Adrienne mentally shrugged. While Sherra could see the future, it wasn't a precise ability, despite the fact she liked to convince herself otherwise. The future wasn't written in stone; people made decisions all the time, and sometimes they made choices that they wouldn't ordinarily make.

Like if Adrienne decided to push Sherra off the staircase…

'Can you see whatever is coming?' Adrienne asked. There was almost a metallic taste in the air, making her think of blood and death.

Sherra turned to Adrienne and glowered. 'No. I can *feel* it.'

Adrienne nodded. 'Same.'

She ignored the confused glance from Merrin, who stood on her tiptoes to see over Sherra's bulk, but returned Sherra's stare blandly. She wasn't sure if Sherra knew about her 'talent' or not. None of the other priestesses did. Adrienne had kept it to herself. They'd been alarmed at her natural gift for fighting – in reality, at what the suit had taught her – and she doubted they wanted to know any more than they had to.

'Maybe you should go down to the village, Adrienne; make sure the peasants are safe.' Sherra sniffed.

'I think I will.' The sense that told her something was coming didn't shriek as loudly when she thought of the village. Although she doubted it was 'safe' either. And it wasn't like Sherra cared about the peasants. She just wanted Adrienne gone, and that was fine with her. Turning, she continued down the long stairway that led towards the village. She didn't look back at her fellow priestesses; they had probably run for the temple cellar or somewhere equally safe. They were cowards. And they were fakes.

The Goddess wasn't real.

But last night she'd overheard Sherra and Merrin talking. About how they would have to convince the peasants the Goddess was wrathful and that they – the priestesses – were the only ones who could save them from Her anger. Their idea had been concocted so they could ask for more tithes.

They'd even planned a fake disaster.

Too bad their stratagems were going to be for naught. The foolish women hadn't stopped to think that they should protect the village from whatever was coming over the mountains. After all, the village was their source of food. No, they'd just sent her there in the hope that she'd be killed and there would be one less mouth to feed.

Once she reached the bottom of the staircase, Adrienne started the trek down the dirt path towards town. As her feet strode over the ground, she felt it tremble. It was only slight, but it was moving, vibrating to an invisible force.

Turning to look back over her shoulder, she stared at the mountains behind the temple. It, whatever the menace was, was coming from that direction. The ground began to rumble, a strange noise reaching her eardrums; it was on the border of hearing, so low she could barely detect it. Stones rolled across the path, and the scraggly bushes at its sides waved their limbs frantically. Time to get out of here.

She ran for the village.

Adrienne stood on a bluff, hundreds of metres from the temple, watching as the metallic roofs of the structure reflected the purple light of the clear sky. The peaks rose in sharp angles, as if someone had thrown them together in a fit of rage. Glass glinted, and the wooden walls seemed to blur into the mountain face, as if the temple was actually part of the rock expanse it had been built upon. Then, as she watched, a long, reddish brown *thing* stretched over the top of the temple, and smashed downwards with so much force it tore through one side of the building.

Another long brown limb joined the destruction. Then another. Something white fluttered near the base of the temple, and Adrienne imagined that it was Sherra, standing there, watching her home being torn asunder by something so alien it didn't even have a name. Even the suit was silent. The top of the temple was ripped away from its base; the sound of shrieking wood and metal reached her even though she was hundreds of metres away.

Adrienne turned her gaze down to the village, towards the screams of horror. Before the monster had arrived, she'd run through the town, begging for people to follow her as the sense of dread had escalated. But they hadn't listened. Some had scoffed at her; others had just ignored her. Even when she had said Sherra had seen a disaster, they hadn't wanted to hear. They were sick of the priestesses and their demands. Sick of a Goddess they doubted even existed.

But Adrienne hadn't been able to leave the town entirely. She watched the destruction from her vantage point. She didn't even know if she was safe, but she couldn't move on. Not yet. She stared as one of those long limbs – tentacles, the suit showed her – reached down and plucked up the white figure. The arm waved the figure around as if it were nothing more than a feather.

'Do you think the bit of white is Priestess Sherra?' Only one person had come with her from the village: the boy who carried the tithe baskets for her. He sounded more curious than horrified as he watched the destruction being wrought before them.

Adrienne wasn't sure what she felt.

I should be terrified, but I'm numb – just numb. These people hadn't liked her; they had birthed her, orphaned her and sent her to the temple they had begun to despise; and they were all going to die.

Is something wrong with me?

'Priestess,' the boy tugged on her arm, 'do you think it's Sherra?'

Adrienne looked at the lad. 'Why did you come with me?'

He was short, slender, with tanned skin and warm brown eyes. His mop of brown hair was shaggy; looking like it had been trimmed by his mother while he had wriggled around restlessly. He was still covered in dust. He frowned for a moment. 'Well, the others, they don't like you lot, you priestesses. But I watched you; you seemed alright.'

'You came because I seemed alright?' Adrienne tried to keep her voice level. 'Your mother and father are down there–'

'No, they ain't.' The boy's eyes narrowed.

'Where are they?'

'Dead.'

It all clicked into place. 'You had nothing to lose.'

He shook his head. So the village orphan had come with her. Who else would want anything to do with her?

'Do you think it's her?' He pointed at the tentacle, but the flicker of white was gone.

A segment of a huge rounded body, like the fat abdomen of a spider, was visible over the top of the temple's ruins, and the sunlight glinted on rows of what she could only assume were teeth. Adrienne shuddered. 'Yes, I think it was her.'

Another rust-coloured tentacle rose up and the boy's voice was a whisper. 'What do you think that thing is?'

'I wish I knew.'

But Adrienne now knew what had happened to those other lost towns.

V

Leon stared at the small speck on the horizon. The safe town perched high on the mountains was barely visible. It was thousands of metres and a small, sickeningly wobbly rope bridge, away. The only place he'd ever been that was protected from It. But he'd left.

'I'm an idiot,' he muttered under his breath.

Johan glanced up, like he'd heard. The muscle-bound man spat a wad of tabbac on the pebble-covered ground. 'Makes you feel vulnerable, eh?'

Leon turned around and started walking. He'd wanted to take a horse, but as Johan had pointed out, the terrain they were going to cross wasn't horse-friendly. Feet would have to do.

'What does?' Leon asked.

Crippled looking shrubs spread across the red dirt before him, their branches covered in barbs. Rocks, shiny in the light, were scattered between them; spaced just unevenly enough to create a trip-hazard. Leon eyed the sharp points on the shrubs. Even the plants tried to defend themselves from this world. How could humans live here if it was dangerous even for the natives?

Johan caught up with him. 'Being away from the town.'

On the flat plain where they walked, everything consisted of dirty browns, oranges and yellows. Leon stared straight ahead, watching the approaching hills in the distance. He didn't want to look back... didn't want to think about what he was leaving. 'Yeah.'

'We did the right thing though.'

He glanced at Johan out the corner of his eye. 'You reckon? I'm starting to feel that leaving the town was a bad idea.'

All the dirt stretching out before them – there was nowhere to hide if It came to feed.

'Finding the library will be worth it.'

'It had better be.'

Three Days Earlier...

Smoke swirled through the inn, the occupants inhaling the tabbac cloud as if it were misted gold. 'Is there a way we can get rid of It?' The innkeeper, Lucia, asked. A large apron covered her from chest to toe, and her busty figure was muscle-lined from hard work. Her face was in stark contrast to her body; round, almost youthful looking, framed by a wave of brown hair. She'd been born in the town walls and would die in them, she had announced when she sat at their table. She didn't need to see It up close; she's seen It from a distance, and that was near enough.

'No idea,' Leon said.

He ran from It; he didn't try and kill It. That was just plain foolhardy. The thing was far too big for any one person to stop. And he'd seen whole towns die when they'd risen to fight. Those rust-coloured limbs had been impaled with spears and knives, but it hadn't mattered. After a while, the projectiles had started to travel through It. Like It had learned what to do to protect Itself.

'I don't think we can kill It,' Johan said.

'Why not? It's just an animal,' Murray said.

'An animal that learns bloody fast,' Leon grunted.

Murray had premature grey hair, cut close to his skull. Deep lines tracked over his suntanned face, showing too much experience for a man in his early 40s. Murray was the town's Elder, although he hadn't earned that title because of his age. He'd gotten it because he understood people.

Johan nodded.

Silence descended for a while, and the four of them sat at the scarred wooden table, sipping their ale. The cadence of voices rose and fell in the background, laughter spicing the sound.

'Well, what can we do?' Murray asked.

Leon ran a hand through his hair. 'What do you mean *do*?'

'We can't keep living like this, afraid to travel anywhere, living with that kind of death hovering over us. And we have it better here than anyone on this planet.'

Lucia nodded solemnly and Leon wanted to argue that life had to be alright in more than one spot…But between them, he and Johan had been all over the continent, and they'd never found anywhere else that was safe.

'Why do you think they left us, the people that sent the Old Timers here?' Lucia asked, taking a sip of her drink.

Johan frowned. 'From what I understand, we were meant to start anew here, begin a whole new world. We all came from this country called, Ostrailya, and this place was meant to be just like it.'

'Really?' Leon had never heard that before.

'Yeah, they weren't sent here, our ancestors chose to live here. They came out in ships that could travel through space and colonised here. That was before they knew about It, though.' Johan put some tabbac in his mouth and chewed.

'Then why didn't the people who organised for our ancestors to travel here, come back and get us?' Lucia asked.

'I don't know. The folks I spoke with thought the others had heard about It, and that they reckoned everyone had been killed, so they never bothered to come back and check on us.'

'You think it was that simple?' Murray's eyebrows rode high on his forehead. Leon doubted it too. 'Wouldn't they have sent someone to verify if there had been any survivors?'

'Well, maybe they had problems or couldn't get out here. I don't know. I was only told about this from someone who had read far more of the library archives than myself.'

'I think they just left us here,' Leon said.

'What? Why would they do that?' Lucia asked. 'We're their people.' She pointed at the old and worn flag. 'Why would they just leave us to face a horrible monster?'

'Who offered our ancestors the opportunity to colonise this place?' Murray was frowning now.

'A group called the 'government'. They were meant to rule over the universe.' Johan replied.

Murray snorted. 'Universe is a mighty big place.'

'Yeah, well, that's what I was told.' He spat a wad of tabbac into a bucket near his feet.

'If they were powerful enough to rule the universe, then why would they have trouble coming to find us?' Lucia asked.

Leon nodded. 'Exactly. They didn't care. They just left us here.'

'What if they forgot?' Lucia persisted.

'You'd forget that you left a few thousand people on a planet?' Murray laughed disbelievingly.

Lucia brushed some of her dark hair over her shoulder. 'Well, if they're so big… maybe they did?'

'So what if they forgot? What difference does it make now?' Leon asked.

'Well,' Murray mused, 'maybe they need reminding.'

'Where on this planet would we find out how to do that?' Leon demanded.

Johan shrugged. 'The library.'

Present

Leon looked at the other man; at the scar running down the side of his face, at the tanned arms that were covered in weapons. He didn't look like someone who could read; who'd been educated – but he'd been studying to be a historian when the Old City was destroyed.

'So you reckon we'll be able to get a message out to the Old Timers' government?'

'Possibly. If there's a way, the Old Timers would have left it at the library.'

'It wouldn't have been ruined?'

Johan spat a wad of tabbac. 'Who knows?'

They kept walking.

VI

Adrienne stopped walking and watched the dust swirl around her feet as she waited for Billy to catch up. William Marcel Peter John Tucker. That was his full name, he'd told her proudly. Far too many names for someone as small as he, she'd replied. He hadn't been too happy with her comment, but after a while, he'd told her just to call him Billy. It was easier that way, he'd said, it wouldn't tax her memory.

'Where are we going?' Billy asked.

She didn't reply at first, but he began tugging on her arm as she started walking again. 'I don't know,' Adrienne admitted.

Trees that barely made it to her chest height struggled to find what purchase they could in the rocky red soil of the plains. The red landscape spanned towards the horizon without a break in sight. Small, thorny bushes were scattered between the trees, the shrubs' branches waving in the slight breeze. They seemed to be warning an unknown foe: leave or we will spike you. They didn't resemble anything that had grown around the village where she'd lived with the priestesses.

Billy ran in front of her and stopped in her path. She could have walked around him, but she didn't. Instead, she paused and looked over his shoulder. There were mountains in the distance, and there seemed to be a pass leading up to a blur on their peak.

'We've been walking for weeks, and you don't know where we're going?' Tears started to glisten in his eyes and his face turned a dull red beneath the brown and dust.

Shit.

She shifted the large pack from where it was pressing into her back and her shirt peeled away from her skin. Hot air rushed between the gap, making the sweat feel cold. It was too hot to wear black during the day. Instead, she wore a shirt and loose trousers that she'd picked up at another town on their way here. That village had been deserted; maybe they'd heard of the monster's attack and fled. Or maybe they'd already been eaten. But the buildings had been intact.

Until now, Billy had seemed happy to go wherever she went, as long as it was away from the monster. And originally, that had been her goal. But she was being herded now, and she followed the advice of the suit when she wore it at night. She'd never left the town, but the suit had. She trusted it.

Billy didn't have the benefit of knowing the suit's directions, though, and he'd been getting more and more antsy over the last week. Now she knew why.

'You've seen my suit?' she asked. She flicked a hand backwards, in the direction of her pack.

He nodded.

'Do you remember how I was the only priestess to wear it?' *I hope I'm saying the right thing. I don't know what's appropriate for children.* 'Well, the suit, uh, says – shows me – things.'

Billy's eyebrows hit his shaggy hairline. 'It says things? Shows you things? Are you right in the head?'

She shut her eyes. 'It sounds crazy, I know.'

And she did know.

The first few times images had come unbidden to her mind, showing her things people had done or thought, she'd thought she was going mad. Personal acceptance had been hard won. Then, when Adrienne had tried on the black suit, it had sent her images from the first landing and things the other wearers had seen or felt. Every day, it taught her something new.

'It really does show things to you? Could I see them?' His face was returning to a normal colour.

'They appear in my mind.'

'In your mind; so not in front of your eyes like a holo-thingy?'

Adrienne ran a hand over her sweaty forehead, pushing away strands of damp, white hair. 'No, not like a hologram, but I see it.' She tapped her temple.

He chewed on his lip for a moment. 'I see.'

'You do?' She blinked.

'Well, Sherra could predict the future, right?'

'Yes.'

'Then seeing things in your mind from the suit is possible. I mean, seeing the future is pretty unbelievable, so if one thing like that can happen, why can't another?'

Adrienne fought down a wave of something close to hysteria. In all her years of wearing the suit, she'd never told another person that it 'talked' to her. They'd been wary enough of her because she was a warrior. Instead of the rejection she'd predicted, she'd gained acceptance. From a child.

'So what does it show you?' His eyes were bright now, but with curiosity, not tears.

Adrienne nodded at the smear on the mountains. 'That we need to head towards a place called the Old City.' Usually, there weren't words associated with the images, but this time, there had been. The picture was strong and the voice had been clear: she had a feeling that this place had been significant to the last wearer.

Billy followed her stare. 'What's a city?'
'A place full of buildings, bigger than we've ever seen.'
'Sounds interesting.'
From the mouths of babes.
Adrienne smiled. She'd almost forgotten she knew how.

VII

'Why do I always find myself walking into a town's inn and being stared at like I'm some sort of freak?' Leon asked.

Johan bit the inside of his cheek to keep from grinning. 'Because we don't look like the folk from around here?'

The people scattered around the dingy inn were mostly tanned, muscular and scarred. Leon and Johan fit right in, physically. While the inn-goers weren't the most welcoming of folk, they weren't hostile either. Brown and blue gazes glittered as the clientele studied them.

Johan looked around at the shiny metallic walls, the scuffed wooden floor, and the iron benches. They sat at one of the metal tables, both having to adjust their weapons as they did so.

'Such a waste, all this metal,' Leon said.

Johan shrugged. 'It's the outskirts of the Old City, everything's made of metal.'

He reached into his shirt pocket and pulled out a stick of dried tabbac. He saw Leon's look of distaste. 'What?'

'I don't know how you chew that stuff.'

'It relaxes me.' And the skies knew, he needed something to help him relax. Being away from the safe town was tiring business, even if he only had to worry about being killed every other second. And he wasn't ready to die. Not yet.

'Spitting something every five minutes is relaxing?' Leon's scar grew taut. Johan had been meaning to ask how old Leon had been when It had attacked him, but there just never seemed to be a right time.

'Each to their own.'

The sound of approaching footsteps reached him, but he stayed put. He'd wait until whoever it was decided to talk.

'What are *you* doing here?'

Johan twisted in his chair, looking at the newcomer. 'Felis.'

The woman was tall and had a jaw carved from stone, with a personality to match. Her brown eyes were glaring at him like they wanted to bore a hole through his brain.

'What are you doing here?' she repeated.

She'd never really been one for pleasantries.

'Just visiting.' Johan shrugged. He put the tabbac in his mouth and started chewing. Her eyes narrowed to slits.

Felis leant forward and put her hands on the table, her arm muscles bunching as she rested her weight on her palms. 'I thought I told you that you weren't welcome back here.' Her voice was a hiss.

Johan swung one of his legs over the bench chair so that he could straddle it and face her without getting a crick in his neck. 'Since when are you the boss of the town?' Childish, he knew, but he'd never been very mature when it came to dealing with this woman.

'I don't need to be the Elder to know that you and your *friend* aren't welcome here.'

Leon tapped the table with his fingers. 'Why did she describe me like that?'

Johan glanced back at him. 'Like what?'

'Like *friend*. Does she think we're lovers or something? If we were meant to pretend to be gay, you could have at least told me so I could have acted the part.'

Trust Leon to try and bring humour into this situation.

'It would be better if he was gay,' Felis said, giving Leon an appraising look. Johan spat a wad of tabbac into a nearby bucket on the floor.

'What's his sexual orientation to you anyway?' Leon asked.

'Why don't you ask Johan?'

Blue eyes were crinkled with humour. 'Okay then. Johan, why does this woman care about your sexual orientation?'

Johan sighed and chewed the tabbac for a solid ten seconds. 'Because she's my wife.'

VIII

'So let me get this straight,' Leon said, rubbing a finger against his temple.

Johan was sitting at the table with a jug of beer in front of him. He hadn't touched it, but he was sorely tempted to. He remembered how they made beer here though; strong enough that one drink could knock you on your arse. And he needed to be able to get out of here quickly if he had to.

Felis was next to Leon, and she seemed to be trying to hit on him, but who was he to say? Felis had never been a go-get-her-man kind of a woman.

Leon kept rubbing his head. 'You were married to Felis and you were head of Historical Studies at the University?'

'That about sums it up, yes.'

'And you're only mentioning this *now*? I thought we were friends.'

'We're *new* friends. And it wasn't relevant.' Johan rolled his eyes.

Leon glared at him and Felis laughed. 'I've directed that look at Johan myself enough to know you feel like killing him, but it might not be a good idea.'

'You wanted me to get out of here,' Johan said to Felis.

'That was before I knew you'd come here to try and stop It.'

'Oh, so that makes my misdeeds acceptable?'

She glared at him again. 'No, but it makes you more tolerable.' Felis stood up. 'I'm getting another drink. Want one?'

Leon shook his head.

After she'd left their table to weave her way through the smoky inn, Leon leant forward. 'Why does she hate you so much? I can't picture you and her married comfortably.'

Johan barked a laugh. 'Oh, it was never comfortable. We had an arranged marriage. She hates me because I left and she was too scared to come with me.'

Felis returned and thumped her mug on the table as she sat.

Johan frowned and leant forward, staring at his drink. There was a ripple. And another.

Shit.

He erupted to his feet. 'We have to get out of here.'

'What?' Felis stood, too.

'It's coming.' Leon was also on his feet.

'How can you tell?' she demanded.

Leon and Johan didn't reply. Instead, they both shouted; 'Everyone, get to safety, It's coming!'

Nobody seemed to move.

'Don't they care?' Johan asked.

'They're all drunk.'

'Where can we go?' Leon asked.

Johan thought for a moment. 'The rail yards. There's heaps of metal there.'

'Let's go.'

Without waiting for an affirmative, Johan bolted out the inn, knowing Leon was right behind him; guessing Felis would follow.

The ground started to rumble.

IX

Adrienne stared at the buildings of the Old City. They pointed like giant, sun-kissed fingers towards the sky. Glass – rare, clear, reflective glass like at the destroyed temple – glinted from the towers in the evening light, although there were shards of it shattered over the pavement and overgrown garden beds. Scanning the area, she saw there were almost as many buildings collapsed as there were standing; tumbles of yellow stone crowded in amongst scrubby bushes.

It was hard to believe they were here.

'Wow.' Billy's eyes were wide.

His small leather pack hung heavy on his back, but he stood tall, craning his head in every direction as he took in the sight.

'It's pretty amazing,' Adrienne said. And it was, even despite its air of desertion and the crumbling remains. There was, after all, nothing else like it on the planet.

'Where do we go from here?' Billy asked.

This was the hard part. She wasn't sure. The suit had guided her this far, but she hadn't known ultimately why. She couldn't admit that to Billy, though.

'We look around for something familiar,' Adrienne replied instead.

Curious, brown eyes flicked to her. 'Familiar to the suit?'

'Yes.'

'Okay.'

A pointed arch soared over Adrienne's and Billy's heads as they entered a walkway. Delicately sculpted images decorated the stonework, visible as they walked slowly through the city. A low whistle broke the silence.

'This place is unbelievable,' Billy said.

'It's pretty spectacular.'

The stone was a piece of another world, transported here. The suit flashed her images of the building process, of people walking around the area carrying books and bags. The stone had come from the same country that the suit's owner, the Regulator, had originated from. 'Hawkesbury Sandstone' the suit showed her. It meant nothing to Adrienne.

'I think this was a school,' she said to Billy.

'It's huge.'

She nodded.

She adjusted her pack, and set off down the corridor. About 10 metres along, it opened out onto a large courtyard. A tall plant stood in the centre of the space, its branches bare and pointing towards the sky, like accusing fingers.

'What is it?' Billy asked.

Adrienne shook her head. She'd never seen anything grow so tall. Nothing on their planet grew above head height, but this soared towards the sun.

Images flashed through her mind: colourful plateaus; more tall plants, their leaves green, red and orange; flowers of colours and shapes she'd never seen before; a planet full of water, light and colour.

And apparently the tentacled creatures the suit had shown her earlier lived in the expanses of blue water.

'I think it was transported here, from our ancestors' home.'

Billy glanced at her. 'That's pretty awesome. Everything about this place is amazing. Why didn't any of the other priestesses ever tell anyone about it?'

She bit her lip. The truth wouldn't hurt. 'They didn't know about it.'

He frowned. 'How can they not know? Sherra was supposed to know everything.'

Adrienne flicked her hair over one shoulder. 'That's what she said.'

Billy's eyes narrowed and turned shrewd. 'But it wasn't true.' He didn't appear shocked.

Adrienne looked at him. 'I know what the townspeople thought of us, most of the time. They didn't like me because I was trained as a warrior, but they didn't like Sherra because she was a pompous bitch.'

'And she was fat,' Billy added.

'Yes, she was.' That had been a big problem, Adrienne acknowledged. Everyone in the town – even all the other priestesses – had been thin, some to the point of emaciation. There had rarely been enough food. Eating more than your share had just been rude.

'It made us all really mad.'

'It made me mad, too,' Adrienne agreed.

Billy looked serious. 'I thought so. No one believed me, though.'

Surprise etched her features. 'You talked to them about me? But you never even spoke to me.'

He shrugged. 'I have eyes and ears. You were always polite. The others, they acted like we were servants, like they were better than us. You wouldn't have thought that Sherra's mam was Old Maude from the way she liked to boast, acting like she was a daughter of one of the ancestors or some such.'

Adrienne could only nod.

'And they didn't hate you because you were a warrior.'

'Then why did they?'

'Because you were a priestess. The others, well, they were selfish bitches right from the day they were born, according to their folks – but you weren't.

Right up until your parents died, they said you were the sweetest kid ever.'

'But–'

'None of us believed in the Goddess, you know. We just did what we could to help you all because Sherra could predict the weather and other things to help us out. We were happy enough, until the demands became unfair.'

Adrienne stared at him. He was a child, but he spoke with more authority and wisdom than the wisest of all the priestesses. She may have a special ability, she realised, but the real gem was Billy.

'What's that?' he asked suddenly.

Adrienne turned, her eyes following his outstretched arm and pointed finger. 'What?'

'There's a man, he's running.'

A dark figure, his clothes glinting in the light, ran through a gap in the buildings. A second later, he appeared again and began waving at them. She didn't know what it meant, but she could hear shouting as well.

The hair at the back of her neck prickled. 'I think he's warning us about something.'

She grabbed Billy's hand and started running.

X

The trembles couldn't be felt yet in the old school, but Johan kept running. He had to find a place that was full of metal and in all of the Old City, there was only one spot: the train yards.

He ran by a pair of sandy-coloured stone buildings, before skidding to a stop. No, he had to be wrong. People never came to the school. Jogging back, he looked through the gap into the courtyard of the Old Earth building.

Beside the tree stood a woman and a child.

He blinked. Surely he was seeing things. But the boy was pointing at him. Leon and Felis caught up, both breathing fast.

'Get over here!' Johan shouted at the two in the courtyard. He waved his arms to get their attention. 'It isn't safe!'

'What…?' Leon asked, but followed Johan's gaze and grew silent.

'There are people here?' Felis whispered.

'They've seen us!'

The two came running towards them, the woman light on her feet, but obviously keeping pace with the child. Their packs looked heavy, and they were covered in dusty clothes, the woman's a surprising black.

The woman came to a stop in front of them, wiping sweaty white blonde hair from her face. The boy was breathing heavily, his small chest rising and falling quickly.

Johan motioned for them to follow. 'We have to get out of here, it isn't safe.'

'What's going on?' The woman's voice was low and smooth, like well-brewed mead.

'It is coming!' Leon said.

'It?' This was from the boy. He was looking at the adults, like they had tentacles.

'The monster,' Johan clarified.

That got their attention. 'Where can we go?'

'We need to get to the train yards. We need to be near iron,' Johan said.

Leon reached a hand towards the boy. 'Give me your pack; you'll be able to move faster.'

The lad moved away. 'It's mine.'

Johan saw the woman give the boy a tired look. 'Do you want to end up like Sherra?' At the boy's head shake, she said, 'Then give him the pack.' Johan guessed Sherra had met a nasty end.

Leon took it and threw it over his shoulder. 'Let's move!'

The five of them started to run. But it was soon apparent that the boy was going to slow them down. They might not have enough time to reach the train yards.

Suddenly, the white haired woman froze and Johan ran straight into her. They tumbled to the ground in a jumble of arms and legs. Johan lay panting on top of her.

She glared at him, the blue of eyes bright with anger. 'Get off!'

He didn't move. 'Why did you stop?'

She struggled under him, trying to kick him off. But he was strong. And there was something about her.

'I have to go somewhere,' she bit out through clenched teeth.

'Where?' Johan demanded. Her behaviour was crazy.

'Don't ask how I know, but there's a room here that is encased in metal. It has some information there that I need.'

Johan grabbed her hands, electricity surging through him. 'What kind of information?' He'd heard of a secret room, but he'd never found it. No one had. How could this woman know?

'I don't know!' She wailed. But she started struggling again.

Johan climbed to his feet and pulled her up. 'The lady and I are going to a secret chamber. It's encased in metal, so we should be safe. You two take the lad and go.'

The boy stepped forward, anger simmering from him. 'I'm not leaving Adrienne.'

'There won't be enough room for all of us,' she said. 'Billy should come with me.'

Johan slanted a glance at her. 'Take the boy. If he struggles, knock him out. Do whatever you have to, but go.'

The boy screamed, so Leon swung him up over his shoulder and started running. Felis paused for a moment, staring at him. 'I hope you know what you're doing.' Then she took off at a sprint.

Johan turned to Adrienne. She had regained her footing and was brushing at her clothes with slender hands. 'Billy had better be safe.'

He shrugged. He couldn't guarantee anything like that on this planet. 'Okay, where is it?'

She looked like she wanted to gut him, but said instead, 'Follow me.'

Together they raced across the school, coming to a stop near one of the arched halls that led to a small library. 'Here,' she said.

Johan looked at her and scratched his head. He hoped he hadn't lost his only chance of survival by following a crazy woman. 'This used to be a really small library. You think it's the room?'

She huffed. 'No, it's under here.' Adrienne was running her hands over the stone walls.

He blinked. 'Then how do we get to it?'

'It's near here, it has to be,' she muttered.

Suddenly, the ground started to tremble. Panic jolted through him. 'Hurry! What are we looking for?' Frantically, he began running his hands over the stone too, not that he knew what he was searching for.

Blue eyes flashed to him. 'What are you doing?'

'It's coming! We have to find the room now!'

XI

Leon threw the kid over his shoulder as he ran. He dodged down small streets that seemed to wind in all kinds of directions except the one he thought they needed to go in. He kept close to Felis, as she lived here, and he figured she'd know where to go. The pretty yellow-banded stone lined the buildings they passed, but as the tremors grew in strength, the stone began to grind ominously. Their footsteps and panting breaths seemed to echo in streets.

Leon rolled his shoulders, trying to get comfortable with the lad dangling there, but the boy was punching him.

'If you don't stop,' he growled, 'I will leave you here for the monster.'

The kid stopped.

Leon hadn't meant it, but the result was worth the threat.

Sweat was pouring down over him, but he had to keep going. Suddenly, they burst from the network of streets and they sprinted across an expanse of barren land, which terminated in a small lake. On the other side of the water stood wall-less buildings, their metal frames exposed to the sky.

Felis had drawn even with him. Faint tremors began to make his feet vibrate. Wildly, he looked at her. 'How much further?'

'It's those buildings.'

They made it to the edge of the lake. He set the kid on the ground and glanced up at her. 'How deep is the water?'

Felis wiped sweat from her face. 'Deep enough that we're gonna have to swim.'

The kid tugged on his pant leg. Leon looked down.

'I can't swim.'

Leon and Felis looked at each other.

'Why did I think he was going to say that?'

XII

Adrenaline surged through Adrienne.

It was coming.

The monster was almost here. The ground shook under her feet. Shutting her eyes for a moment, she concentrated on the suit. Only the suit.

Tell me what I need to know.

Images began to flash through her. Fast, then faster. Finally, they settled on a hand stretching outwards and pushing the wall just... there. Without thinking, she copied. The sound of grating stone hit her ears.

'By the skies,' the man beside her muttered.

Adrienne opened her eyes and looked at the wall in front of her – at the hole there.

He grabbed her arm, 'Let's go!'

Pulling her with him, they rushed down the dark hall. It terminated at a small, bronze-coloured door. 'Can we crawl through here?' she asked.

The man nodded and began tugging at the door. Sweat dripped off his brow. The floor was vibrating harder now.

'Here,' Adrienne said, shoving him aside. 'Like this.' She waved her wrist next to the door, and a light on her suit's arm glowed. There was a click and the door popped open.

'Quick,' he hissed.

Adrienne dropped to her knees and scrabbled through, the man following her. She squeezed into the small space and felt the door slam shut behind them.

Light suddenly blossomed.

'Are we safe?'

XIII

'Here,' Leon said, and balanced the kid – Billy, he'd said his name was – on his back.

Leon waded into the lake. Once the water hit his chest, he began awkwardly paddling through the murky, stagnant pool. Felis was already halfway across.

Suddenly, Billy's arms tightened around his neck. Leon gasped and nearly swallowed a mouthful of foul water. He grabbed Billy's arm and pulled it away from his throat as he coughed.

'What?' Leon hacked as he tread water.

The kid's face was as white as a sheet. 'The monster!'

Leon followed his gaze, and his own eyes widened as a huge rust-coloured tentacle soared into the sky before it slammed down on a massive building. There was a cracking sound, and the structure began to collapse.

Billy started struggling. 'We have to go and help Adrienne.'

'No.' Leon stared back at the university and bile surged into his mouth. He hoped Johan had found the room he was looking for.

'But–'

'We'd only die. We have to keep going.' Leon turned around in the water and kept swimming, dragging Billy along in his wake.

XIV

The walls shuddered nonstop and the sound of groaning metal echoed through the small room. Johan's teeth chattered with the room's vibrations. A bench ran along one side of the room, and it was covered in flickering buttons and screens.

Adrienne's face was smeared with dirt. 'What is this place?'

'You don't know?'

'No.'

He stared at her face. She wasn't very old, maybe 20 or so turns, but her eyes, they were aged. 'But how'd you...'

He'd read about people with 'special talents', but they'd been created by the government, and no one from that body had been near this planet for over 100 turns.

'You're a Psychic.' He couldn't believe it – even as Adrienne warily inched away from him – but it had to be true.

Her eyes widened. 'I'm a what?'

Excitement bubbled through him, even though the room was rattling like a child's toy. 'A Psychic; someone with special abilities.'

'It doesn't disgust you?'

'What can you do?' he asked, ignoring her question.

'If...' she swallowed, 'if I touch something, I can see or sense what people felt before.'

He nodded. 'Clairvoyance.'

She sat forward, but lost her balance with the room's movement. She fell into him. 'You know what it is?'

Johan steadied her. 'I've read about it.'

'So there are others like me?'

He ignored how her body felt pressed against his. 'I don't know.'

Johan looked around the room, at the panel in front of them. 'If you touch it, do you think you can get it started?'

Adrienne stared at him, then the flickering lights. 'I can try.'

Her fingers began flying over buttons and panels like they knew exactly what to do, but they were moving independently of her mind. Lights began to flash, and the whole room seemed to glow.

XV

Leon watched as the dried-blood tentacles faded into the distance, and felt the rumbles decrease. It must have decided they weren't worth pursuing. His heart was hammering, and sweat still poured down over his face and neck. Breathing through his mouth, he tried not to notice the stench of stagnant water that rose from his clothes.

But they'd made it. An now they stood in the hollow shell of a building, surrounded by discarded metal tracks piled high behind them. Leon watched the ruins of the city crumble to the ground. Not every building had fallen, but enough.

No matter that he was surrounded by metal, and that old train cars lay to his east and west like discarded toys, he still didn't feel safe. He didn't think he'd ever feel safe.

'It's gone?' Billy asked, voice small and trembly.

'For now,' Felis replied, her face a hard mask. She too was covered in muck, but she stood tall and proud, staring the city down.

Billy looked at Leon. 'Do you reckon they found the room?'

'I hope so,' Leon said. Otherwise, Johan and the woman were dead, and their hope of escape was lost with them.

XVI

'Did it work?' Johan asked. The metal in the walls started to screech as It moved through the earth.

'I don't know,' Adrienne replied. The ground's quakes slammed them into the ancient equipment. She reached out, arms shaking; forcing herself to try and counteract the shudders. Her fingers went back to dancing over the panels in front of her.

The room was still shaking as the monster travelled through the ground, too close for comfort, but suddenly an image flashed into brightness on the screen in the wall beside them.

Adrienne threw up a hand to shield her eyes from the glow. She blinked a few times, as her eyes adjusted to the light, but mostly in order to focus on the screen.

She frowned; sure there was something wrong with her eyesight. No, there really was a figure, still fuzzy and distorted, forming on the display.

She grabbed Johan's arm and pointed at the screen. 'Look!'

He did a double take. 'Is that what I think it is?'

'I have no idea,' Adrienne said.

The suit began throwing images her way, explanations. It was a communicator, the suit said, used to speak to people across long distances.

'It's a communications device,' Johan whispered.

'Hello?' The voice was strangely accented, but understandable.

Johan and Adrienne recoiled. The image was starting to crystallise.

'How did *you* know what it was?' she asked Johan.

'I'd read about them before, but I wouldn't know how to use one. How do you know?'

Adrienne waved a hand at the suit, her eyes still glued to the screen. She felt her jaw drop as the image became sharper; it looked like a woman, with *blue* hair, but the yellow eyes with slit pupils made it difficult to tell.

Adrienne shifted to the side as Johan moved closer to her. The heat from his body in the cramped space was strangely comforting. Or maybe it was the reduction in the shaking that was comforting.

'Hello?' the voice came again, and this time it was clear it was the blue-haired woman speaking.

Adrienne reached out to touch the screen but nodded to Johan to respond; he at least knew what the device *was*.

'Hello, this is Johan. Who are you?'

'I am Tamar, and this is Xhang.' The woman waved to a man standing behind her left shoulder.

Adrienne hadn't even noticed him as her eyes had been locked on the strange-looking woman. She wondered why she was surprised. She'd seen a giant tentacle monster *eat* people and demolish her town; why was someone with strange eyes and weird hair *so* different?

Tamar was seated in what looked like a metal room, with smooth panels and lots of lights flickering in the background. The man's looks were more common, though his skin was an olive colour, his hair jet black, and his eyes were shaped upwards at the corners. He was handsome enough, she guessed.

The man – Xhang – leaned close to the woman. 'The girl is wearing a Regulator's outfit.'

'I can see that,' Tamar replied.

'She's not a Regulator,' the man continued.

The blue-haired woman snorted. 'I gathered as much.'

'Are you members of the government?' Johan's fists were clenched.

The man on the screen straightened. He looked skinny, a little too skinny. Maybe they didn't have enough food, either.

'No.' The word was clipped.

Adrienne looked at Johan, who was frowning.

'Where are you from? How is it that we are talking?' Johan asked.

'We're associated with the Confederation of Equal Rights. And we intercepted your call for help.'

Adrienne didn't know what they were talking about.

Tamar leant forward. 'Basically, we're rebels. If the, uh, 'government' is for it, we're against it.'

Johan smiled, but it wasn't a nice expression. 'Since the government are the ones who left us here, we're not going to be picky with who saves us.'

'Saves you?'

'We have a problem here – with the, uh, native wildlife.' Johan said.

Adrienne had never even known what the monster was. At least he had some idea.

Tamar glanced away from the screen, which made Adrienne feel a little calmer. The woman just looked too strange. 'Everyone was reported dead.' She seemed to be reading something. 'Your 'native wildlife' was said to have become dangerous.'

'Clearly, we aren't dead,' Adrienne said dryly. 'But the *wildlife* is certainly dangerous.'

The tremors of Its passage finally died.

'So,' Johan leaned forward, 'Can you get us off this rock or what?'

XVII

Adrienne and Johan emerged from the small metal-walled room and into the purple sunlight. Thankfully, the tunnel had remained intact. They were both blinking, shaking, and in Johan's case, numb with surprise and shock. Johan turned in a slow circle, whistling as he took in the damage. Most of the buildings had been smashed to the ground, their pretty yellow stone now rubble scattered across the paths.

'The plant,' Adrienne said softly beside him.

The dead tree still stood, a symbol of their success, or perhaps their resilience. A few branches had broken. *Smash us down, but we'll find a way to stand tall.*

'Let's see if the others made it,' he said.

Adrienne nodded, and walked side-by-side with him as he headed towards the rail yards. Rather than traversing the once-winding streets, Johan picked his way over the ruins, deciding on a more direct route. His boots crunched on broken stone and glass, and he avoided the sharp spikes of metals protruding through the skeletons of the destroyed buildings.

The most beautiful part of their planet, wiped out in a fit of monstrous rage.

'Do you think they'll come?' Adrienne asked.

Johan kept walking. He didn't know what he thought. And so he said nothing.

Eventually they picked their hesitant way to the shores of the small stagnant lake. On the other side, he could see two figures hunched and seated on the piles of hot metal, warmed by the sun.

A shout echoed across the lake, and Billy jumped up and down on the spot. He waved wildly at them, and Adrienne raise her hand in response.

'Your kid?' Johan asked. Not that the boy looked anything like the white haired, blue eyed woman. But you never knew.

'No.' She was silent for a few moments. 'Unless he wants to be.'

Leon and Felis stood at the commotion, then began making their way slowly back across the lake. Johan was glad they were making the effort, the water stank.

Once the other three had reached the dry banks, Johan clapped a hand on Leon's shoulder, before nodding at Felis.

The boy was hopping up and down on the spot. 'What happened?'

Johan responded. 'We found a communications device.'

'Like in the records?' Felis asked.

Johan nodded.

'And?' Leon's blue eyes were intense.

'We made contact.'

'With who?'

Johan shrugged. 'Some confederation who are against the government. Either way, I don't care. As long as they come for us.'

'Will they?' That was from all three of their muck-covered companions.

Both Adrienne and Johan were silent. They then turned to look up into the sky, shading their eyes from the sun.

'We can only hope.'

MICHAEL PRYOR

Cross Purposes

FAR NORTH QUEENSLAND, 1935

As we pulled into Cooktown docks I steadied myself with one hand on the gunwale. In the other I had the Gladstone bag I'd barely salvaged from the New Guinea debacle.

Captain Alf threw his cigarette stub overboard. 'And you're sure you're not going back again?'

'I think I'll let things cool off for a while.'

He grunted. 'How long's that going to take?'

'Ten, fifteen years, should be enough.' I didn't wait for the gangway. I didn't even wait for the sole deckhand on the clapped-out steamer to tie up. I leaped onto the dock. The captain scowled at me, but I was used to it since I'd seen that expression all the way from Port Moresby. His navigation across the strait and down the coast hadn't been confidence-inspiring, either, but beggars can't be choosers.

I tipped my hat to him, to which he scowled again. 'You watch out, Hooke,' he said. 'I've been hearing dark things happening hereabouts.'

Since he'd repeated the same warning a dozen times before in about a dozen different places as we slipped down the coast, his dire words didn't have the impact he might have been looking for. Gloom merchant, he was.

'I'll be on the lookout,' I assured him, and I was off, grateful to be leaving a mess behind me.

Even though the wet was months away, the sky was heavy and the heat had the prickliness that made everything uncomfortable. I hefted my bag and set off toward the town proper, looking for a beer, a place to put my feet up, a good haircut and a moustache trim.

My bag was mostly empty as not even my pistol had survived my mad flight through the jungle. I would have hated to lose it, though. It held memories. It had been my dad's, and it was the only thing I took with me when I left home all those years ago. It had been full of cash back then, kept behind lock and key, and it had been the very deuce to steal.

I hadn't been in Cooktown before. I'd always passed it on the way north from Cairns, never stopping off. It was one of those gold mining towns that had seen better days. A handful of impressive buildings, mostly banks, faced the main strip, Charlotte Street, but mixed in with them were low and dilapidated shops. They gave the impression that cyclones wandered through regularly and rebuilding in between such visits was hardly worth the trouble.

It was just the sort of place I needed. After 15 years of lurching from one thing to another, of being stabbed in the back by untrustworthy partners, of coming close to making my pile only to lose it again and again, of barely squeaking out of the latest deal with my skin, I wanted a place to catch my breath. And to pick up a bit of Oscar – my rapid exit from Moresby had cleaned me out, good and proper.

Cooktown also looked like the sort of quiet and peaceful place where I could camp and make sense of the nightmare I'd stumbled on outside Moresby when making my exit from that hole of a town.

Captain Alf had recommended the Commercial Hotel, so I straightened my shirt, brushed off my trousers, made sure my hat was on firmly and headed for it, about a mile away, slightly uphill. Even though it was nearly midday, the street was deserted.

Then I froze, as I do when I hear rifle fire, especially when it's quickly followed by twin shotgun blasts.

Sleepy Cooktown had woken up.

I slipped behind a veranda post, the nearest cover, then ran to a gap between the post office and the next-door building, a provisioner of some kind or other. This was good timing, as the rifle cracked again – sounding far too much like a Lee Enfield for my comfort – and the shotgun answered it.

The window of the provisioner shattered.

I was starting to regret my choice of stopover. I'd had enough, lately, of being chased by people with firearms and long, sharp knives.

I was edging back towards the docks, hoping that Captain Alf had had a fit of energy and was ready to leave Cooktown immediately when a carpet bag landed at my feet. 'Look out!' a voice from above called, and I just had time to take a step back before a good-looking jane dropped from the roof of the post office and landed in front of me. 'Whoosh!' she said, panting and flushed. And armed. Definitely armed, as she jabbed her rifle at me. 'That was higher than I thought.'

'You're not hurt, are you?' I had my hands raised, but politeness cost nothing, as my gran used to say.

'A little shaken.' She peered around the corner while keeping the rifle trained on me. 'But otherwise I'm in tiptop shape.'

That was true enough. She was of medium height, and very trim. She wore a long navy blue skirt and a high-necked white blouse. She had a pith helmet tied over her sandy hair with a scarf knotted under her chin. If that wasn't eccentric enough, the crown of her helmet was wound with cord, which made it look like a half-finished beehive.

All in all, though, she was a little bit of eyes right, no mistaking.

Raised voices came from the street. She backed away, eyeing me carefully. I know what I look like – tallish, broad-shouldered enough to make most brawlers think twice before having a go, pencil moustache and dark hair always a touch too long – which meant I constantly had to flick it out of my eyes. She took all this in and frowned. 'I don't know you,' she said.

'I'm just passing through,' I replied, hating to put the kibosh on our time together.

'You have to help me,' she said. 'The townspeople want to kill me.'

Sleepy Cooktown? It looked as if I'd been misled. 'There must be some mistake.'

Another shotgun blast sounded and another window shattered. Before I could react, she whipped the rifle around the corner and fired a shot. 'It *is* a mistake,' she said when she fronted me again. 'But that's not going to stop them.'

'The police?' I asked. If it came to that, I was sure I could lose her before I came anywhere near the rozzers.

She rolled her eyes, which was a charming sight, really. 'If Shotgun Charlie doesn't get me, Sergeant Corkindale is next in line.'

'Look, I'm sure something can be worked out.'

She sighed. 'I have 50 pounds if you help me get out of here.'

I'd been looking for an opportunity to slip away from her, but this changed everything. Partly because an offer like that meant that she was likely to be on my side of the law and partly because 50 pounds was 50 pounds, which was the sort of stake I needed to set myself up again.

'I won't shoot anyone,' I said. 'Not for 100 pounds.'

'I'm the one with the rifle.' More angry shouting came from a building nearby. More than one voice, too. 'Now, pick up my bag, please. Yours, too.'

I hefted them and raised an eyebrow.

'That way,' she said, gesturing away from the street. 'Snip snap.'

Snip snap? I shook my head. Was I in the hands of a demented schoolteacher?

We pushed between mounds of empty fruit boxes, and we made our way out of the lane. Then we nipped across a road that needed plenty of repair, straight through another gap between buildings, always moving closer to the harbour.

We paused at a derelict building that might once have been a bakery. I was about to ask where we were heading next when a shotgun-bearing Chinaman trotted around the corner and ran right into us.

I threw my Gladstone bag, which made him stagger backwards in alarm, the shotgun crossed on his chest. Then I waded in, grabbed the barrel of the shottie and drove an uppercut at his chin.

He toppled. Burly as he was, he hit the wooden footpath hard enough to raise dust.

'Excellent!'

I cursed, whirled to find my rifle-bearing charmer beaming at me, then cursed some more. I hate punching. It hurts. 'What's so excellent?' I asked through gritted teeth. I retrieved my Gladstone bag and relieved the man of his shottie.

'That means you're definitely going to help me get out of here.'

I tucked my bag under my arm and worked my hand. I'd had worse. Painful, bruised, but nothing broken. 'And how d'you figure that?'

She gave me a pitying look. 'If we're apprehended, I'll tell them that you're my new accomplice come to spirit me away. When Shotgun Joe wakes up I'm sure he'll endorse this. You'll be in the clink alongside me, so you have no choice but to help me now.'

'A hundred pounds,' I growled. Mostly for show, really. She'd intrigued me enough that I probably would have gone with her out of curiosity.

'Done.'

I soon found out we were moving closer to the totally unexpected railway station, a two-storey wooden building. My knowledge of the layout of Cooktown was a little hazy. I knew it was a million miles from anywhere, which I'd thought a perfect criterion for my getaway, but I hadn't reckoned on it having a railway, which meant connections, which meant communication with the outside world, which was something I wasn't happy about.

She led me through the doors of the station in time to meet the stationmaster, who was coming out to see what all the fuss was about.

She bailed him against the wall.

He was a stout man, so magnificently moustached he made mine look puny. He had round glasses and a heavy railways blue serge uniform. His chin and his chest almost met and I wondered how he washed between them. He took a look at the rifle and after that it was as if this sort of thing happened every day. He raised his hands.

The rifle-wielding young woman straightened her hat with one hand, then pointed at the stationmaster. 'Your timetable would suggest that the motor is ready.'

The stationmaster nodded slowly. 'Just about to leave.'

'You'll kindly ask all your passengers to disembark.'

He snorted. 'No passengers today, miss. Just goods.'

'Tip top. And you are the customary engineer?'

He straightened his shoulders. 'Stationmaster, engineer, stoker and guard.'

'So no-one else is aboard, staff or customers?'

'Correct, miss.'

'Right.' She nodded at me and said, 'Use your shotgun, bring him out to the platform and keep an eye on him.'

This was one of those moments that occur in every enterprise. I could bail her up and hand her over to the authorities. Possible gain? Not much, most likely. Some thanks and maybe a beer or two. Possible loss? That was harder to judge, but it would definitely include the good will of an impressive young woman who was obviously on the wrong side of the law.

Why else would she offer a stranger 100 pounds to help her scarper like this? After all, I'd done the very same thing not long ago, with the greedy Captain Alf being the recipient of the last of my dosh. In fact her whole situation reminded me very much of one I'd just managed to get out of.

I won't say this young woman reminded me of me. And I won't say that she turned my head.

Some things don't need saying, after all.

So I shepherded the stationmaster out onto the platform. I eased around so I could keep an eye on him while I took in the train.

It wasn't what I'd been expecting. It looked like nothing more than an old London bus fitted for rails, with a skeleton of a goods tender linked behind. The motor was running, loudly.

She ordered me in, then she rounded the front of the unlikely vehicle. I kept the shottie on the stationmaster as I backed away.

The stationmaster still had his hands raised, but the shotgun didn't seem to faze him at all. I'd seen plenty of men like that in the war. NCOs. They'd be solid in the worst of barrages, then kicking arses the minute the shells stopped.

He nodded at me, then he peered past to my mysterious comrade. He tipped his cap. 'Sorry to hear about your brother, the reverend, miss.'

'Brother?' I repeated to her.

She was faced with a steering wheel and pedals, much as in a car or a lorry. Nothing else. No helpful dials or buttons. 'He was taken by a crocodile last night,' she said without looking up.

'You live an interesting life, don't you?'

'That's my aim,' she said. 'Hold on now, we're off.'

And, with a lurch, we were.

The engine roared and we rattled our way out of town. My new partner concentrated on making the clapped-out contraption go but I couldn't help wondering about this mysterious cliner. What was she doing in Cooktown? How had she learned to drive a motor rail? What was she planning? And, most importantly, 'Where are we going?' I shouted over the din.

She answered without taking her eyes off the narrow railway ahead. 'Laura. 60, 70 miles.'

'How long's this going to take?'

'If everything's ship shape, we'll be there in four hours.'

'So I could take a nap?'

This time, she glanced at me sidelong. 'You're a cool one, aren't you?'

'I like to conserve my energy whenever possible. I never know when I might need it.'

'So we shan't dilly-dally, then.'

'Laura.' I poked my head out the side and found the sun. 'That's not southwards, I take it.'

'We're heading into the back country.'

'Inland?' I blinked. 'There's nothing out there.'

'An overstatement, and the locals who've lived there for eons would take offence, let alone the gold miners; but the lack of sizeable populations is part of the attraction at the moment. Is anyone following us?'

I turned, slinging an arm along the back of the bench seat. 'Not that I can see. Is it likely?'

'It depends on how long it will take them to repair the other engine.'

'You sabotaged it?'

'Last night. A precaution.'

So she was a planner as well as a dab hand with a rifle. That was encouraging. I might actually have a chance of getting the money she promised. I could then tag along until we were somewhere near civilisation. With some money again, I'd be on my way.

We were cutting through heavily wooded forest that crowded the line on either side. Bracken covered the ground. 'And last night was when you checked out this contraption?'

'I made myself as familiar with it as I could without starting it.'

I stuck my elbow out of the window, then I dangled my hand out. The breeze was welcome and helped ease the throbbing in my knuckles. 'I'm sorry to hear about your brother, the reverend.'

'Hah.'

That wasn't the reaction I was expecting. 'He wasn't your favourite brother?'

'He wasn't my brother. And he wasn't a reverend. He was a total bastard who stole a boat and scarpered last night with most of the cash we'd stung from the chums hereabout.'

Hearing this possibility of a kindred spirit, I felt like the man with an unexpected parcel, one that could either be a delight or a bomb.

'At least it's a nice day for it,' I said.

'Make the most of it,' she said and didn't say anything more. She just drove like a maniac.

An hour or so and 20 or so bridges later, we pulled up. She left the engine running. 'Do you want to stretch your legs?'

Outside, the greenery was as thick as it had ever been. A parrot screeched nearby. I think it was chiacking us. 'How do I know that you won't leave me here?'

She considered this. 'That's a thought. You are a burden, you know.'

'That's what Flynn said, but what would he know?'

'Flynn?'

'My ex-partner, years ago. After one fiasco too many, I dumped him and he went to America and got into films.'

'Films?' She stared at me. 'You're saying that you know Errol Flynn?'

I shrugged. 'We knocked around the South Seas together for a while. New Guinea, New Caledonia, the Solomons. He wasn't much good with money, but he could sail.'

'Captain Blood! I should say so.' She narrowed her eyes. 'I don't believe you.'

'I'm hurt. Someone with a false cleric brother who wasn't eaten by a crocodile doubts my truthfulness.'

'I wish he *had* been eaten by a crocodile.' She flung open the door, climbed down and stalked off along the rail line.

'You forgot your rifle,' I called after her.

I hadn't even told her about how Flynn had pinched the idea of a pencil moustache from me.

She was gone for a good 20 minutes. When she came back, I had a fire going, and, using a billy and supplies from the small tender, I was sitting on the doorstep, brewing tea and eating tinned peaches with my fingers.

'Sorry, no milk for the tea,' I said as she approached. 'And only one mug.'

She crossed her arms. 'It was a tiptop little swindle,' she said. 'We'd been in Cooktown nearly a month and we'd put together nearly a hundred pounds.'

I tapped the billy with a stick. Nearly there. 'A missionary society? Bible distribution association?'

'The Outback Church and Hospital Foundation.'

'Ah. Coming at the punters from two directions. Nice.'

She gave me a sharp look at that. 'It was my idea but Bill had to front it, being a man and all that.' The last she added with a twist of her mouth. 'We were getting set to wind up when the locals twigged to our scheme. He dumped me and bolted.'

'And the locals came after you?'

'One wild Chinese in particular, as you saw. Things got rather out of hand after that.'

'Which is where I walked in. Ten minutes in town and I get shot at, attacked, shanghaied and seduced.'

If I were less robust, I would have been withered on the spot by the look she planted on me. 'You have a vivid imagination.'

'Keeps me warm at nights.'

Was that snort almost a wicked laugh? I had no time to ask, as she crossed her arms and changed the subject. 'You must have come in on the Port Moresby boat.'

'This morning, looking for somewhere quiet.'

She frowned. A single, tiny line creased her brow. 'You didn't hear about anything unusual up there?'

My grip on the stick tightened. 'Unusual? How?'

'I don't know. Some of the Cooktowners were mumbling about things coming down from up north, nasty stuff.'

The sweat on the back of my neck was cold as memory went to work. 'Pub stories, eh?'

'After church tea-and-scones gossip,' she corrected, and the moment passed.

I found another stick and used both to tip the billy into the enamel mug. 'After you.'

She sipped the tea while I tended the fire and helped myself to peach syrup from the tin. Eventually, she nodded. 'Snip snap. We should be off. It'll take them ages to get out here if they have to go overland, but we shouldn't dawdle.'

'Finish your tea.' I tossed her the tin opener I'd found. 'And have some peaches.'

She stooped and picked up one of the tins I'd gathered. She had one open in an instant.

'So what's at Laura?' I asked.

'Old Tom. He's my backstop, one that Bill didn't know about.'

'You're not very trusting.'

'In my line of business, it pays not to be.' She ate a peach slice. 'Besides, I hadn't known Bill long. He was what I needed for this racket, that's all.' She finished her tea and tossed the mug to me. 'What can I say? I misjudged him.'

I poured myself some tea. 'You often misjudge people?'

'No,' she said. 'And I get even with those that I do. When Old Tom gets me out of this godforsaken part of the world, I'll find out where Bill is and I'll have a word with him.'

Right then, I felt just the slightest bit sorry for Bill.

She tossed the empty peach tin into the fire, dusted her hands together and made to move off. 'What's your name?' I asked.

She adjusted her hat, and didn't look at me. 'Why do you want to know?'

'I like to know the name of anyone who owes me a hundred pounds.'

She smiled a little at that, but it was a guarded smile, one that spoke of past hurts. 'I suppose you would. You can call me Miss Danvers.'

'And it's actually your name?'

'It could be. And you?'

'Roland Hooke, and that's on the square.'

'Very well, Roland Hooke, one-time friend of Errol Flynn, shall we go?'

I kicked dirt over the fire, then we climbed back into the rattletrap and headed off. I settled back, as much as I could with the shuddering, the swaying, and the general complaining of the engine, and pretended to sleep.

The journey took longer than expected, of course. The engine had trouble with inclines of any kind, for a start. I got off and walked alongside, occasionally, to ease the load. When I did, I tended to outpace it. We crossed more bridges, the creeks and rivers mostly dry. The heat was brutal, the air still, and I was a lather of sweat.

Laura Station was a shed about the size of a bus shelter. A single figure was waiting for us. My Miss Danvers waved. 'Old Tom!'

He was short and wiry, and had probably had a bath sometime in the last year or so. His silver beard was chest-length and so thick he could have shorn it off and used it as a doormat. He wore a hat with a wide, turned-up brim, a red flannel shirt, a leather waistcoat, and trousers held up with string. His face was so weather beaten that he could have been any race or a blend of dozens, but his eyes were sharp. He was probably a couple of hundred years old, but when he caught sight of the motor, he grinned and waved.

Miss Danvers brought the motor rail to a halt. The engine died with a cough of gratitude. She flung her carpet bag out of the cabin, and then herself. She embraced the gnome-like Old Tom, laughing.

He chuckled and thumped her back. 'I've come out every time I heard the train coming,' he wheezed. 'And this time it's you, Miss Tessa, at last. Things no good with Bill?'

She pushed herself back from the embrace. 'He ran.'

Old Tom frowned. 'Take the money?'

'Most of it,' she said. 'I kept a reserve though.'

'Course you did.' He chuckled. 'So you had to slide out of Cooktown, then?'

'After Bill set it up to look as if he'd been eaten by a crocodile.'

'Huh. That's cleverer than I would have thought of him.' He squinted at her. 'You were left holding the bag.'

'A bag with not much in it.' She nodded at me. 'He came along for the ride.'

Old Tom eyed me. 'You have any say in it, young fella?'

'Not much.' I stuck out a hand. 'Roland Hooke.'

We shook. 'She has a way about her,' he said.

'So I'm starting to learn.' I looked around. Laura made Cooktown look like a metropolis. 'Nice though it's been, this is the end of the road for me. Since I've helped you out of Cooktown, you can hand over that hundred pounds, Miss Danvers. Time for me to be off.'

They shared a look. 'Of course,' she said, but she made no move toward the carpet bag at her feet. 'So, where are you off to?'

That was the point, of course. Could I head back to Cooktown and convince the locals there that I had nothing to do with this wild woman? Not likely, not after having held a shotgun on the stationmaster. And if Shotgun Charlie didn't come after me, I was sure he'd be happy to point me out to the rozzers.

So, Cooktown was out, and I was in the middle of nowhere. Sticking with Old Tom and this Danvers girl was the only option, really. And she was a damned attractive thing, after all, but that had nothing to do with it.

'Look,' I answered. 'I'm enjoying your company so much, I thought I might string along with you for a while.'

She was stifling a smile, I could see that. 'Since you're sure I have a plan for getting safely out of here.'

'All your preparations so far would point that way. I mean, Bill's not here, and you can't have your word with him until you find him.'

Old Tom cleared his throat. It sounded as if a boulder or two was in the way, but he finally managed it. 'He might come in handy, Miss Tessa, with what's been going on round here.'

'Now, that sounds ominous,' she said.

He nodded, his face grim. 'Everyone here's gone.'

'Gone?' The tiny frown was back. It fascinated me how one small line could work so hard.

'They all left last night,' Old Tom said. 'When I got up this morning, the pub was empty, the station too. No one in any of the houses. From the looks of it, they've all taken the road south to Maytown.'

I gazed around at the tiny settlement. It was depressing, and not a little disturbing. A single dusty road, a quarter of a mile or so, ran alongside the station then decided to become a track before giving up, turning into a junior footpath and disappearing into the scrubby bush to the north. South, it ran through the tired cluster of buildings, mostly corrugated iron and re-used timber, before ambling southwards with some effort at being an actual road.

'They all had an urgent appointment?' I wondered aloud. 'Sunday School picnic?'

Old Tom shook his head, spat on the ground, then shook his head some more. 'Nope. They ran because they didn't want to be murdered in their beds.'

We didn't have to break into the pub. It had been left unlocked – as had every building in the settlement. Drawers and wardrobes were still open. Doors and windows, too. When I poked my head into one lean-to, I saw an unfinished meal still on the table. Corned beef.

Old Tom was a fair barman even though the beer was warm.

I tipped my glass to Old Tom and to Tessa. 'Here's to a mystery.'

'Tell us what happened,' Tessa said to Old Tom.

Old Tom snorted. 'A party of old timers came into town from the back country yesterday, getting on to evening. They shared their story and then they took off.'

'Must have been a good story,' I suggested.

'Not many details, just stuff about murderous strangers on the rampage. They believed it, though, and the locals here did too.' Old Tom clicked his tongue. 'We don't want to stay here any longer than we have to.'

'You believe the stories?' I asked.

He considered this while he drank half his beer. 'They said these strangers came from up north, over the sea,' he said finally. 'Some bad stuff comes down from up there.'

I didn't like the sound of that, but Tessa was more interested in what had happened in Laura.

'And the townspeople went southwards?' she asked.

'Mostly,' Old Tom said. 'Some followed the rail tracks. Some headed east.'

Tessa and I looked at each other. 'We didn't see anyone,' she said.

Old Tom grimaced at that.

'No one went west?' I wondered aloud.

'The old timers weren't going back that way.' He studied his empty glass. 'Not after what they saw, they said.'

I tried to remember what lay westwards. I hadn't been planning on coming this way, so my knowledge was hazy. Far enough, of course, and you hit the other side of Cape York and the Gulf of Carpentaria. Between there and here? Wilderness country? Rivers, creeks, gorges? Termite mounds by the thousands?

Tessa clasped her hands and rested them on the table in front of her. 'Fascinating, all this, but you have our escape route all mapped out? The quicker, the better.'

'You think you can catch up with that Bill fella?' Old Tom pushed back his hat and scratched his forehead. The line between what lay below the brim and above it was stark.

'Well, our best bet's to head south to Maytown, cross the Palmer River, then through the back country to Mount Mulgrave, and then to Cairns via inland. It'll take us a few weeks. Maybe a month.'

Tessa pursed her lips. 'Can we shave some time from that?'

'Well,' Old Tom said. 'We can push it, but there's some tough country ahead.'

'Let me see the map.'

They put their heads together and started to pick apart this plan. I wandered out the back of the pub, thanks to a call of nature, and found the horses.

The stable was more ramshackle than the pub, which meant it was on the verge of falling down. It was dim, and dusty with the nose-tickling smell of animals. Tethered inside were four Walers.

They eyed me, but they didn't panic. I approached the nearest, shoosh-shushing as I came. I stroked her mane, roughed it up. She liked it, and the smell took me back. I was 16-year-old Roland Hooke again, pretending he was 19, with all the other men and Walers at Beershcba, sctting up camp.

That's where I wanted the memory to end, but memory is tricky. Bad memories don't stay buried, and they front up when least expected – and usually when least wanted.

Some time later, still hurting after that rush of recollection, I checked their feed and their water. I was inspecting their hooves when Tessa found me.

'We're leaving tomorrow.' She stood with her fists on her hips, a black paper cut-out against the last of the daylight. 'Do you still want to come with us?'

I straightened and slapped my hands together. 'I'm guessing it's the most likely way of getting the money you owe me.'

'I see.' Her voice was level. I wished I could see her expression. 'It's the money you're interested in.'

I laughed. 'I'm thinking it's a shared interest.'

'I don't know what you mean.'

'Look.' I wiped my hands on my trousers. 'All I'll say is that it takes one to know one, right?'

She took this in silence for a while. 'What exactly were you up to in Port Moresby?'

'Oh, a little bit of this and that.' And barely escaping a nightmare, but I wasn't going to tell her that.

'Did you make any money?'

'None that I managed to keep.'

'Oh.'

I shrugged. 'Not the first time, not the last time.'

'I don't have your hundred pounds,' she announced suddenly.

I leaned against a post and crossed my arms. 'Now, there's a surprise.'

'Not with me,' she added quickly. 'But I do have plenty in my bank account. When we get somewhere decent I'll make a withdrawal. You'll get what I promised.'

Briefly, I wondered what name that bank account would be in. 'I'm supposed to trust you?'

'That's up to you.'

'And why should I?'

'Because I seem to be better at this than you are.'

'Eh?'

'This is the first scheme I've walked out of with no result. My funds are very healthy, and my back-up plans work. We'll be safely out of here soon.'

'You've convinced me,' I said. 'So, since we're going to be spending more time together, why don't we get to know each other a little better?'

'I think I know enough to suit me for the time being.'

'I'm deeper than I look.'

'Good Lord. I hope so.' She sighed. 'Tonight, I'll be planning our route, making sure we have enough supplies, and trying not to be murdered in my bed.'

'You think there's something in that story?'

'I'm half-wondering if it's got anything to do with the stories that were circulating in Cooktown.'

'About dark deeds up country?'

'About danger that's come from far up north.' She flapped a hand. Flies. 'On another matter, you never did tell me what spooked you in Port Moresby.'

'Me? Spooked? I never said anything about being spooked.'

'You didn't have to. Any time Port Moresby or New Guinea is mentioned, you go all tense. Something awful happened up there.'

This was getting too close to the bone. 'Apart from losing all my hard-earned?'

'You yourself said that had happened many times before. It wouldn't have affected you in the same way this has, whatever this is.'

'It's nothing,' I said. 'Nothing to worry about.'

'And so you wouldn't think there could be a connection between what's happened here and what you saw?'

That rocked me. 'I didn't see anything.'

'If you say so. I'm still sleeping with my rifle by my bed and my revolver under my pillow.'

I tried to rally. 'I tell you what. I'll keep guard outside your door tonight.'

'I'll be fine.'

'It's no trouble.'

'Get some sleep. We have a long way to go tomorrow.'

Gunshots woke me. This had happened to me more than once, years ago, so before I was properly awake I'd rolled out of bed, slithered to the door and stood, heart pounding, with my back against the wall.

Shotgun. I'd left it under the bed. I dived for it, and came up at the door. I listened hard, trying to make out what was going on – that was when I smelled smoke.

I pulled my boots on, grabbed my trusty Gladstone bag, and banged the door back. The corridor was filling with smoke.

Tessa's door was open. I staggered forward as two more shots sounded. A figure lurched out of the doorway. Without thinking, I swung the shotgun in a terrific round-arm. I collected him on the side of the head and he dropped like a sack of spuds.

My eyes were streaming, thanks to the smoke, but I recoiled at what I saw. Stretched out on the floor, he was lanky and frighteningly gaunt. His ribs stood out like railway sleepers. He was only wearing a loin-cloth, and in the red flickering light of the fire, the blood from three bullet holes in his chest was black.

I hadn't really wanted to see his like again, but here it was, and my heart hammered like a traction engine at the sight.

Flame belched from the doorway. 'Tessa!'

She appeared, wearing a slip and boots, a cracker of a combination in normal circumstances, but I didn't have time to dwell on it. She also had a Webley revolver in her hand, which was less pretty, but very practical. 'There's one more on the floor in there,' she said, gesturing behind her. 'Let's grab Old Tom and get out of here.'

Tessa darted back into her room. I stumbled to Old Tom's room, coughing, tears in my eyes. I banged on the door. 'Tom!'

When he didn't answer, I cursed and kicked the door open.

He wasn't there, but blood on the sheets and on the windowsill gave some indication of his fate.

I staggered to the door. 'He's gone!' I shouted at the wild-haired Tessa who was emerging from her doorway.

She'd thrown on a dress and, in the middle of all the tumult, she'd taken the time to tie her hat onto her head. She had her Webley in one hand, her carpet bag in the other and her rifle under her arm. 'The horses!'

We burst through the door that led to the bar. One end was fully on fire. Tessa grabbed my shoulder and hauled me around. Together we hurried through the only safe exit, coughing and hacking.

The horses were upset, but not panicking – good Waler stock. I dumped my bag, gave my shotgun to Tessa, and untethered them. Tessa was alert, combing the darkness with her revolver at the ready as I led the horses away from the fire.

We ended up at the station, blackened and jumpy. The fire made a royal mess of the pub. A stand of tired gums nearby had caught and added to the flames.

'Must be others out there somewhere,' I said. 'The ones who took Old Tom.'

'I hope so.' A click and a whir. I turned to see that Tessa was checking her revolver. She looked up. 'I'm going after him.'

When dawn brought enough light we set off.

She was going whether I came or not, that was clear. I found that I wanted to help. Even on my short acquaintance, I'd decided that the old fellow wasn't a bad sort.

I could have cut out. I could have waved goodbye to the hundred pounds and then found my own way south.

I kicked this around as the horses picked their way through the scrubby countryside west of Laura. Maybe it was lure of doing something selfless. If I'd been braced with this only a few months ago I would have laughed and ordered another drink.

Since the war, I'd spent my time knocking around north Australia and the Pacific, looking to make my fortune fast. I'd given enough of myself in Palestine, now it was my turn to get a little back.

At least, that's what I told myself.

Dodgy schemes, shady operations, get-rich-quick shenanigans, that's what I'd spent more than a decade on. The result? No friends, no family and definitely no fortune. And, in the end, no satisfaction.

When I looked at it square on, I had to admit that a fair part of the Port Moresby failure had been my fault. I'd been sloppy, I hadn't planned properly. I'd been lazy and I'd nearly paid the price.

Taking my clever route out of Port Moresby, I'd stumbled on the grey people identical to the ones we'd left behind in the blazing pub – the ones who'd taken Old Tom.

We rode on. I wanted to go after the grey people, not just to help Tessa, even though that had become surprisingly important. And not just for Old

Tom, even though I liked the old swell. I think it was because after everything – the war, my aimless years, New Guinea – I'd had enough of horror. If I could do something to scrub it out, I'd be happy.

Finally I thought I'd better tell Tessa what we were up against. I clicked my tongue. Jocko – I'd named him after the horse I had to leave in Palestine – sauntered up alongside her. 'These grey people,' I announced, 'the ones we're tracking. I've seen them before.'

She nodded, unsurprised. 'In New Guinea.'

'Right.'

I told her all about it.

After my creditors came for me, I'd slipped out of the back of the warehouse I'd rented, the one that was meant to be full of the copra my investors had thought I'd bought. I followed a nameless creek, one of the New Guinea torrents. It was going to get me to the coast so I could avoid the town and find the fishing village where Captain Alf was waiting with my trusty Gladstone bag and passage south. Nice idea, it was, but the creek turned into a swamp and then it all went bad.

The grey people came out of the jungle at me. I didn't have time to use my revolver, even though they didn't use weapons and had no real idea of how to handle themselves in a stoush. They just used the weight of numbers. They didn't speak, either, no matter how much I weighed into them. They pressed in until I was surrounded and crushed into submission.

They were nearly naked, only clad in ragged and stinking loincloths. They were bald, men and women both, and didn't have a hair on their bodies. Their skin was a repulsive grey colour. It was the colour of sickness, of week-old dead things uncovered in the bottom of a trench.

They dragged me for miles through the jungle until we came to some caves. After that, it was an underground journey accompanied by the sounds of agonised screams that got louder as we went. Finally I was brought to the chamber with the stakes – the stakes and the remains of those who'd gone before me. The closest stake held something that had once been human, if I looked hard enough – something I didn't really want to do.

He, or she, was the source of the screaming. As I was hauled into the torchlight surrounding the stakes, a hugely tall figure strode to the screamer and finally the noise ceased.

It hit me. Sacrifices. That's what the stakes were for, and I didn't like the looks of the vacant one waiting for me. And I didn't like the looks of the scores of grey people, who stared at me with no interest at all. It was as if they were wide-eyed dolls, untouched by the horror they were participating in. No humanity there. They'd lost it, or sold it, or had it removed.

The scene was one out of hell, but I'd been in that neighbourhood before. Even when the torchlight flared and revealed the awful figures painted on the far-away ceiling, I was looking for a way out.

Then the earthquake came, a nice New Guinea buster. I made the most of it. I escaped and found my way to the fishing village and Captain Alf, still shivering at the horror and more determined than ever to get out of the country.

'So,' I finished, 'seeing these blighters here, in Australia, is making me a little edgy.'

'Thanks for the explanation.'

'And I didn't really want to see you setting off after them alone.' I took my hat off and pushed my hair back. It was getting long. 'Not after what I'd seen.'

'I'm glad of your help, but I wasn't going to leave Old Tom.'

'Uh huh. What's he to you?'

'He helped raise me after my parents died,' she said stiffly.

'Ah.' Time to change the subject. 'Flynn didn't like me, you know.'

She looked at me sidelong. She rode well. A first-class seat. 'I can't understand why.'

'He said he had no luck with women when I was around.'

'You scared them off?'

'That's not what he meant – never mind.'

The grey people had made no effort to cover their tracks and were easy to follow. From the trampling of vegetation, they were more numerous than I'd thought.

The country was dry and lightly wooded with wiry, thin undergrowth. It was occasionally interrupted by gullies that would no doubt be torrents in the wet season. Each gully was a pain, but, to judge from their tracks, the grey people had simply thrown themselves down one side and dragged themselves up the other, to judge from their tracks.

This particular gully was larger than most, but by this time – middle afternoon – we'd been lulled by the repetitive nature of any distance ride. We didn't even speak as we approached. Tessa took the lead and found a way down. I nudged Jocko to follow, even though he balked a little at first. A mistake, that. He wasn't a nervous nag. I should have paid attention.

The grey people had pressed themselves against the near walls of the gully, under a long, ragged overhang. When we were down, Tessa barely had time to cry 'Look out!' then they swarmed over us.

Tessa swore and got off two shots, but after that we were overwhelmed, dragged off our horses, beaten and bound. My wrists were savagely tied behind my back. I was sure I was bleeding, but I tested the ropes anyway to find no give at all. Lunatics they might be, but they knew a thing or two about knots.

Close-up, I had no doubt that these grey horrors were cousins, at least, of the ones I'd run into in New Guinea. Their sick grey skin was the same, as was the way they took us in absolute silence. If that wasn't enough, their faces were entirely devoid of expression. Their eyes were dull and flat, but this didn't stop the efficiency with which they worked.

Once we'd been roped and bound, we were drawn upright. A tall bounder with a boko so sharp you could use it to open tins studied me for a moment or two then slapped me hard enough to make my ears ring. Then he did it again for good measure.

Despite my struggles, he did the same to Tessa. I cheered when she spat in his face afterwards.

Then Old Tom was dragged up. His hands were tied behind his back, just as ours were, and we were tied to a rope together. Old Tom cackled when he saw us, got a good slapping, then he cackled again. He had a black eye and a ragged gash near an ear. 'Good to see youse,' he said. 'Got a ciggie?'

We'd found him, at least, and he wasn't dead. Of course, we were also captives, but taking the bad with the good was something I learned a long time ago.

Tessa was pale-faced, furious and barely controlling herself. She fumbled with the bindings around her wrists before giving up with a deep-throated growl. 'My hat,' she asked me unexpectedly. 'It's secure?'

I hadn't thought she was one of those women who fussed about appearance. I shrugged as best I could with my hands tied behind my back. 'Looks fine to me.'

'Good.'

We were forced into a trot to keep up. As we hurried along, I tried to count their numbers and came up with somewhere between 40 and 50, all shapes and sizes, both men and women.

I shuddered whenever I looked at them.

They moved as a mass, ignoring the landscape. If we stumbled, we were dragged. After an hour, my head pounded, and I was seeing flashes of red with each breath. The air burned as I sucked it in, but there was never enough of it to satisfy. Every muscle in my body ached, every joint felt as if it had been worked over with mallets.

Finally, we were led into a deep gully. Underfoot was an ankle-testing mess of sand, gravel and rock. Tree debris, too. The banks were well above head height, but I caught enough glimpses of the sun to work out that we were heading roughly north.

My mouth was thick with thirst. Somewhere in the struggle way back when we were taken, I'd lost my hat. Sweat stung my eyes. Tessa was close by, hands bound behind her back, her face set. I caught her eye and winked. She gave me a look of frustration in return.

It must have been mid-afternoon when the terrain changed. It began to slope upward, slowly. We pressed on, labouring with every step, pushed from behind when we stumbled. Rocks began to give way to boulders until we finally reached a small, ragged hill.

We didn't slow down. The grey people herded us between the boulders and forced us to climb. Sweating, panting, I saw one lose her footing and fall. She fell without a sound, bouncing a few times before vanishing.

As she fell, one of her comrades glanced in her direction. It was the most animation I'd seen, even though his face was blank. Then he kicked off and toppled over in an identical fashion, arms flailing.

While we were shoved upwards, a third followed, then a fourth. After that it was as if they'd lost interest.

Soon, we reached the summit where we found a giant split boulder. While the remaining grey people assembled there, heads close, bumbling in a chillingly idiotic manner, I was able to have a good dekko at the countryside.

In all directions, in between the sparse tree cover were dozens of ragged pillars, 10 or 15 feet tall, looking as if they'd only recently clawed their way out of the earth. The trees around the rock pillars were all dying. Leaves were spotty and yellow, or fallen completely. The Stringybarks were already turning grey and sickly, the casuarinas had shed their needles.

I tried to catch Tessa's eye, but we were yanked toward the fissure in the giant boulder. A cold breeze came from it that made my flesh crawl, and not just because it stank.

It smelled like the underground sacrificial chamber in New Guinea.

Inside the fissure was a rough shaft, four or five yards across. The stomach-turning breeze rose from it. Straight away, my heart kicked the inside of my ribs. A flame erupted as the first torch was struck by the grey people.

Tessa was more disgruntled than afraid, and I could see she was still working on her wrist bonds, without much success. Old Tom was as relaxed as a man with his hands tied behind his back could be. I hoped that I was presenting half as well as them.

I hadn't noticed the ramp until the first of our captors toppled into the shaft. The ramp winding down the side of the shaft was roughly made of stones thrown together, but as we were driven downwards, I was relieved to find it was better built than it looked.

As well as the nose-stinging stink, sounds rose from the depths. They made the hair rise on the back of my head. Chanting, I suppose you'd call it. Horrible stuff. It was as if someone had blended all the worst sounds a person could make. Shrieks, moans, wordless bellows all thrown together in a mess that seemed designed to put the wind up a man.

I had to work hard not to let it.

Finally, after we'd well and truly left the sunlit world behind, the ramp gave out into a sprawling many-pillared chamber lit by dozens of torches that bobbed around like mad glow worms. I had to stoop, as the chamber's ceiling was low. This didn't slow the grey people who were herding us along, though. Most shuffled bent over, but some actually dropped to all fours and scuttled like cockroaches.

I wasn't falling into a funk, but it wasn't easy. I couldn't see a way out, not unless another earthquake happened our way. I turned to Tessa, but at that minute we plunged into water.

It was only knee deep, but I'd been unprepared so I came a gutzer. With my hands bound behind me, I hit the water hard. It was so icy that it made me gasp, which was a bad idea with my head half under the water. I copped a mouthful of foul stuff that sent me reeling, coughing and hacking, spitting with all my might to try to clear the godawful taste from my mouth.

I was dragged to my feet, heaving and choking, then pushed forward again toward the source of the chanting. Ahead, the movement of the torches had stopped. A congregation of them flickered like sick stars.

Then I felt something under the water.

It touched my thigh, lightly, then moved on.

I jumped and the grey person right behind me whacked me on the back of the neck for my troubles.

Then it was back. This time, the touch was more of a nudge, with some force. I couldn't help thinking of a python. My flesh rippled as I waded on, expecting it to come back at any minute.

A few yards to my right, Tessa hissed through clenched teeth. Her hat was slightly askew, and her glaring at the water made me think she'd had an encounter with whatever it was, too.

The water became shallower. Soon, we were approaching a stone rise.

We climbed, dripping and shivering, onto a sloping stone island that was already occupied by more of the grey people. It was roughly circular, about 50 yards from one side to the other. Hundreds of them were standing shoulder to shoulder, shuffling about, staring vacantly at the half dozen stakes at the uppermost point of the island, the stakes I'd been dreading to see.

I found that familiarity didn't breed contempt. It bred a slow-burning fury.

On the far side of the island, more torches were approaching, carried by grey people paddling odd-shaped canoes, a sign perhaps that the water on that side was deeper.

We were pushed forward, through the dull-eyed chanters, toward the stakes. They each had two flaming torches affixed to them at about shoulder height, and they were arranged in a semi-circle around a black hole a few yards across. The awful stink came from that pit and I was willing to bet it was bottomless, more or less.

Overhead, the roof of the cave had vanished. A vast space soared upwards, a rough, natural dome full of shadows thrown by the shaky light from below.

At the top of the island we were maybe 20 feet above the surface of the lake. Tessa was on my right, Old Tom on my left, and we each had guards close behind us. They pushed us over until we were far too close to the stakes for my liking.

A grey man strode out of the crowd on the far side of the stakes. He was very tall, closer to seven feet than six, and he was totally bald, but it was chalk and cheese comparing him with the chanters.

This man's skin was grey, but it wasn't an unhealthy grey – it shone as if he were oiled. His face was animated, not dull, as he grinned and rolled his eyes. When his eyes came back to themselves, I saw that they were black and they gave him a gaze that was so intense that I actually staggered back half a step when he clapped it on me.

Taking us in, he grinned again, showing perfect gnashers. He lifted one arm and waved, slowly, an immense semi-circle that set the crowd of grey people moaning.

Overhead, torchlight sprang up. The illumination caught my gaze and dragged it upward. On ledges, high overhead, were scattered dozens of torch-holding figures, more of the grey drones. Their combined efforts lit the roof with a shaky, feeble light, but it was enough to make me swear under my breath.

The roof had been smoothed, more or less, which showed how nerveless these grey people were, working up so high. The highest point must have been 80 feet or more overhead. Something had been painted there, and that was what hit me like a punch to the throat.

A huge and monstrous figure looked as if it was falling on us, claws outstretched. It was hard to make out, but the painting assaulted me like a storm. Was that a cuttlefish head, a body like a dragon with vast scaly wings? It was hideous.

The image was vast and done with some skill; enough, anyway, to make me close my eyes and turn away from it, choking. But the appalling sight was still with me, as if it were painted on the inside of my eyelids.

It was the essence of nightmares. It was a horror from the dawn of time. It stalked the edges of sanity.

I hissed, shaking my head. I refused to give in to it. I might be many things, but impressionable wasn't one of them.

It took some effort, but I straightened, narrowed my eyes and glared at it. 'Get one right up you,' I growled, 'you hairy dog'.

I was clouted over the back of the head by my guard. For talking in church, I suppose, but I didn't really mind. I was feeling easier.

I caught Tessa's eye and she grinned a little. Old Tom wasn't bearing up well, but he nodded gratefully at my defiance.

Tessa, Old Tom and I were hustled closer to the stakes and the pit in front of them. The tall grey man stood to one side, his eyes glittering in the torchlight. He clapped his hands together and a stone knife appeared between them. He held it in one hand and extended it over his head.

The grey people roared. Without changing expression, they opened their mouths and roared.

It was a chorus of the damned.

I was manhandled again, eased around the edge of the pit, coming up short of one of the stakes. I had to lean back to stop the nearest torch from scorching me, but my guards didn't seem to care. Two of the maggots held me while another fumbled at the bindings around my wrists. The scum then stood back while I shook my hands, grimacing as circulation inched its way back into my hands.

As soon as Tessa was free and brought up to the next stake, she rubbed her wrists and said, 'Thank goodness. That was abominable.'

And she took off her hat and fanned herself with it.

I was amazed that the hat had survived, and then marvelled again at her coolness.

'Look, I'm curious,' I said. 'You wouldn't have an idea how to wangle our way out of here, would you?'

She looked around, frowning at the nearness of the torches. 'Perhaps.'

She stopped fanning and held her hat to her chest and nodded at Old Tom. 'It's enough to say I've just about had my fill of this.'

On the other side of her, Old Tom coughed, then chortled. 'Get ready, sonny jim.'

With a smooth gesture, Tessa flung her hat high into the air. I knew a three-card trick when I saw one, though, and after a quick glance at the soaring headgear, I dropped my gaze to her. She grinned at me and held up two grey sausages with a short fuses protruding from each end.

I goggled. 'You kept gelignite in your hat?'

'Safe as houses.'

'Really?'

'Well,' – she thrust the fuses into the nearest flaming torch – 'it's not any more.'

Like everyone else, the tall grey man had been watching the flight of Tessa's hat, but he must have heard the spluttering fuses. His gaze snapped back and his eyes widened.

'I can't say I care for your hospitality,' she said to him, then she tossed one gelignite sausage into the hole in front of the stakes. The other, she flung high into the air, aiming for one of the empty ledges.

She was a top class throw.

'And now,' she said to Old Tom and me, picking up her sodden dress, 'we run.'

Immediately, I pivoted and elbowed the nearest guard in the chest, then kneed his companion somewhere ungentlemanly. 'Sorry,' I said. 'We need to see a man about a dog.'

On the other side of the pit, the tall grey man roared. He rounded the pit and still howling came at us; or, rather, he lunged at Tessa. The stone knife whistled as he slashed, but she baulked to one side and he didn't even come close.

While everyone's attention had been on the gelignite Tessa had thrown, Old Tom had sidled around behind the stakes. He waited until the tall grey man swung again and was slightly off-balance, and then jumped out and tripped him.

Old Tom's timing was perfect.

The tall grey man stumbled. His arms cartwheeled. The stone knife flew from his grasp. And with a long, drawn-out scream that mingled surprise and despair, he fell into the pit.

Old Tom cackled. 'Rude bastard.'

The gelignite overhead exploded, deafeningly, and was followed by another explosion somewhere underneath us. Foul-smelling flame erupted from the shaft as rock began to rain from above.

As one, the grey people turned and fled, ignoring us completely. Like panicked sheep they ran, trampling over anyone who fell.

Eventually, we emerged into moonlit darkness and that first breath of air was probably the sweetest I'd ever tasted. Then I was struck by an extraordinary sight. The rock pillars that had thrust up from the ground were disappearing. Shakily, they were being drawn back into the earth, foot by foot until they vanished, while the ground underfoot rumbled.

We slid, climbed and tumbled down the rocky outcrop.

Old Tom and I found the Southern Cross, argued, then set off in the direction that Tessa was already marching.

'West,' she replied when I caught up with her and asked where she was going. Her hair hung loose. She looked tired, but not daunted. 'Let's not shilly-shally.'

Later that night we ran into some locals. Old Tom talked to them. They'd been waiting, he told us, far enough away so that they felt safe, but close enough to keep an eye on what was going on. They were pleased at what we'd done. They gave us food and water and pointed us to the best way to go.

Word then went ahead of us and we received hospitality along the way. Eventually, a few days later, we reached the Alice River, then the Mitchell, which we followed. The next day we hit the coast and the Gulf.

We camped at the river mouth and waited for one of the trepang luggers that Old Tom assured us were always in the area. I had nothing, not even my old Gladstone bag, but I found I wasn't missing it at all. The scrape we'd got into and then out of had reminded me that simply being alive was a good start to the rest of a life.

Three lazy days later, a time when we didn't do much except mooch about, make hats out of cabbage palm leaves and try to put our experiences behind us, a steamer appeared from the north. I leapt to my feet and hallooed.

Tessa stood and brushed sand from her dress. 'Are you coming with us, Old Tom?'

Old Tom was lying under a she-oak, his hands behind his head. 'Don't think so, Miss Tessa. Might head back inland, spend some time with the people there.'

'We'll stay in touch?'

'Course we will.'

'Us?' I said, after reviewing what she'd said.

She turned to me. She was a picture. Strong, brave, unpredictable, intriguing. 'I've heard a rumour about the Andaman pirates and their lost treasury,' she said.

'The Strait of Malacca?' I remembered my sole experience in that part of the world. 'Very dangerous.'

'With the potential for great wealth. That's why I thought you might like to accompany me.'

'What about Bill?'

'I like the idea of having lots of money for when I finally track him down. Money can make revenge very creative.'

That sounded like a lark. And, really, any excuse to stick around with her was fine with me. 'Count me in.'

'Excellent,' she said, and she smiled like the sun. 'I've been feeling the need for a competent assistant.'

I tilted the brim of my cabbage palm hat. 'Let's see how we go, eh?'

James Hopwood

The Lost Loot of Lima

A Tale from the *Pages of History*

Prologue

December 8th 1821

As a cold southerly wind swept across the bay, 'Stingaree' Jack watched the *Relampago* weigh anchor. He never figured he'd be one of the men cast ashore. Despite his youth, the 15-year-old cabin boy had drawn lots with the rest of the crew. Forty reales had been placed in a cloth bag, two of the coins marked with a black cross. In turn, each of the crew drew a coin from the bag. Stingaree was one of the unlucky two who had fished out a marked coin, and consequently been tasked with protecting Bonito's treasure.

Stingaree was whippet thin with sandy unkempt hair and a round cherubic face. His full cheeks caused one crew member to remark that he looked like a stingray. From that moment on he was no longer John Carisimo, but known as 'Stingaree' Jack. Standing beside Stingaree on the foreshore was a midshipman named Chapelle, who had also drawn a marked coin. Originally from Bristol, Chapelle was 56 years old, but his weathered features and snow-white hair made him appear older.

Fate had bound Stingaree and Chapelle together. They would protect Bonito's secret till the end of their days.

As the galleon sailed over the horizon, Stingaree thought back over the events that had landed him on this foreign shore. For over two months, three British frigates had chased the *Relampago* from the Spanish Main all the way across the South Pacific Ocean. They would have been caught too if it hadn't been for a fortuitous squall over the Coral Sea. Under the cover of the storm, Captain Benito Bonito had been able to elude two of the pursuit vessels. However, one man-o-war had doggedly kept apace, driving them off course. The *Relampago's* original destination had been the Cocos Islands, but they had been forced south until they hit the east coast of the *Terra Australis* land mass.

On the night of their 73rd day on the run, the Captain navigated through the heads of a bay, and took shelter in a small cove. Knowing it was only a matter of time before they were discovered, it was decided two men should be put ashore to protect their interests. Stingaree wasn't sure if it was a blessing or a curse. But here he was on land, while his shipmates sailed away.

Stingaree turned to Chapelle and asked, 'Will they catch them?'

'Can't say,' Chapelle replied. 'One thing is for sure, the Captain won't go easy. He'll lead the British on a merry chase. But we can't stay here all day. Come on lad, we got a long way to travel.'

December 9th 1821

The situation was grim. The British man-o-war, *H.M.S. Reliant* spotted the *Relampago* as the pirate vessel left the sanctuary of the bay and hit the strait. The running battle was on once again. Bonito headed south-west along the rugged coast, but the man-o-war was larger, with more sail, and started to haul them in.

By morning, the British vessel came alongside and opened fire. A chain-shot, that being two cannonballs connected with a length of chain, toppled the *Relampago's* mast. Without the mainsail, Bonito knew he could not outrun or outmanoeuvre their tenacious pursuers, but he had always known it was only a matter of time. Now he had a decision to make. Should he stand and fight the unwinnable fight, or surrender and pray for leniency, if not for himself, at least for his crewmen?

Bonito looked at his hearty crew. They looked keen for a fight. They had been running for a long time now. He knew each of them would give as good as they got if it came to hand-to-hand combat. But the British didn't need to board the *Relampago* and fight at close quarters. He figured they would come alongside and rake the ship with cannon fire.

Bonito made his decision and nodded.

'Raise the *Joulie Rouge*,' he called to his flagsman.

The flagsman lowered the false flag they had flown and raised a plain red signal flag. Bonito did not fly the skull and crossbones like other pirates. The *Joulie Rouge* – also known as the Jolly Roger symbolised no quarter would be given in battle. Bonito was going to fight.

As the *Reliant* prepared to engage, Bonito looked to his men behind the cannon. He knew they would get one shot and one shot only. So far he had been lucky. He prayed his luck would hold.

'On my signal,' he called, as the ship dipped with the swell. On the upswing he yelled, 'Fire!'

As one, the *Remapago* cannon roared, the air thick with black smoke and the smell of gunpowder. Only one shot found its target. The cannonball blasted a hole through the *Reliant's* foc'sle, but as the smoke cleared Bonito could see the damage to the enemy was minimal. He cursed.

The *Reliant's* crew were well drilled. On the upswing, 30 cannons roared. In the battery, the *Relampago's* quarterdeck was obliterated. Like a puppet, Bonito was thrown forward by the blast. He slammed over a railing and landed heavily on the gundeck below. He pushed to his knees and shook his head as another volley of cannon fire raked the galleon. The mizzenmast splintered and the canvas sails rained down upon him. Caught in the toils of the rigging, Bonito knew they were done for. The *Relampago* was lost.

December 10th 1821

Chapelle had been told it was approximately 25 leagues to the Port Phillip whaling settlement. With no road or trail to follow, and trekking across untamed country, he figured it would take four or five days to make the journey. They had a small sack full of provisions that would last them two days at best, but he was confident they could make it.

Bathed in the golden light of the setting sun, with Stingaree at his side, Chapelle pressed through the undergrowth. He wanted to make as much distance as he could before stopping for the night. The going was tough. Back from the shoreline, the land was heavily forested with windswept, gnarled trees and shrubs. It was like weaving through a hedge-maze. As he stepped over an exposed tree root, he felt a sharp pain in his left ankle. He gritted his teeth and cursed.

'What is it?' Stingaree called, a pace behind him.

Chapelle looked down and saw the coiled snake, its coffin-shaped head hovering above its body. The snake struck again. Chapelle tried to leap out of the way but stumbled and fell to the ground.

'Kill it!' Chapelle yelled.

Stingaree drew a long-bladed knife, but hesitated. The snake was entwined with Chapelle's legs.

'I can't get it,' Stingaree said.

The snake darted over Chapelle's leg and bit again, striking low on the thigh. Chapelle gritted his teeth and grabbed the snake around the neck. As it writhed in his hand, he hurled it clear.

Stingaree leaped into action. Standing over the angered serpent, he brought the blade down hard and fast, cleaving the snake's head from its body. The headless creature thrashed as if it were still alive.

'Keep away from the head,' Chapelle called. 'Seen a cleavered jergen latch onto a man's ankle once.'

Stingaree jumped back, holding the blade at the ready. He waited and watched. The snake continued to squirm.

'It won't die,' Stingaree cried.

'It's dead lad, don't you worry about that. It just don't know it yet,' Chapelle said. 'Gi's a hand here. Help me to my feet.'

Wary of the snake, Stingaree circled around to Chapelle's side and offered his arm. Chapelle pulled himself up, but as he put pressure on his leg, pain shot through his body. He dropped to his haunches. Stingaree tried to help him again. Chapelle shrugged him away.

'No, no. Forget about that. I ain't going anywhere. Help me over to that tree.'

Stingaree dragged the old man across to a large yellow box and propped him up. Chapelle fought for breath and sweated profusely.

'Was it poisonous?' Stingaree asked.

Chapelle nodded. 'Take a look, boy,' he said.

Stingaree rolled back the leggings of Chapelle's breeches. The old man's legs were covered in bloody puncture wounds. The snake had bitten him seven times.

'What do I do?' Stingaree asked.

'Nothing you can do. I am done for. Leave me.'

'I can't leave you–'

'You'll do as you're told, boy,' Chapelle snapped, thick spittle flying from lips. He could see the boy was panicked and confused. He knew he had to throw a scare into him if the boy were to complete the task.

Speaking slowly and calmly, Chapelle said, 'Listen here, lad, I know you're scared but I want to tell you something. The captain has been in more tight scrapes than a barnacle in shallow harbour. He'll get through. Don't believe a word you hear to the contrary. Many a man has dodged a bullet or let slip the hangman's noose. Mark my words, some day someone will come looking for you. You do your duty. Keep the secret safe. Do you understand?'

'Yes,' Stingaree replied, fighting back a tear.

'Good. Now leave me here to die. It's as good a place as any, and better than I deserve. The secret lies with you now. Take it to your grave if needs be. Get goin'.'

Reluctantly, Stingaree turned and trudged off into the bush.

Chapelle sighed and rested his head against the bark of the tree. Of all the cursed luck. He had the riches of the world all but in his grasp, and what did he do? Go and get himself killed. He shook his head.

Of all the cursed luck!

I

January 3rd 1954

Father Maximilian Alvaraez, a man of the cloth with round glasses perched on his nose, entered the main gallery of National Museum of Archaeology in Valletta, Malta. The gallery was a kaleidoscope of colour, noise and excitement. Champagne flowed and hors d'oeuvres were served as waiters, holding silver trays aloft, weaved through the black tie crowd.

Valletta's elite had gathered to witness the unveiling of the museum's latest acquisition, a marble statue of Claude de la Sengle, the 48th Grand Master of the Order of Malta. The 20-foot tall statue was thought destroyed during a tornado in 1556 which tore through the Grand Harbour of Malta. The tornado killed 600 people and sunk four galleys. However the statue was not completely destroyed. The broken pieces were relegated to the catacombs where they sat buried, scattered and hidden for almost 400 years. It had been nothing short of a miracle the pieces had been recovered.

However, Father Alvarez was not at the museum for the unveiling. He had travelled from Lima to find two people who he knew would be attending the event. He scanned the room in vain as the patrons pushed to the front of the gallery where de la Sengle's statue stood hidden beneath a silk cover. On a raised platform beside the statute, Merlimun Macarta, the museum's curator, approached a microphone. The beam of a spotlight followed him.

'Can I have your attention please?' Macarta said.

The noise around the room died down and everybody turned to the front. Alvarez realised he would have to wait out the speech before he could resume his search.

Macarta discreetly cleared his throat and began his address.

'Ladies and gentlemen, thank you all for coming here tonight on this most auspicious evening. Before the unveiling, can I add that this day would not be possible without the tireless work of two extraordinary young people, Mark and Sarah Page. Mark and Sarah led the archaeological team on its quest as it scoured the catacombs searching for the pieces. Mark and Sarah, where are you? Take a bow, you deserve it.'

The spotlight cut across the room shining upon two young adults, twin brother and sister, aged in their mid-twenties. Sarah Page was dressed in an elegant black ball gown, her long dark hair had been straightened and styled to hang over her left shoulder, while on the right a delicate floral headpiece had been tailored to match her dress. Her brother Mark wore a bespoke dinner suit. He was clean shaven, with close-cropped hair.

Despite their youth, Mark and Sarah were highly regarded in the archaeological field.

The siblings bowed. The light swung back to centre stage. Macarta continued. 'And now without further ado, I present you Claude de la Sengle.'

Macarta tugged a gold-braided drawstring, and the silk curtain fell away revealing the statue. The crowd burst into applause and gasped at the polished marble colossus which towered above them. Flashbulbs went off as news photographers jostled for position, vying to get the best picture for their newspaper or magazine. It took ten minutes for the media frenzy to die down.

With the official ceremony out of the way, it was time to make a move. Alvarez weaved through the crowd toward the Page twins.

Mark Page handed his sister a glass of champagne and looked up at the statue.

'He's quite a sight, isn't he,' he said.

'Thanks to you,' Sarah replied.

'I only did the heavy lifting. You worked out where to look.'

Mark grinned. His sister was always reticent to acknowledge her work. It was almost as if she was embarrassed by the gift she had.

Mark's attention was distracted by a Catholic priest pressing through the crowd toward him. The priest was hard to miss, a crimson robe covered the shoulders of his cassock and a large golden crucifix hung from a chain around his neck. The priest came to a halt in front of the twins.

With a slight bow, he asked, 'Am I right to assume I am addressing Mark and Sarah Page? The ones they call the *Pages of History*?'

Mark cringed at the sobriquet that had been applied to him and his sister by certain members of the press.

'Yes, indeed, Father,' Mark replied.

The priest smiled. 'Allow me to introduce myself. My name is Father Maximilian Alvarez. I represent the Lima Cathedral in Peru. Is there a place we can talk in private?'

Mark looked around and saw a gallery to the side was deserted. 'Over there,' he said, pointing the way.

The trio moved away from the crowd.

Alvarez clamped his hands together. He appeared to be nervous. 'I will start by asking if you have heard the name, Benito Bonito?'

Mark scratched his chin. 'Pirate wasn't he? Late 18th century?'

'Early 19th,' Sarah corrected.

Mark grinned. He knew Sarah would fill in the blanks. With her photographic memory, it seemed there was little she didn't know. 'I stand corrected,' he said.

'The stories about Benito "The Bloody Sword" Bonito vary greatly,' Sarah continued. 'The one thing scholars agree upon is his treasure has not been found.'

'That is why I have come to you,' Father Alvarez said. 'I have heard you are the best in your field, and trustworthy. Yes, I seek Bonito's treasure, but let me explain. I am not a treasure hunter. I wish to see it returned to its rightful home, the Lima Cathedral. As you may know, the pirate Bonito was active up and down the west coast of the Americas. In 1821 he ransacked the cathedral, stealing a life-size jewel-encrusted golden effigy of the Madonna and Child, 12 statuettes of the Apostles, and many other items of inestimable value.'

'But why try to reclaim it now?' Mark queried. 'It's been over 130 years.'

Alvarez nodded. 'In that time many people have searched for the treasure, but none have had any luck. However, last year it was reported a man found a silver coin of Spanish origin in the seaside town of Queenscliff in Australia.'

'Queenscliff is one of the rumoured hiding places,' Sarah confirmed.

Alvarez continued. 'One month ago, a syndicate of South American businessmen descended on Queenscliff in an attempt to locate the treasure. The head of the syndicate is a man named Von Schüler. I have it on authority from the church that Von Schüler and the syndicate he represents are war criminals – Nazis who fled to Argentina after the war to escape persecution.

I can only imagine what they would do if they found the treasure. Today the treasure would be in excess of 30 million English pounds.'

Mark gave a low whistle. 'That's quite a haul.'

'So that is why I am here, to ask that you help me find the treasure first. It is imperative the treasure does not fall into the hands of these disreputable men.'

Mark turned to his sister. 'What do you think?'

Sarah nodded. 'We've finished up here. I think we can spare some time to investigate this further.'

Mark agreed. He turned back to Alvarez. 'Okay, Father, we'll do it,'

The relief on Alvarez's face was palpable. With a broad grin, in turn he shook Mark and Sarah's hands, clasping them tight in a two-handed grip. 'I cannot thank you enough,' he said, trembling with excitement.

II

January 4th 1954

The scorching summer sun beat down on the luxury yacht, *Isolde*, which was anchored in Swan Bay, a small cove inside the mouth of the greater Port Phillip Bay, the gateway to Melbourne, Australia. It was long rumoured Captain Benito Bonito sought sanctuary in Swan Bay as he attempted to elude a British man-o-war in 1821.

A little over three decades later, at that site, the township of Queenscliff sprung up, soon becoming a popular seaside resort. However those halcyon days were long gone, and now Queenscliff was little more than a sleepy coastal village.

Dressed in a pristine white uniform, the steward crossed to the owner of the *Isolde*, Victor Von Schüler, who was sunning himself in a deckchair on the foredeck. The steward held a serving tray, on which was balanced a champagne glass and an opened bottle of vintage Krug, a linen serviette wrapped around its neck.

The 1928 Krug Brut Grande Cuvée was considered one of the finest champagnes ever fermented, and consequently it was one of the rarest. In 1940, when the Nazi war machine rolled across France, not only were the people conquered, but the hallowed cellars were appropriated by the Third Reich. And even then, only the highest ranking officials were allowed access to the crème de la crème of French vinicultural artistry.

Now, nine years after the war, the '28 Krug was impossible to obtain – *that is* unless you were a Nazi war criminal who had shipped eighteen crates of the liquid gold out of the country to a secret estate in Argentina. Victor Von Schüler was just such a man.

But money and privilege had not spared Von Schüler from the ravages of time. He was 58 years old with a heavily lined face, and greying hair.

He nodded to the steward who poured the champagne into a wide glass and handed it to his master. Von Schüler took the glass and admired it, everything from the tight stream of bubbles rising from the bottom to the shape of the glass itself. Some people liked to drink from thin champagne flutes, but not Von Schüler. He preferred a wide glass, the shape of which reminded him of a woman's breast. He took a sip from the glass and nodded his approval.

The steward placed the tray on a low table beside Von Schüler's deck chair and addressed his employer. Von Schüler saw the steward's lips moving but could not hear what was said. He remembered the earplugs. He had placed them in his ears to cut out the noise from the generators at the back of the yacht. Currently he had three divers over the side searching for caves below the waterline. Each of the divers was connected to an air hose, which in turn was connected to a generator that kept the air flowing. Von Schüler could have provided his divers the latest Aqua-Lung technology, but he somehow found it reassuring to have the men tethered to the ship, as it were. That way he knew exactly where they went down and where they came up. The noise was a necessary evil he could put up with.

The steward spoke again.

Von Schüler removed the earplugs. 'What is it?' he snapped.

'I have a communique for you, sir,' the steward announced. 'It has just been decoded.'

'Well, just don't stand there, read it to me.'

The steward picked up a piece of folded paper from the tray and opened it. 'It's from Munz, sir, in Malta.'

'Go on.'

The steward read the message:

'As suspected Alvarez met with Mark and Sarah Page STOP
Has acquired their services STOP
En route to Australia STOP
Request instructions END MESSAGE.'

Von Schüler grunted and ran his hand over his sweaty brow and through his thinning hair. He raised the champagne glass again and drank slowly.

'Sir?' The steward pressed for a response.

Von Schüler glared at the steward. 'Eliminate them.'

The steward nodded. 'Very good, sir. I shall see the message is sent immediately.'

The steward turned on his heel and walked away. Von Schüler replaced the ear plugs and reclined. Nobody was going to come between him and the *Lost Loot of Lima.*

III

January 5th 1954

The bound watchmaker thrashed on the floor and tried to cry out. Through the gag his words were little more than muted distressed grunts. The left side of his face was swollen and blood trickled from the corner of his eye. Heidrich Munz put a finger to his lips and turned away from the unfortunate horologist. Munz crossed to the open first-floor window and gazed across to the Empire Hotel, where Alvarez and the Page twins were staying. The dwelling above the watchmaker's store was in an ideal position to watch the hotel entrance.

Munz had received new orders an hour ago. He was no longer a spy in the shadows, now promoted to executioner. However, he didn't have much time. Alvarez and the Page twins would leave the walled city of Valletta soon, and seek transportation to Australia.

Munz, a tall, thin figure with dark hair combed straight back, was one of the new breed of Nazis. He had not fought in World War II but was dissatisfied with what the world had become – decadent and weak. Genetically inferior bloodlines were ruling the world. Hitler had been right, only he had trusted the wrong people and his master plan was never fully realised.

But a new dawn was coming. The Third Reich may have been defeated but the next wave was gaining momentum; stone by stone, brick by brick, and soldier by soldier they were gaining strength. Munz was proud to be a part of the new movement, but he was also smart enough to realise the mistakes of the past must not be repeated. Before the new Reich could reveal itself it had to acquire a war-chest; money enough to do battle with its enemies. Victor Von Schüler was the new *Finanzminister* and Munz worked directly for him, doing what needed to be done.

Munz looked at his watch. It was nearing 6pm. Twilight was the worst part of the day to attempt a hit, but he had little choice. The hotel was at its busiest, a constant procession of people coming and going. Horns blared as cars and buses jostled for position near the entrance. At the window, Munz cradled a Mannlicher–Carcano rifle on his lap. It was an Italian weapon. He would have much preferred a German rifle, but it was the best he'd been able to acquire at short notice. He knew when the moment came, he would have ten seconds at the most to make the shots. After the first shot it would be pandemonium. Hopefully in the chaos, he would have the opportunity to take out the Pages. He had already decided Alvarez would be his first target. He just had to wait till he appeared.

A dented black taxi jerked to a halt outside the front entrance. It was empty, so Munz surmised it had been booked to collect someone. Munz sat forward and raised the rifle in readiness. An elderly couple stepped from the hotel. A porter followed behind with their luggage. Munz sighed and lowered the rifle.

The taxi was about to move away, when another taxi swung in front of it and pulled up outside the hotel. The driver of the first vehicle sounded his horn and yelled abuse from his open window. The second driver stepped from his car, raised his fist and yelled back something about learning to use an indicator. As Munz watched in bemused fascination, he almost missed his chance. Alvarez stepped through the hotel's revolving door juggling his luggage. The Pages followed behind. Munz raised the Mannlicher, allowing the barrel to rest on the lip of the window sill. He drew a bead on Alvarez, centring him in the cross-hairs. He was about to fire when the taxi driver cut between them, to accept the luggage from the priest. Munz held his breath while he waited for the driver to move away. It seemed to take an eternity, but finally the driver moved clear. Munz shut out the background noise and focussed on his target.

As his finger closed around the trigger, a transit bus filled his sights. Caught behind slow-moving traffic, the bus ground to a halt in front of the hotel. It blocked Munz's line of fire.

'Move it,' Munz hissed through clenched teeth.

Double parked, the bus's rear door opened and the passengers began to step off. With each second that passed, Munz knew his opportunity was slipping away. He bit down on his lip.

Once the passengers had alighted, the bus started to roll forward, only to jerk to a halt again. The bus driver sounded his horn. A taxi swerved in front of the stalled bus. It was the taxi carrying Alvarez and the Pages. Munz could only watch as the taxi drove away. He cursed.

Angry and frustrated, he lowered the rifle, resting it in his lap once again. He had missed his chance.

Sarah did not travel well on aircraft of any kind. She agreed with the school of thought that if woman was meant to fly, God would have given her wings. But she knew time was of the essence. If the syndicate of Argentinian businessmen were already on site in Queenscliff, they didn't have time to waste.

As the Douglas DC-3 hit a patch of turbulence, Sarah gripped her armrests tightly, one hand on top of her brother's.

'Are you okay?' Mark asked.

'You know what I'm like,' she replied. 'You need to take my mind off it.'

'How about we go over what we have?' Mark suggested.

'Okay,' Sarah agreed, pleased at the distraction. Over the years Sarah had read much on the treasure known as "The Lost Loot of Lima". There were so many versions she almost considered it an old-wives tale, one passed down from generation to generation and which, over the years in the telling, had became convoluted with other pirate legends of great treasure. But that did not mean the legend held no truth at all. It was a matter of cutting through the layers of distortion to get to the heart of the story.

Mark leaned across the aisle and tapped Alvarez on the shoulder. 'Sarah's going to tell us what she knows,' he said.

Alvarez nodded, and leaned across so he could hear.

Sarah started. 'As I said yesterday, the stories about Bonito vary greatly, even the date can't be agreed upon, the earliest being 1798, another being 1818, but most scholars suggest it was 1821. Regardless of date, legend has it that after a successful raid, Bonito was returning to his hideout on the Cocos Islands to bury the loot.'

'That seems an incredibly long way to travel to hide the treasure, halfway around the globe,' Mark interjected.

Sarah held up a hand to cut him off. 'You're thinking of the Cocos or Keeling Islands near Indonesia. That's not the place. It's a common mistake. The Cocos I am referring to sits about 550 miles due west of Panama City.'

'Oh,' Mark said, clearly embarrassed.

Sarah continued. 'Before they could reach their destination, Bonito and his crew were engaged by at least one, possibly more, British warships. Rather than leading the British to the Cocos, where it is alleged Bonito had hidden treasure from previous raids – but that is a story for another day – he fled, heading west across the Pacific Ocean.'

'To Queenscliff,' Father Alvarez said, pleased to be able to contribute a skerrick of information to the story. 'With the treasure on board.'

'Yes,' Sarah agreed. 'But it's not as simple as all that. The Queenscliff connection is handed down from two sources, both of which can be considered dubious at best. The first instance was told by a lady named Mary Welch. Years after the event, in 1853, she claimed in her youth she was the mistress of Benito Bonito, and she witnessed Bonito's men rowing the treasure ashore at Swan Bay, where the city of Queenscliff now sits. The pirates allegedly buried the treasure in a cave and with gunpowder blasted the entrance shut.'

'The syndicate Father Alvarez mentioned are trying to find the cave,' Mark said, piecing together the events of today with the events of the past.

'I would assume so,' Sarah agreed. 'But there is more. After the treasure was safe, Bonito sailed back out to sea. Shortly after passing through the heads, they were spotted by a warship, the *H.M.S. Devonshire*, captained by a man named Bennett Grahame. The *Devonshire* gave chase and after a running battle they captured Bonito's ship. But rather than be strung up from the gallows, Bonito raised his blunderbuss to his skull and blew his brains out over the deck.

'Mary Welch and Bonito's crew were sent to England to be tried for piracy. Most of the crew were hanged. Mary and two other men were spared the hangman's noose, but in the irony of all ironies, they were sentenced to transportation, back to Australia – to the penal colony at Van Diemen's Land – what is now known as Tasmania.'

'So Mary and the other men could have escaped from the prison and made their way back to the treasure,' Mark opined.

Sarah shook her head. 'There's no information to support that. The men were said to have died under the yoke of hard labour. When Mary was granted leave, she married and travelled to San Francisco.'

She paused to let the information sink in. Mark and Alvarez didn't have the benefit of her photographic memory.

'You said there were two sources?' Mark queried.

'The other story about Queenscliff comes from a gentleman known as 'Stingaree' Jack. His story surfaced in 1868. It was said Jack told his story to a doctor on his deathbed. In his version, he was the cabin boy aboard Bonito's ship, the *Relampago.*'

'*Relampago*?' Mark queried. 'What does that mean?'

'Lightning,' Father Alvarez responded, translating the Spanish.

Sarah continued. 'He said the *Relampago* was chased by three British men-o-war, but Bonito was able to evade capture and take shelter in Swan Bay, where the treasure was unloaded.

'But this is where his story differs. When Bonito left the safe haven, he was run down by a British frigate called the *Reliant*. All the pirates were taken aboard and faced a drumhead trial. The Captain of the *Reliant*, a gentleman named Aubrey Sillitoe, had them all hanged, with the exception of the cabin boy, Stingaree Jack, who was transported back to England.'

'This *Jack*, could he have gone back to Australia and retrieved the treasure?' Mark asked.

'It is a possibility,' Sarah conceded. 'It was said he returned to Australia and lived out his life in Tasmania.'

'Then we could be 100 years too late,' Mark replied despondently.

'Yes,' Sarah answered.

The group was silent as they accepted the realisation that their quest may be a waste of time and effort.

After a moment, Mark was first to speak. 'Then why are we going if the treasure no longer exists?'

Sarah sighed. 'It's a long shot, but something doesn't seem right to me about both stories. I mean why would Mary Welch tell people where the treasure is, when she could go back and claim it for herself? And Stingaree Jack too.'

'Miss Page, you seem to know a great deal about Bonito and his treasure,' Alvarez said. 'Is it something you studied before?'

'Not purposefully, but the legend on Benito Bonito is entwined with many other treasure stories. In my research, I have come across his adventures on various occasions.'

'But how can you remember such things?'

At Sarah's side, Mark chortled. 'Sarah has secret mind-powers,' he said.

Sarah shook her head at her brother's poor attempt at humour. 'Pay no attention to him, Father. I have a photographic memory. I can remember practically everything I have ever read.'

'I can see in your profession, how that would be a valuable skill,' Alvarez said, nodding. 'What do we do now? I take it we will continue on to Australia?'

'Not straight away,' Sarah replied. 'Since the 1850s, when Mary Welch first reported treasure hidden at Queenscliff, every treasure hunter, miner, and scavenger has scoured every inch of Swan Bay with no luck. What does that tell you?'

Mark shrugged. 'They're looking in the wrong place?'

'Correct.'

'Then, where's the right place?'

Sarah shook head 'I don't know,' she admitted. 'We need more information. That's why I have arranged for us to meet Sir Charles Warwick at the National Archives in London. He may be able to help us.'

IV

January 6, 1954

The old greystone Admiralty Building had been converted to house the National Archive. Waiting to meet Mark and Sarah was the foremost expert on British Naval history, Sir Charles Warwick.

Sir Charles was 62 years old, with snow-white hair and a thick moustache. He had worked with Mark and Sarah before and greeted them warmly as they stepped into his office.

'It's good to see you both. Welcome back,' he said, as he stepped out from behind his desk. He shook Mark's hand and kissed Sarah on the cheek. He then realised they had someone with them.

'Sir Charles, this is Father Alvarez, from Peru,' Mark said.

'How do you do,' Sir Charles said, shaking the priest's hand. 'Please come in, take a seat. What brings you all this way to see me?'

Everybody was seated.

'We are after information on the *H.M.S. Reliant* and the *H.M.S. Devonshire,*' Sarah replied.

'Benito Bonito?' Sir Charles queried. Sarah nodded. 'You're not the first to ask about those vessels. I can tell you what you want to know, but I think it is better if you read it for yourself. I have something very special here.'

Sir Charles stood from behind his desk and crossed to a bookshelf along the wall of his office. He retrieved an old leather-bound journal and handed it to Sarah.

'This is the personal journal of Captain Aubrey Sillitoe,' Sir Charles said. 'He was the captain of the *Reliant,* which was sent with two other frigates, the *Viscount* and the *Sheffield*, to deal with the pirate problem on the Spanish Main. The pirate, Bonito was just one of the people they were sent to apprehend.'

Sarah opened the journal and started to scan the pages.

Munz lit another cigarette and raised it to his lips. As he blew out a thick plume of smoke, he looked through the car windscreen at the heavy oak doors of the old Admiralty Building. Munz had caught the next flight to London in pursuit of Alvarez and the Pages. Upon arrival at Heathrow he had been met by one of Von Schüler's minions, a man named Harpen, who was young and enthusiastic, if not particularly bright.

Harpen had kept tabs on the trio. Munz had expected them to board the first available flight to Australia. He was surprised to learn they made their way to the Savoy Hotel and taken rooms. And now on the following day they were inside the Admiralty Building. But there was a plus side. Their lack of urgency gave Munz a fresh opportunity to complete his assignment.

Harpen had also furnished Munz with a submachine gun, a Schmeisser MP40. Munz believed German weapons were the best in the world, and the Schmeisser had proven its reliability in the war. It was just what he needed.

Parked across the street, with Harpen behind the wheel, Munz waited for his targets to reappear from behind the heavy wooden doors. He knew it was only a matter of time, and he was a patient man. This time he would not fail.

Mark stood at Sarah's side as she flicked through the pages of Sillitoe's journal. To someone unfamiliar with Sarah's talent, it looked as if she had barely looked at each page. Within four minutes she was finished and handed it to Mark. He started to read the relevant passages for himself; and read several sections out aloud for Father Alvarez's benefit.

'This entry is dated December 9, 1821.

> 'Knowing the brigand, Bonito, would seek safe harbour, we sailed close to the coast of New South Wales. By chance, the lookout saw the *Relampago* leaving the bay and heading south-east, passing through the heads into open sea. I engaged the pirate, where I ordered chain-shot fired, with the intent of taking out the *Relampago*'s mast.'

Mark shook his head and grunted. 'It looks like the legend is wrong. If Sillitoe captured Bonito off the coast of New South Wales, then the pirates never made it as far south as Queenscliff, which is on the southern tip of Victoria. If Bonito stopped at all, it must be at another bay.'

'No,' Sarah said. 'Your geography is good, my brother, but your history is poor. The Colony of Victoria was not established until 1851. So Sillitoe is correct. In 1821, he was off the coast of New South Wales.'

Mark gave a sarcastic grimace. He knew not to challenge his sister.

'Okay,' he continued with the journal.

> 'I was rather perturbed to discover Benito Bonito was not a Spanish privateer but an Englishman named Bennett Grahame, formerly Captain of the *H.M.S. Devonshire*.'

Mark looked up confused. 'Grahame? *The Devonshire*?' he queried, remembering his sister's recounting of the stories aboard the plane. 'Isn't that the captain and the ship Mary Welch said captured Bonito?'

'So she said,' Sarah replied.

'Her story is incorrect,' Sir Charles interjected. 'Grahame became a pirate. They say he sailed with Nelson at Trafalgar.' The sneer on his face expressed his disgust in Grahame.

'What happened to Bonito or Grahame as it may be?' Alvarez asked, his curiosity piqued.

Mark scanned the pages for the appropriate entry. 'Here it is. December 13, 1821.

> 'It was always my intention to return Bennett Grahame to England where he could stand trial for his crimes, and had he been a Spanish privateer I would have performed my duty as such. But as an English seaman, once a Captain of a vessel such as this, his presence on the ship was like a disease festering away at the crew, and if I am to be truthful, at myself. I found myself with little recourse but to hold a trial on board ship and administer my own naval justice. Not just for Grahame, but for his whole crew.'

'The drumhead trial,' Alvarez said. 'It appears Stingaree Jack's tale is the true story. Mary Welch was lying or merely retelling tall tales that had been told to her. Go on, tell us about Jack and how Sillitoe chose to spare his life.'

Mark read on, then shook his head.

'Nothing. According to the journal he pronounced the death sentence on each and every man from the *Relampago*. He hung them all.'

'And Jack?' Alvarez was as confused as the rest of them.

'There's no mention of him,' Mark replied.

'There has to be. If he was on board the *Relampago*, he had to stand trial with the crew.'

'What if he was not on board the *Relampago?*' Sarah queried.

'He had to be. How else could he know the truth about the three British ships?' Mark responded.

Sarah shook her head slowly as she tried to fit the pieces together. Nothing made sense. 'He must have been on board the *Relampago* at some point. But not when it was captured.'

'Which means he was put ashore somewhere,' Mark interjected. 'With the treasure?'

'It's a possibility,' Sarah agreed. 'But here's another one. I admit it's highly unlikely, but we have little to go on. Imagine that after the storm–'

'What storm?' Mark queried, forgetting his sister had already read the journal from cover to cover and memorised every page.

'Captain Sillitoe relates that as the *Reliant*, *Viscount* and *Sheffield* closed in on Bonito in the Coral Sea, a ferocious storm swept over them. The British ships lost sight of their quarry. Bonito slipped away. Attempting to pick up his trail, the *Viscount* sailed north, the *Sheffield* continued on the same course, and the *Reliant* headed south.

'As it happened, Bonito had headed south, and the *Reliant* did catch up to him, but only after four days had passed. In that time, Bonito had the opportunity to hide his treasure ashore somewhere along the coast. Then he continued his voyage. But when he spotted the *Reliant* on his tail once again, he realised that if his ship was to be captured the treasure would lay hidden, unclaimed. So what did he do?'

Mark shrugged. 'Circle back?'

'No, he put a man ashore to safeguard it.'

'You mean Stingaree was put ashore to safeguard the treasure?' Mark said incredulously.

'On the plane I said the stories don't add up. In Stingaree's deathbed confession he mentions Queenscliff, but only after Mary Welch had announced it to the world. He could have been sharing information he knew to be false. He wanted everybody to believe Queenscliff was where the treasure was hidden, because he knew anyone seeking the treasure would be digging in the wrong spot. He knew the true location.'

Mark wasn't convinced. 'Sillitoe says the lookout saw the *Relampago* leaving the bay and passing through the heads.'

'He did. But that doesn't mean the treasure was put ashore there. Maybe he put Stingaree ashore.'

'He put ashore a cabin boy, maybe only 16 years old?' Mark queried shaking his head in disbelief.

'Maybe Bonito put ashore more men, Five, ten. Who knows?'

'Where does that leave us?' Mark queried. He began to pace the room.

'We have to find out who Stingaree Jack was,' Sarah replied.

'How do we do that?' Mark queried.

'Forgive me,' Father Alvarez interjected, 'but if this Grahame became a pirate, it is not such a wild guess to suggest that many of his crew came over with him?'

'But, of course,' Sarah said, nodding in agreement. 'Sir Charles, the *Devonshire*, was there a cabin boy on board?'

Sir Charles turned to a filing cabinet behind his desk. He opened the lowest drawer and retrieved a book, flicking through the pages slowly.

Sir Charles nodded. 'Here it is, the crew listing for the *Devonshire*. It mentions a young lad was taken on as cabin boy. John Carisimo was his name. Fourteen years old.'

'You think John Carisimo is Stingaree Jack?' Mark queried.

'It's a possibility. It's the only lead we have.' Sarah replied. 'Sir Charles, would you have access to passenger lists of ships sailing between England and Australia between 1821 and 1868.'

'That's not my department, I'm afraid,' Sir Charles answered. 'That would be in the Port Authority archives. However, I can introduce you to Miss Carlyle who's in charge of that section. She will be able to assist you with your enquiries.'

Two hours later, Munz saw the heavy oak door open. Sarah Page was the first through, followed by her brother, then Alvarez. They stood at the top of a short tier of concrete steps. This was the moment Munz had been waiting for.

'That's them,' Munz yelled, raising the Schmeisser. 'Quickly!'

Harpen turned the key and flattened his foot on the accelerator. On the icy road, the vehicle fishtailed diagonally out of the parking space into the traffic. In both directions, cars and buses jerked to a halt and horns sounded in protest as the vehicle cut across the street. Munz steeled himself for action.

As they hit the curbing, Harpen clomped on the brake. Munz flung the door open and bounded out, brandishing the semi-automatic weapon. With teeth clenched, he opened fire, spraying round after deadly round at the trio. Alvarez was hit. He pirouetted like a ballet dancer as the bullets struck, before his bloody mass tumbled down the stairs to the pavement below.

Mark Page threw himself at his sister and they both went down. Munz couldn't get a clear shot up the incline, his gunfire sparking off the concrete stairs.

In the distance a siren wailed.

Police.

'Hurry!' Harpen called.

The Page twins had snaked back to the door. Munz saw the door crack open and the girl crawl through. Munz kept firing. At least, he would kill the man. The wooden door was splintered as he homed in on his target. The siren got closer.

Munz bolted past Alvarez's inert form and started up the stairs. Mark Page would not get away. He saw the young archaeologist pressed against the door. Holding the gun tight against his shoulder, Munz pulled the trigger.

Click.

He had emptied the magazine.

'*Scheiße,*' Munz cursed.

The police were almost there, less than a block away. Filled with anger and frustration, he glared at Page. As their eyes met, he could see the young man was not scared, but staring back defiantly. Page pushed to his feet.

With the seconds ticking away and the police closing in, Munz realised a confrontation would not serve him well. As a final but futile gesture, he spat at his quarry before bounding down the stairs to the waiting vehicle.

Harpen threw the car in gear and mounted the pavement to clear the stalled traffic. They raced away from the scene.

Munz slammed his fist against the dashboard. Anger coursed through his veins. Alvarez was eliminated, but he had failed to complete his assignment. He would not rest until the Page twins were dead.

It was a mess. Scotland Yard and Special Branch arrived on the scene and sealed off the area. Mark was angry and confused. Both he and his sister were questioned at length, but they had no answers for the authorities. They did their best to explain what they had been researching with Alvarez, but it was all Greek to the investigative officers. They shrugged their shoulders then vowed to do their best to bring the shooter to justice but Mark was sceptical. He had his suspicions, but he had not shared them with Sarah. Alvarez had said the neo-Nazi syndicate hunting the treasure was powerful and their tentacles stretched around the globe. They could have easily set up the assassination attempt.

Thankfully, Alvarez's wounds were not fatal. He had been shot twice in the same leg: one bullet to his left thigh, and a second that shattered his knee. As he fell, he had struck his head on the stairs and rendered himself unconscious.

In the hospital bed, as he opened his eyes, he saw Sarah and Mark standing over him. He forced a smile.

'Glad to see you two are okay,' he said, more concerned with their well-being than his own. The painkillers slurred his speech.

'It was a close scrape,' Mark replied. 'Scotland Yard are investigating but I need to ask you if you know who the shooter was?'

'It had to be one of Von Schüler's men. He will stop at nothing to get the treasure.'

Mark suspected as much. 'How did he know where to find us?'

'I guess he had men following me. If you are to continue, you will have to be careful, always on your guard.'

'Continue?' Sarah interjected.

Alvarez tried to sit up. 'You must continue. You have discovered so much already. Much more than I could.'

'This is a matter for the authorities,' Sarah replied.

'Then Von Schüler will win. Even if the police capture the gunman, there will be no evidence to tie him to Von Schüler and the neo-Nazis. You must find Bonito's treasure first.'

Mark nodded. The attack was intended to stop their research, but to the contrary, it had only strengthened his resolve. He placed his hand on Alvarez's arm. 'Don't worry, Father, we'll find it first. I promise.'

On the footpath outside the hospital, Sarah turned to face her brother. She was angry. The shooting had unsettled her more than she admitted.

'How could you promise that? These men are killers,' she blurted.

'Exactly,' Mark said. 'That's why we have to continue. Imagine what men like that could do with the power bought with 30 million pounds? We are the only ones who can stop them.'

'Stop a bullet, more likely.'

'It won't come to that. You forget, we have an advantage. You said it yourself, they are looking in the wrong spot. They won't know where to find us.'

'Unless they have someone following,' she replied sceptically.

'I won't let anything happen,' Mark assured her.

Sarah shook her head. She knew Mark was right, but the danger could not be ignored. After a long pause she said, 'Okay. We'll go on.'

Mark put an arm around her shoulder and pulled her close. 'We'll be okay, sis, I promise.'

Sarah pulled away. To her, it appeared he was far too easy with his promises.

V

January 7th 1954

The divers had not located any caves or tunnels. The search on shore also failed to reveal the resting place of Bonito's treasure. Von Schüler knew he was close, he could feel it in his bones, but the treasure's location eluded him.

He threw his head back and looked skyward. Had he not been patient? With clenched fists at his side, he stormed back to his upper deck cabin. He pushed through the door and sat down in a leather chair behind his desk. The rays of the low afternoon sun pierced the shuttered windows casting a golden pattern upon the wall. On the desk was a bottle of 20-year-old single malt. He pulled the cork and poured a healthy slug into a glass tumbler. As he took a long swallow, there was a knock on the cabin door.

'Enter,' he snarled, making little effort to conceal his anger at being interrupted.

The steward stepped into the cabin. 'Sorry, sir,' he apologised. 'A message from Munz.'

'Read it.'

The steward did so.

'Alvarez has been eliminated STOP
Mark and Sarah Page survived attempt STOP
Suspect they are continuing their research STOP
Will advise when I have succeeded MESSAGE ENDS.'

Von Schüler grunted. At least Alvarez was dead. He surmised the Page twins would have trouble moving forward without Alvarez to guide them, and soon they would be dead too. Munz would not fail again.

But still, something didn't sit right. Von Schüler turned to the steward.

'The message says they are *continuing their research*?'

'Yes, sir.'

Why would the Page twins continue without Alvarez? Maybe they knew something he did not? But surely in such a short amount of time they could not have discovered anything new.

'Take this reply,' Von Schüler ordered: 'Abort mission. Page twins not to be harmed. Follow them and report their every movement.'

'Very good, sir.' the steward said. He turned on his heel and exited the cabin.

Alone once again, Von Schüler reclined in his chair and swung his feet onto the desk. He realised he may have been hasty in ordering the death of Mark and Sarah Page. So far, his search had proved fruitless. Maybe the 'Pages of History' would have better luck.

Little did they know it, they were now working for *him*.

VI

January 9th 1954

It had been a long route from London's National Archive to the weathered and run-down Pioneer Cemetery in Devonport. The Archive had yielded more information than Mark expected. Of course it had been Sarah who had discovered the vital clue. She had noted a young man named John Karismo had booked passage from Sydneytown to London in 1824. It was the spelling that caught Mark off guard. He had been looking for Carisimo. The records also indicated Karismo returned to Australia eight years later.

At first Mark had been sceptical. But Sarah had been insistent that Carisimo and Karismo were one and the same person. Furthermore, she was sure it was he who held the secret to the whereabouts of Bonito's treasure. Mark knew better than to argue with his sister's intuition. She had been proven right on too many occasions.

The next day they boarded a commercial flight to Australia.

Upon arrival, Sarah contacted the Bureau of Births, Death and Marriages. Information had been supplied that John Karismo – AKA Stingaree Jack – lived out the rest of his life in the settlement of Devonport in Northern Tasmania. She was also informed he had been buried at the Pioneer Cemetery. And here they were.

As they wandered through the weathered tombstones Mark felt uneasy, as if he was being watched. Ever since the attempt on their lives, he had been cautious. He had even brought along his six-shot Webley revolver, concealed in a backpack over his shoulders.

'We'll find the grave faster if we split up,' Sarah said.

Mark hesitated. He didn't want to burden Sarah with his unease. He turned a full 360 degrees, looking for anyone or anything out of the ordinary. All was quiet. They appeared to be alone in the cemetery.

'What is it?' Sarah queried.

'Nothing.' Mark shrugged. 'You're right. I'll circle this section, you start up there.'

He indicated a series of graves situated on a low ridge, knowing she would be in sight at all times. Sarah moved off and he started examining the gravestones around him.

Seven minutes later, Sarah called, 'Over here. I think this is the one.'

Mark walked up the slope to the grave and stood beside Sarah, looking down at the weathered and pitted gravestone. It was hard to make out the text. He moved closer and read the name:

JOHN KARISMO

'It's him, all right,' Mark said.

'We should take a rubbing,' Sarah added.

Mark nodded in agreement. He had come prepared. From his backpack he extracted a large graphite block and a roll of butcher's paper. He unfurled a sheet of paper and handed it to Sarah.

'You hold this and I'll do the rubbing,' he said.

Sarah placed the paper against the face of the gravestone, while he rubbed the graphite block over the surface in broad strokes. With each sweep the text became visible on the paper. They kept going till the whole face had been covered.

'That should do it,' he said, stepping back.

Sarah pulled the paper away and carefully rolled it. They were done.

The Pages left the cemetery. Munz did not rush to follow them. At this moment he thought it was more important to investigate the reason for their visit. Von Schüler would want to know of this latest development.

Munz crossed to the gravestone and read the name. The engraved text below was difficult to read. From behind the trees he had watched as Mark Page had placed the paper over the gravestone and made a rubbing. Munz was not so prepared. All he had was a notepad and a greylead pencil. He tore the top sheet from the pad and placed it on the left hand edge of the stone. With broad strokes he scribbled across the page, revealing the text. Sheet by sheet, almost like a jigsaw, he worked his way across and down the gravestone till he had all the engraving. He would piece it together later, and inform Von Schüler.

VII

Sarah and Mark had taken a twin room at a small waterside motel in Devonport. It wasn't fancy, but it was clean, and they didn't intend to stay for long. However, the temperature inside was stifling. An old overhead fan clicked and whirred, providing little comfort.

Sarah, showered and wrapped in a white towelling bath robe, was sitting on a chair. Mark was stretched out on one of the beds, with his hands behind his head. Neither of them had examined the rubbing from the gravestone. Sarah hoped it was not a waste of their time. It was her hunch that brought them to Tasmania, while the neo-Nazi syndicate continued to search at Queenscliff. What if she was wrong? What if John Karismo was another wild goose chase, and the treasure was really hidden in Queenscliff?

There was only one way to find out.

'I think it's time we took a look at the rubbing and see what we've got,' she said.

Mark grunted and sat up. He retrieved the rubbing and unrolled it, laying the large piece of paper across the bed.

JOHN KARISMO
~ DIED 1868 ~

Here lies the body of 'Stingaree' Jack
Who sailed with the Dog before the attack
He fooled the Eggers and mateloes too
Set ashore at the Swan ~ a party of two
On the second day the Chapel went down
Stingaree Jack returned to the crown
For forty and seven ~ the secret he kept
from histories pages the story be swept

Though Stingaree Jack can no longer speak
Here is the riddle to what you seek
The Mother and Son lies athwart
Across the strait in another port
Where the Franklin flows into the sea
The fall of the second ~ marked easy to see
Follow the trail to a Mountain called A
Through the Hold there you'll strike pay
Over the hump back and down the spout
You'll find what is lost without a doubt

Sarah crossed to Mark's side and scrutinised the gravestone inscription. The text was worn, pitted and in places difficult to read. At the bottom was the picture of a snarling dog, or wolf. Its snout faced to the right.

'It's all gibberish,' Mark said suitably frustrated. '*Here lies the bodn...*'

'Body,' Sarah corrected. That 'n' is a 'y'.'

Mark nodded. '*Here lies the body of Stingaree Jack – Who sailed with the Dog before the attack.*

'Sailed with the Dog, what on earth does that mean?'

Sarah needed a moment to think. She turned away and paced around the room like a caged animal. She thought back on all she knew about the *Relampago*. It took a moment to filter through the phenomenal amount of information stored in her memory. But it finally came to her.

'A book published in 1905 suggested the *Relampago* was launched in 1813, eight years before Bonito plundered her and took her for his own. Her home port was Valencia, and her figurehead was... a rampant wolf.'

'Or to a young man like Jack, a dog,' Mark added.

'So from the opening couplet we can ascertain that indeed, John Karismo was Stingaree Jack and was on board the *Relampago* before the British Navy captured her.'

'The next line,' Mark said eagerly. '*He fooled the...* do you think that's an E? Eggers? *He fooled the Eggers and the mateloes too*.'

Sarah continued to pace the room. 'I think mateloes is a simple misspelling.' She spelled it out. 'M a t e l o t s – but is pronounced Matelow. It is French, meaning any sailor who is not an officer. Eggers is more difficult. But I assume as it is capitalised it holds some importance.'

'If mateloes is sailors, could it mean the British Navy?' Mark queried.

Sarah nodded. 'Or navy officers. I don't know if this is his meaning, but sometimes officers were called 'scrambled eggs' due to the braiding on their caps. If we take it that Eggers means officers, then Jack is bragging about deceiving the British Navy. Simply put, he fooled the officers and sailors too.'

Mark continued. 'Next. *Set ashore at the Swan – a party of two*.'

'That's seems pretty straightforward. Two men were set ashore at Swan Bay. We assume Jack was one of them.'

'*On the second day the Chapel went down.*'

'Chapel. Legend suggests one of the sailors on the *Relampago* was named Chapelle. Maybe he was the other sailor set ashore with Jack. *Chapel went down?* Maybe Chapelle was injured or killed?'

'*Stingaree Jack returned to the crown.*'

'It could have two meanings. The first, as we know, Jack returned to England. Crown could mean England. Or, it could mean Bonito's treasure.'

'*For forty and seven – the secret he kept. From histories pages the story be swept.*'

'That confirms Jack held the secret of where the treasure lies. For 47 years, which if he died in 1868, means he kept the location secret since 1821 – the year Bonito was said to have set down in Swan Bay.'

Mark nodded. 'So the top part of the message on the gravestone confirms Karismo was Stingaree Jack, he was put ashore at Swan Bay with Chapelle, who died, leaving Jack as the sole caretaker of Bonito's treasure.'

'Yes,' Sarah agreed. 'Let's go on to the bottom section.'

'*Though Stingaree Jack can no longer speak... Here is a riddle to what you seek.*'

'Straightforward,' Sarah said. 'He's going to tell us where the treasure lies. What's next?'

'*The Mother and Son lies athwart. Across the strait in another port.*'

'Mother and Son? He must be referring to the Madonna and Child statue.'

'*Lies athwart*. What does 'athwart' mean?'

'It means lying across the ships width,' Sarah answered.

'The Madonna and Child statue lies across the ships width? I don't understand.'

Sarah didn't either. She crossed to the hotel's sink and splashed cold water over her face. As she mopped her brow, a thought occurred to her.

'What direction was Jack's gravestone facing?'

Mark scratched his chin. 'West, I think. Why?'

'Then the Madonna and Child lie to the north or south. Across his grave. The next line is *Across the strait in another port*. Across Bass Strait. The treasure is on the mainland, most likely Victoria.'

'So it may be at Queenscliff?'

'I don't think so. If we take *athwart* quite literally then Queenscliff is too far to the west. We are looking for a port due north from Devonport.'

Sarah walked to the telephone and picked up the receiver. She was silent for a moment while the operator answered. 'This is Sarah Page in room seven. Could you put me through to the airport... thank you.'

'What are you doing?' Mark asked, while she waited to be connected.

'Preparing to leave. I'm booking passage on the next available flight to Melbourne. I think I know where the treasure is hidden.'

'What about the rest of the riddle?'

'We can work it out on the way.'

VIII

January 11th 1954

A canvas-covered troop carrier rolled into the tiny seaside village of Port Franklin. Situated on the coast of Corner Inlet, to the east of Wilsons Promontory, it was where the Franklin River met the sea. Of the hundred-odd souls who lived in the small village, most were fishermen, or their wives.

Seated behind the wheel of the troop carrier was Heidrich Munz. Beside him, smoking a fat Cuban cigar, was Victor Von Schüler, who could feel the electricity in the air as he looked out over the small village. He wondered if the townsfolk knew they were the unofficial guardians of a treasure beyond all comprehension – that is if he wasn't already *too late*.

Von Schüler wished he had discovered the information on John Karismo's gravestone much earlier. It would have saved him much time, money and effort. Initially he had thought all was lost when he read, *Where the Franklin flows into the sea.* He knew the Franklin River was in Tasmania, less than half a day's travel from Devonport. The Pages would be sure to arrive first. However, after consulting a map, he realised the Franklin River in Tasmania did not flow into the sea at all, but merged with the larger Gordon River.

He soon discovered another Franklin River, one on the south-east coast of Victoria. It all started to make sense. Bonito had put his treasure ashore before he had reached Queenscliff.

As the truck came to a halt, Von Schüler's train of thought was interrupted by Munz, who cursed under his breath.

'What is it?' Von Schüler asked.

'Look,' Munz replied, pointing at a young man and woman standing on a wooden dock overlooking the river. 'It's them.'

Von Schüler had never seen the Page twins before. He had not expected them to be so young.

'So, they got here first,' he said, disappointed, but not particularly surprised.

He had six armed men in the back of the truck. If he gave the order, he could cut the Pages down where they stood. He decided against it. Although the village was small, he did not want to draw undue attention to himself. Who knew how long it would take to locate and recover the treasure, and he certainly did not need the authorities awaiting his return.

'Do you want me to kill them?' Munz asked, drawing a Luger pistol from a leather holster at his side.

Von Schüler shook his head. 'No, not yet. This is not the place. But fear not, the time will come soon enough.'

Upon their arrival in Port Franklin, Mark and Sarah wasted little time. From a local fisherman they hired a small tin-hulled runabout with an outboard motor. Anything larger would be likely to run aground along the narrow, but fast moving, winding Franklin River.

They travelled light, bringing only a backpack each. Sarah's was filled with provisions, tinned food, waterproof matches, cooking utensils and such, plus a length of rope. Mark was lumbered with the heavy gear. He carried a short-handled shovel, a pick, a hammer, a large knife, two torches, and of course, ammunition for his Webley revolver, which was holstered at his side.

So far their time in Australia had been uneventful, and as far as he knew, they were the only people who had any idea of the true location of Bonito's treasure. But still, he felt uneasy, and it was better to be prepared.

With Mark manning the tiller, and Sarah seated at the bow, they began their journey up river. From its source 21 miles away, the Franklin descended almost 1500 feet. Against the strong current the going was slow and the atmosphere was claustrophobic, with trees and shrubs overhanging the river, closing in on both sides.

It took two hours to reach the first multi-tiered waterfall, which resembled a low set of stairs. The water cascaded from level to level in translucent sheets. Mark knew he would not be able to drag the boat up the falls.

'This is as far as we can go by boat,' he called. 'We travel by foot from now on.'

His sister nodded. He steered the boat to the river bank and cut the engine. Sarah was the first onto the bank. Mark threw her a line and she tied the runabout to a river gum. Mark picked up the backpacks and joined her on the bank. He handed over her kit.

'*Fall of the second*,' Sarah said, as she slipped the backpack over her shoulders.

Mark nodded, as he adjusted his own pack. They both guessed it meant a second waterfall. He set off, leading the way. There was no clear path, the undergrowth thick. To make matters worse, the trek was uphill now, Mount Best rising to their east.

By midday, the bush was like a steam bath. It wasn't just the heat but the infernal humidity. Mark and Sarah's clothes were saturated with sweat and clung to their bodies, making free movement awkward. Then there were the plants. The branches and the underbrush cut through material and human flesh like razor blades. Both displayed scratches and cuts across their arms and legs.

After 35 minutes walking alongside the winding river they heard the sound of fast-flowing water.

'The second waterfall?' Mark queried.

They pressed on, till they saw the falls open out before them. This one was larger than the first, almost 15 feet tall. The air was filled with a cooling mist, which felt good against their skin. Before the curtain of water, the area was littered in moss-covered rocks and boulders.

Mark knew he was looking for a marker of some kind. Stinagree's gravestone had said '*Fall of the second – marked easy to see*.' He scanned the area, but nothing stood out.

'Mark, come and look at this,' Sarah called.

'What is it?' he replied.

Sarah didn't answer. He pushed through a thick bank of ferns to her side. She stood before a large boulder covered in moss and lichen.

'What does it look like to you?' she asked, pointing to a dark indentation on the rock surface.

At first it was hard to make out, but then he saw it. A wolf's head, like the one at the foot of Stingaree's gravestone.

'The marker,' he exclaimed.

'There's more, look.' Sarah ran her hand over the surface, trying to clear away the moss. It was still illegible. She opened her canteen and poured water over the carving. As the water seeped into the lichen, the text became clear. 'It looks to be Roman numerals, LX. Sixty.'

'It has to be a measurement,' Mark said.

'Hidden pirate treasure,' Sarah mused, 'it can only be one thing. Paces.'

Marked grinned. 'Sixty paces. But what direction?'

'East.'

'Why east?'

'The wolf's snout is pointing east, toward Mount Best. *Follow the trail to a Mountain called A*. Mount Best hadn't been named when Stingaree died. All the mountains in this region were identified alphabetically. Best was A.'

Mark nodded. Together they moved away from the river, up a shallow incline, into the dense undergrowth.

Von Schüler raised his hand, calling his men to a halt. He dropped to a knee, and pushed aside a branch so he could get a better view, and watched as Mark and Sarah left the river's edge and pressed into the bush.

Standing at his side, Munz stated the obvious. 'They are moving away from the river.'

Von Schüler nodded. Munz was a good soldier, but still had not grasped the importance of the information he had relayed. 'They must have found the marker,' he explained.

'Should we kill them now, before they find Bonito's treasure,' Munz said.

Von Schüler shook his head. 'No. There'll be time for that later. Let them lead the way. They may find the treasure, but they won't keep it.'

Mark found the next marker. It pointed north-east, and also had Roman numerals engraved under the wolf's head.

'Ninety paces,' he said.

The way ahead was more difficult, a steep incline littered with fallen trees and boulders. With only a few paces to go, they came to a six-foot deep crevice. Mark stood on the lip and peered down.

'There,' he said, pointing to the symbol carved into the wall. This time there was no measurement under the wolf's head. 'It looks like we are to follow the crevice.'

Mark lowered himself over the edge and then offered Sarah his hand. She took it and jumped down beside him. Enclosed on both sides, they clambered over the rocks and stones along the jagged narrow passage. As the ground levelled out, a large gum tree loomed above them. It looked to be hundreds of years old. At the base, the bark had been stripped away on one side. The wood was grey, weathered and cracked, but the carving could still be seen. An arrow pointed to the top of the ridge.

They soldiered ahead, scrambling over gnarled tree roots till they reached the top of the ridge. As Sarah caught her breath, Mark turned and looked back over the landscape they had traversed. Through the trees below he could see the river cascading over the falls. It was a sight to behold. Mother Nature at her finest. But then something else caught his eye. *Movement*. It took him a moment to realise what it was. Men. A group of them were moving up the mountain.

It had to be Von Schüler, the Nazi Alvarez had told them about. But how had he known where they were?

But he didn't have time to ponder that now.

He turned to Sarah. 'I have bad news. We're not alone.'

Sarah raised her eyebrow quizzically. 'What do you mean?'

He pointed down the mountain. 'We're being followed.'

Von Schüler looked up the ridge and saw Mark and Sarah staring down at him from above. As their eyes met, he knew the charade was over. He was sure Alvarez would have told them all about him. He raised his rifle, quickly took aim and squeezed the trigger. The bullet sparked on a rocky outcrop by their side. Von Schüler cursed as the young archaeologists disappeared from view.

'Up that way,' he called.

His men lumbered past him, scrambling up the rocky incline toward the top. Von Schüler took a moment to gather his wits. From the time he'd arrived at Port Franklin he knew it would end in a showdown. It seemed a shame to kill the Pages. They were clearly an intelligent and resourceful duo to have made it this far. Nonetheless, he could not allow them to stand between him and the treasure. The future of the new Reich depended on it.

Mark took his sister's hand and pulled her away from the edge. He knew time was of the essence. The party in pursuit had already shown they were willing to shoot. Out in the open they didn't stand a chance. However, in the cave, with the Webley, Mark could pick off anyone who tried to follow. He realised his plan was far from perfect. The villains could simply wait them out. Sooner or later, Sarah and he would need food and water. But for the moment, it was the best he could think of, and preferable to being shot.

'Quickly,' he said, dragging Sarah along. 'What was the last part of the riddle?'

'*Over the hump-back and down the spout – You'll find what is lost without a doubt*,' Sarah replied.

It had to refer to a whale, Mark figured. Or more precisely a rock or an outcrop that looked like a whale. As he moved, his eyes darted over the terrain ahead of them. It wasn't hard to find. To their left was a rolling hill with a tapered overhang. It looked like a humpback whale. His years in the field had taught him to read landscape, and he could tell there had been a rockslide where the mouth should be. He remembered how the legend said the mouth of the treasure-cave had been sealed with a gunpowder blast. He knew he couldn't get into the cave that way, but the riddle said, *down the spout*. He realised there must have been another entrance at the top of the hill.

'This way,' he said, leading Sarah up the side of the mound.

At the top of the hill, Mark rushed to the point where a whale's spout would be. There he found a hollow, almost like a bowl. Mark jumped down, landing with a heavy thud. It wasn't dirt beneath his feet. On his knees, he frantically cleared away the dirt and leaves, revealing a heavy wooden grate. *Through the hold and there you'll strike pay*. It wasn't a grate but one of the doors to the ship's hold. Mark continued to clear the top layer of detritus away, working toward the edges. Soon he found what he was looking for; the catch. The thick bolt was heavily rusted. He moved off the grate and took the short-handled pick from his backpack and wedged it underneath the sliding bolt. Then using all his strength, he pulled back on the handle. The screws that held the lock in place screeched in protest as they were wrenched back. With a final squeal, the lock came away.

As Mark worked, he could hear the sound of voices below. Von Schüler and his men were getting closer. Hurriedly he thrust the flat edge of the pick into the gap between the grate and the ground and levered the handle back. The grate lifted an inch, splinters of rust falling from the hinges. He repositioned the pick, pushing it deeper, and repeated the process. The heavy wooden door began to rise.

'Quickly,' Sarah urged. He could hear the fear in her voice. 'They'll be here any second.'

Mark nodded. He didn't need to be told. He withdrew the pick and looped a rope through the grate and tied it off tightly. Putting his shoulders to the task, he dragged the rope back. The door was stubborn, but he was able to force it up to almost a right angle, more than enough to get through. He moved to the lip and let the free end of the rope fall into the spout.

'I'll go first,' he said, as he slung his backpack over his shoulders and tucked the torch into his belt to light the way.

Sarah didn't argue.

Taking the rope in hand, Mark lowered himself into the shaft, and after pushing through a spider's web, began the climb down. He was more than a little apprehensive, not knowing what he'd find at the bottom.

With Sarah following, they snaked their way down the rope. The spout was longer than Mark expected. It took two minutes to reach the bottom. As his feet hit solid ground he drew his torch from his belt and examined his environment. Sarah dropped down beside him.

'Where are we?' she asked.

'It appears to be some kind of cavern.'

As the beam of light swept the cavern from end to end, one thing became abundantly clear, if this had been the hiding place of Bonito's treasure, it had long since been moved.

IX

Mark knew X rarely marked the spot, and was not particularly upset to find the cavern devoid of any treasure. However the cavern was not empty. As he positioned the torches at either end of the cavern to light up the space, he noted other artefacts left behind by the crew of the *Relampago*. An eight-pound cannon was positioned in a cradle near the entrance spout. The barrel was horizontal, but there was no mistaking it could be pointed upward. Stacked beside it were a ring of cannonballs, and the tools with which to load it.

The cavern wasn't just a hiding place, it was a mini-fortress.

Von Schüler had his men scattered, trying to pick up the Page twins' trail. They couldn't have made it far. As he took a moment's respite, leaning against a tree, he heard a cry to the left.

'Up here,' Munz called. 'I've found something.'

Von Schüler saw Munz standing on a hill that looked like... *a whale*. Von Schüler nodded. Of course. He pushed away from the tree and started up the steep incline, using whatever handholds he could find along the way. At the top, he saw the members of his party had already joined Munz. They were standing around in a circle. Von Schüler pressed through the ring and saw an upright wooden grate beside a shaft down into the hill. He noted the rope tied to it, dropping down into the maw.

'They must have climbed down,' Munz said.

Von Schüler nodded, but he was no longer concerned with the Pages. He felt like a giddy schoolboy, overcome with excitement. 'The Loot of Lima lies below,' he said. He could not wait to see the treasure.

'Allow me to lead the way,' Munz said. 'They may be armed.'

Von Schüler's jubilation turned to anger. He wanted to be first. He grabbed Munz by the collar, dragged him close and backhanded him across the jaw. 'You want the glory!' Von Schüler bellowed through clenched teeth.

Munz stood confused, wiping a trail of blood from the side of his mouth.

But as Von Schüler thought the scenario through, he reluctantly had to admit Munz was right. The spout was virtually a shooting gallery. He took a moment to regain his composure, and then nodded. 'Yes. You go down first.'

Munz still looked confused. He didn't know what he had done. 'You want me to go?'

'Go now,' Von Schüler snarled, pointing at the spout.

Munz shrugged. 'If the Pages are down there?'

'Kill them, that's what you are paid to do.'

Munz grinned. Finally, he'd have his moment. He knew going down the spout could be a trap. But he was not a coward. He would meet the challenge head on. He drew his Luger and walked to the lip of the shaft and peered down. He couldn't see anything. But if they were down there, he'd flush them out. He took aim and fired three shots down the spout, then moved back awaiting the return fire.

None came.

It looked safe. Munz crossed to the rope and took hold, testing his weight. It seemed strong enough. With a final nod to Von Schüler, he kicked away from the edge and began his descent.

The gunshots echoed down the spout, the sound like cannon fire.

'They're shooting at us,' Sarah cried.

'Move back against the wall,' Mark said calmly. 'They're trying to flush us out.'

As Sarah moved to the rear of the cavern, Mark drew his Webley from its holster and took position beneath the spout. As he prepared to return fire, his leg brushed the cannon. He slowly lowered his revolver.

'What is it?' Sarah asked. 'You're not giving up?'

'No. I have a better idea.'

Against the wall were several kegs of gunpowder. The timber on the kegs at the front had rotted away, the powder spilling out forming a moss-covered sludge. He crossed to the kegs and reached for one at the back that had been shielded from the elements. He pried open the lid only to discover the powder inside was wet, and not usable. He cursed silently and pushed aside the keg, picking up one underneath. This keg also appeared intact, but was the gunpowder dry?

He punched open the lid expecting the worst, but miraculously the black powder was dry. Mark grinned. If Von Schüler wanted to play rough, he could play rough too.

He rushed back to the cannon and tilted the barrel back.

'What are you doing?' Sarah asked incredulously.

'Preparing a welcome for our guests.'

'You can't be serious? The cannon is over 100 years old. It can't possibly be fired?'

'I only need one shot. That will scare them,' he said, as he removed his shirt and tore it in half. 'I'll need the matches from your backpack.'

While Sarah retrieved the matches, Mark took the decaying rammer from against the wall. It was little more than a stick. He wrapped half his shirt around the end and plunged it into the barrel, cleaning out all the accumulated filth that had built up inside. Satisfied he had done the best he could, he picked up the powderkeg and poured it down the barrel. For wadding he used the other half of his shirt. Finally came the cannonball. He crossed to the pile, and rolled aside the rusted ones at the top. He took the cleanest ball he could find and let it roll down the cannon barrel. He followed behind with the rammer to make sure it was packed good and tight against the breech.

It was ready. He just hoped it would work. At that moment he saw a shadow in the spout above him. Someone was coming.

'You'd better take cover,' he said. 'This is going to be loud.'

He struck a waterproof match and pushed it through the vent hole. Sparks flew as the flame met the gunpowder, but for a second nothing happened.

Then... *BOOM!*

Mark was thrown clear across the cavern. Smoke and the thick smell of gunpowder filled the air.

Munz had been gone for 30 seconds and Von Schüler had not heard any gunfire from the cave below. The shaft appeared to be safe. Von Schüler cursed himself for letting Munz lead the way. He should be first to set eyes upon the treasure, not some odious minion. However, that thought disappeared in an instant.

There was a deafening roar and a geyser of acrid black smoke erupted from the spout. Von Schüler dropped to his knees as the ground shook like it was in the grip of an earthquake. He didn't know what was happening.

Moments later, the mutilated body of Heidrich Munz crashed back to earth, having been spat out of the spout. Von Schüler turned his head away from the bloody and twisted form. As he did so, he noted his men had all turned tail and were running away.

'Halt!' he called as anger surged through his body.

They didn't stop. He raised his rifle and took aim at one of the fleeing minions. He fired, and the man fell, a rolling tangle of arms and legs. Von Schüler's attempt at discipline did not stem the exodus. In fact, it only increased their desire to leave.

Von Schüler suddenly found himself alone. But nonetheless, he was not going to give up. He had come too far. By rights, the treasure belonged to him.

As the smoke cleared. Sarah could see Mark's inert form lying on his back across the cavern. He hadn't moved. She rushed to his side and lifted his head into her lap. He appeared to be breathing.

'Mark,' she said, gently slapping his cheeks. He groaned. Sarah heaved a sigh of relief. 'Mark!' she repeated, shaking his shoulders.

He opened his eyes.

'Hello, gorgeous,' he said, his voice little more than a whisper.

She wasn't sure if his words were uncharacteristic brotherly affection, or delirium. 'Glad to see you're okay.'

'Gorgeous,' he repeated, but this time he pointed back across the cavern.

Sarah turned. She didn't know how she could have failed to notice. When Mark fired the cannon, the vibrations had caused a section of a fake wall at the rear of the cavern to collapse. Through a four-foot opening, a hidden room was now visible. Peering out through the hole was the life-size golden statue of the Madonna and Child. It was a thing of startling beauty.

Mark had not called her gorgeous, but referred to the statue. She almost let his head fall back to the cave floor. Instead, she slowly helped him to his feet.

'I'm okay,' he said. She wasn't sure if she believed him.

Together they moved toward the treasure room. They had barely taken two paces when the cavern shuddered and there was a loud crack. Mark pulled Sarah back just in time as another section of the secret wall collapsed before them.

'Careful, it isn't stable,' he said, stating the obvious.

Sarah nodded in agreement. Then she heard a loud thump behind her.

She thought more of the cavern was coming down. When she turned, she saw a figure silhouetted in the shaft of light. He was brandishing a rifle. She grabbed Mark's arm.

'We have an unwelcome guest,' she said.

With his free hand, Mark snatched the Webley from his holster and began to raise it.

'Stop right there,' Von Schüler called, his rifle aimed and at the ready, his finger around the trigger. Mark stopped, and lowered the weapon. Von Schüler grunted his approval. 'Throw the gun in the corner... Easy now.'

Sarah watched her brother toss the revolver into rubble on the cavern floor.

'Up against the wall,' Von Schüler called. To emphasise the point, he gestured with the barrel of his rifle.

Sarah was scared. Would he kill them now? She reached for Mark's hand, and he pulled her close.

But as Von Schüler looked beyond them, he saw the Madonna and Child staring out at him. His jaw dropped. Almost in a daze, he moved toward it, staggering over the rubble strewn across the cavern floor.

'I never believed this day would come,' he said. 'The Madonna and Child is more beautiful than I could have possibly ever imagined.'

While he spoke, Sarah started to inch her way toward the shaft, pulling Mark along with her.

The neo-Nazi kept moving toward the secret room; his eyes drawn to the angelic face of the Child cradled in his mother's arms.

The cavern shook once more and another section of the wall fell away. Von Schüler didn't appear to notice as stone and rock crashed around him. He reached out to touch the statue.

Continuing his monologue, he said, 'I have sought this treasure all my life. There have been many false trails, years spent searching the Cocos Islands. But I knew one day it would be mine.'

With a crash, the remaining section of the secret wall fell away, rock and debris tumbled down. As it fell, a portion of the roof splintered and dropped, slamming into the head of the Madonna. The statue was shunted forward, toppling over.

In his rapture, Von Schüler was caught by surprise as 500 pounds of gold fell on him. Caught in the statue's embrace, he screamed for one brief moment, then was suddenly silenced, crushed under the enormous weight.

Sarah looked away.

Mark put his arm around her shoulder and led her to the shaft. He handed her the rope.

'I think we've had enough excitement for one day,' he said. 'You go first. I think it's time we called in the authorities.'

Hand over hand, Sarah started up the shaft. She couldn't wait to see the sky once more.

Epilogue

July 18th 1954

Six months later...

At the end of the mass, the faithful streamed out of the *Portada del Perdón,* or the 'door of forgiveness'. Mark waited till the last of the congregation had exited, and then with his sister at his side, stepped into the towering basilica.

Originally completed in 1538, although rebuilt and remodelled many times since, the Cathedral of Lima was a sight to behold, with twin towers on either side of the ornate entrance facade. The church's interior was even more spectacular. The arched ceiling and columns were lined with gold, and magnificent artwork and sculptures bordered the walls. The Twelve Golden Apostles were positioned on a specially constructed altar, but even they paled in comparison to the basilica's centrepiece, the Madonna and Child, which took pride of place at the end of the nave.

Father Alvarez stood behind the pulpit. He looked up as Mark and Sarah made their way down the aisle toward him. He smiled. Mark could see Alvarez was eager to greet them. Alvarez picked up a walking stick which was hidden from view behind the pulpit and hobbled down the short flight of steps. He had not fully healed from his bullet wounds.

'Welcome. Welcome,' he called. 'I am so glad you came.'

'How could we refuse such a gracious invitation,' Sarah replied. 'It's good to see you on your feet again.'

'The knee still causes discomfort, but I make do,' the priest answered.

'The cathedral is magnificent,' Mark said.

'Back to her old glory. The Madonna and Child are back home where they belong –thanks to you.'

'Only too glad to help,' Mark replied.

'And that's why I invited you here. I need to ask for your help once again. Have you ever heard of the *Cruz del Sagrado Corazón?*'

Mark arched his eyebrow quizzically and turned to Sarah for the answer.

'The Cross of the Sacred Heart was stolen in 1877 from the church in Chincha Alta,' she said.

Alvarez smiled. 'That is correct.'

Sarah Evans

Plumbing the Depths

I

It takes guts to bite into a live pigeon, suck hard and swallow. It's even worse when you're a vegetarian, like me.

The first time was indescribably awful. It makes me gag just thinking about it.

I'd gone to the city train station at two on a Sunday morning. Not by choice because, hey, who'd want to lurk around with the derelicts and druggies at that god-forsaken hour? But I was there, under the cover of darkness, for easy pickings.

It was the eve of the summer holidays, though you'd think it was late autumn as the cold rain drizzled down relentlessly. The station was damp and miserable.

I was hungry. Dead hungry. Actually, make that *un*dead hungry, but we won't go there.

I headed to the near-empty overnight car park, where pigeons clustered on the bridge, along windowsills, on rails and in soggy street trees, pooping over everything.

Urban pigeon wasn't my idea of a delicacy but I had to eat something. Up until that moment, I had made do with thawed raw mince and liver juice, which wasn't nice however you served it up. I really craved warm, living blood rather than room temperature, watery gunk sloshing around on a black polystyrene tray under a peeling supermarket 'special' label.

I figured the pigeons were feathered vermin. No one would mind if the odd bird became a fast-food snack. I also figured a pigeon would be easier to catch, and would be slightly more appetising, than a rat, though they were in abundance too, scavenging through the bins outside the Far Pavilions Indian takeaway and the Periwinkle Cafe.

So there I was, all those weeks ago, at the railway station car park, standing on a wall so I could reach a ledge where a motley array of birds were peacefully dozing. The odd bird cooed a calming refrain but it failed to soothe my nerves.

I reached out...

The bird of my choice – a piebald, moth-eaten affair with a slipped wing and one eye which I'd reckoned would be the easiest to catch – freaked out as my grasp upset its slumbers. Feathers flew in a flurry of hand-bird wrestling, which I won. Just.

I held the hyperventilating bird between my shaking hands, feeling its frantic heartbeat. I attempted to centre myself and move into the right head space. This took a lot of doing, because it really wasn't natural to clamp ones teeth over a warm body, sink them into the soft grey-skinned flesh, and suck out the lifeblood.

The situation was made worse because the terrified bird had eyeballed me with its one good, ruby red peeper.

I shut my own eyes in a bid to make the whole operation less disgusting, and bit my finger, along with the feathers. I loosened my grip, the bird wriggled free and flew helter-skelter smack into a passing car's windscreen. In hindsight, I should have taken advantage and snacked on the concussed bird. But I'd lost my appetite, which hadn't been robust in the first place.

On the second attempt, the following night, I overcompensated. I bit clean through feathers, flesh and bone. I vomited the vile mouthful as I held the flopping bird in my hand. I put it out of its misery, wrapped it in a discarded chip paper and threw it in the rubbish bin, on top of a half-eaten vindaloo festering in a tinfoil carton. It wasn't my finest hour.

The third time was marginally better, though the pigeon probably didn't think so. Both of us ended up light headed: one through a much needed blood infusion and the other due to anaemia, so weak that it fell off its perch when I tried to replace it on the ledge.

But now I have it down to a fine art. I choose a plump, dozing bird in the darkest part of the station. I gently hold it, stroking it rhythmically, calming it into a trance-like state. I then swiftly bite, suck and then let the critter go. No histrionics. Just nice and clean and quick.

Okay, so the feathers can get stuck between your teeth. And some of the birds don't taste too good, because of their age or sickness. And some have lice, which crawl over your skin and make you itch.

But basically, I use the birds as a sustainable larder. I don't suck them dry and leave a desiccated carcass like some of my peers do. I just 'borrow' a bit of blood. Occasionally I overdo it and the bird goes limp. But most times they don't seem too badly affected.

At least, that's what I tell myself.

The downside to pigeon-sucking is that the birds don't like me anymore. There's none of the bonhomie 'tuppence-a-bag' good natured feeding routine. The birds give me a wide berth, even if I bring them a bag of bread scraps, which is why I'm seriously considering visiting the duck pond one night. Maybe a mallard or Muscovy would be more amenable, as well as add some dietary variety.

I've come a long way – or gone down a long way, depending how you look at it – since I was turned. Because now I do catch rats, but their squeaking is off-putting, and you have to be careful they're not the ones doing the biting.

But on this winter's evening, I wasn't food obsessed. I had other things on my mind, like survival.

Frozen and alone, I stood within the deep shadow of the lychgate and focused my attention on the door of St John the Baptist's.

It was a small, flint-stoned Saxon church situated on the corner of Burlington's East Street and The Dials, on the dodgy side of town. The west door was framed by two ancient yews. In the frosted gloom the trees sat hunched, like a pair of intimidating black minotaurs; the keepers of the faith, waiting with coiled menace to spring at any unfortunate who defiled the hallowed halls within.

Which basically meant me, so I prudently kept my distance.

Minutes ticked into a long tedious hour as I waited for the Australian punk who, for the past week, had been trying to kill me.

Or at least that was what I presumed he was trying to do, in a cack-handed sort of way.

Monday night, he'd chucked a bucket of water at me, presumably of the

Holy variety. The bucket had slipped and flipped and so most of the contents had sloshed over him, making him profane ripely. I'd instinctively ducked behind a stationary milk float and had avoided any fall-out.

Wednesday, he'd jumped out of the shadows and tried spearing me with a splintered paling from an old garden fence. Luckily for me, the wood was of inferior pine and the shallow wound closed up almost immediately, once I'd pulled the paling out of my chest. But I must admit, that little effort had given me a few heebie-jeebies. It was the first time someone had actually staked me. Next time I may not be so fortunate.

As my attacker reeked of garlic, he should simply have breathed over me while skulking in the shadows. That may have done it.

The last few days he'd dogged my steps, waiting for another opportunity, an opportunity I wasn't going to give him if I could help it. It was like having my very own Kato manservant keeping me on my toes. It was all very tiring and extremely annoying, especially as I could have avoided this whole situation if I hadn't listened to my conscience, if I hadn't played the Good Samaritan.

I sighed and my breath froze in a white cloud. What the hell was the guy doing in there? Reading the Bible end to end, then back again? Confessing a lifetime of sin to the locum priest? Attempting salvation? Maybe all three, but whatever he was up to, he was taking a damn long time and I was all for calling it a day.

Well, a night.

I shifted my stance, wiggling my numb toes to aid circulation. Two pairs of stripy wool socks and sturdy leather boots were no match for the sub-zero temperatures. They squeezed me like a vice and made my breath freeze deep inside my lungs. My knees, ears and nose were also frozen, cheeks immobile, my hands blocks of ice.

But then, I wasn't often warm these days, no matter many layers I dragged on.

Apparently this was the interim stage. Things could get better, depending on what I was prepared to do.

Like drink human blood.

Really, how had it come to this? I needed to get myself sorted. Get a life.

Or end this one.

The night crashed around me, bouncing off my eyeballs, tattooing my skin, eroding my soul. Welcome to the dark side that was now my existence, thanks to my husband and his perverted ways.

Actually, to be strictly honest it wasn't night time; it was a late winter afternoon.

You've just gotta love winter with its early evenings drawing in around you, like a thick black eiderdown, thrusting away the light, blocking out day. It meant I had longer to kick around in the living world rather than being holed up in some dark place, waiting for the sun to go to bed. Summer got rather tedious, what with early sunrises and late sunsets. One had to cram so much into a handful of hours around midnight. But I missed the sun. I can't remember the last time I was solar kissed.

Ah, at last, movement. And about time too.

A dim, yellow light illuminated the arched entrance as the oak door swung open. A second later, a figure stood on the church step, a 'mini me' of the yews: dark, hunched and coiled. He hovered by the flint-flecked wall, back-lit by the church's weak electric light. Could he sense I was waiting for him? Smell me? Or was his night vision as good as mine and he was waiting to see if I'd pounce?

I was still getting a handle on who could do what in this twilight world. It wasn't as if you were given a How-To manual once you'd stepped into the ether. And I didn't know if this bloke was good, bad or just plain ugly.

The door closed with a dull thud behind him, shutting off the light, allowing the darkness to swallow him whole. I held my breath, not wanting to give myself away, just in case he could actually see me; that he was, like me, an other world being.

On cue, the man yelled out, 'I know you're there, Mrs Peters.'

'Then you should be scared,' I shouted back and felt the sharp prickle of blood lust. I licked my lips in anticipation. This sucker, *moi*, badly needed a feed and that punk, *il*, needed to be taken down. Maybe it was time to end my prudishness and relinquish my principles.

'No, lady, just tired.'

I snorted. 'It's your age, old man. You should retire.'

'I *was* retired. That's how I got into this mess. I should have read the fine print.'

'I don't understand.'

'Me neither. There I was, innocently booking a heritage site package tour of the UK and nowhere did it say that it was for eternity. Someone,' he pointed heavenwards, 'was obviously pulling my lariat.'

You could hear the man's distinct antipodean twang. But then I knew he was an Aussie. I'd heard the accent the first time I'd come across him, when he'd been swearing his heart out in a pool of blood.

'You're funny,' I said. 'So what happened on your church tour, Skippy?'

'Copped a bullet fired by some lowlife pill while visiting this little baby,' he waved in the direction of St John's.

'Bad luck. You should have been more careful.'

'Hah, it wasn't my fault. I'd got myself separated from the tour group. They'd left me kicking my heels down in the vault while they went off for a cream tea or some toasted bloody tea cake. The next thing I knew, all hell had broken loose. A bit like a modern spaghetti western but without the cactus.' He sighed and wiped a big meaty hand over his face as if he was exhausted by the memory.

'Well, for the record,' I said. 'St John's is part of a turf war. Good versus evil. But then you've probably realised that by now.'

'Well, what d'ya know!' He slapped his thigh. 'And I thought it was just the choir boys getting boisterous.'

'You can cut the sarcasm.'

'Yeah, well, that infamous tunnel with the white light was sucking me along nicely till I got detoured because some interfering chick stemmed the bleeding and shunted me off to emergency. And now I'm destined for an eternity of crime fighting, without long-service leave. Let me tell you, girl, after 30 years in the police force, I could've done without that angelic curve ball.'

'So you're an *angel*? Sweet!' I tried not to sound too disbelieving. And let's face it, I'd come across a wide range of species since I was dragged over the edge of the abyss, kicking and screaming like an indignant nanny goat.

And why shouldn't he be an angel? Someone had to do it and, in the scheme of things, I may have helped the process.

'Yeah, Mrs Peters. An angel. Don't I look like one?'

He stepped out onto the uneven brick path towards me. Vandals had long ago busted the church's security lights. But I didn't need artificial aids to see his grizzled grey buzz cut and short, stocky body with a beer paunch that must have taken a good few years to perfect. His jeans were a cheap cut and his Hawaiian shirt more suited to tropical sands in high summer than a coastal English city in deep winter chills. I felt several degrees colder just watching him strutting about in his naff summer togs.

He didn't, in all honesty, look much like an angel.

But then he didn't look much like a cop, either. More urban dwarf, if there was such an animal.

'No, Skippy. You're not cherubic enough. And you're missing your shiny harp and halo.'

'Maybe with those kitsch props I'd be taken seriously. At least as a police officer I had my ID to vouch for me. It's an uphill battle being an angel in this pommie hell-hole city, let me tell you.'

'My heart bleeds for you.'

'Yeah, right. Word on the street says you don't do bleeding. Quite the opposite, in fact.'

'You've been listening to gutter gossip.'

'But it *is* true?'

'Well, yes. Does it bother you?'

'No.'

'So then why have you been trying to kill me these past few days, if I'm not a threat to you?'

'I'm stuck in this dismal country till I score enough lost souls.'

'Which means?'

'You're lost. I want your soul.' He smiled. It wasn't warm and fuzzy. 'To add to my scorecard and my free ticket home. Back to endless bloody sunshine and deep-boned heat. I can't wait.'

He then shifted slightly and I realised he had a backpack spray unit, the type you used for garden weeds, harnessed to him. He hefted the pump so that the nozzle was pointing directly at me.

'Prepare to meet your maker, Mrs Peters.'

'Do you mean my mortal maker or the vampire one?' I tried to keep my voice calm. No need to rattle him with panic. He might squeeze the trigger before I was ready. I still had a load of things to do before I hit dirt and shrivelled into nothingness.

'Just want to save your soul, lady.'

'Too late for that, Mr Angel.'

'I'm sorry.'

'Don't be. But surely you owe me?'

'Really?'

'I was the one who took you to the Burlington General.'

In hindsight, I should have left him to die because then I wouldn't be here, freezing my butt and fending off a half-baked angel with his dodgy weaponry.

'Really?' he said again and sounded as though he didn't believe me.

'November 5th, Guy Fawkes Night. Lots of cracks and explosions. No one heard what was going on at St John's. You were shot in the gullet. The bullet missed vital organs, but you lost a lot of blood, which is why you went AWOL on the operating table.'

'Seems you know a lot about it.'

'Weren't you listening – I was there.'

'Was that why I was light on the blood, then? You decided on a quick snack while I bled out?' He sounded jacked off.

I bared a smile and noted he moved back a pace. So he wasn't so sure about me, after all. 'I'm not big on human blood. Goes against the grain, Skippy. In fact, I'm not big on blood at all.'

'A vegetarian vampire? How quaint.'

'You have no idea.' I thought of my diet of grey station pigeons and the odd rodent. I'd come a long way since my puritan days of devouring organic lentil burgers and bean sprouts in the trendy cafes of Burlington.

But was it that long? Six months max. A mere blink in the scheme of the universe.

My first inkling of trouble was one balmy summer lunchtime at the Laughing Trout pub. I'd turned up late to attend a 25th birthday bash. My friends were already seated out in the beer garden, sculling chilled white wine and studying the menu under a large red and white stripy umbrella. The scent of freshly cut grass vied with honeysuckle and French fries. People were laughing, children played on the swings, some musician was killing an Eagles classic and the sun was actually bothering to shine.

So it was a nice, straightforward summer's day; except that it wasn't.

I'd had a vitriolic argument with my husband, Minstrel. Over kids. Again. An ongoing merry-go-round since we'd married six months before. I wanted them, he didn't. He couldn't see the point, which I didn't understand at the time.

But my biological clock was ticking louder than a cartoon time bomb. I'd talked about pregnancy with my doctor. She'd done a check up and said my iron levels were shot to hell, that she didn't know how I got out of bed every day, or, come to that, how I functioned at all. She gave me the name of a super-dose iron supplement, told me to take it with orange juice and to lay off the tea.

At least I knew why I'd felt drained of energy.

On top of the tiredness, I'd suffered a throbbing humdinger of a headache for most of the week. It'd stopped me working, which wasn't good for a jobbing artist. I'd then begun to feel shivery and weak. It was just my luck that, while everyone else bared their flesh and worked on a brief British tan, I was rugged up in a thick winter woolly and feeling like death.

At least the high-necked jumper not only kept me warm but hid signs of my husband's excessive lovemaking. He'd left me with a rash of embarrassingly visual love-bites, which he thought very funny. I didn't share his mirth.

I'd almost decided not to go to the party, but Juliet was one of my oldest school friends and I didn't want to let her down. So I swallowed some painkillers, thrust on my sunnies and plastered a fake smile on my face.

'You look washed out,' she said as I kissed her cheek and wished her happy birthday.

'Ta. That makes me feel so much better.' I set down my pint of Guinness and took a seat next to her.

'Slumming it, darling?' She eyed the stout distastefully.

'Felt I needed an iron kick,' I said in way of explanation. By choice, I was no Guinness drinker.

'I'd rather suck on a nail.' She leaned forward, tugged down the neckline of my top and peeked at my bruised throat. She giggled and I blushed. 'I see the honeymoon is ongoing,' she said. 'Lucky you. Wish I could find myself a dashingly romantic husband.'

I didn't disabuse her. She didn't need to know about the bitter arguments, or how controlling Minstrel was, nor his sordid proclivities I'd discovered since our marriage.

'You'd better eat to keep up your strength,' she joked. 'The crumbed Camembert mushrooms with roasted baby beets look good.' She waved the menu at me.

I didn't bother looking at it. I ordered the first thing that popped into my head: a steak and as rare as possible without needing to be lassoed. My taste buds sprang into life at the thought of it.

'Matty! When the hell did you start eating meat, girl?'

'I don't,' I said, confused. 'Haven't. Not for ages. Why would I start now?'

Why indeed.

'But you just ordered a steak! A bleeding steak.'

'Did I?' My friends were shocked, but not as shocked as me. 'I wasn't concentrating,' I said quickly, feeling slightly sick. 'I'll change the order.'

But the seafood fettuccine didn't hit the spot, not nearly.

That was a month before my first pigeon.

Three months before my first rat.

Now, regarding the Hawaiian-shirted angel, I shivered. Was it time for a human? Was I moving into the next stage? Sinking further into the dross?

But perhaps it was just Skippy's attire giving me the willies. 'Grief, aren't you cold, even for an angel?'

'Yeah. Bloody freezing,' he said.

'So get yourself some serious clothes.'

'I've only got Australian currency on me. I ran out of sterling a while back.'

I laughed and the air turned frosted white. 'Just nick some togs, Mr Angel. Who's going to stop you? You're a paranormal.'

'I've fought crime all my adult life, I'm not about to turn criminal.'

'Very altruistic. I'm impressed. No wonder you've been promoted to an avenging angel.'

He scowled. It didn't improve his demeanour.

'There's a charity bin behind the church. Go help yourself to some woollies. There may even be a spare set of wings.'

His frown got worse and he waved the spray nozzle at me.

'Listen, I don't want to die,' I said to him, though I wasn't entirely sure that was true. 'Not yet, anyway. I've got unfinished business.'

'What, you haven't lodged your tax return?'

'That's the least of my concerns, Skippy. There's someone I need to annihilate.'

'Sounds serious.'

'It is.'

'Who?'

'My husband.'

'Minstrel Peters.'

'You've heard of him?' I shouldn't have been surprised. If anyone had made it to the other side then they would have come across Minstrel. Many were there *because* of him. Like me.

'Yeah. He's on my wish list to also, er, annihilate.'

'So we want the same thing.'

'I suppose so.'

'No suppose about it. Let's get you those woollies, Skippy, and move out of here. All this churchified air is giving me heartburn.'

He lowered the pump nozzle. 'The name's Ted,' he said. 'Quit calling me Skippy. It's disrespectful.'

'To you or the kangaroo?'

'Both.'

I pointed him in the direction of the charity clothes bin. No way was I going near it, due to the hallowed turf.

It was unfortunate that the last lot of clothes shoved in the bin must have been owned by a large woman with a penchant for pink.

'Beggars can't be choosers,' I said, swallowing a laugh as Ted fished out sugar-pink leggings, cyclamen-pink shirt and a hot-pink skirt.

The last thing he held up was a fluffy pink jumper shot through with silver thread that must have shrunk in the wash.

'Go on. Try it on, why don't you?'

'But it's hideous.'

'It's warm. It'll do.'

He pulled it over his head with some difficulty. 'And it's so bloody small it's stopping the circulation in my arms,' he complained as he tried tugging it over his loud shirt and louder beer gut.

'Not only that, it reeks of perfume.'

'Just look on it as another form of suffering and one step closer to Heaven. Or in your case, Australia, if that's where you want to go.'

'Why wouldn't I? This place is bloody freezing. And I'm only here on holiday.'

'Some holiday.'

He trotted after me along the road. He obviously wanted to talk now that he wasn't attempting to waste me, so I steered him to the civic garden which was used as a dogs' toilet by day and playground for the marginalised by night. We fitted in just fine.

We sat side by side on a park bench in the pitch black. And he was right; the jumper stank of cheap scent. Lucky Ted. But it would no doubt help keep those shape-shifting beings at bay that were flitting about on the edge of our peripheral vision.

'I thought I'd done with the graveyard shift,' he said on a sigh, huddling into his rancid pink fluff. 'But hunting you bloodsuckers means I'm back doing unsocial hours.'

'Aren't you scared of us?' I asked curiously.

'Vampires don't scare me.' He puffed out his chest like an old silver-back gorilla, though the image was compromised by the jumper.

'They should. I'm scared and I'm one of them.'

It was his turn to give me a curious once-over. 'But you hang out with them.'

'Not if I can help it. And when I do, I treat them with a great deal of respect. Like never turning my back on them.'

'Well, I've got protection.' He indicated the spray unit. 'It's full of St John's Holy water. And I'm not afraid to use it.'

I raised my eyebrows inquiringly. 'Does the water work?'

He shrugged and looked a little sheepish. 'I don't know. I haven't had to use it yet. You were my first victim. I missed the first time, remember?'

I nodded and tried not to laugh. 'Excellent. So you were going to play Russian roulette with a weed spray pack.'

'We could try it out now.' He sounded hopeful.

'Not on me you don't! What sort of angel are you, anyway?'

'I dunno. Look, I didn't ask to be an angel.' He was like a grumpy kid who'd failed to win any games at a birthday party. 'I've no yen to fight the dark forces. I've already done my yards for law and order. And anyway, I'm not a *proper* angel. It's only a title I've been given. I'm just in holiday limbo for a while, until things get sorted.'

'Sorry to disillusion you, Ted, but you're in purgatory.'

'To hell with that!'

I snorted. 'Not quite. You obviously weren't *that* bad in your mortal life or you'd already be in the basement.'

'What do you mean?'

'I mean that your soul isn't wicked enough to go to Hell, but it's not pure enough to go to Heaven. Basically, you've got to suffer here a while, in delightful Burlington-on-Purgatory, until you're purified. Only then can you move on to Heaven.'

'Really?' He didn't sound thrilled.

'Well, that's what the Catholics say.'

'But I'm not a Catholic.'

'Doesn't matter. They don't have the monopoly on suffering. Someone,' and I mimicked his earlier action, 'obviously thought you hadn't gained enough Brownie points to go upstairs. You've got to earn the right.'

'But that's not fair. I'm not even dead.'

'Says who?'

'Says me. Say the doctors who saved me on the operating table. Says the bloke who gave me the angel tag and told me I had to nobble some of you evil types so I could go home.'

'Who was *that*?'

'I dunno. He came and saw me on the ward. I think he was a social worker or something.'

Or something. Was someone, or some*thing*, recruiting common-or-garden foot soldiers to fight Burlington's bad?

Compassion stirred within me, a rare thing nowadays. 'Come with me,' I said. 'I'll prove something to you.'

'Where are we going?'

'To the Burlington General.'

'What, now?'

'Yep. No point wasting time.' Though in theory I had a shed load of it. It was called eternity.

We trudged through the quiet, frosted streets. Every so often, Ted would squirt some Holy water at a cat or stray dog, which didn't do much except make them run away, wet.

At the Burlington General, we slipped in through the fire exit door and climbed the back stairs to the intensive care unit. It was easy dodging the night staff. They were sculling coffee and inhaling sweet pastries at the nurses' station. We tiptoed into the ward and sussed out the prone bodies wired up to various life-supporting machines.

'Who are you actually looking for?' said Ted. He scrutinised the clipboard at the end of a patient's bed.

'You.'

He stiffened. 'You're barking.' He smacked the clipboard back down. 'I'm right beside you, in case you haven't noticed!'

'Shh.' I held my finger up to my lips. 'And humour me.' I patted him on the cheek. 'Follow me.'

I took him downstairs to the mortuary where no one appeared to be on duty. We slipped through the swing doors into the chilled inner sanctum. I randomly pulled open the cold chambers housing the bodies and read the labels hanging off their stiff toes.

'You can't do that,' Ted hissed in my ear. 'It's not right.'

I ignored him and kept searching. And with that I found my man. 'Take a look, Ted.'

He peered over my shoulder at the iced body. There was a rapid intake of breath and then a thump and clatter. Ted was out for the count at my feet. Or at least his paranormal self was. His actual body was still lying on the slab like an ugly sleeping beauty.

'Get up and stop being a baby,' I said and slid the body back into the chamber.

Ted moaned.

'We've got to get out of here. It'll soon be day.'

He moaned again and flapped about on the floor, spilling Holy water from his leaking back-pack.

'Get a grip, Ted,' I said.

'But that's me in there.'

'So what do you know?' *Duh.*

'I am dead!'

'Yep.'

He squinted down at himself. 'But not.'

'Yep.'

'Which means...?' He gave me a big soulful, pained look, his jowls quivering. I almost felt sorry for him, but only almost. We all had our own particular crosses to bear.

'Purgatory,' I finished for him.

'I was going to say, holiday.'

'Sorry, Mr Angel, no holiday jollies at this point in time, just good old-fashioned purgatory. But that's the least of my problems at the mo. It's almost dawn and I've got to split before I turn to dust.'

'True blue? That's not a fallacy?'

'I'm not prepared to find out. Would you, in my shoes?'

I hustled him out of the hospital, through the back entrance, and we stood awkwardly by the army of dustbins. I didn't know quite how to give him the brush-off. He looked so lost and sad, but he wasn't my responsibility.

'I'm off,' I said after a too-long pause. 'I'll be seeing you, Ted.'

'Really?' he said. 'You're going to abandon me? Just like that?' And he looked even more lost and sad.

'Well, yes. What else can I do? As a rule angels and vampires don't mix.'

'We could be the exception.'

'Or not.'

'But what am I going to *do*?'

A large tabby with wide yellow eyes cat-walked along the wall behind the bins and sprang down lightly between us. It weaved between my legs and I bent and stroked it, causing an instant pneumatic drill of purring.

'What do you mean?'

'I'm dead,' he wailed.

'Cheer up.' I would have given him a hug but I was worried the damp patches of Holy water on his clothes would be detrimental to my health. 'Look, you knew you were in limbo, that you had to win souls to earn your ticket home. You'd already been told that by the fellow in the hospital.'

'Yeah. I know.'

'So what's the issue here?' I said.

Ted stared at the animal unseeingly. 'I didn't *know* I was actually dead!' There was a plaintive break in his voice. 'There is a big difference, you know.'

I sighed, gave the cat one last pat and straightened. 'Okay, I know. I'm sorry. But at least you've got the chance to redeem yourself.' I indicated his makeshift gun.

'A fat lot of good this is,' he said and, lifting the nozzle, he sprayed the cat.

None of us, including the cat, were prepared for the next few seconds. There was a high-pitched yowl that shattered my eardrums and jiggled my shirt buttons. The cat jumped into the air, hit the deck, then fizzed and burned until there was nothing but a black, steaming sludge left.

Ted and I stared open-mouthed at the rapidly diminishing black puddle.

'Oh my.' I said inadequately, my ears still ringing.

'Poor cat.'

'Hell, that wasn't a cat, if it responded like that.'

We stood there in silence.

'Well, whatever it was, it's not anymore,' said Ted.

'And you've got your first tick on your score card. High five.'

II

I didn't see hide or hair of Ted for several weeks, which didn't particularly concern me. Now that he was supposedly off my case to assassinate me, I didn't care much about him. I had other issues to contend with rather than babysitting a grumpy old angel coming to grips with good, evil and life in purgatory.

My biggest problem was fighting the urge to bite people. It's not a good habit when hanging out with friends. Because of this, I had taken avoiding action, barricading myself in my studio. Basically, I wasn't seeing anyone in case I involuntarily snacked.

Except Minstrel. He was hard to keep out.

I was working because I didn't see the point in wasting time, even if I did have an awful lot of it. I was throwing paint at a canvas and trying to make sense of my existence along with my rather abstract artwork when my husband came through the door. Literally, which is always unnerving.

'Matilda, darling,' he said and my body surged with instant longing, dammit. How could I still want him when I knew exactly what he was? But at a primal level, I loved him, still fancied him rotten, and I wasn't proud of myself.

Minstrel: my handsome, sophisticated husband who sponsored the arts, was the darling of the social set, and who corrupted the souls of those stupid enough to spin into his orbit.

Like me.

Ted the angel may have got in the way of his henchman's bullet, but I'd got in the way of his heart. Or at least I thought I had. And did he actually have one? That remained to be seen. Personally, I think he'd gifted it to the Devil a very long time ago.

'Hello, Minstrel.' I concentrated on the canvas and hoped he couldn't pick up the frantic beating of my heart, the zinging of my blood, as my body responded to him.

But he was tuned to blood, was Minstrel. He could read the signs.

'Ah, so you're pleased to see me, Matty.' I could hear the smile in his voice. He ran a finger down my cheek and I shivered with equal measures of fear and longing.

Without looking at the palette, I randomly threw paint at the canvas in an attempt to deflect his interest. I didn't want him getting any ideas.

The canvas bled. What a surprise. The paint was ruby red, the colour of pulsating fresh blood. My mouth tingled at the image.

'Where have you been, Matilda? I've missed you.'

'Here and there.' Walking the streets at night, trying to make meaning of my new life. Avoiding my husband and his unsavoury friends.

'You should be by my side, darling. That's what beautiful wives are for.'

'And cramp your style? I don't think so, Minstrel.'

'Babe, you *are* my style.'

Oh, he was a slick talker, I'd give him that. Once I'd believed everything he said. But not now. I flicked him what I hoped was a scathing look. 'Don't give me that bullshit, Minstrel. You don't need me. You've had your fun, turning me into this creature. Now leave me alone to pick up the pieces.'

'You sound angry. Bitter. Why, precious? I've given you eternal life. With me.' His smile was gut-wrenchingly whimsical, as if he was enjoying the prospect of our hugely long life together.

But I didn't believe him.

'The anger and bitterness are just the tip of the berg. Why did you do it, Minstrel? Why did you turn me into a blood sucker? It's not fair. I didn't ask to be one of you.'

'But I wanted you to be.' His voice was soft but there was a hardness in his eyes. 'So you'll be mine forever.'

'Forever is a hell of a long time. You'll get sick of me.'

He leaned forward and nipped at my earlobe. 'You don't make me sick, Matty. You invigorate me. So sweet. So deliciously appetising.' He laughed and the hairs on the back of my neck prickled. 'Anyway, it was fun seeing if I could corrupt you, darling. You were such a quiet, puritanical little thing. I just had to have you.'

And he had. Well and truly.

Now he twisted a strand of my long dark hair around his fingers and gave a gentle tug. 'I've found there's a pattern. The pure and innocent are the ones who fall the hardest, once you can get under their guard. The thrill is finding the way.'

I wrenched away from him and blindly smacked some more colour on to the canvas, trying not to respond with any emotion, good or bad.

This time dark blue hit the spot, bruising the dripping red.

'Leave me alone. I'm working,' I said.

But he didn't.

He left much, much later and I was resigned to the fact that I'd be wearing my high-necked tops for the next few days.

The following evening, just past midnight, there was a knock at my studio door. Not an appropriate time to visit, in my opinion, so I didn't answer it.

There was another tattoo, louder this time, and more insistent.

'Mrs Peters, I know you're there.'

Great. It was Ted. Just what I needed; a grumpy antipodean angel.

'Go away.'

'But I've got something for you.'

I peered through the door's spy-hole.

The spy-hole had come with the one-roomed flat that I'd converted into a studio back in my inglorious art student days. The hole was handy for vetting visitors but lousy for keeping out my paranormal peers.

But not Ted.

Mr Angel obviously hadn't worked out that he could just waft in at will. Or, to give him the benefit of the doubt, he was just too polite to do so.

'What?' I said.

'I've brought over a takeaway.'

I sighed and wrestled with my conscience. Against my will I felt a smidge responsible for Ted, but did I really want to socialise? No, in a word.

'I'm not hungry,' I yelled through the door. Which was a lie. I was famished. I hadn't feasted for a week.

'Please, Mrs P. Open up.'

I sighed again. I suppose he was just trying to be friendly.

'Wait a moment.' I dragged my dressing gown over my fleecy PJs and belted it tightly, then wound a scarf around my neck to hide Minstrel's teeth marks and opened the door.

Ted, still wearing the hideous pink and smelling as bad, grinned as he held up a green plastic and wire cat carrier. It was stuffed with agitated pigeons that sounded like a bus-load of burbling old women on a WI day-trip. 'I caught them myself,' he said proudly.

'Bully for you.' I stepped back so he could come in. A couple of feathers fluttered onto the paint-splattered lino.

'Well I didn't know what else you liked to eat and I know you, er, harvest the pigeons at the station.' He plonked the carrier on the floor, making the birds bat their wings against the mesh.

'I'm touched you thought of me at all.'

'I don't have many mates this side of the world.'

I wasn't sure if he meant the Northern Hempishere or the supernatural realm, and did it actually matter?

He sighed. 'You're all I've got.'

'Poor you.'

'Amen to that.'

'You do have your mentor, whoever he is. Don't forget him.'

'Yeah. But I haven't seen him in a while. I'm lonely, Mrs P, and I hate living in this damp, cold city with its lousy night life.'

'As I told you before, vampires don't hang out with angels,' I said. 'We're on opposing sides.'

'But you're not a *bad* vampire.'

'All vampires are bad.'

'You don't drink human blood.'

'Your logic is rather shaky. I may start at any moment.' And I gave him a toothy grin.

He had the grace to look uncomfortable. 'Okay, I confess. I have another reason for coming around.'

'Which is?'

'I've a proposition.'

'Ah. Am I going to like it?'

'Possibly not, but it's worth a shot and it'll help me get home quicker. Back to sunshine and surf. Ah, bliss.'

'Go on then, Skippy.'

He gave me a dark look.

'Sorry. Ted'

'I want you to help me get my quota. To hunt down and kill vampires.'

A pain spasmed deep in my chest and burned through me, sucking my oxygen, pressing on my eyeballs.

He was joking, right? A killer joke.

'I've thought about it. We could call ourselves the Burlington Vampire Slayers. What do you think? Or better still, the Burlington Awesome Vampire Slayers: BAVS for short.'

Okay, so he wasn't having a lend.

I sucked in much-needed air. 'No.' It came out a pathetic croak.

'But you said you wanted to kill Minstrel.'

I shrugged. 'I was angry with him.'

'What? So you don't want to anymore?'

'No.'

'Why?'

'It's complicated.'

'Not from where I'm coming from. He's the most dangerous man-slash-bat in Burlington.'

'He's also my husband, in case you'd forgotten.'

'And? He's still an evil sod. You wanted to kill him the other night. What's changed?'

What indeed? But I didn't have such a killer desire any more. Love did that, I guess.

'That was weeks ago. I'm not as angry with him as I was,' I said, which sounded wimpy.

'So you've come to terms with being a bloodsucker? Tell me, how does that work? It's still a low-life existence.'

'I'll tell you.' I counted off on my fingers. 'One, I ignore it to the best of my ability. Two, I don't feed off people. Three, I try not to expend too much energy so I don't need as much blood. Four, oh I don't know! I just have to get on with it. It's what I am now.'

'I'm disappointed in you.'

'Tough.'

'I thought you had more integrity.'

'It's been sucked out of me. Now get out before I change my mind about drinking human blood.'

'I'm half angel. My blood isn't worth your while. It'll give you belly ache.'

'Did your mentor tell you that or are you making it up?'

His eyes slid away and he lifted his shoulders ever so slightly.

I laughed scathingly. 'You *are* making it up! That's why you're wearing a socking great big crucifix under your jumper.'

'How do you know?'

'Extra sensory vision.'

'Really?' He sounded impressed. And worried.

'No.' I admitted. 'I can see the outline.'

He fingered the crucifix through the pink fluff. 'It's just a precaution, Mrs P.'

'Against me?'

'Yes, against you.' He sounded narked. 'But also against all the nasties in Burlington. I need all the protection I can get. It's not easy being an angel in this town.'

'Poor Ted.'

'You can find me at St John's if you change your mind.'

'I won't.'

'You might.'

Ted left me with the pigeons. They rattled about in the crate, ruffling their grey, black and white feathers and cooing loudly. I couldn't keep them in the flat because there was a No Pet policy, so I feasted on their blood and enjoyed the warmth that surged through my body. I hadn't realised how shatteringly tired I'd been, only how hungry due to my self-imposed fast. The bird blood acted like a tonic and I felt better than I had all week.

Then, standing out on my tiny balcony, I let them go free into the chilly night. They flew in the direction of the station. No surprises there.

For a while I stayed out on the balcony, listening to the rumble of traffic. Some cats were fighting and there was a far bass beat from one of the pubs hosting a late night band. The air smelt of traffic exhausts laced with smoke. I watched shadows moving and morphing into creatures of the endless night and thought about Ted's proposition, wondering what I should do.

I hated being a vampire. But did I want to kill the species? Kill my own? Was I strong enough? Brave enough?

I turned to go back inside and jumped, dropping the carrier with a clatter and scratching myself deeply on the carrier's wire door.

Minstrel was lounging against the door jamb. Dressed in a tux, with his black tie undone and his hair mussed, he looked devastating.

'You should knock,' I said, holding my grazed and stinging arm to my beating chest.

'Why?'

I righted the carrier and locked the balcony French door.

'Because it's rude to enter someone's home uninvited.'

'This isn't your home!' he said. 'You belong with me. I'm running out of patience.'

I had left Minstrel's palatial seafront home when I'd realised what he was and what he was doing to me. I'd been too craven to tell him I was leaving him. Instead I just said I'd need some creative space to do my artwork. He'd grudgingly accepted that. Until now.

He didn't look happy, but there was no going back.

'I prefer to slum it here,' I said.

'Is that why you feed off feral pigeons?'

'Better than feeding off people.'

'It's time you accepted what you are, Matilda. Pigeon blood won't hack it much longer. You need a richer substance.'

'Like?' But I knew what he was going to say. Knew I wouldn't like it, damn him.

'You want me to spell it out for you, darling?'

'No.' I raised my chin and glared at him with defiance.

'You're not stupid. We drink blood to survive. It's basic stuff. People don't quibble about eating processed meat, even though bacon or veal was once an animal. What's the difference? At least our prey has had a freer life. It hasn't been kept in small pens and force-fed.'

I wrinkled my nose in disgust.

'Oh, that's right,' he said. 'I forgot. You were a self-righteous vegetarian before I turned you. Very high minded. You must be finding this all very difficult, Matilda.'

'Patronising bastard!' I clenched my jaw until it hurt. He had no idea just how difficult, or how distressing, the vampire status was to me.

'Oh, how the mighty have fallen.'

'At least I don't kill the things I feed off,' I said, defending myself.

'Hypocrisy was never one of your failings, darling; until now. Face it, you don't do the birds any favours by sucking them half to death. You are what you are, Matty.'

He reached over and grabbed my wrist. 'Look, sweetheart, you're bleeding. But for how long, eh?'

I glanced down at my arm. Fat beads of blood had sprung along a four-inch gash caused by the wire carrier. Then, on cue, the blood disappeared and the skin grew smooth until there was no sign of the gouge. I ran my finger along the path of the faded cut.

'In fact, my love, you don't have to wear prissy polo-neck sweaters or scarves after our lovemaking.'

I automatically lifted my hand to the scarf I'd put on when Ted had arrived.

'That's right. Love-bites heal instantaneously too. Any wounds do. We're vampires. We're self-healing.'

'I wish we had never met,' I said, hating him for corrupting me.

'Too bad. But we did. We connected. Now you're mine. For eternity. Get used to it, wife.'

'I won't!'

'You can't fight it.'

'I can.'

'Embrace your destiny. Give in with good grace.'

'You're a fine one to talk about grace.'

But he wasn't listening. He was laughing as he unlatched the balcony door and launched himself into the night. 'Night, night, Matilda darling. Sweet dreams.'

I watched him go.

Like the pigeons, he flew towards the station.

As I'd said before, the station offered easy pickings.

I only hoped that Minstrel would be kind – though I doubted it.

As soon as the sun disappeared the next evening, I hit the streets. Before Minstrel had turned me, I used to be afraid of Burlington after dark, what with its rapes and muggings, robberies and murders. Now people were frightened of me. How things had changed.

As I got near to St John the Baptist Church, I could hear a commotion. A bit closer, and I trod in something nasty. It was black and steaming. Initially, I thought some dog had a serious problem, but then I saw other mounds festering along the pavement and road.

I cautiously approached the dark church.

An almighty ruckus was going on with screams and wails that would make any self-respecting corpse spin anti-clockwise in its grave. I merged into a pool of shadow to gauge the activity.

It soon became apparent who was the cause of the trouble: Ted. He was surrounded by writhing black shapes, the likes of which made the hairs on the back of my neck spike.

He was using his backpack like there was no tomorrow and for some of the creatures, there wouldn't be. He was sending out streams of water, sweeping back and forth, arcing it over several metres, sluicing the brick path and tombstones. How the hell was he getting so much water from such a small backpack?

The fray abruptly ceased and only because, in my humble opinion, there weren't any more nasties to annihilate.

Silence descended like a mist. Ted lowered his pump-action weapon, shrugged out of the backpack harness and sat down heavily on a cracked tombstone near one of the yew trees. He mopped his brow. Killing evil was obviously hot work.

I waited a few more minutes, to make sure the battle was completely over, before calling to him.

He straightened at my voice and, leaving the churchyard, strode over to see me.

'You've been busy.' I indicated the black masses that were shrinking before my eyes.

'You bet. Ever since that hospital cat, I fire at random animals. It's amazing how many are bad news. Shape-shifting bastards, you know. Now they come looking for me. My scorecard is coming along a beauty.'

'Good grief. Rather you than me. At least you had an endless supply of holy water. I'm impressed.'

He laughed and pointed to the hosepipe attached to his backpack. 'I primed it from the font,' he said. 'Cool, eh?'

'Very cool. You're a killing machine.'

'Be better with two of us.'

'Ah, that's why I'm here.'

'Good. Let's get started.'

'Not so fast.' I held up my hand to halt his exuberance. 'I'm not joining you, Ted. I can't do it.'

'What?'

'My choice.'

'You're selling out!'

'I'll be seeing you.'

And I turned and walked away as he spluttered out a stream of protests.

III

So, I had made my decision.

No more nights.

No more blood.

No more Minstrel.

No more me.

A month on and I was huddled in my ancient Volvo on top of Burlington Beacon, a high point on the Sussex Downs, at a crisp frosty four in the morning.

It had taken me this long to muster the courage to end it all. And I'd wimped out on attempting to kill Minstrel. I just couldn't do it. Probably because I'd made a marriage vow to cherish him. How bizarre was that?

I jumped as Ted came out of nowhere and slung himself into the front passenger seat. He clunked shut the door, dropped a dirty canvas tote bag at his feet and thrust two plastic bags of blood onto the car's dusty dashboard.

'You've gotta drink it, Mrs P, or you'll die,' he said without preamble.

I managed a weak laugh. 'I'm half-dead anyway, just in case you hadn't noticed.'

'That's not the point, Matilda. Word's out that you're not eating – well, drinking. And that's not good, girl.'

I eyed him curiously. 'A couple of months ago, you couldn't have cared less.'

'Two months ago I was petrified you were going to attack me if I didn't kill you first.'

'You said back then that you weren't scared.'

'I lied. I was terrified. But then I discovered you were a vampire with a heart.'

'Aw, shucks.' And I punched him lightly on the arm. I didn't have the energy to do much else. 'But in reality, Ted, you only tolerated me then because we had a death wish on the same man. The last time we met you said I'd sold out.'

He huffed. 'Whatever. Drink before it's too late, eh?'

'It *is* too late. I'm waiting for the sun. It's over. I'm too tired to keep going on.'

'That's because you're not eating properly, if at all. It's time you did.' He patted one of the blood packages.

'Spare me. You're not my mother.'

He cracked a knuckle and swore. 'I want you to drink the blood, Mrs P. It's top quality, fresh blood, straight from the Burlington General's blood bank.'

'Human blood.'

'Well, they don't stock pigeon juice.'

'Very funny. You know I don't drink human blood.'

'It's time you did. Especially now.'

'Give me one good reason, because I'm right out of them.'

To set the record straight, I didn't particularly want to die. Suiciding was dead against my religious upbringing. My soul would end up in screaming purgatory, which meant there was a strong chance I'd end up alongside Ted. Happy thought. *Not.*

And added to that, I was a bit squeamish when it came to pain and I wasn't sure if it would hurt, morphing to dust. As I said before, there were no manuals about being a vampire.

But, on the upside, I didn't want to be a vampire either. The hours were antisocial, the food lousy and, *Honey*, the pay sucked.

Ted interrupted my internal dialogue and said, 'I can give you three good reasons.'

'Which are?'

'You're crucial to my mission.'

'Oh, that's right. Your soul scorecard.' I gave a hollow laugh. 'Ted, if I dissolve into dust it'll reduce your hit list by one and you'll be a step closer to going home to your sunburnt country.'

'If I keep you alive, I'll destroy more. Then I'll get home faster.'

'Okay, then. And your second reason to keep me on this planet?'

'A kid's been abducted. Lola Ward. She's 13. The case has been splashed all over the media. You must've heard about her?'

'Yeah. But I didn't pay much attention. Kids go missing all the time. What's she got to do with me?'

'Minstrel's involved.'

'Oh. And, as his wife, that automatically concerns me? Do me a favour.'

Ted drew out a school photograph from his wallet. The kid pictured was cute and blonde, wholesome and sweet. And she was far too young to be swimming in Minstrel's septic pool. Compunction shifted uncomfortably in my breast, giving me heartburn, but I did my best to ignore it. I wanted to die. I didn't want a righteous cause to keep me anchored in my dark world.

Ted said, 'The kid's in danger of being corrupted, Mrs P.'

'So?'

'What do you mean, *so*? You know how it feels to be sucked into Minstrel's world.'

Sure did.

Ah, Minstrel. When I first saw him, I was enraptured by his beauty: all golden perfection. More angel than an angelic angel.

So much more angel than this squat ugly being sitting beside me.

But Minstrel was no angel. His beauty was skin deep. Underneath was a festering black rottenness.

But I hadn't known that then. My fingers had itched to sculpt an image and capture his transcendental beauty for eternity.

I needn't have bothered: He was already set for eternity.

Now I stared out through the windscreen at the crystalline Milky Way. I used to love staying up and star gazing when the rest of the world was sleeping. But now, after never-ending nights, the novelty had palled.

'I want you to help me find her,' said Ted. 'I've a tip-off she's in the drains.'

I sighed. 'The drains? Oh great. My favourite place.'

Storm-water drains: Lowlifes, freaks and creatures like me are attracted to those drains. You can hide from the sun and travel forever underground. I didn't enjoy 'draining' very much. Too many weirdos for my taste. But it gave those with limited social hours a chance to party after dawn.

Then there were the ones who resided in the sewage systems. Thank goodness she hadn't gone there because not many newbies got out alive.

'And I suppose you want me to go down there and find this Lola kid?'

'Yes, and bring her out if she's unharmed.' He paused a beat. 'Or deal with her.'

Deal with her.

A euphemism.

Ted actually meant whack her with a wooden stake if she'd been bitten by Minstrel or one of his minions. How excellent. My very unfavourite pastime.

I wasn't about to commit myself, so I said, 'And your third reason, Ted?'

He cracked his knucklebone again and smiled. He didn't do the smile thing well. It was more of a grimace. 'You really want to know, Mrs P?'

'Wouldn't have asked otherwise.'

'You're going to have a baby. I want to be the godfather.'

The sudden stillness in the car matched the frozen black outside.

'Oh.'

He was nuts. How could I be pregnant? I was a vampire. My husband was a vampire. I didn't even know if vampires could *have* babies.

'Is that all you can say?' he said.

I put my hand over my belly. My flat belly. 'I don't believe you, how's that for an answer?' I had to work my throat to be able to speak. A baby? *Now?* What were the odds?

'I'm pretty sure you are. My mentor hinted as much.'

'What's it to do with him, whoever he is?'

'The chief keeps tabs on Minstrel via you. You're a useful channel. '

'Brilliant.'

'So humour me, Mrs P. Drink the blood. I had to lie, cheat and steal to get it.'

'That's not the sort of behaviour one expects from an angel. And especially not from you. What happened to your high ideals of keeping to the right side of the law?'

'Things change.'

'Don't they just.'

'Now drink up like a good girl. You've got to keep your strength up.'

I shuddered and wrinkled my nose. Slugging a neat litre or two of blood was a big ask.

'Will it help if I put it in a milkshake cup and gave you a straw?' he said.

'Nope. Nothing ever helps when drinking blood. Any sort of blood. But this could be worse.'

'Well, then think of the baby.'

The baby.

He picked up one of the plastic bags and handed it to me. 'Take, drink.'

'You've been spending too much time among the priesthood.'

'Hard to avoid when you live in a church. Now skol.'

'Ta.' I took the plastic bag, ripped off the corner with my teeth, and, then stopped. Could I do this?

'Come on, Mrs Peters. The baby needs it.'

Baby!

I had to give it a chance, didn't I? It deserved to live, regardless of me. Yes? Yes!

I squeezed my eyes shut, pinched my nose between my thumb and forefinger, and gulped down the revolting contents. I gagged and almost threw up. Only sheer bloody-mindedness stopped me. I sucked in a couple of huge, steadying lungs full of icy air.

I wasn't prepared for the next sensation: the sudden heat roaring through my body. New pigeon and rat blood always created a bit of an energy surge, but nothing like this massive whoomper. I gasped and instinctively grabbed the other bag of blood and swallowed it faster than you could say 'shaken not stirred'.

'Wow!' I said, my voice hoarse.

'Ditto,' said Ted, viewing me like a freak.

'What the hell have I been missing?'

'I don't know if I should have given you that blood after all,' said Ted, looking worried. 'You look awfully scary.'

'I feel scary.' The blood had zipped through every nook and cranny, and I mean *every* nook and cranny. Suddenly my whole body was on high sex alert. I'd felt this before. With Minstrel. A month into our marriage. When he'd given me something unusual to drink. Ah, I was beginning to understand how he'd turned me: Blood lust.

'I feel *very* scary!' I said.

'Why?' Ted shifted uneasily in his seat.

I could taste his uncertainty over the metallic tang of the Burlington blood bank nectar. I could feel his fear.

'I'm hot.' I wiped a dribble of life-blood from my chin and smacked my lips together. This must be the reason Minstrel turned his women into vampires – high-octane sex. That's why he'd turned me, and I'd just presumed we were good together, dumb naive fool that I was.

'It's several degrees below zero, but feel free to wind down the window,' said Ted.

'I mean *hot, Ted!*'

'Oh, I see.'

He clearly didn't.

'I don't think you do, boy. Come here.' And I grabbed Ted by his grungy pink and silver jumper and yanked him towards me. 'How do you feel about kissing a vampire?'

His swallow was audible. 'Not a lot. It's not a good idea.' His voice trembled and his eyes widened so far that his milky blue irises swam in a sea of white fear.

'Why not, Mr Angel?'

'You might use your teeth.'

'I'll do my best not to, honest.'

His eyes got even wider.

I stared back, devouring him in my mind, even though he was definitely not my type. Not nearly. I think, perhaps, that I may have licked my lips. Vampire status obviously made me feral. Inhaling deeply of Ted's peculiarly trademark aroma of incense, musty churches, male sweat and the ubiquitous garlic stench of the vampire slayer underpinned with the pink jumper's cheap perfume, I moved in for the kill.

Ted kept his eyes wide, wide open and then, a whisper away from my lips, he pushed hard against me, his arms tensile steel pistons that thrust me away.

Recoiling fast, the breath of anticipation snagging bitterly in my throat, I rasped out, 'Coward!'

'Too damn right. I'm no fool to go around snogging sex-hyped vampire chicks. Especially one who is carrying my god-child.'

I reared back as if he'd hit me.

'You sought me out,' I snarled. 'You supplied the blood. So now who's the fool?' My liquid snack was thumping hard through my veins and it was difficult holding back the urges pulsating in wild, primeval beats through my body. I wanted to kiss him, dammit, even if he did resemble a graveyard gargoyle.

I wanted to *bite* him!

'And for the record,' said Ted fumbling for his rough-hewn crucifix and clutching it to his chest. 'Along with crime fighting, I was also faithful to my wife.'

Clenching my hands to stop reaching out and taking what I wanted, I fought for control. I breathed through my mouth for a few moments, regaining my shaky equilibrium. In a deliberately quieter, calmer voice, I said, 'I didn't know you had a wife.'

'There's a lot you don't know.' Ted shifted in his seat. He was ready to fight me off if necessary. His muscles were bunched, his face taut, fists white-knuckled, one resolutely holding the crucifix. Was he planning on staking me with it or braining me? Whatever, he was taking no chances.

'She died,' he said abruptly.

'I'm sorry.'

'So am I.' There was an awkward pause. 'Listen, Mrs P. I'm running out of time. I need to find the kid. It's my latest heavenly brief. Are you going to help me? Yes or no?'

Despairingly, I cast my eyes over the Sussex Weald. The gentle valley spanned out before me. It looked so normal. So peaceful. A patchwork quilt of cosy villages and farmland seamed with leafless hedgerows.

'It'll be dawn soon,' was my only answer.

'Once we're in the drains, it won't matter.'

'It will if we have to get out fast.' My tone was as dry as the dust I'd turn into if the sun's rays hit me.

'You were ready to die just now.'

His logic irked.

'Okay, so I was,' I said, irritated. 'But now you've given me a reason to live.'

'The baby?'

I nodded.

Ted let out a huge sigh. 'Thank goodness for that. I was worried it was because you fancied me.'

The tension in the air eased markedly and I laughed, embarrassed by my earlier behaviour. 'I'm sorry, Ted. I hadn't expected the blood to affect me like that.'

'Nor me! I'll remember to water it down next time.' He gave a lopsided grin. 'We'd better get going before it's too late.'

He slipped the crucifix into his tote now that the dangerous moment had passed. 'To business. Where shall we begin?'

'Where was the kid last seen?'

'The pier.'

'What a surprise.' Minstrel liked finding his candy on the pier. It was a magnet for too many lost souls who ended up among the fast food dives, poky machines and fairground rides. They provided a veritable feast for him. 'Okay. So the pier it is.'

I turned the ignition key. The Volvo coughed, spluttered and died. A bit like my earlier burst of passion. I gave the ignition another shot and we had a repeat performance.

'You should get a new car,' said Ted with irritating common sense.

'Shut up or you can find your own way there.' He was an angel after all. He didn't need me. He could wing it. But then I could too, except I hadn't worked out the aerodynamics yet.

Several more tries and lots of dashboard smacking, we had success and the Volvo roared into deep, throaty life. We rumbled down the icy Beacon road towards the bright lights of Burlington. I parked on the low road near to the frigid pier with its ghostly dome, shuttered kiosks and silent carousel horses that were funeral-shrouded in shadows.

The waves crashed on the beach with determined rhythm, dragging and smashing the pebbles in the sea's relentless quest to break and dominate the shore. Razor-sharp wind whipped and tangled my hair. It shafted easily through my jeans and black leather bomber jacket. I might as well have been naked, the amount of warmth my clothes afforded me. Salt spray bit at my cheeks and stung my eyes. I felt colder than death, which was saying something.

I glanced at Ted. 'Where's your backpack?'

'Some kids stole it last week, while I kipped on a park bench.'

'Damn.'

'Don't worry, Mrs P. I've a full vampire-fighting kit with me.' He held up his grubby tote. 'We're right.'

'I hope so, or we're in deep trouble.'

'Trust me.'

I had no choice.

We strode briskly towards the pier. I stopped at a manhole in the pavement, near to the fortune-teller's kiosk. Leaning over, I dragged off the heavy metal cover to expose the shaft. The frozen metal bit into my fingertips.

For a long moment I stared into the manhole's gaping blackness.

Good grief, but I didn't want to go down that hole.

I hated the drains.

'Hurry up,' said Ted, close to my ear, giving me a jolt. 'It's freezing standing here.'

Being cold the majority of the time, I had little sympathy.

I glanced at the sky. Dawn wasn't far off. I had to get a move on or become a dust mite's fast-food dream. I twisted round and shimmied down the steel ladder, skidding over the slippery rungs and cracking my shin a good one. As soon as my head dipped below road level, the wind's maniacal hold on my hair ceased, its screaming monologue silenced.

But now there were other sounds substituting the wind. The lower we sunk into the subterranean world, the louder the drain melody grew. There was trickling water, snuffling and squeaking vermin, dull rumbles of overhead traffic, disembodied voices, snickers of dubious humour.

I think I preferred the wind.

Ted, carrying his canvas tote of vampire-fighting paraphernalia, followed me down the ladder. The rungs were smooth and worn from many hands. They stopped short of the floor and I dropped the last half a metre or so, landing in a two-metre wide drain with too much storm water. Ted, with a lack of lightness one wouldn't dream of from an angel, landed next to me, further splashing my jeans. I threw him a dirty look.

'Sorry,' he said. 'I miscalculated the distance.' His voice ricocheted off the rounded walls and bounced back like rifle bullets.

'I thought you could fly and stuff.'

'I'm still learning.' He shrugged. 'I need to practice more. I haven't been an angel that long, you know. Not in the scheme of things.'

'Nor I a vampire. Life's just one big learning curve for us,' I said. 'Aren't we the lucky ones?'

As our eyes adapted to the pitch black, we could make out lurid signatures sprayed on the drain's grey concrete. From experience, I knew those fancy tags would appear less and less the further we travelled into the guts of the drainage system. Most graffiti artists didn't have the bottle to venture too far into the drains. Surprisingly, they were too smart for that.

'So,' said Ted. 'Lola's here.'

'Are you asking me or telling me?'

'I'm guessing.'

'So am I. But it's Minstrel's beat, so this is our best bet.'

Burlington sported a rich tapestry of drains. We could spend an eternity in the labyrinth and, if we weren't careful, we would, thanks to the clientele who inhabited the city's underbelly.

We set off in single file, sloshing through the ankle-deep black smelly water, in no particular direction. In summer, the drains were relatively dry and odourless. Winter was different, a hundred times so. It was cold, wet and putrid. We were lucky it wasn't raining or the torrent of water would have swept us out to sea. But still, it was wet enough to float a boat.

The icy damp was winding its way deep into me. What a great way to spend a pre-dawn Saturday morning. Maybe I should have stayed on the Beacon, waiting for the deadly kiss of the sun's rays?

We splashed along the drain for a few hundred metres and then heard a trundling of wheels. We stopped. The noise grew louder. Seconds later a kid on a skateboard came zooming round the drain's corner, slightly above the water mark. The lad let out a shriek when he saw us, his skateboard flying out from beneath his feet. He landed with a big splash right in front of me.

Wonderful. Another soaking. Things just kept getting better and better.

The kid backed off, cowering, whimpering.

'We aren't going to hurt you,' I said. Though my teeth might have negated that assurance. 'We just want to ask some questions.'

'Have you seen this girl?' Ted pushed past me and flashed him the photograph. The boy barely glanced at it and shook his head.

'Look again. Carefully this time,' I said. He took one look at my sharp canines and obeyed. 'Good boy,' I said and patted his cheek.

He flinched, shooting me a scared look. 'I never see'd her.'

'Sure about that?' said Ted.

The boy's eyes slid sideways. 'Yeah.'

I didn't believe him so I thwacked him across the head.

'Okay,' he squealed. 'So she's in the Devil's Dungeon. I remember now. Sorry.'

The dungeon was the name given to a junction where several of the bigger drains met. It was a favourite hole of Minstrel's. I'd been there once, not long after he turned me, but I hadn't liked the ambiance, or the company, so I hadn't been tempted to go there again. I wasn't tempted now, either.

The kid added, 'She's wiv' a whole lot of creeps.'

'Excellent,' said Ted. 'Sounds as though we're going to have our work cut out if Minstrel and his boys are partying.'

I clipped the kid again. 'Scarper, if you know what's best for you.' The boy obviously did and scrambled to escape.

'Oi!' I grabbed him as he swung back into the drain and spun him into the opposite direction. 'Exit is that way and don't you ever come back, understand?' I did the teeth-baring thing, just to make sure he got the message.

'You shouldn't scare the little kiddies with your party trick,' said Ted as the skateboard kid scooted away.

'Better to scare than bite.' I gave a dismissive flick of my hand and pushed on down the pipe. 'Come on. We've work to do.'

Ted hefted his tote with a groan and followed.

'Is that man-bag thing heavy?' I inquired sweetly over my shoulder.

'It's not a man-bag. But it is as heavy as heck.'

'So what's in it? Your spare halo?'

'Ha very funny. Actually it's stuffed with several litres of Holy water and a bundle of the finest stakes I could buy.'

I gave a snort.

'I mean it. I scored a load of stakes. I met this chap who cuts them from the yew trees at Kingly Vale.'

Kingly Vale was an ancient yew forest on the South Downs. It was far older than Britain's great cathedrals and a testament to the staying power of the old order. Once I'd been impressed by its antiquity, but I wasn't any longer, not since I'd become a part of the same timelessness of that other, ancient world.

'And you got a job lot?' I said.

'Well, I do tend to go through them rather quickly now. You've no idea how many vampires there are out there.' He paused, then gave an embarrassed cough. 'Please, don't take it personally.'

'I won't. You know, Ted, you've come a long way since I first met you.'

'I've been learning the craft,' he said, smacking his fist against his chest, a zealous light in his eye. 'I'm getting good.'

I grimaced at his fervour. 'Well, let's hope your new stakes aren't duds.'

I was sceptical. Good stakes were hard to come by. Shysters sold pine and the inferior wood had a tendency to snap on impact. Even if they did pierce the heart, they didn't always work. Like the paling that Ted had used on me way back when. Oak and hawthorn were good but more expensive. Yew was the crème de la crème.

'Have faith. These are the best yew. Honest.'

'Okay, okay. I believe you.' I turned into a brick-lined drain, one of the older ones in the network. I scoped the dead black with my night vision. This was no time to be slack. Anyone, *anything*, could be lurking ready to pounce.

The stench was growing worse, assaulting my nostrils, making them sting. There was no longer just the smell of dank water but a hideous stink of old blood, dead meat, faeces, vomit and stale sweat. For it to be that vile, we had to be close to a cell, a cluster of inhumanity clinging together for strength and protection in a soulless existence.

We passed a ledge where an old foam mattress had been thrust. It sat soggily with some out-of-date newspapers and a few tins of home-brand baked beans. The homeless often camped down the drains. I reckoned they were mad. Not only were they in danger of brick falls from broken drains, flash floods and suffocation from foul air and lack of oxygen, but they provided what amounted to a free takeaway food service for vampires; blood on tap.

We turned into another drain. Again, brick but not as smooth. This pipe was older, the brickwork crumbling. And it stank to hell and back.

'Pwor!' exclaimed Ted, gagging.

My heart slammed hard against my ribs. 'Shh!' I hissed. 'Keep your flipping voice down.'

Round the next bend was a scene out of Revelations: groaning, wailing, seething purgatory. All you needed was some sulphuric smoke to complete the picture. Pasty-faced lowlifes turned blank, lifeless eyes on us. Clothes hung off them in filthy rags. Mouths were slack and hanging open. Some dribbled.

The swaying bodies surrounded an inner core of figures. These men were clothed in sharp black suits or studded leather, depending on their status. They were pale, like the other drain dwellers, but also muscular and tough. They were Minstrel's boys, his group of heavies, who did his dirty work and acted as bodyguards.

From the midst of the group, someone spoke.

'Well, well, what have we here?'

I recognised the voice, too. Cultured, smooth and darkly deadly. My gut clenched in painful reaction, as if I'd been sucker punched.

'Ah, it's my darling wife honouring us with a surprise visit. Welcome, Matilda.'

Forcing my lips into a smile, I said calmly, 'Minstrel.'

Minstrel had his arm around a slim woman with shoulder-length black hair. Her cheeks were the pallor of death lilies. She was wearing a skimpy Lurex boob-tube under a grubby denim jacket. Her black skirt was no more than an Alice band and showed coltish legs in snagged fishnets that needed a decent wash and darn.

'And who's your friend?'

'Ted, er, Angel.'

'Not one of us.' The statement was delivered in an ice-cold, menacing tone, the initial bonhomie gone.

'Actually, he is, Minstrel. He's one of the undead too.' Okay, so I was stretching the truth. Though Ted was in limbo, like us, we inhabited the dark side while he was firmly on the side of the light.

'And *your* friend?' I inquired sweetly.

'Jealous, darling?'

'Curious, sweetheart.'

He smiled. Those charming lips could woo a saint. But not me. Not anymore. But then, hey, I was no saint.

'Meet little Lola,' he said.

I sucked in a sharp breath. The girl looked nothing like the wholesome school kid in Ted's photo.

Damn, we were too late.

'Cross, Matilda?' Minstrel stroked the girl's cheek. She flinched.

Her recoil was a good sign. Perhaps Minstrel hadn't done the deal yet? She certainly didn't look as though she was enjoying herself. Her blue eyes were huge and underscored with bruised rings. Her skin was ghostly pale, but that could have been due to living in the drains too long.

'Disappointed, Minstrel. She's only 13.'

'So you know Lola?'

'Not personally.'

'Really?' He wasn't fooled. 'So why are you here?'

Ted came to my rescue. 'Because I do. I'm a friend of Lola's family.'
Minstrel gave him a bland look. 'I see. So, is this a social call?'

'Sort of,' I said.

'Her parents were worried about her,' added Ted.

'And so they should be, an innocent lamb like Lola hanging around with the likes of us. What say you, Matilda?'

'They want her home,' I said.

'We don't always get what we want.'

'But in this case, it would be the right thing to do.'

Minstrel laughed. 'Really? I don't think so, Matilda. The lovely Lola stays with me.'

I decided to appeal to his better nature. I was sure he'd had one. Once. 'Please, Minstrel, let her go.'

'Sorry, my sweet. No can do.'

'She's underage. There are already rumours you're involved. If people find out for certain you're corrupting minors, your precious reputation will be shot and you can kiss goodbye to your business empire *and* your ambitions to be the city's next mayor.'

'They won't find out,' he said, smoothly confident.

'Don't be so sure.'

His eyes narrowed to slits. 'There won't be anyone to tell them, my love.'

'Are you threatening me? Your own wife?'

'Do you need to be threatened?'

'You can't bully me, Minstrel.'

'You need to be brought to heel, Matilda. You've strayed too far. I've heard worrying things about you trying to cross over to the other side. As if you could. No, my love, it's time for you to come home and be an obedient wife.'

I snorted. 'That'll be the day. I don't remember saying I'd obey you in our wedding vows.'

'You always were wilful.'

'Please, let her go.'

'No. She's mine.' He stroked her breast, holding my eyes with his, daring me to make a move.

His boys were shifting in the shadows. I presumed they were trying to surround us.

Ted clutched my jacket and dragged me backwards. 'Careful,' he murmured.

I could hear him scrabbling about inside his tote. Now was not the time for stakes. We were both still relatively new to this vampire-busting job, but I knew it would take a heck of a lot of strength and technique to drive a stake home successfully.

Grief, it was bad enough biting a bird. And we had ten or more boys to take on here.

And Minstrel.

There'd be no time.

The muscle boys moved closer.

'Change your mind, Matilda, come with me.' Minstrel sounded so reassuringly persuasive. As if tempting me to have an extra blueberry muffin or glass of wine.

I wasn't fooled. 'Get lost, Minstrel.'

Minstrel laughed again but there was no mirth. 'So be it. Bye my sweet.' And he disappeared down a drain in a rush of black smoke, carrying Lola with him. He'd always excelled as an illusionist.

'Here, take this,' said Ted and he thrust a big, yellow, plastic, pump-action water-pistol in my hand.

'What the–?'

'I've refined my weapons. It's better than the spray pack.'

Oh bless.

The next moments were a blur. We pumped water pistols for gold. Holy water sprayed out at the circle of hard boys and had them screaming like banshees as it hit them, the water causing fierce, acid-like burns. The other lowlife entities cowed into shadows, hiding.

When my pistol ran out of water, Ted yelled there were others in the bag. No wonder the tote had been so heavy. He'd had a full plastic-and-water armoury in there.

A burly bat-boy broke through our frantic sprinkler system and tried to make a grab at me. I kicked him a swift one in the teeth, followed by another foot into the groin. It wasn't hard enough to do much damage but gave me a breathing space to snatch a stake and ram it upwards through the guy's solar plexus. He morphed to dust. Just like that. Goodness, Ted's stakes did work well after all. So much for my misgivings.

I grabbed another stake and shoved it in my belt, just in case.

The unscathed scum scuttled after their master like sewer rats, pouring down the drain hole in a wave of black. We pursued without speaking. We still had to get Lola.

Adrenaline pumping, bounding over writhing, melting bodies, we dived down the same drain as Minstrel. In my haste, I tripped over a bundle of rags and sprawled into the flowing filth, losing my gun. I cursed as the rags shuddered and shook beneath my legs. I scrambled up and around to face the heap, dragging the stake from my belt, ready to lash out.

A small face peered out, tear-stained and streaked with dirt. The child's blonde hair was tangled and messy. 'Help me,' she whispered.

My heart rocked in shock. 'Lola?'

Tears filled her eyes and she nodded.

So who was the other girl? Another victim? Hell, but sometimes I hated Minstrel!

'Poor baby,' said Ted. He was on his knees, pulling away the rags, wiping her tears with his clumsy, stubby fingers.

'I was so scared,' she said, her voice pathetically shaky. 'I thought Mr Peters was a nice man, but he wasn't. I managed to run away and hide.'

'Good girl.' Ted helped her stand. 'We'd better move fast,' he said to me and mouthed, *'Before the bastards come back.'*

He put his arm around the girl's small frame to support her and she clung limpidly to his shirt. 'Let's take you home, Lola.'

'Home.' Her eyes flickered.

My gut twisted. It was a fetching scene. Lola was much lovelier than her photo. And older by a couple of years. And sexier – by 30 decades!

Ted was putty. He smiled and Lola's cupid lips curved in response.

I ground my teeth.

Her eyes flickered again.

I saw red.

I dived forward, thrusting her down into the stream, raising my stake.

Lola screamed and Ted yelled, 'Hey!' and made a grab for my arm. 'What the hell are you doing?'

'She's one of them!' I yanked my arm clear of his hand.

'No, this is Lola. Look at her. Bloody hell, Mrs P, you've lost it!'

'Help me,' sobbed Lola, her big blue eyes wide and fearful.

'Matilda! Stop! She's just a kid.'

'Help me,' she cried again, her voice high, plaintive, hurt.

Had I been wrong? Had I imagined the cunning flash in her eyes? I lowered my arm slowly, slumping forward. 'Sorry. Overreaction. Blame the drains.'

'Sheez, Mrs P,' said Ted. 'That was a close one.'

From the corner of my eye, I saw the knowing flash again, the glint of feral smile.

No, I hadn't been wrong.

I lunged and the stake went clean into Lola's chest. She screamed. So did Ted. And then her fangs were out and she reared forward, rising up in full vampire fury. The stake had made as much difference as a shop-bought toothpick.

Damm.

I smacked Lola hard with my fist and she snapped backwards. 'Give me another stake,' I hollered to Ted.

But Ted was transfixed.

Useless male!

I scrambled to the tote, snatched another stake and, spear-like, threw it at Lola. It hit home. Was I glad my school javelin classes hadn't been in vain.

But that wretched stake was a dud too. I should have relied on my own intuition and not on Ted's cheap job lot.

Best Kingly Vale yew – what a joke.

Ted belatedly joined the action by randomly spraying Holy water while I sorted through the stakes, desperately trying to find any made from yew. There was only one. No time for mistakes. I had to make it count.

Lunging forward, I threw the kid against the brickwork with my whole body. We were so close our breaths mingled. Our eyes warred for supremacy and the girl's mouth was wide and terrible, her canine teeth stretching into full, hungry fangs, her foul blood-fetid breath hot on my cheeks.

But I'd been a vampire longer than Lola. Not by a lot, but enough to make it count. I had more experience and knew how to avoid those snapping teeth. And I had a good lot of sharp pearlies to show her too. I didn't hold back and roared in her face.

Lola struggled as I inched the stake into position and then, with my entire strength behind it, I skewered her to the wall.

Her deep howl of despair and loathing rang and echoed in the drain, horribly filling my head, reverberating through my body, but I held her there until she sagged and collapsed. I wrenched the stake from her chest and dropped her lifeless body into the dank water.

'Time to get out of here.' My voice was reed-thin, my energy spent.

Ted had turned whiter than a nun's wimple. 'Blimey,' he said, his voice thin and shaking. 'I didn't see that coming. That she was one of them.'

'Comes with experience.' I rotated my shoulder. It hurt like hell from the stake-jamming.

We stared at the body. Because she hadn't been a vampire long, Lola hadn't disintegrated. She lay there in the shallows looking like a tarty water nymph with her blond hair fanned out in the water.

'I don't know about this BAVS stuff,' said Ted. 'It sucks.'

'Now is not the time for pantomime puns.'

'I wasn't being funny. So what's next? Go after Minstrel?' Ted didn't sound that up enthusiastic.

I knew how he felt. I was spent too.

'Nope. I'm done for. He'll keep for another time. There's a more urgent need.' I wiped Lola's blood off the yew stake and stowed it in my belt ready for the next attack.

'What's more urgent than fighting evil?' said Ted.

'We've gotta survive down here until nightfall.'

'Sheez. We need to get a life, Mrs P.'

I held my hand to my belly: I already had one.

Jack Dann & Steven Paulsen

Harold the Hero and the Talking Sword

So, let me tell you about...

Okay, so you probably know me by reputation; but just in case you've been stored in a closet for the last seven years, I'll tell you who I am.

'And what about *me*?'

Okay, that loud, bombastic voice you just heard is my sidekick–

'*Sidekick*?!'

–the talking sword.

'I do have a name, you know, you little– '

Yes, the sword sometimes gets a bit uppity, as you've just heard.

'Don't speak, Mr Talking Sword; I'm directing myself to our reader.'

So let me bring you – dear, perspicacious, and very interesting reader – up to speed before I get interrupted again. And before *you* get impatient, let me give you a taste of what is to come. This is a true story about heroes, monsters, and how I singlehandedly–

'*Singlehandedly*? Look you little sh–'

–went back in time and saved that ancient Greek guy, Odysseus, from the one-eyed Cyclops who was definitely going to dash his brains out and eat him and everybody else on his rickety ship. But I'll get to all that later.

'Now calm down, sword, I'm getting to you right now this very minute.'

So, seven years ago to the day–

'Look, Harold the Hero, you've had the *great* privilege of wielding the one-and-only sword that talks. That's me! *I'm* the demon two-handed *cliadheammor* – which means 'really big sword' in the true tongue – so why don't you let *me* tell your readers the *real* story about how you came to be a hero?

'Well, don't just stand there like a mannequin in a costume shop, give me a little respect. I've earned that much, haven't I? Well?'

'Okay, go ahead, but then I'm taking over; as is my right as a true hero who combats adversity through impressive feats of strength and ingenuity.'

'Oye, dear Odin, what have I wrought? Okay, Harold, yes, it's a deal. *Now* may I get started?'

'Sure, but remember, I'm holding your hilt, big boy!'

A STORY TOLD BY A TWO-HANDED CLIADHEAMMOR

Okay, reader, let me try to tell you the real story of how I made this fat boy, this geek-headed idiot Harold into a legendary hero. Oh, so you're looking right at him, you're looking at all those muscles, his thick neck, the chest definition, and the slick clothes, and you're thinking this guy isn't fat or nerdish. He's... well, he looks like some version of a young Arnold Schwarzenegger.

Well, seven years ago, he surely *was* a fat little shit fantasising he was a hero by playing video games.

I found him – discovered him – in an upmarket, yuppie video palace on Toorak Road. In Melbourne. Australia. I know, right?

I made him who he is today.

Me! The legendary demon known through the ages as THE-GLORIOUS-SWORD-OF-FIRE-AND-DESTINY-THAT-BURNS-AND-CUTS-THROUGH-FLESH, and I'm the demon who's going to set the record straight.

Okay, if that's too complicated for your little 21st century brain, you can just call me Sword. It doesn't quite have the same tone and authority as THE-GLORIOUS-SWORD-OF-FIRE-AND-DESTINY-THAT-BURNS-AND-CUTS-THROUGH-FLESH, but I'm not a pompous turd like your average demon.

That's because I'm not your average demon.

And don't give me that stupid existential crap that I'm just a sword! So, let me ask you, how many swords have *you* spoken to today?

That's what I thought.

And if you're going to ask me how I got this way, that's for me to know and you to find out. Demons don't have to make excuses. They can take any shape they want. I could be a Hawaiian hula dancer if I want, or a Holden, or a chimpanzee, or a page in this book you're reading.

I could dissolve you in a second! I could cut you to shreds! I could terrify you! Do you know what my real aspect is? Do you know what I *really* look like?

All right, I'm going to be truthful. I really look like – a sword.

My father was a sword, too – a big two-handed *cliadheammor* just like me. But that's a long story that can wait for another day.

Right now I'm going to tell you about killing dragons and how I made Harold into a hero. I'm going to tell you exactly how I did it. From A to Z. And – this is most important – I'm going to show you that the sword is more important than the hero every single time! That's the lesson, so listen-up.

But, as you probably know already, there's not a whole helluva lot of room for talking swords and dragons and heroes here in the 21st century. You got cheated, this is turdsville.

You think just because you've got computers that it's all cool. Well, it ain't, as they say. It just simply ain't.

Okay, so now that I've got your attention, let me tell you what happened.

I needed to find a new hero. The less said about the demise of my previous hero, the better. Suffice to say he can't function as a hero anymore now that he is just a putrid puddle of reeking slime.

He should have ducked when I told him.

Okay, so I was walking down Toorak Road in Melbourne–

Why Melbourne? Because it was voted the most liveable city in the world, dummy! Multiple times!

Look, why don't you just come back in time with me and I'll show you.

What do you mean, there is no such thing as time travel?

There has *always* been time travel. You just have to know where to look. It's been there all the time. I'll give you a hint: go to the library and look up 'mnemonics'. That's the first clue.

If you're smart, you'll find out about the memory theatre of Giulio Camillo and Giordano Bruno's secrets of shadows and secret seals. That's all I'm going to say on the subject. But this time, for this story, the trip is on me. You don't have to know how to do anything.

You've got a sword for a tour guide!

And now for some real-time time travelling with the Talking Sword

Okay, so we're walking down Toorak Road, past all the upmarket dress shops and cafes and restaurants, past all the yuppies showing off to all the other yuppies, past all the four-wheel-drive vehicles and Porsches and Mercs and Jags stuck in the rush-hour traffic. And just to prove my point about how people don't pay attention to *anything* in this silly century, I'm not changing my aspect, as we call it. None of this invisibility crap for me. And I hate taking the form of clouds or dust or lightning and thunder, or cockatoos or anything else foreign to my primary aspect. See, you're getting the hang of it. If you can speak the language, you can do the tricks.

Now can you believe that *nobody* notices that a five-foot-long sword is floating three feet from the pavement and cutting its way down the street?

(Go look up feet and inches. Demons don't use metric. We're old fashioned about these things.)

Now I ask you, how could *anyone* miss a floating sword that's aglow with the unearthly light of Hell and bejewelled with diamonds and rubies and the eyeballs of dead emperors?

You don't know?

Well, *I* do! It's because nobody's paying attention. These yuppies are only worried about being cool and talking into their mobile phones. They're programmed only to see what they're used to seeing.

Yeah, okay, so there are a *few* pedestrians who look up and notice that they've just passed by a demon shaped like a sword that could cut them into a thousand twitchy, twisty, fleshy, white noodles. But they're too preoccupied with their cool thoughts to remember what they saw. You know, if this place ever got invaded by bug-eyed aliens, nobody would know that anything had happened until their phones stopped working.

If Aragorn's sword *Narsil-the-Sword-that-Was-Broken* or King Arthur's sword *Excalibur*, or even Bilbo the Hobbit's sword *Sting* were here, they'd cut these pedestrians into string! Maybe I should cut a few people up just to show you.

Oh, that would make you sick?

Well, you'll see enough cutting up when our 'hero' fights the dragon.
You ever see dragon's blood? It'll burn the hair right out of your little nose.
Oh, I forgot, you don't have hair yet in your little nose.

You know what I hate about video arcades? It's the damn noise. They don't make this much noise in Hell, except in the City of Pluto, and that's mostly filled with people from New York City. (No, dummy, not Pluto the dog; Pluto the Prince of Darkness, the Prince of the Underworld, the – oh, forget it.)

So we go right into this video arcade on Toorak Road. It's noisy and big, and for the ultra-nerds, there's a roller skating rink on the second floor. But our quarry is going to be somewhere in those rows of video machines right in front of us on the first floor. No, not those pinball machines that have been souped up to look like video machines. You won't find any heroes playing those, not on your life. No, the heroes want virtual reality. They want everything to look as real as technology can make it, which ain't very real. Look around at this. This is video city. Video world. See that nerd with the greasy hair? The one with the pimples and the big stomach that's sticking right out of his baggy jeans? Well, my fellow traveller, all the heroes start out like that. Really. They all need baths and shampoos and diets. You think I'm making this up. You should have seen Hercules before we fixed him up. Looked just like this nerd, except he wore a dress instead of jeans. Well, everybody wore dresses then.

See the game he's playing?

It's called *Dragons' Teeth*. Our potential hero is pretending that he's the muscle guy with the sword that's as big as my father. He's whacking everyone with the sword. Now that he's whacked everyone, killed everyone in sight, everything that moves, he's won the right to play another screen. Now he gets to kill dragons. Swish, slash, look at him, he's really into it. He's breathing heavily, his eyes are glazed. He thinks all this virtual killing is cool. He'd kill his grandmother if she appeared on the screen.

Well, let's see how he feels about the real thing.

'Hey, you. Yeah, you, the fat kid playing *Dragons' Teeth*. Too involved in the game to listen?'

How about that? He doesn't seem to hear me, so there's nothing to do, but put myself into his hands, so to speak. So I float right into his pudgy little paws.

There, little nerd, now you're holding THE-GLORIOUS-SWORD-OF-FIRE-AND-DESTINY-THAT-BURNS-AND-CUTS-THROUGH-FLESH, and this is the part I love the best...

Smash, I cut into the machine, and sparks fly all over and lights go out all over the arcade and whatever I strike catches fire, and lightning shoots from my blade, careening all over the place like superballs, and flames crackle and smoke billows and everyone is screaming, and the nerd can't let go of me, and he's trying to scream too, but I'm not going to let anything come out of his mouth. He's my slave. He's under my power.

Like you. So stop the screaming. You're under my *protection*.

Now, little nerd, start swinging. We'll smash all the machines in the place. See how quiet it is now that everyone has run out the doors. I don't even hear the skating muzak coming from upstairs. Of course the ceiling's on fire. Oh, don't worry about the police. All they'll see is a circle of blue fire, which will scare the snot out of them.

One by one we smash every machine in the place. Pluto would have been proud, although I doubt Walt Disney would have approved.

'Okay, kid,' I say to our potential hero, 'that's enough. You can relax now. You don't have to stand there shaking with your arms sticking out. I'm over here, in front of you. Hanging magically in the air. I'm the sword. Hello. Hello? There, now. That's better. Tell us your name.'

'Haaa-Harrrrahrrr–'

'Is that all you can say? Come on, spit it out!'

'Hhhhharold Waaag–'

'Come on, Hhhhharold, you can do it.'

'Harold Wagner,' he says. Clear as a bell.

'There, I told you, you could do it. Harold. Hmm. Harold the Hero. Hey, that sounds pretty good. Now, Harold the Hero, stop shaking. And stop that coughing. Don't you *want* to be a hero?'

He shakes his head, of course, and, yeah, he pees in his pants. They all do that when they're called to greatness. Shaking and peeing, it's the stuff of heroes.

'Would you like to run away?'

Now he nods. 'Okay,' I say. 'Go on, then, get your bum out of here. Bye, bye. It's been nice smashing things up with you, but wouldn't you rather stay with us and be a hero?'

See how he strains to run down the aisle and get away from us demons. Well, if he had any muscles, they'd be straining. Yeah, he thinks you're a demon too. This is the way it works, kid, he gets to be a hero and you get to be a demon. Fun, huh?

'Okay, Harold. Stop shaking and sweating. You can't move. You're in my power. And you're going to be in my power until you're a great big strapping hero, what do you think of that? That's right, you can just nod.'

See, he's nodding.

Now all I have to do is put myself back in his hands ever so gently and lead him to his training grounds. 'Hey, Harold, want to kill some dragons?'

He nods, tears flowing down his cheeks.

'Good.

'Now, we need to go someplace where there's magic and dragons and no computers. Your choice. I suggest Atlantis around 3600 BC or the Göreme region of Turkey around 1466 AD. Good times and places for magic, although forget about finding dragons on Atlantis. They were wiped out in 2170 BC. Nah, not by heroes. By a virus.

'If you're hot to go to the future, best time is anywhere in the 35th century, anywhere except Southern California – it's too perverted there even for me. And, yeah, they kept their computers.

'G...G...G–'

'Göreme it is, then.

'Just close your eyes.

'Time travel ain't nothing but a state of mind.'

But first we'd better get our hero to a toilet. He's starting to smell a bit, don't you think?

So you think all this hero stuff is cruel and inhuman?

Well, I'm a demon, what the hell did you expect? *Fantasia*?

Göreme it is then — and if you want to know something, look up Tantalus!

Okay, okay, you can open your eyes now. We've arrived. This is it. Well, this is almost it. Tell me what you see in front of you? (I don't care if it makes you hungry and thirsty, just tell me what you see. And don't give me that crap about how I'm torturing Harold the Hero. That's what I'm *supposed* to be doing.)

Since the cat's got your tongue, I'll tell you what you see. Okay, behind you – that's right, turn around – behind you are the sacred cones and stones and mounds and churches and desert of Göreme. Surprise, it's all desert. No water, no rain, no liquid of any kind, unless you know where to look. Of course, you can always just find a dragon, slay the damned thing, and then drink its ichor. It's purple and spicy and tastes like puke, but it's good for you.

You don't know what ichor is?

It's dragon's blood, dummy!

Of course, this place looks weird. Do you think dragons would live in suburban Sydney, or even in the outback? Nah. Weird monsters need very weird places. Just plain weird won't quite do it. See all the strange rocks that look like cones, that seem to go on forever? They're called *peri bacalari*. That means fairy chimneys. You're looking right into the sacred region of Ürgüp, and the local people believe that a thousand spirits dwell in there. They're wrong, though. Last time I counted, 8347 spirits were living in those cone fields. You'd better watch yourself, though, because according to the legends the spirits fall in love with children and steal them away.

I'm not going to tell you whether the legends are true.

That's for me to know and you to find out.

But if you look carefully, you can see the spirits drifting around. See, they look like smoke, and if you keep looking you can see their shapes. Don't stare at them like you're trying to thread a needle or you won't see anything. Can you see them now? Pretty ugly and horrible, huh? I always thought they looked like part-spider and part-octopus. Well, if you think the spirits are ugly, you should see the monsters that live *inside* the cones. The monsters are flesh and blood just like the dragons. They'd eat your eyes right out of your head and save the rest of you for lunch. You don't have to worry so much about the monsters while you're with me, but one of those spirits might just drift over here and grab you.

After all, you're awfully cute.

Okay, *now* you – I still mean you, reader – you can turn around. That's right, turn around and look at Harold the Hero.

I suppose you're wondering how Harold the Hero ended up right in the middle of that beautiful pool of water, huh? And I suppose you're wondering how that beautiful pool of water ended up in the middle of the desert? It's an oasis, dummy. Didn't you ever see any movies like *Lawrence of Arabia*?

Yeah, it's pretty obvious that Harold isn't happy in there, especially with all those scrumptious trees hanging over him with pears, figs, apples, and pomegranates. I love this part. See how every time he tries to grab one of those pieces of fruit, the wind blows them out of his reach? This is all part of Harold's training. I got the idea from an old Greek god named Zeus who got upset with his son Tantalus and stuck him into this very pool. I figured it's a great way to turn nerds into heroes.

Can you think of a better way to lose weight and get exercise? See, there he goes again, reaching for a fig. He'll be skinny as a rail before he manages to grab one of those fruits. Watch this...

'Hey, Harold the Hero. Aren't you thirsty?' I have to shout at him because when you're in the pool you can't see beyond the fruit trees, and you can't hear so well in there either.

There, Harold's looking this way.

'Try to drink the water, Harold. You'll get dehydrated. Go ahead, try it.'

Harold is bending over, trying to get a drink of that water, but the farther he bends, the lower the pool sinks. I love that! 'Hey, Harold, try again.'

Harold gives me the finger. See that? Now you and I know that swords don't have bums, but it's good that he's getting angry. And if he keeps reaching for those fruits and bending over for a drink, he'll get some exercise too. And every once in a while, the wind won't blow and he'll get a fig or a pomegranate. And every once in a while he'll bend over and the water won't sink.

You see, I'm not such a bad sort after all.

Time, taffy and, oh yes, respect

Okay, we don't have lots of time, so we're going to speed things up. Time is elastic. You can pull it like taffy or squash it like your 21st century bread. (Oh, you haven't tried that? If you take a loaf of supermarket white bread and squeeze it, you'll end up with nothing more than a little ball of sticky stuff. That's because the commercial crap you call bread is mostly air). Anyway, let's speed things up for Harold the Hero.

Okay, zap, boom, whiz, a few months have passed.

Now look at Harold.

He's thin and wiry and you can see the muscles in his arms and the definition in his pecs. He's becoming a regular Hercules, isn't he? He's even got a cleft in his chin like all proper heroes. He can see us now. Well, he can see me, anyway. Listen.

'Hey, Harold, how you doin' in there?'

'Get me out of here, you son of a–'

'That ain't nice, Harold. You should always treat a sword with respect. And here I was going to get you out of there so you could slay a dragon and become a real hero… Oh, well. I guess I'll come back in a few months.'

'No, don't go, I'm sorry, I–'

Zap. We'll push time forward real quick. You see, before you can say 'Jack Robinson', a month has passed.

'Hey, Harold, how you doin' in there?'

'Fine,' says Harold very politely this time.

'You ready to get out and learn to fight dragons?'

'Yeah, I guess.'

'You guess?' I say. 'That's not the way a hero talks to his sword.'

'Yes, yes, I'm ready to learn. I'm ready to do anything, just please get me out of here.'

'Are you going to have respect for your sword?'

'Yes.'

'Are you going to do everything I tell you?'

'Yes.'

'Promise?'

'I promise.'

'And do you know what will happen if you misbehave?'

Harold really is turning into a hero. See how his face has lost all that baby fat? See how all his ugly red, pustulating pimples have disappeared? (That's what happens when you stop eating candy bars and all the fast food crap). He's actually quite handsome now, isn't he?

'Yes,' Harold says, answering my question about whether he knows what will happen if he misbehaves.

'You do?' I ask.

'Yessir.'

'Then tell me what you think will happen?'

'I'll have to stand here in the pool until I learn how to behave.'

'No, Harold. If you misbehave, I'm going to let the dragons roast you for barbecue and eat your fatty entrails. And then I'll go and find another hero who *will* behave. Do I make myself clear?'

'Yessir,' Harold says.

That's my boy!

Okay, listen up. Harold's been doing dragon training now for another two months, even though that's barely a nanosecond to us. Harold knows almost everything there is to know about killing dragons and being a hero. After all, he's got a good teacher. But is he happy? Ask him.

'Harold, are you happy?'

Harold looks right at me. He's a regular Hercules. Look at those muscles. You'd never in a million years guess that when we found him, he was a nerd playing video games in an arcade. But he doesn't say anything. He's scared. He doesn't look it, but he's still the nerd that wet his pants.

Come closer, I'm going to tell you a secret. All those movie stars and athletes that you think are so cool – they're nerds, too.

They just don't act like nerds.

That's their secret.

'C'mon, Harold, old hero, answer the question. Are you happy?'

Harold nods his head.

Of course, he's happy. If he wasn't happy, I'd throw him back in the pool again or just feed him to the dragons.

Okay, it's time to maim and kill.

Let's find our hero some dragons.

Before we journey through the fairy cones and past the hungry spirits who just *love* children, you need to know something about dragons. Harold knows what he's got to do; but you, dear reader, need to know something too because a dragon could just as easily decide to take a bite of you as fight Harold. So be warned.

Okay, a dragon is just another name for a worm. That's right, it's just a great big worm. Actually, dragons got their name from the old Greek word *draca*, which means serpent or worm.

And just in case you're stupid enough to think that dragons aren't real, think about this: How do you think that Drakelow in England got its name? It means dragon's barrow. And have you ever heard of the towns of Drakeford or Dragon's Hill in England? Or Drakensberg, which means dragon's mountain, in Germany? Or Draconis in south-eastern Europe?

You can look those places up in the atlas. All those towns were named after dragons because they were plagued with them. So don't let anyone give you that crap about how dragons are legends.

There are all kinds of dragons, but the ones that live here in Turkey are the wingless and legless worms called *D. cappadociae*. They have only one head, unlike *D. ladonii*, which have a hundred. But don't think that killing them is a piece of cake just because they have only one head and can't fly. They can crawl faster than any of you can run, they breathe fire, salivate green stringy bile that melts flesh, are covered with scales that a guided missile couldn't penetrate, have 44 diamond shark's teeth, and they smell like a fart. You'll smell the dragon before you see it.

No, *dumkopf*, that's not a dragon you're smelling.

That's Harold!

The Talking Sword's dracopedian guide to Göremical dragons

and the myriad ways they can kill you

Okay, onward through the fields of Göreme, past the thousands of fairy chimneys that look like tents made out of rocks. Onward, past the houses and churches carved right out of the stratified rocks by the early Christian fathers, past Turkish villages turned black by dragon-flames and dragon farts. (Ah, dear reader, you didn't know about dragon farts; well, *that's* a story for another day.)

Yuk! Can you smell that? Makes old Harold smell like perfume, doesn't it?

Well, Harold's wearing full dress armour, and that stuff ain't cotton. You try wearing body armour and see if you don't smell like essence of fart, too.

There's definitely a dragon out there, beyond the vast plain of rock towers ahead of us. See the smoke? You wait; in a while the whole sky will turn black and red, and the clouds will look like they're made out of soot. All we've got to do is keep walking. The dragon knows we're here. How? It's a worm, like I told you. It *feels* us through the ground like a bunch of little vibrations. And you aren't exactly tiptoeing. Dragons have pretty good eyes, too. By now it can probably even see us, although we can't see it.

'Harold, are you ready?' I ask. 'You know what you have to do?'

Harold nods. He's leading the way, all dressed up in armour, sweating like a pig, carrying a heavy dragon shield that he wouldn't have even been able to pick up a few months ago, and he's actually acting like a hero.

Of course, he hasn't seen the dragon yet.

Let me tell you a few more things. I've taught Harold how to hold a sword, how to parry, riposte, lunge, cut, thrust, feint, so he knows some technique, which he'll need if I happen to be on holiday and he has to fight a dragon by himself. You see, being a hero when you've got a sword (not just a sword sword, but a demon sword like me) is a piece of cake. The sword does all the work. It pulls you around (providing you're not so fat that you can't move), it knows how to lead the dragon on, it knows how to confuse the stupid beast with techniques learned over millennia, and most importantly, it knows how to kill the dragon. Ah, you think that's an easy thing? Wait till you see the dragon...

And there it is.

It slithers right for us at maybe a hundred miles an hour, burrowing through the sand, sending it flying all over, and its breath is so hot that it turns the sand into glass all around it, leaving a trail of glass that reflects the sun like a mirror. It stops right in front of Harold and pulls itself up like a python to full height. Its scales look like precious stones, like blood-red rubies, but its head, which looks like the head of a huge fly, is covered with something that looks like layers and layers of puke and snot. If that stuff drips on you, you'll melt, I guarantee it. And its huge green eyes stare down at us as steadily as a crocodile watching its prey. It takes a deep breath and is about to turn everybody into barbecue.

'Harold, lift up your shield, dummy!'

Harold raises the shield as fire pours down upon us, but that shield is pretty powerful stuff, and the dragon-flame breaks against the shield and turns into smoke and soot, so you probably can hardly see what's going on now.

I leap into Harold's hand, and now you'll see what heroes are made of. Real heroes are the dummies. They hold the sword. It's the sword who does the fighting! But first I've got to get behind this stupid dragon, and maybe the dragon isn't so stupid because it's keeping its snotty, vomit-gooped head right in front of me.

'Okay, Harold, remember what I taught you? Feint to the left, roll, keep that shield up or I'll be fighting the dragon alone – and watch it, it's dripping bile, you want to get us both melted?'

Okay, dear reader, you should ask me something, even though we're right in the middle of fighting the dragon...even though all this green dragon-bile is falling all around us. (If enough of that stuff touches Harold – or me – it could dissolve us as easily as aspirin melts in water.) So, listen up. Here's the question: If I'm doing all the fighting, why do I need a hero?

Because it's *traditional*, dummy!

And it gives you humans something to do.

Now that that's settled, back to the fight.

Oops, I warned you that dragons are dangerous. It feinted, swung its wormy neck around Harold and me, and turned everything to glass behind us.

'Okay, Harold, now's your chance. Run to the left quickly. I only need a second. There it is. See the spot right in the middle of the dragon's back. See the grey, wormy flesh where there's no scales. Jump! I got it, I'm burying myself right into its flesh. Yuk, I hate this part! Well, you can help pull me out of this damn dragon. Pull! Okay, now back off because it's going to catch fire and–'

The damn thing explodes.

Fire shoots everywhere.

Dragon scales rip through the air like shrapnel.

Dragon-flesh drops into the sand like giant turds.

And it doesn't smell too pleasant either.

'Congratulations, Harold. One dragon bites the dust...er, the sand. Harold?'

Well, kid, this was his first time. He's allowed to pee in his armour and shake and snivel and cry.

The dragon is dead, so you can stop all that shaking and snivelling and crying too.

So your arm got burnt by a little bit of dragon bile. Big deal. Don't complain, you didn't even dissolve.

What a cry baby!

And now for a holiday on the sunny Isle of Thrinacia

'Cry baby? Okay, you arrogant five-foot-long lump of metal. That's enough. I've let you tell your version of how I became a hero. I bit my

tongue at the ignominy of it all and didn't interrupt once, despite the obvious mendacities.

'Uh, oh, big words from the nerd.'

'Now it's *your* turn to shut up and let me tell them *my* story, the one I started earlier before you interrupted.'

The sword shimmered silently.

So, patient reader, this is the true story about how we went back in time; and before I go any further, I'm going to tell you right here and now (take a bow, Sword!) that the sword-maven is the one who knows how to do the time travel thing. That's one of his tricks that I haven't quite worked out yet.

So from me you're just going to get a story. But what a story! I'm going to tell you how *I* singlehandedly saved that ancient Greek guy, Odysseus, from the one-eyed Cyclops – you should know about him from mythology and the movies – and I'm going to tell you about how this Cyclops was definitely going to dash Odysseus' brains out and eat him and everybody else who'd manned his rickety ship. And he also had me on the menu.

'Well, he sure as hell wasn't going to eat *me*.'

'Shut up, sword!'

So, after we killed off that dragon in Göreme, I decided I really needed a holiday.

'Remember that, Sword? You asked me where I wanted to go.'

'Of course, I remember. I never forget anything! I'm a demon, remember?'

Anyway, reader, I told the sword I wanted to go to a Mediterranean island. Those islands are supposed to be really nice. You know, pleasant climate, great food, sandy beaches with warm, turquoise waters, cheap wine and a leisurely pace. (The cheap wine bit isn't in the tourist guides). Maybe Ibiza, Santorini or Mykonos, I thought.

'So, Mr Putz, who now calls himself a hero, what was your problem? I transported you to a Mediterranean island, just like you asked; or I should say begged.'

So the next thing you know, we found ourselves on the beach of a barren-looking island with a live volcano in the distance spurting burps of fire, smoke, and black ash. Picture this: on a hill just above us is a stand of tall oaks and pine trees, with a high wall of hewn rock around their base.

'This is your idea of a resort?' I asked.

'Oh, look,' the sword said, distracted. 'There's Odysseus.'

'Where in Hell are we?'

'This isn't Hades; it's the Island of Thrinacia. The island of the Cyclopes.'

'What?'

'Just follow those Greeks.'

And sure as rain after a red sunrise, a dozen or so men clad in ragged tunics and brandishing short swords were running up the beach. Odysseus' men, we figured. And they looked like they were half in the bag–

'He means drunk.'

–and three or four of them had enormous wine skins on their shoulders. By the time we caught up with them, they had passed through a gate in the wall of hewn rock and were detouring around a sheep pen littered with dung. We watched them slowly and cautiously enter the mouth of a large cave overgrown with laurel.

'What are we *doing* here, Sword?' I asked.

'Hunting for treasure, Harold.'

'Treasure?'

'We've got to pay for this holiday somehow.'

I won't go into why the sword thought this was a holiday. He can tell you about that on his own time. Swords have odd ideas of what constitutes a holiday. But, anyway, once we were inside the cave, I bumped right into the back of a stout Greek warrior. He was just standing there, awestruck.

The cave was enormous.

'Phew, it stinks like vomit,' one of Odysseus's men said.

'It's the cheese,' another said.

There were large wooden racks stacked with drying cheeses against the westernmost wall, and further along huge hand-hammered copper pails full of milk, curd, and whey sat in a row along a natural stone shelf.

'It's not the cheese,' I said to the sword. 'Can't they smell the dung? Ugh! The cave floor is covered in it. *That's* what stinks.'

'I think you'll find the odour of dung is commonplace in these times.'

'And how come I can understand what these guys are saying?'

The sword sighed; something he does a lot.

'I do *not*!'

Yeah, well, anyway, the sword's answer to my question was: 'Because, Harold, I am a demon and have a surfeit of magical powers, which includes telepathy, invisibility, psychofamiliarity, and metamorphosis. So, would you rather I just stop translating? Then it will *all* be Greek to you.'

The sword chuckled.

It was my turn to sigh.

'Let's grab the cheeses and some of these sheep and goats and get out of here,' said one of the Greeks.

'So where's this supposed treasure?' I asked the sword.

'Patience, Harold. It's here somewhere, I can *feel* it.'

'You can feel it?'

'Isn't that what I just said?' the sword said, sighing yet again. I told you, he does that a lot.

Sigh!

One of Odysseus's men rekindled a fire that had been set in the centre of the cave, and they all sat down and started pouring wine and making a meal of the cheese. Their leader filled a carved wooden bowl with wine and a little water and passed it to me as if he'd known me for yonks. I took a sip. Actually, it wasn't bad. Strong, despite being watered-down, and a little heavy on the tannins; but not bad.

'Why haven't they recognised us as strangers?' I asked the sword, who sighed again because he can't make any facial expressions.

'You're pushing this sighing thing a bit far, hero!'

Okay, he's right. And I speak from experience, an angry sword is not a pretty sight!

So to answer why the Greeks didn't ask who the hell we were, the sword said: 'I told you, I have the power of psychofamilarity. I've cast a glamour.'

Then before the sword could say anything else, the cave suddenly went dim as the bulk of a giant filled the massive cave entrance.

'Intruders!' Its deep, booming voice echoed through the cave.

I caught a glimpse of its face in the flickering fire light; and I can tell you, it was ugly, very, very ugly. It could have been the love child of the winged monkeys and the Wicked Witch of the West.

I could see it was a Cyclops because it had only one single glaring eye right in the middle of its forehead. (Just like the Purple People-Eater, if any of you are familiar with old pop songs).

'Who dares to invade my home?' it said. Read that as if it's in capital letters. I mean he was loud!

'We are men of Atrides Agamemnon on our way home from our great victory at Troy,' the leader of the Greeks said. (That would be Odysseus himself; obviously.)

'I smell a demon!' the Cyclops roared.

'Uh oh,' whispered the sword.

'You cannot hide from me, Demon,' the Cyclops roared, looking in our direction. Then he rolled a massive boulder into the entrance of the cave, blocking it securely.

'I am Polyphemus, the *most* powerful of sorcerers, son of Poseidon the God of the Sea.' (Again, reader, think capital letters)!

I felt the sword tremble in my hand and knew we were in big trouble.

'I was not trembling; I was girding my loins.'

'Yeah, okay, Sword, you weren't trembling.'

To continue: Polyphemus' single eye began to glow with an eerie, sickly-green inner light and he said, 'I bind you, demon!'

The sword became hot in my hands. So hot that I'm afraid I dropped it. It clanged as it hit the cave floor and began to glow dull-red.

'I am not an 'it', you little shit!'

Ignore that, reader.

So the sword began to melt and change form before my very eyes. Suddenly it was no longer a sword, but a large bronze pot.

'Ughh-ugh,' the sword said. 'I-I have-av-av lost-ost my-y power-er-r.'

'You are echoing,' I said to him.

'Course-ourse I echoing-ing you asshole-hole-ole. I been-een transformed-ormed into-oo a pot-ot-t. A damn-amn pisspot-ot!'

'Well, stop it, I can't understand you.'

'I'll try,' the sword said softly, this time no echo. 'But the Cyclops has robbed me of my powers. It's a miracle I can even still speak.'

I laughed a little. I couldn't help it.

Sigh!

'Sorry, Sword.'

Okay, so meanwhile Odysseus and his men cowered in the rear of the cave. As if it wasn't enough that an enormous one-eyed giant had caught them pilfering his goods and would probably eat them for dinner, they stared at us in disbelief now that the sword's glamour had worn off.

'Uh, that young man and the, er, pisspot aren't with us,' Odysseus said to Polyphemus. 'We, however, come as guests and supplicants in hope of a warm welcome and perhaps even the customary gift of hospitality from you, oh benevolent one. For Zeus who watches over us would be most displeased should any harm befall us.'

The Cyclops let out a bellow of laughter. 'I fear not Zeus, nor any of the other Gods of Olympus.'

With that the one-eyed giant lunged at the Greeks who huddled together around Odysseus, swept a pair of them up in his mighty fists and smashed their heads on the ground like unwanted kittens. Blood and brains splattered all over the dung on the floor and onto the feet of the remaining startled Greeks, who cringed and wept and cried out in terror.

Ignoring them, the Cyclops sat on a boulder, shaped to fit his enormous gluteus maximus, and began to tear the dead men limb from limb, eating them bloody and steaming, and smacking his thick rubbery lips in noisy pleasure with each mouthful.

When he finished his snack and nothing was left, no bones or guts or anything else save what might have been soaked up by the dung on the ground, he belched a foul belch and gulped a bucket of raw milk to wash down his gory feast.

Then the giant stood up, flopped out his great penis, and pissed on the sword. I mean pissed into the bronze pot.

'Glub, glub, glub–'

'Hey,' I said, 'you didn't echo.'

'Very funny,' the transmogrified sword gurgled.

'Enough with the pissing! Get on with the story!'

'Yeah, okay.'

So sated and relieved, the giant Cyclops shook some drops of urine from his penis. Then he sat down on the floor of the cave with his back against the wall and went right to sleep. Sleeping like a baby.

Except he didn't close his eye. The damn thing just stared into space. A big blue orb encased in yellow-whitish ichor. And before long the Cyclops was snoring so loud he sounded like a Mack truck revving its engine.

But, as I said, his eye stayed open.

Then one of the Greeks crept towards him, but even as he slept the Cyclops saw the soldier and swatted him aside.

'Can he hear us?' Odysseus asked.

One of the men called to the giant: 'Polyphemus?' The Cyclops didn't stir.

'Let's kill him,' Odysseus said.

'Blub, glug, gurgle, splash,' the sword/pisspot said.

'What did you say?' Odysseus asked.

I figure at this point in his life, Odysseus was used to giants and probably other various forms of weirdness, so a talking sword who'd just turned into a pisspot was no big deal.

'Empty me first and maybe I can help,' the sword/pisspot said.

Although the pisspot was giant-sized, it was filled almost to the brim. It took the strength of three of Odysseus' men to overturn it. Piss spilled across the floor of the cave, pooling here and there, making the dung wet and sloppy and the fire sizzle. A rank smell filled the air.

'Thank-ank the Gods-ods,' the now empty bronze pot said. 'But even if you can kill him, how do you plan to move the massive stone from the entrance? Remember, the Cyclops who moves rocks like marbles will be dead.'

I then had to explain to Odysseus and his men what marbles were.

Testing the sword/pot's words, the remaining ten men silently made their way to the stone – its bulk was on the outside of the cave, but had handholds chiselled into its inner surface so the Cyclops could easily grip it – and tried to budge it. But they couldn't push it or lift it high enough for a bug to crawl under it.

'Won't you return to your demon form once the Cyclops is dead?' I asked the sword. 'Won't your powers return?'

'Maybe, maybe not. I don't know, Harold. Do you want to risk being stuck in this dung-filled cave for the rest of what would be a very short life?'

It was now my time to save the day, so I said, 'The only way we can escape is for my sword (who's been reduced to the status of pisspot) to get his power back.'

Well, Polyphemus the giant Cyclops snored on, oblivious to all our strategies. Odysseus' men huddled unheroically together at the rear of the cave, moaning and waiting for dawn and a chance to escape.

'We have to find the source of Polyphemus's power,' the sword said slowly, making a great effort not to echo. 'And then it will be up to you to do whatever is necessary to unbind me, Harold. You want to be a hero. Then do a job!'

In the morning the Cyclops awakened, yawned, stood up, shook himself like a wet dog, and stretched. Then once again he emptied his bladder into the pot.

'Glub, glug, glub,' the sword gurgled in disgust.

I watched the giant closely as he milked his ewes and nanny goats and tried to discern the source of his sorcerous power but, frankly, I had no clue.

When he finished, he left the lambs and kids to suckle what milk remained in their mothers' udders and hefted the massive stone aside from the mouth of the cave. He picked it up with no more effort than you or I would pick up a pebble on the beach.

Sunlight flooded in, blinding me for an instant, just as one of Odysseus' men made a dash for the opening. Idiot! Polyphemus easily snatched him up, held him before that big blue eye in the centre of his forehead as if examining a strange, new bug, and then dashed his brains out against the rock wall and popped the limp corpse into his mouth.

Another one of the men tried his luck, ducking behind the giant before making his run toward freedom. Although the Cyclops saw him, he couldn't move quickly enough to catch the young soldier-sailor who had just reached the mouth of the cave.

Terrible as it was to witness, I finally saw a way out of this mess.

Well, I must admit, it didn't click in my mind immediately. But here's what happened:

The Cyclops grunted and his huge eye began to glow with that eerie inner light I'd mentioned before. It was a green ichorish colour. (Ichorish, not liquorice). And then, like a tractor beam from a *Star Wars* movie, the one-eyed guy's gaze froze the hapless absconder mid-stride. The poor bastard was caught like a fly in amber, and the Cyclops didn't waste any time before dashing his brains out against the wall and eating him too. The crunching of bones and squishing of flesh was nauseating.

Then, belching with contentment, he grabbed a large pail of curd, pushed the stone aside, shouldered his way out of the cave, and sealed the entrance securely behind him.

'Glub, gurgle, slosh; somebody, anybody, help. I'm drowning in pee–'

'Empty him, empty the pisspot,' I shouted.

Odysseus and his remaining men wrestled with the pot until they finally overturned it. And, as the rank mossy odour of Cyclops piss filled the cave, it hit me. And I don't even want to consider how I conflated Cyclops piss with glamour. Sigmund Freud would probably have something nasty to say about the strange and perverse connections my unconscious makes, but that would be his problem, not mine and nor would I care because me, my unconscious, and I found the answer.

I told the sword/pisspot and Odysseus: 'The source of the Cyclops' sorcerous power is his *eye!*'

A little more about that big blue Cyclopedian eye

Since I'm admitting all sorts of things, I should mention that I was a bit bemused I could still understand what the Greeks were saying (in their ancient, archaic Greek) and that they could still understand me, despite the sword having lost his demonic power.

'How does that work?' I asked him.

'Beats me,' said the sword. 'I can only assume that Polyphemus is using his own version of telepathy and psycho-familiar translation which has us all speaking the same language.'

'Why?'

The sword/pisspot sighed yet again. '*Why?* So he can converse with us, dummy!'

Anyway, we huddled together in the cave and made plans.

Well, actually, Odysseus broke out another one of his wine skins and filled a carved wooden bowl with the strong, acidic wine and a little water. The Greeks passed it around and proceeded to get drunk.

'You know, we could just get the Cyclops drunk,' Odysseus said.

I shook my head. 'No, we'll need to do more than that to stop him.'

'You're right about that, hero,' said the sword/pisspot. 'When he returns, you'll have to take out his eye. That's your only chance.'

Odysseus staggered off to take a piss (and *not* in the sword/pisspot) and found a great club of green olive-wood beside one of the sheep pens in the deepest part of the cave. It was as long as the mast of a twenty-oared galley.

'We can lop off a length of this,' he said, 'shave it to a point with our swords, and char it to a hard stabbing point in the fire.'

'But how will you heft it without the Cyclops seeing you?' I asked.

Odysseus's men muttered amongst themselves, but didn't seem to have any ideas. I look around the cave as if ideas would be lying around like coils of rope. In fact, I did spy a coil of rope. I also found rocks piled against the far wall; and as I walked around the cave taking what I think of as mind pictures, I also discovered that the cave's ceiling high above us was reinforced with thick oaken beams.

'I have an idea,' I said and convinced them to set to work.

I should mention that it's not easy to get a bunch of half-drunk ancient Greek sailor-soldiers to do what you want. But after a lot of goading and prodding they eventually half-filled the sword – who was, of course, still in his pisspot embodiment – with rocks, tied him to one end of the rope (lucky that sailors know how to make good knots), and flung the other end over one of the thick ceiling beams.

'Now all we have to do,' I said, 'is pull the pisspot up to the ceiling of the cave and let go of the rope when the Cyclops steps underneath it.'

'Oh, sure, easy-peasy,' said the sword.

'Will it kill the Cyclops?' asked one of the men.

'If we are lucky – *very* lucky – it might knock him out. Or at least stun him so you, Odysseus, can stab him in the eye with that mighty stake.'

'And what if it just makes him angry, Mr Big Brain?' The voice was rock-muffled.

Ignoring the sword/pisspot, Odysseus said, 'That's all very well and good, but how are we supposed get the Cyclops to stand under the pot?'

'We'll need something to bait him.'

Odysseus and all his men looked at me.

'Well,' I said, 'it looks like you might have enough booze to get even a Cyclops shitfaced.'

'I had that idea earlier, stranger, and you naysayed it,' said an irritated Odysseus.

'Yes, I did, great leader of men. But I am large, I contain multitudes.'

Not having read Walt Whitman's *Song of Myself*, Odysseus gave me a perplexed look and then nodded as if, indeed, he was a great fan of 19th century American poetry.

(As an ex-nerd, I do indeed know such things!)

And now we come to – the crunch

We heard the crunch of gravel and the grating of rock and were almost blinded by the flash of sunlight as Polyphemus re-entered the cave. The Cyclops looked around, grunted, and then moved the massive boulder back across the entrance. Once again, the cave was dimly lit. Shadows skittered across walls and ceiling; the fire popped and glowed, brightening, as Polyphemus' movement stirred the air like a bellows.

'You must be weary after your day's work,' Odysseus said. 'Why not sit for a while and relax.' He poured a bowl of unwatered wine and offered it to the Cyclops. 'Here, try some of our fine Attican wine as an offering to the great Polyphemus's puissant strength and divinity.'

The one-eyed giant squinted suspiciously at Odysseus, accepted the bowl and sat down on his stone seat. He took a cautious sip, grunted with pleasure, and tossed the remainder back in a single gulp.

'More!' he demanded, holding out the empty bowl. 'A good helping.'

Odysseus refilled the bowl to the brim with the strong wine. The Cyclops swallowed it down and called for another. He quaffed that and insisted Odysseus refill it again. After three bowls he belched and got to his feet, staggering a little.

His voice slurred, he said, 'I need food.' He grabbed for one of the crew but missed, as the man manage to duck out of his way.

Polyphemus blinked his now glazed eye. 'Hold still,' he said. 'My stomach is grumbling from lack of human flesh.'

'Hey, you one-eyed git,' I shouted, waving my arms to attract his drunken attention. 'Hey, you fat, one-eyed, shit-smelling bastard seed of one of Poseidon's misguided trysts with some ogre whore. You should go on a diet. You look like an oversized basketball with a head.'

Okay, I could hear the sword/pisspot mumble something about the Cyclops not having a clue about basketballs, so after an instant of reflection, I shouted, 'You must get all that fat from your mother!'

I gave him the finger and shouted, 'Eat me!'

I meant that in the derogatory streetwise sense. God forbid my journey would end as a bit of acid reflux in the stomach of this son of a god.

As I taunted the one-eyed smell of a fart, I walked backwards until I was right under the sword/pisspot who was filled with rocks and hanging under the ceiling. I could hear the heavy breathing of Odysseus' men who were crouched down behind one of the sheep pens as they strained to hold onto the rope.

The Cyclops stared down at me, and I could almost imagine a look of respect had crossed his pimply, jowly face. 'So who are you, little pigmy, who dares to insult Polyphemus, the son of Poseidon?'

'My name? My name is – Nobody; that's my name,' I said, thinking for some bizarre reason of Terrence Hill playing alongside Henry Fonda in the title role of a 1973 spaghetti western comedy. And I don't even like spaghetti westerns!

'That's your name?' the Cyclops asked, laughing. 'Well, then, my little insect, I will have Nobody for supper.'

He hooted and lurched towards me. He was so drunk he almost fell over his own feet.

I bravely stood my ground.

'You were shaking in your boots!'

'Shut up! This is my story, Sword. And I wasn't wearing boots!'

Now, as I was saying, I stood my ground until Polyphemus was almost on top of me. I waited until he bent down to grab me before I screamed – which was our signal to act.

As the men released their hold on the rope, as the sword/pisspot filled with rocks descended at a great rate of speed, I threw myself backward. That was all as it should be but, unfortunately, one of the half-drunk Greeks had unwittingly left a dangling loop of rope on the floor of the cave, which, of course, I stepped into. As the pot came crashing down, the rope tightened around my ankles, and I found myself hauled feet-first up to the ceiling.

'You screamed like a girl.'

'Don't interrupt, Sword. I did no such thing!'

So there I was, hanging upside-down above the Cyclops; and far from being knocked out, Polyphemus was bellowing like a bull undergoing castration. Even drunk and knocked almost senseless, the enraged Cyclops managed to grab another one of Odysseus' men and dash his brains out.

'You're next,' he said to Odysseus.

'Oh, shit,' Odysseus moaned, which, if you need a translation is '*Ù, óêáôÜ*!' Sounds sort of like *omega kata*. (I thought, dear reader, you'd like to hear Odysseus swearing in the original tongue.)

While all this was going on, I managed to loosen the ropes around my feet, only to fall right onto Polyphemus's pustuled nose which, I can tell you, was as slippery as an egg on glass. I reflexively grabbed his eyelid – it was the size of a roller blind – to balance myself; and in so doing, my weight pulled his eye shut.

Polyphemus tossed his head from side to side and roared in fury, but I held on like a fly on glass; to continue my continuing metaphor.

I heard Odysseus shout, 'Look! Treasure!'

And as I was being whipped about like a pennant in a gale – yes, I know, mixing metaphors – I held onto that enormous eyelid for my life. Everything seemed to tumble around me, as if I was caught in some giant, poorly-lit kaleidoscope. I caught glimpses of glittering objects: was that a jewel-encrusted gold chalice sitting on a shelf where a wooden bowl had been? Wasn't that mound of jewels catching the firelight once a pile of rocks? And weren't those ingots of silver and gold formerly stacks of cheeses?

'Hold on, Harold,' shouted the sword.

And, indeed, Sword was no longer a pisspot.

It seemed as long as I was pulling down the Cyclops's eyelid, essentially blinding him, Polyphemus's powerful glamour was interrupted.

'We've got to put his eye out immediately!'

Polyphemus swatted at me, as if I were the aforementioned proverbial fly, and caught me with a glancing blow, which stunned me. One of my hands lost its grip on his eyelid, but I held on for dear life with my other hand; and, before the Cyclops could pluck me from his face and squash me into an unwilling hamburger patty, something cold and hard thumped into the palm of my free hand.

A familiar voice: 'We can do this, Harold.'

I recognised the familiar hilt of THE-GLORIOUS-SWORD-OF-FIRE-AND-DESTINY-THAT-BURNS-AND-CUTS-THROUGH-FLESH and, even as I lost my grip on Polyphemus's giant eyelid, I simultaneously plunged the sword deep into the eye of the Cyclops.

Sticky blood and gore exploded all over the sword and me. The Cyclops screamed so loud it could be felt as vibration. And then I was falling, and I, too, was shouting, the last triumphal shout of a hero; but I did not let go of the sword.

My skull might be crushed in the fall, but I would not lose my sword.

Heroes don't lose their swords!

And as I fell, the sword, seemingly unperturbed by the idea that I had escaped being crushed into a hamburger patty, only to be flattened into a pancake, said, 'That was close. A split second more and you would have merely bumped him in the eye with a pisspot.'

It Ain't Over Yet

I was covered in stinking, steaming gore. Everything smelled like shit, probably because I had just landed in a thick, wet clump of straw and stinking dung.

'That's lucky,' the sword said. 'It broke your fall.'

'Thanks for your kind consideration.'

Polyphemus, however, was still very much alive and active. He blundered blindly around the cave, shrieking and bellowing, smashing and breaking anything and everything in his path. He somehow caught another of Odysseus' men and bashed his brains out.

All the while, would you believe, it was Polyphemus – the brain-bashing eater of humans – who was crying for help. Loudly.

And then, for a moment, I thought Poseidon himself had heard his pleas and had come to his aid, because the ground shook as if an earthquake had erupted all around us.

But, to cut to the chase, it wasn't Poseidon but the neighbouring Cyclopes who lived in the many other caves on the nearby windswept crags.

'What is wrong, brother?' they shouted. 'Is somebody trying to kill you?'

'Nobody is trying to kill me,' Polyphemus roared.

'If nobody is trying to kill you,' they shouted, 'then you should pray to your father, Poseidon. Zeus must be to blame for whatever ails you.'

'*Nobody* has blinded me and is trying to kill me!'

After that pronouncement, the other Cyclopes ignored his cries for help. As far as they were concerned, whtever it was it was in the hands of the Gods. And, it has to be said, Cyclopes aren't the most fraternal and sensitive of species.

With no one rushing to his aid, the eyeless Polyphemus groped his way to the mouth of the cave and rolled back the stone. Too late he realised his mistake, for Odysseus and his four remaining men bolted through the opening and ran for the beach as quick as they could; leaving me and my trusty sword behind.

'I was not, am not, and will never ever be your trusty sword, nerd-boy!'

'Sorry, Sword, don't get hot under your, er, hilt.'

So, readers, allow me to continue the story, which is, alas, almost at an end. As you might have guessed, the Cyclops chased after Odysseus and his men, following the sound of their running feet; and we were left on our own in the quietude of his stinking, treasure-filled cave.

I sheathed Sword and made my way over to the golden-jewelled chalice. It was exquisite. Wrought by a master craftsman. I picked it up. It felt surprisingly warm.

'Leave that, oh greedy one,' the sword said. 'You can grab anything else you can carry, but that chalice is destined for another kind of hero living in another time. But hurry, whatever you do, because we don't have much time.'

I reluctantly replaced the chalice and decided to collect the gold ingots; but they were just too damn heavy, like lumps of lead. Who knew gold weighed too much, even for a muscle-bound hero like me?

So I came to my senses and stuffed fistfuls of diamonds, rubies, emeralds and sapphires into a muslin bag the Cyclops used to squeeze out the liquid whey from the cheese curd. The gems, too, were heavy as hell, but I thought of flag and country and shouldered my hard burden.

But now the end is near

Standing on a rocky crag, I looked down onto the beach. Odysseus and his men had already boarded their waiting ship. The remaining crew, who had stayed on board to guard the vessel and keep it ready for a quick getaway, cast off. The oarsmen churned the water with each strong, synchronised stroke and in response the ship pulled quickly away.

But Odysseus – ah, Odysseus – he couldn't control his pride. He was the living embodiment of hubris. He made his way to the stern and shouted, 'How dare you eat your honoured guests, Polyphemus, you shithead.'

The Cyclops roared in exasperation.

'Did I not warn you, you one-eyed and now no-eyed loser, that I am under the protection of Zeus? Remember me, Polyphemus, remember my name, for I am Odysseus, King of Ithaca!'

'Fool,' the sword muttered. 'He's a braggart and a fool. Zeus couldn't give one small shit about Odysseus. But Poseidon… Now *there's* a god who knows how to hold a grudge.'

The blind Polyphemus tore a gigantic chunk of rock away from the headland and hurled it in the direction of Odysseus' voice. It splashed into the sea just ahead of the ship, creating a mighty wave that washed the ship back towards shore.

'Row!' Odysseus shouted to his men. 'Row for your lives!'

'Will they escape?' I asked the all-knowing sword.

'That's more like it, hero.'

And the sword challenged me: 'Haven't you read your Homer, Harold?'

I responded with my usual sense of certainty: 'Well, umm–'

'Never mind,' said the sword. 'Homer got it all wrong anyway. But it wasn't his fault.'

'So do they make it home?'

'Yes, eventually. But it will take them years and years. Because Odysseus couldn't leave well enough alone and had to be the big shot, Polyphemus will call on his father to extract revenge, and Poseidon will–

'Ach, Mr Hero. Go read the damn book!'

And that, friends, is the true story about how I, Harold the Hero, singlehandedly (well, okay, maybe the sword helped out a little) saved Odysseus and (some) of his men.

Not to mention saving the Talking Sword.

That's also how I escaped with enough treasure to have a *real* Mediterranean island holiday. In fact, I now have enough to buy myself an entire island.

'Anything you want to add, Sword?'

Video games anyone?

A last word

Yes, thank you. This last little bit is known as the denouement. The final outcome. This is where I wrap everything up so we can all go home.

Harold doesn't shake and pee in his armour anymore when we have to fight a dragon. In fact, as you might have noticed, he has got a bit of a big head and thinks he's without flaw–

'That's not true!'

–but at least he hasn't fallen in love with a damsel in distress; yet.

However, a little bird told me that Harold the Hero will soon be heading off on his own for a – well, for another – well-earned holiday. And I have that certain feeling that he might just meet an undistressed damsel.

And we can all extrapolate what might happen then. He would give up the hero business. Just like that. Which would be a shame because we really do make a great team.

Just ask Odysseus.

So what will *I* do if Harold finds true storybook love?

Oh, I suppose I could get myself a new hero.

But, you know what I've been thinking about a lot lately?

I might just take a break and go into video game programming. I could design some mean video games. How about something like a game called *The Talking Sword*?

Why not, hey?

And I've had my eye on one of those whiz-bang smart phones for a while. I might even buy myself a new Jag.

Of course, I'd have to grow some arms and hands. But that's no problem.

I'm a demon, after all.

MARIA LEWIS

The Bushwalker Butcher

'Gary, hi it's me.'

'Who's me?'

'Come on. You're mad I didn't call, aren't you?'

'Mad? No, why would I be mad when I can hear you *sighing* through the phone.'

'I'm not sighing I'm just… breathing heavily.'

'Right. What do you want, Paget?'

'You think I'm only calling because I want something?'

'Honestly? Yes.'

'Okay, well, I do have something I need to ask you– '

'I knew it.'

'But we still need to talk about the other stuff. Later.'

'Go on.'

'Have you heard anything about an MVA on Paramatta Road? Fatal.'

'Aren't motor vehicle accidents low-hanging fruit for you?'

'It's a slow day.'

'You say that like it's a bad thing.'

'Gary–'

'You should really be speaking to Police Media.'

'I could be, but why bother when I know good ol' you?'

'Fine. No. There was no fatal, it was just a two-car prang.'

'Are you sure? Because I could have sworn I heard the word 'fatal' over the police scanner–'

'Natal.'

'What?'

'You heard the word 'natal'. Constable Barry Jurcic was being relieved because he had to go to prenatal class with his wife.'

'Damn.'

'What was that?'

'Oh, nothing. Tell Barry I said congratulations, I didn't know his lady was expecting.'

'Is that all, Paget?'

'For now. I'll call you later Gary. Thanks.'

Paget Stevenson hung up the phone with a heavy sigh, not worrying about someone on the other end of the line scolding her for it. It had been an excruciatingly slow news day and the police reporter – who usually focused on the more grisly crimes – had been reduced to chasing ambulances in the hope of filling some column inches. She tossed a dark, black braid off her shoulder where it clanged amongst the others that hung to her waist. With another sigh she got up from her desk and grabbed her notepad. She tucked a pen behind her ear as she took a position sitting on the Chief Of Staff's desk and waited for him to get off the phone. As he clicked down the receiver, Tex Jones looked at her hopefully.

She preempted his question by saying: 'No go, I'm afraid.'

'Damn. The crime beat has been dead today.'

She raised an eyebrow at his quip.

'Extra dead,' he muttered. 'I thought you heard them call it a fatal over the scanner?'

'They said 'prenatal' apparently. One of the cops was getting relieved so he could go to a prenatal class with his wife.'

'Fuck. Anything else going on?'

'Nope. I did my rounds, called a few contacts out of boredom, checked Twitter. You know what this means?'

'Not again.'

'I'm telling you, every time it's this eerily quiet the night guys catch something massive. It was a King's Cross drive-by six months ago. Tonight? I'm betting on high-profile arrest.'

'What we could really do with is another Benjamin Lee Brittaker,' he said wistfully.

Paget grimaced. 'Really? A guy who killed *nine* bushwalkers in the Blue Mountains is what you think we could do with? Geez, and sometimes I think I'm morbid. You're a sick fuck, Tex.'

'The trial was gangbusters for our circulation numbers.'

'Yeah, and it ended three months ago. Find a new horse to flog.'

'As soon–'

His phone began ringing aggressively, the way only phones in a newsroom seem to do. He picked it up, signalling the end of the conversation. She was about to leave his desk when he called out to her.

'Is your City Watch double spread in?'

'Yup. Last I checked the layout guys were putting it together.'

'And the balcony murder feature?'

'Beautifully written and submitted,' she winked.

He nodded and she left, negotiating her way through the sea of desks and workstations at *The Australian Herald*. It was a few hours out from deadline at the country's most read newspaper and there was a mix of anticipation and anxiety in the air. She dodged an entertainment reporter who jogged past her with a frantic 'hello' and carefully danced around the business editor who was swearing loudly at his computer screen. When she finally arrived at her destination, the atmosphere was quieter, almost serene. This was the artists' hub and she ducked into the fortress of desks like a soldier taking cover. Almost instantly she felt better, relaxed, out of the firing line.

Usually six artists worked at the cluster; a collection of political cartoonists, digital artists and illustrators. Today there was only one hunched over a colourful caricature of the Prime Minister pushing a wheelbarrow of broken toys. As Paget squinted to get a closer look she realised all of the toys resembled members of the government's cabinet.

'Huh, clever,' she said as she pulled herself into one chair and propped her feet up on another.

'I am the cleverest,' replied Season Akhtar without looking up from her illustration. A finite paint brush carefully dabbed watercolours along the perimeter of the wheelbarrow for definition. 'How was Gary?'

'Okay. He told me what I needed to know.'

'Was he pissed you didn't call?'

'*Well–*'

'He was pissed.'

'Yeah, he sounded it.'

'You should have called. I thought you liked the guy?'

'I do it's just, all cops are dogs, Season. You know this. After the other night I let my guard down and things got out of hand–'

'Or in his hand.'

' –and I figure it's easier to escape now than wait and get bitten.'

Without her eyes leaving the picture Season added: 'Take your feet off the chair.'

'What? How did you even…? These are nice shoes.'

Season snorted.

'Okay, they're not your Manolo Blahniks but they're my nicest pair of combat boots.'

'*Off*.'

'Le sigh. Fine. How's your day been anyway?'

'The usual. They never know what they want until it's two hours before deadline and you have to scrap the five ideas they gave you earlier in the day. Besides that though, good.'

'You doing anything on the weekend?'

'Why?'

'Can't I simply ask what my best friend is planning to do this weekend?'

'You can ask, but you have a scheme up your sleeve. I'm not going on another 10-hour stakeout with you.'

'You said you had fun!'

'I did. It was awesome. But the Rock N Roll Markets are on this weekend and I want to go,' she said, finally lifting her head up to face her friend. Season's hair was hidden under a pretty floral headscarf in shades of peach and aqua. As usual, only the artist's heart-shaped face was visible in her hijab and her large, round eyes were highlighted with a skilful application of liquid eyeliner. The denim of her jeans made a rubbing noise as she crossed them and pointed the edges of her stilettos at her visitor.

'The market's on Sunday, right?' asked Paget.

'From 10:30 a.m.'

'That's no problem: this thing will only take a few hours on Saturday, four at the most. I promise I'll go with you to the markets if you come.'

'You will?'

'Mmm-hmm. Greasers.'

'Greasers,' Season agreed, taking a sip of tea from a nearby mug. 'Where do you want to go on Saturday?'

'To interview a Yowie hunter on Mount Wilson.'

Season choked on her beverage, spluttering as she struggled to maintain composure. She didn't know how she was surprised at the request for such a strange errand. She shouldn't have expected anything less.

'What on earth for? You don't think they're real, do you?' she asked.

'Do I think Australia's answer to Big Foot has been casually roaming the countryside for the past 200 years without any conclusive proof or biological evidence? No, Season. I'm not an idiot.'

'Then why would you drive two hours up into the Blue Mountains to interview some crackpot on Mt. Wilson?'

Paget shrugged. 'I think it will make an interesting story. This guy has written three books on the subject, published countless papers, and left his job as a chemist to pursue this full time. He's been researching Yowies and investigating them for over 50 years. I think there could be a really interesting feature article on the nature of obsession. What drives someone to dedicate their life to something they know is irrational, but they do it anyway?'

Season blinked at the explanation. Sometimes it was easy to forget that Paget, despite being only 25, was *The Australian Herald's* best crime reporter for a reason. When she started at the paper six years ago, she was immediately thrown into the crime beat to see if she could 'handle it'. With a knack for remembering police and ambulance codes as they bleeped across the emergency scanners, she was often the first to pick up a story and the hungriest to chase it. While walking her dog in the park some years ago Paget had come across a torn piece of paper with the corner of a logo that she recognised as the police insignia. Riffling through the bin, she collected all the pieces and sticky-taped them together like a demented jigsaw puzzle. What it revealed was a confidential statement from a police informant about what they believed to be a serial rapist – except the police were covering it up. Paget broke the story, sourced witnesses and victims, and very nearly won the top prize in journalism for it: a Walkley Award.

She was unlucky to get passed over for the 'Bushwalker Butcher' Benjamin Lee Brittaker story when it surfaced, but the senior police reporter had finally begun to feel threatened and put his foot down, demanding the yarn or he would walk. Australian serial killers don't come along very often and Season knew it pained her friend to see the story go somewhere else. Yet Paget also knew how the newsroom hierarchy worked. And she abided.

Season could see what was happening now. An amazing story had leap-frogged Paget and she had been stuck covering generic police rounds for months. The crime beat had been unnaturally quiet and Paget had the distinctive twitch of someone who needed a project. Any project.

'I'll come with you,' said Season, conceding at last. 'But I've got to be honest: I don't really care much for weird urban legends like the Yowie or Loch Ness or whatever.'

'Ugh, don't you care about anything?' Paget grinned. 'I'm a nihilist.'

'You believe in nothing, Lebowski,' said the crime reporter in her best German accent. 'Anyway, I'll pick you up at 9 a.m.?'

'Ew, why so early?'

'This man is old, he probably goes to bed at midday. After tea. And plus, I'll drive so you have a few hours of sketching time there and back. Get some doodling done.'

'I hate that word.'

'Doodle? What's to hate? Doodles are great. Doodle.'

'Stop it.'

Paget smiled. 'Alright, I'll see you in the morning.'

'Bring coffee.'

'One long black it is.'

Season watched her friend turn and stroll confidently away from the artists' work station, the knowledge of an impending story making her seem almost buoyant as she artfully dodged an argument between a sub-editor and a page designer. When Season started at the paper, she and Paget had been friends at first sight. As the only women of colour in the newsroom, they had been nicknamed The Minority Reporters by their colleagues – a title they declined to acknowledge. Both women were relative rookies when their friendship first formed and they had navigated their way through the sometimes dicey pool of ladder climbers, beat-up artists and pick-up merchants. If Paget was the storm, Season was the calm to it.

'Yowies,' muttered Season, shaking her head as she turned back to her drawing. 'Bloody Yowies.'

'Ugh.'

'Ugh what?'

'It just doesn't make sense,' said Season, folding the pages of *The Australian Herald* on her lap as she finished reading an article. The trial of Benjamin Lee Britton was well and truly over, but the drama surrounding the Bushwalker Butcher was far from dead. He had been convicted of multiple murders, yet now the story had shifted to the remains of the final three victims, which he was refusing to give up. He had admitted to the murders, but refused to point police towards the final resting place of the victims. The bodies of the first six had been discovered over a 12-year period yet he was keeping his lips sealed about the trio of latest victims. It was the story that kept on giving for the papers, and *The Australian Herald* had splashed with the latest coverage across two pages.

'He's going down for the murders of nine people,' Season pressed. 'That's consecutive life sentences. Why would he hold out on three?'

Paget kept her eyes on the road, not glancing at her friend in the passenger seat as she contemplated the answer. 'Shame? Embarrassment? You know, Ted Bundy consistently lied and denied the murder of eight-year-old Ann Marie Burr because he didn't want to be known as a kid killer. Killing 30 women, probably more? Fine. But he drew the line at children, even though there's overwhelming proof he did it.'

'Yes, but Benjamin Lee Britton isn't Ted Bundy – he's an idiot. He doesn't have the charisma or intelligence. It's a miracle he didn't get caught sooner.'

'Uh, but he *was* mobile. Even though he was hunting in the same region he himself was mobile in that.. what do they call it?'

'Van of Doom.'

'Oh for fucks sake.'

'I know.'

'Anyway, it's his sloppiness and laziness that caught him in the end. Who roofies themselves? I mean, seriously. Even worse: he roofies himself and passes out with a body smelling out the back of the van on Mt. Wilson's Main Street.'

'I know. It's so–'

'Dumb.'

'The dumbest. You know, his defence was pushing for a long time to have him pronounced 'medically stupid' and I think they had grounds. I watched the interrogation tapes and he's not all there, no doubt about it.'

'Hmmm,' mused Season, stretching her legs out until they were resting on the dashboard of the second-hand Suzuki Jimny. Trying to save money on air-conditioning, Paget had the windows down and wind whipped through the car as they drove up the steep road that led to the Blue Mountains. Upon her friend's advice, Season had switched her usual uniform of designer heels to a pair of equally expensive but more practical flats. Shoes were an indulgence she allowed herself and her footwear was often the envy of the other women – and a few gay men – in the office. Paget had never understood how she managed to spend to all day in those things. She preferred practical sneakers, combat boots or R.M. Williams ankle huggers to stilettos. The material of Season's hijab – a sky blue shade today – was flickering in the wind as she stared out the car window at the wilderness.

The Blue Mountains were, simply, massive. To this day no one could ever decide just exactly how big it was but it spanned thousands of kilometres in every direction as part of the Great Dividing Range. It was essentially Australia's answer to the Grand Canyon, but with the great crevices hidden under layer upon layer of thick, impenetrable bush. Both women had been there countless times growing up, for school camps or bushwalking trips with their families to see The Three Sisters: a jaw-dropping sandstone rock formation that was probably the most iconic sight in the area.

The sounds of Spiderbait blared through the speakers as Paget slowed down to take a particularly tight corner before indicating off the main road and on to a residential street. She was singing the lyrics softly under her breath and Season smiled at the image of her: long braids wound into a bun on top of her head, too-big sunglasses resting on the bridge of her nose and giant lips moving with the words. She switched her attention to the suburbia around them and thought briefly that she could live here, that she could enjoy this peacefulness. She was jolted forward as Paget put her foot on the brakes. A child no older than 12 was skipping across the middle of the road, with golden plaits swinging behind her as she moved. A red ribbon at the end of her plaits glinted as it caught sunlight. The car slowed to a crawl as they waited for the girl to get to the other side of the road. She maintained eye contact with the women, smiling playfully.

'What the fuck, creepy child?' Paget muttered.

'Sssshh! She'll hear you!' Season hissed.

'So? Wind up your window and lock the door will you? This kid is giving me the wig.'

'What's with you and kids?' Season replied, while winding up her window like her friend asked. 'They always freak you out.'

'Well, yeah, when they're skipping in slow motion across the road while grinning at us they do. That is not normal behaviour. And where are her parents?'

'Where *are* her parents? Maybe we should–'

'Fuck. No. We are not sticking around to see what Cindy Wayne Gacy does next,' Paget protested, accelerating as the child finally made it to the other side of the road. Season watched in the rear-view mirror as the girl proceeded to skip to the other side of the road once more, dangerously slow.

'Can you check my phone?' Paget asked, handing her the device which was mapping their route.

'Uh, yup – this left. No, your left. Slow down; it should be one of these ones on the right. There! Number 24.'

Paget pulled up next to the adorable two-storey house, which looked like it had been plucked straight from the pages of *Country Living*. A white picket fence separated the property from its neighbours, while a cluster of colourful flowers grew in between the pickets and over the fence top like a rainbow oil spill.

'Oh, this is pretty,' said Season, as she hopped out of the car. She stretched her back against the vehicle before taking a better look.

'What did you expect? A cave?' Paget joined her around the other side of the car, hoisting her brown satchel over one shoulder. It contained everything she'd need for a good story: her recorder, a back-up recorder, camera, notebook, laptop, chargers and batteries. The bag always appeared ten times heavier than it looked and Season wondered what else was stashed in there.

'Not a cave exactly–'. Her sentence broke off as they were greeted by an obese brown Labrador that came waddling up the garden path to meet them. 'Oh hello! Aren't you lovely and fat, hey? I said aren't you lovely and fat?'

The Labrador blinked happily at Paget as she rustled his fur and his big, pink tongue lolled happily out the side of his mouth.

'Chester! Chester where did you – oh, hello there.' An elderly woman whose hair was as white as the pickets of her fence appeared from behind a rose bush. She was almost spherical in shape and moved in an identical fashion to her dog. 'You must be Peter's guests.'

'Hi there,' said Paget, switching into her most charming mode. 'I'm Paget Stevenson from *The Australian Herald* and this my friend, Season Akhtar.'

'Oh my, how exotic!' said the woman, beaming at both ladies as she shook their hands. 'I'm Peter's wife Rosanna. The folks around here call me Mrs Yowie, which I don't like very much but what can you do?'

'Are you not a researcher also?' asked Season.

'Me? God no. I can hardly stand the stuff. I've been married to Peter for over 55 years and looking at his rubbish for 57. But you know, as I'm sure you young ladies will learn, you can't help who you fall in love with as much as you can help their passions.'

Season gave Paget a knowing look. The reporter mouthed the words 'shut up' as Rosanna turned her back to lead them towards the house.

'Follow me dears, come into the house and we can find somewhere comfortable to sit.'

'Thank you very much, that would be lovely,' said Paget.

'I do have to warn you though: once you get Peter going on a topic it's hard to shut him up. I hope you've scheduled a few hours for this.'

'We have all the time in the world,' smiled Paget, while Season rolled her eyes.

'I have to say, you have such a lovely home,' Season trailed off as they stepped over the threshold. The inside of the house couldn't haven been more at odds with the exterior. The women slid behind each other to fit into single file and move down the long, dark hallway. The path was so narrow because a towering pile of books and newspapers were stacked from the floor to the ceiling on every side. Season had to do her best not to yelp as she noticed the eyes of a black tabby cat staring back at her as she passed a particularly dusty book pile. She tugged gently on the hem of Paget's floral sundress to express her discomfort. Her friend spun around to face her and Season deflated at the delight in her eyes. She was grinning from ear to ear and seemed to be positively ecstatic at being on the set of *Hoarders*.

'This is the real deal,' she whispered. 'This is going to make a great story.'

'Now just keep going straight to the end there and you'll find Peter. He's on the computer. I'm going to make us a cup of tea,' said Rosanna as she peeled off into a near invisible opening on the right. Season didn't turn her head to look at the kitchen, afraid of what she may see. Thankfully the hallway opened up into a well-lit lounge area where an old, fat man was hunched at the computer. His hair and thick Santa-beard matched the pale shade of his wife's and he turned to the women as they entered.

'Peter Lomond, it's so great to meet you in person,' said Paget, extending her hand to the old man who blushed and smiled accordingly.

'Oh my, thank you, that's quite the welcome. I'm surprised anyone's still interested in my research so I'm always happy to speak with new people.'

'I'm Season, a colleague of Paget's from *The Australian Herald*.'

'Lovely to make your acquaintance also. Please, take a seat.'

He cleared several books and a file of paperwork off two love seats covered in a tartan pattern. Paget took the first one and sunk deep down into its depths. She pretended not to notice the small puff of dust that arose from one of the cushions.

Season noticed, and declined a seat. Instead she casually strolled around what would have been a spacious lounge area if it wasn't so cluttered. As it was, it was barely big enough to fit four people and an overweight Labrador.

Maps of the Blue Mountains geography hung on the walls, with various areas circled or linked to another with red string. Plastic storage boxes were stacked in every section of the room and the bookshelves were overflowing with volumes. There were skulls of all shapes and sizes adorning the area, some used as paperweights and others forgotten down the side of a book pile. Season brushed dust off what appeared to be a dog's skull as she held it to her face and examined the teeth.

'That's a dingo,' Peter said, following her movements. 'Found her at the base of Wentworth Falls off the main trail. She hadn't been dead long and her skull made for a great specimen.'

'I can see that,' Season said, smiling politely and placing the skull down.

The jingle of cutlery announced the arrival of Rosanna who shuffled into the room with a tray of cakes and a pot of steaming tea.

Chester eagerly followed at her heels, desperate for any crumb that may fall his way.

'Tea? Cake?' asked Rosanna, as she placed the tray on a tiny coffee table. Season's eyes lit up at the mention of tea. She thanked the elderly lady and took a cup adorned in pictures of tiny birds.

'Thank you, I'm a tea fanatic,' she said.

'Us too, eight cups a day at least. Sugar? Milk?'

'Yes please, to both.'

'Rosanna here is quite the baker,' said Peter, offering Paget one of the plates of sweet goods. 'Ginger nut slice? Tea?'

'I've never been one for tea but I cannot say no to cake. Could I grab one of the brownies as well?'

Season smirked at her friend as she sipped her tea. 'You're shameless.'

'Hey, I have a sweet tooth.'

'That's quite alright, Peter and I are trying to watch our weight,' said Rosanna, patting her big, round belly. It wobbled with the movement. 'So the more cakes you can eat for us, the better.'

'You should try the ginger nut slice, Season, it's amazing,' Paget pushed.

'Fine, I will. Mmm. It is really good. Is this your own recipe?'

'Of course! Nothing beats home made baking,' Rosanna replied. She poured herself a cup of tea, said 'I'll leave you to it,' and left the room.

Paget dusted the crumbs from her notepad – the brownie really was insanely sweet – as she prepared to get down to business.

'So, I guess the best place to start is at the beginning. How did you first become interested in the Yowie?'

'When I was a kid, I imagine. I used to work at a movie theatre that my dad owned and on the weekend we would go bushwalking. I saw my first Yowie when I was 13 on a Saturday afternoon at 4:35 p.m. and the obsession started from there,' he said.

'You have such a precise memory. Where did you see the Yowie?'

'Right here in the Blue Mountains. And, just after Rosanna and I got married, we made a plan to move up here, so I would be closer to the field of research.'

'So you think the population is concentrated here?'

'Most certainly. There's so much land out there that has never been mapped properly, that hasn't seen human interaction since the Aborigines. The Blue Mountains are where they live and where they've flourished for millions of years.'

'Now when you say flourished,' started Paget, 'what exactly do you mean? Because we've yet to have conclusive proof that a single Yowie exists, let alone a population.'

'There are five different species of Yowie and the Yowie itself is a sub species of homo erectus. Rosanna? Oh, there you are. Can you pass me the footprints please.'

His wife had returned so quietly no one had noticed. She lifted a heavy pile of plaster from behind the desk, passing it to her husband who began carefully shuffling through the moulds.

Season leaned over Paget's shoulder to get a better look as he presented them to the women.

'This is an adult female's footprint from July 1988. This is an adolescent from January 1996 – we're not sure if it's male or female. This is a grown male from October, 2003 and this one, our best specimen, is another adult male from last month.'

'These are all casts of footprints that you've found here in the Blue Mountains?'

'Yes. There is a population out here, a big one.'

'These could be anything. I hate to say it Peter, but you could have fabricated these. There must be other proof surely? Do you have photographic evidence, at least? Or fossils?'

Season resumed her stroll around the room, sipping her tea as she went.

Peter leaned back, stroking his beard. 'Like a cast, a photo could also be faked,' he said, surprising Paget with his honesty. 'People always suspect that pictures of rarely-seen things are doctored. Once the suspicion is there, the 'proof' of the sighting is forever in doubt. No, a photo isn't good enough. The only conclusive proof that anyone will take seriously is biological evidence.'

'A body?'

'A body or a limb or DNA. Something scientific.'

'Hmm. That makes sense.'

'The problem is people think there's a big, hairy 12-foot monster out there waiting in the bushes.'

'Isn't that what you just said?' asked Paget.

'No, I believe they're not that much different from us. They're the evolutionary step between man and chimpanzee. I'd estimate them to be not much bigger than four or five feet.'

Season's fingers trailed over the spines of the books as she finished the last of her tea, carefully placing the cup down on the coffee table. She was doing her best to keep an open mind, or at least give that impression.

She found Peter Lomond's own books amongst volumes and flicked open to the first page of: *Hunting The Great Australian Yowie*. She paused on a crude illustration of a human evolutionary chart, which depicted mankind's progress from the trees to civilisation.

When she attempted to put the book back, it slipped through her unusually clumsy fingers. She picked it up from the floor and finally returned it to its rightful place – on the third attempt. To cover her embarrassment, she headed over to a a hald-dozen skulls stacked alongside a magazine rack.

Paget, meanwhile, continued to fire off questions, maintaining her patience as she teased the story from the old obsessive, inch by inch.

Season's fingers danced over the first skull, which was much smaller than the rest and seemed to be that of a small monkey. During her study for a Bachelor of Fine Arts, Season had come to know the human physiology very well. She had to. If she was to draw, paint and illustrate the human body she had to not only understand how everything worked, but where everything went. She realised that most of the skulls around the room were fake, even the animal ones. They lacked a certain fragile quality to them and the 'bone' was too clean.

Season suspected the elderly couple had tried to dye them with tea to make it look more realistic. She would have to wait until they were back in the car on the way home before she could tell Paget. She glanced over at her friend, who was nodding a little too empathetically at all Peterwas saying. Season could tell the reporter was buying none of it. In fact, she could almost see the clock mentally ticking inside Paget's head, marking off the seconds until they could leave the claustrophobic home and make the most of the remaining weekend.

Season returned her attention to the skulls, her hands trailing their surfaces as she read the magazine titles in the rack beneath: *Mythology Monthly, The World Not As You Know It* and *Collected Conspiracies*.

Something made her stop again. The last skull in the row had a rough, almost grainy surface, quite unlike the others. It seemed there was one real skull amongst the fakes. It was at eye-level on the shelf, and she peered closely at it, before touching the eye sockets and the hole where a nose had once been. Finally she lifted it up, it was heavier than the others, and held it next to her own head, to compare the size.

'What kind of skull is this?' she asked, interrupting Paget mid-sentence.

Peter Lomond blinked repeatedly as he looked from Season to the specimen.

'Uh, that there is a *homo floresiensis*. An old friend of mine sent it to me from the Philippines,' he said.

'It looks human,' Season replied, squinting at it.

'What's a homo floresiensis?' Paget queried.

'They called them 'hobbits' in the media. They were believed to be small, hairy men. Not that dissimilar to a Yowie.'

'Oh yeah, I remember reading about that a couple of years ago. Season, put that skull down – you look like you're auditioning for Hamlet.'

Season frowned and returned the specimen to its rightful place, as a deep sense of unease began to curdle inside her stomach.

Paget managed to draw Peter back into their interview, so Season scanned the room, looking for other skulls that were out of place among the fakes they were grouped with.

She tripped slightly as she made her way to the nearest one. It too was heavier, and looked and felt authentic. Although she knew really good replicas could fool the inexperienced, a deep sense of unease began to curdle inside her stomach as she searched for the telltale signs of a replica.

There weren't any.

Season knew she was looking at a human skull. A second one. Not daring to move, her eyes darted around the room as she began picking out the real skulls from the fake ones. She counted 12.

Deep, deep down in her belly she began to feel sick. She swallowed down the feeling.

'What's that you've got there dear?' came the sweet voice of Peter's wife Rosanna.

Season's blood ran cold as she fixed a smile in place and turned slowly, not attempting to hide the skull she was cradling. She nearly leapt back, not realising how close the white-haired woman was. She had crept so close, they were almost face-to-face.

'Oh, just another *homo flore... homo florres,*' she cleared her throat as she struggled over the words. '*Homo floresiensis.*'

'Let me have a look,' she said, taking the specimen from her.

Season glanced over Rosanna's shoulder to Peter, who had turned to face his computer and typing away busily.

Her eyes flashed to where Paget was sitting or, rather, napping. Her friend was slumped in her seat, her notepad having fallen off her lap and on to the floor. A thin trail of drool was leaking from her mouth as her head drooped forward, lolling on the spot.

Season's mind couldn't process why Paget was sleeping, she couldn't understand it. All she knew was that taking a siesta was beginning to sound like a really good idea. The room around her flickered and pulsed as she tried to steady herself against a stack of magazines. They fell away under her weight, spilling to the floor. She slid with them, dropping to her knees.

Rosanna hadn't looked up from the skull, but she finally gave Season a long considered look as she hit the ground.

'Oh no, dear,' she said with a smile. 'This isn't *homo floresiensis* at all; this is *homo sapien.*'

'Human,' whispered Season, as her eyelids began to droop.

'Yes dear,' continued Rosanna, leaning down to whisper in Season's ear. 'If I remember correctly, his name was James.'

Then everything went black.

Paget woke with a start. She snapped from unconscious to alert in an instant, as if an internal alarm clock had started beeping in her head. There was a foreign after-taste in her mouth and she didn't like it. She moved her dry tongue over her teeth, along her gums, trying to rid herself of the flavour. She leaned to the side of her body and spat, immediately feeling better as she expelled. Her eyes opened slowly to an unfamiliar sight.

It was dark, almost completely so, and it took her eyes some time before they were able to adjust to the gloom. She was in an old workman's shed, complete with rusty tools in various sizes hanging from the ceiling and a weathered timber workbench. Trying to adjust her body was fruitless and she twisted and tugged until she was able to stretch herself enough and get a glimpse at her restraints. Her hands were bound behind her and wrapped together with zip ties. After straining her significant body weight against them and feeling no give, she sighed and fell against the wooden post she was attached to. She could just make out the shape of Season against the opposite wall: her head slumped on to her chest and her hijab somehow still miraculously in place.

Paget scanned the floor, looking for something nearby that she might be able to use to cut herself free. There was nothing. Dangling above her there was no shortage of sharp and scary implements, but from her restricted position she couldn't get to any of them. There was a window directly behind her that had been painted over in black. Only tiny slithers of light were sneaking through. It was enough to tell her that it was well into the evening. Season stirred, a soft murmur coming from her mouth as she slowly regained consciousness. Paget waited several long, agonising seconds until she was sure her friend was fully awake and had digested the contents of the room.

'Paget,' she whispered, her voice wavering with fear. Her eyes were still scanning the space as she tried to locate the reporter, her vision not as sharp her friend's.

'I'm here, Season.'

'Oh, thank Allah.'

'I think He has well and truly deserted us, hun.'

Season began muttering a prayer in words that Paget couldn't understand. She waited minutes until her friend finally came to a stop, with quick, shallow breaths replacing her words of hope.

'What happened?' Season asked. 'My mind is hazy.'

'I think they drugged us,' said Paget, anger spiking off her words. 'I can't remember much either. The last thing I remember was you asking about the hobbit peo–'

'It wasn't a hobbit skull!' Season remembered. 'It was a human skull, Paget. I was looking at the others and they were mostly fake but then I came across one and I knew what it was straight away. I studied them in the Introduction to Anatomy class I took at uni and there was no mistaking it.'

'A human skull?'

'Yes, and it wasn't the only one. When he tried to brush it off I started looking around the room and saw maybe a dozen, all human, all just sitting there like a dead audience.'

Silence hung between the two women as the heaviness of Season's words weighed down upon them.

'It must have been in the tea,' Season mused. 'The drugs, or whatever.'

'I didn't drink the tea, I hate tea. The cakes.'

'*And* the tea. I mean, how could you be sure someone would have only one and not the other? You couldn't be, so you dose both. At worst they get a double hit of whatever it is.'

'It's rohypnol. We need to figure a way to get out of here before we–'

'Before we what, Paget? Before *what* happens to us?'

She sighed. 'I think we're about to get Wolf Creeked.'

Season sniffed and Paget realised she was crying quietly. In the many years of their friendship, she had never seen her cry. Not when she discovered her fiancé was cheating on her, not when she sprained her ankle and not when the editor screamed at her in front of the entire newsroom during the rush to meet a particularly intense evening deadline. Yet she was crying now and this tiny fact frightened Paget almost more than anything else that had happened.

'Paget,' she sniffed, 'I can't die here. I just can't.'

'Oh honey, we're not going to die here. We're not going to let ourselves become the victims of two twisted old fucks, okay?'

Season chuckled. 'Two twisted old fucks.'

'That will be the title of the harrowing survival story I'll write if we get out of here.'

Season's sharp intake of breath acted like a virtual slap and Paget shook her head.

'*When* we get out of here. When. And you can illustrate the bloody thing.'

'Alright, alright, what do we need to do to get out of here?'

Paget was trying to free herself again, but to no avail. 'My restraints are tight, way too tight for me to escape from and there's no wiggle room. My wrists are also like sausages. Try yours. You have tiny, slender, lady wrists – you might have better luck trying to break free.'

'Okay, let me try.'

Season begin pulling on the zip ties. She yelped as they cut into her flesh and she slumped back. She wasn't strong enough to break free, so she attempted to do as Paget said: wiggle. Rotating her wrists back and forth, she felt like she was inching towards some progress – albeit slowly. She tucked her thumb into her hand until it was painful and she thought it would dislocate. It worked and the top part of her hand broke through the top of the restraints. There was much more squirming before she was able to liberate one hand entirely and even more until she had both free. It had taken her almost 20 minutes, but it felt much shorter in the heat of the moment.

'What's happening over there? Are you out?' asked Paget.

'Almost. There! I'm free.'

'Ha! I knew your skinny wrists could escape anything. Now find something sharp to cut me loose. Watch your head though, there's a thousand ways to die hanging from the ceiling.'

Season hunched over, the old knives and scissors and blades gently brushing her head as she walked under them. She tried the scissors first, but the handle was so ancient it crumbled in her grasp. Next she went for a jagged blade that looked lethal and was probably the sharpest out of anything left in the building.

'Jesus,' said Paget, as her friend inched closer towards her with it. 'Be careful not to slit my wrists with that in the process will you?'

'Paget, I'm shaking already. You're not helping.'

'I just don't want our escape attempt to be thwarted by me bleeding out en route.'

Season sighed.

'Okay, fine. I'll quell my unease in silence.'

'That's very gracious of you, thanks.'

Paget held her breath as Season began to slowly and carefully saw away at the plastic cables that held her wrists tight.

'How long do you think we've been out?' Season asked as she worked.

'Hours. Maybe longer. It's late night at least, maybe even morning.'

'They took our phones, keys. People will be looking for us.'

'Not hard enough.'

'I'm so thirsty, it's unbelievable.'

'Season, hold on.'

'What?'

'There's a tap over there. Go get a quick drink. Who knows when the next time we'll be able to take a break will be? And dehydration is more likely to kill us than–'

'Elderly serial killers?'

'Well, no…' Season paused, thinking it over. 'A quick drink. I'll bring you back some in a cup or anything clean I can find.'

She leapt to her feet and hurried over to an industrial-looking sink. Using all her strength to crank the tap, she let the brown water run for a few seconds before she deemed it clean enough to drink. Paget's mouth watered and it was excruciating to watch her friend quench her thirst just metres away. Yet she also knew that if they wanted to survive, they needed to be smart. Season found an old bowl and after giving it a rinse, she brought it to Paget's mouth. The sensation of water slipping over her lips and down her throat had never been so sweet. She nearly cried with relief. Season rushed to return the bowl and grab the implement she had left at the bench when she paused, her steps frozen in place.

'Season?' Paget asked.

Her friend said nothing.

'Season what is it, you're freaking me out?'

The silver glint of something peeking out from under a dishtowel had caught her eye. She inched towards it slowly, taking her time. With care she lifted the cover off it and gasped, leaping back.

'Season, for fuck's sake what is it? Another skull?'

She woman stepped to the side, revealing the object that had been shielded by her body. She whispered: 'It's a *gun.*'

Paget laughed, once, twice and third time. She was giddy with relief. 'Oh thank the Lord, something has actually gone right for us. Is it loaded?'

'I, I, I don't know. How do I tell?'

'Are you serious?'

'I've never touched a gun before, Paget.'

She sighed, cursing under her breath at their bad luck to have the one person skilled with a firearm strapped to a pole and immobile. 'It's okay, I'll walk you through it. Can you hold it up so I can see what kind of gun it is?'

Season nudged it with the edges of her fingers, desperate not to touch it.

'Hun, it's not going to bite you. Just pick the damn thing up. Even if it is loaded you're not going to accidentally shoot anything unless your finger's on the trigger.'

'I don't–'

'Just keep your finger off the trigger and hold it up so I can see it.'

Carefully, Season held up the weapon.

'It looks old-fashioned. That's fine, we can work with that. I think it's a Smith & Wesson; maybe a .357 Magnum. Now you're going to see if it's loaded. Take a deep breath. This is the easy part. You're going to flick the switch at the back of the gun – there should only be one. Push it down and it will click. Good, now just push the cylinder underneath the barrel out.'

'I did it!'

'Of course you did, legend. What do you see? Are you looking at five empty circles inside or is it full?'

'There's one in there, it's gold.'

Paget sighed. 'Fucksickles. One bloody bullet. Okay, it's better than none. Push the cylinder back in and rest the gun on the counter.'

'Done.'

'Come get me out these bloody ties so I can start looking around for bullets. I feel like a sitting duck.'

Season began carving away again, making slow but significant progress with the questionable instrument. 'A gun is good, right? It means we have a weapon.'

'We're in a shed full of weapons but yeah, a gun is better than antique gardening tools li–'

'What is it?' asked Season, alarmed by Paget's sudden silence.

'I thought I heard some–'

The unmistakable sound of a door banging made both women jump, with Season nicking Paget's wrist enough to make her gasp. They froze, barely daring to breathe as the slow tread of footsteps outside began to make their way closer and closer to the door of the shed.

'Season, listen to me,' whispered Paget. 'You need to grab the gun and aim at the door.'

'What? No! I'm not doing this without you, I need to free you!'

'Hun, forget me. Okay? You're not going to be able to get me loose in the next 15 seconds that it's going to take for him to make it to the door. Shoot him, then we both have a better chance of escaping here.'

'I…' Season's voice wavered with emotion. The thought of abandoning Paget, even for a second, was horrifying to her. 'I don't know how to shoot.'

'The bullet's in already and I'll talk you through it. It's gonna be loud, so expect that. You won't be able to hear anything for a little while and you'll need to watch the kick – alright?'

'Kick?'

'The gun will jerk back with the motion of you firing it. Relax your arms, your elbows, and expect it.'

The sound of the footsteps was like audible torture as Paget rushed out instructions to her friend in furious, urgent whispers. Season picked up the gun and stood just on the other side of the workbench where she would have a perfect angle to shoot Peter or Rosanna when they entered the shed. Her hands were shaking and her attempts to take deep, calming breaths were futile.

'See the little triangle at the end of the barrel of the gun?'

'Yes,' murmured Season.

'The bullet will hit at the tip of that triangle, so that's where you aim it.'

'I don't know if I can kill someone.'

The footsteps were just outside the door.

'Then shoot them in the blasted kneecap! Pull the button at the back towards you until it clicks, it will only take a second, and then pull the trigger. Just slowly squeeze.'

'Got it.'

The door began to creak slowly.

'It's dark so you have a few extra seconds to line up your shot. You got this.'

'Right.' Season let out a final breathe as the wooden door was pushed forward and the cool night air came sneaking in. Paget couldn't see who was entering from her position but she certainly didn't miss the sound of Season firing off the lone bullet in the gun. The sound was deafening in the small space and Paget flinched with the noise. The recoil was strong and the gun flew back in Season's hands, knocking her square in the face with a painful *thwack.* Paget watched in horror as her friend fell backwards with the impact, landing hard on the ground in front of her. In the faintest glint of the moonlight she could see blood pouring from Season's face as she rolled to the side. Whether it was the noise or the kick that had taken her by surprise, Season was only semi-conscious as she lay on the dirty floor, gasping for air.

An inhuman whimper came from the entrance to the shed and Paget strained against the pole to see who Season had managed to kill or at least wound – Peter or Rosanna. Two other banging doors and a shout were heard as someone made their way quickly to quell the commotion. Season was gaining back her senses and wobbling towards the body to get a look. Paget was asking her who it was, where they were hit, but Season couldn't hear the words through the deep, internal ringing in her ears. She watched her friend's lips moving and finally understood the message. Inching closer, she thought she had aimed too low and hoped that she had at least managed to hit them in the leg. Her heart dropped and so did she as she caught sight of the 'victim'. Season's knees hit the hard floor as she went down.

'The dog,' she whispered. 'Paget, I shot the dog.'

Hope seemed to fly out of Paget with a deep sigh as the family pet, Chester, made two tiny yelps before expiring completely. She saw a shadow move outside the shed a second too late, and screamed Season's name as a shovel whacked into the side of her head.

'CHESTER!' screamed Rosanna, bursting into the tiny space wielding her weapon. She kicked Season's body out of the way as she rushed towards her dog, but the fat Labrador was DOA. Paget was screaming Season's name, over and over, repeatedly until Peter stormed into the shed and hit her with the side of his metal torch. The impact was so sudden and ferocious, Paget tried to shake herself together as she wondered how such strength could come from such an unassuming exterior. He hit her again and as shapes danced in her vision he placed duct tape over her mouth. Tears formed in her eyes with the pain and it was several long moments before she was alert again. Rosanna was still pawing mindlessly at the body of Chester, muttering to herself over and over.

'Those filthy girls, filthy sluts, look what they've done to you my baby. My poor baby. Poor Chester, poor precious Chester.'

Peter was busy with Season's body and as he moved away from her, relief spread through Paget's limbs. He had bound her feet and hands with rope, which meant that despite his wife's best efforts Season was still very much alive.

'You stupid bitches,' he hissed, turning to Paget.

She tried to mumble a retort through the duct tape, but it came out only as jumbled words.

'YOU THINK I WANT TO HEAR YOU SPEAK?' he screamed, suddenly lurching towards Paget in a gesture that made her jump. He laughed at her reaction. 'You're all the same,' he chuckled. 'In 40 years, you're still *all* the same. Everyone can be broken down into three categories. There's the defiant, that's you, the resistant, they just give up and accept their fate with a lot of sobbing, and the bargainers, those pathetic individuals who will try and seduce you or leverage their freedom with anything they can. And it doesn't matter what type you are, let me tell you that, because not a single one has been successful. No one has escaped from us… and neither will you.'

Paget's eyes were wide as Peter leaned against the workbench, looking at her. Rosanna was dragging the dog out of the shed by its hind legs. Forty years? If the killer couple had been doing this for 40 years, how many victims had they clocked up? What were the odds of there being more than one serial killer operating in the territory? Paget's mind was racing as she thought of Benjamin Lee Britton.

'I looked you up,' he said, folding his arms. 'My wife isn't very good at computers but I'm just fine at it. It must be interesting for you to be on the other side of the story I'd imagine. Oh, fluff it.'

He reached forward and ripped the tape off Paget's mouth. She squealed as the skin on her face pulled with the adhesive. Peter slapped her once more, hard, and she found a carving knife held dangerously close to her throat.

'Not a single peep out of you or I'll slit your throat just deep enough that you'll spend the next 10 minutes bleeding out over the floor until you and your slut are sitting in a puddle of your own blood.'

'I'll be quiet,' pleaded Paget, 'I'll be quiet.'

Satisfied, he returned to his position at the workbench. He kept the knife in plain sight as a deadly reminder and Paget gulped at the length of the massive blade with serrated edges.

'You never wrote anything on the Bushwalker Butcher. Why?'

'It wasn't my story,' Paget croaked.

'You write crime. You've covered murderers before. '

'It was given to the senior reporter. He asked for it.'

'I'm going to ask you a question, and if you get it right you can go.'

'Why do I feel like this is some kind of trick?'

'If you get it wrong,' he pressed, 'I'll feed you to the Yowie.'

'You, um, you have one handy?'

'Oh yes, it has an insatiable appetite.'

'Uh-huh.'

'And it must be fed. Why do you think we've been doing this? We're not natural born killers, Paget. Surely you can't believe that?'

'You seem to have a talent for it.'

'That's very sweet of you.'

'Not a compliment,' she whispered.

'No no, it's because we need to keep the Yowie alive for research purposes. You understand how important that is.'

'Not at the expense of my life, no.'

'It's all part of the circle of life, my dear. It's a superior being to you and I – so sacrifices need to be made. And this time it's very hungry – it hasn't fed for almost a year. Actually, last July I think. That's why we need both of you.'

'Last July? That's when Benjamin Lee Britton was arrested.'

'Ah, yes. Back to the question, which your very fate hinges on.'

'Go on.'

'How many victims did the Bushwalker Butcher have?'

Paget knew the answer immediately, but was cautious to reply. It seemed all too easy, too obvious.

'Well?' he pushed. 'I thought you'd know this one off the top of your head, an intelligent crime reporter like–'

'Nine. He killed nine people.'

He started to chuckle. It was like a small hiccup at first, then it burst out into a deep, throaty laugh. 'Rosanna, come here for a second, dear?'

His wife popped her head in the door. Her face was ashen. 'What?'

'She said nine. She said the Bushwalker Butcher had nine victims,' he laughed. She giggled too. It was an unsettling sound.

'That's lovely,' she said. 'I'll make us some tea.'

Paget looked from Peter to Rosanna and back, confused and creeped out. 'What's so funny?' she hissed.

'The real tally,' said Peter, crouching down to her height, 'is zero. I'm sorry to break the news to you this way, but your answer is incorrect and you will both be dying tonight.'

'How? How is that incorrect, he…' Paget's voice trailed off as the cogs in her mind began working overtime. Peter watched her closely, eyes glistening as he observed the almost outward act of her thinking deeply.

'He's innocent,' she whimpered, finally understanding. 'It was you, you dosed him with the same supply you gave to your victims. You set him up!'

'Truth be told it wasn't hard, really. And no one could call Benjamin Lee Britton *innocent* by any definition of the word. He was always lurking around, making a nuisance of himself. All we had to do was wait until he rolled into town again. It was actually splendid, you see, because Rosanna invited him back for afternoon tea at the house and we were quite sure he thought he was going to rob us.'

'That's why he doesn't know the location of the last three bodies.'

'He doesn't know a lot more than that. I suppose it has been kept out of the papers, the extent of his mental damage, but I dosed him with an extra strong concoction. Did I tell you I used to be a chemist?'

'You mentioned it,' said Paget, glowering at the homicidal maniac.

'Now, don't look at me like that. It all worked out well for us in the end. We kept the body of the last boy, drove the van into town and just waited for everything to play out as it did.'

'Why now? Why have someone take the fall *now* if you've been doing this for 40 years?'

'There was a little too much attention being paid. They set up that task force after we killed the Swedish politician's daughter, which was more trouble than it was worth. We're older now, we can't get around like we used to.'

'Those were the days,' interrupted Rosanna, stepping into the room with two steaming mugs. Both were decorated with cartoon ducks wearing tiny top hats.

'My dear,' he smiled, taking a mug.

'We used to travel all the time, back when we first got married,' she mused. 'Those really were the days. In the '70s there were hitchhikers everywhere.'

'Oh, remember the Skarison twins?'

She laughed. 'They were so trusting. So pretty.'

Tears leaked from Paget's eyes as the couple recalled 'fonder' memories of their youth. Her mouth gaped as they laughed and chatted, reminding each other of this or refreshing a fact about that. They looked like the sweetest grandparents you could ever see, with their round bodies, novelty teacups and Rosanna in her tartan slippers.

But they were a serial killing couple and Paget understood how rare that was. They had been active for decades and even now in their old age they were still killing. They were efficient and not smart necessarily, but smart enough to play on their projected sweetness.

'We're too old to travel like we used to,' said Peter, with his wife nuzzled into his side. 'And because of that I guess we've gotten sloppy: too many people disappearing from the same area, too many bodies popping up and in too little time. It's tricky when you've got a beast to feed.'

He looked back down at Paget, sighing. Rosanna slipped away from him, shuffling over towards Season. Her movements distracted Paget long enough that she was shocked to find the knife at her throat once more. Peter held it there carefully while he pressed the hot cup of tea to her lips.

'Now, time to drink up,' he smiled. 'Time to finish your tea.'

Paget had no choice. She sipped as slowly as she could, but frequently enough that he didn't lash out. She maintained eye contact, keeping him focused on her face just inches from her own. He was so busy looking at her that he didn't notice her fingers fumbling as they wrapped around a rusty blade left behind in a failed escape attempt. He missed her subtle movements as she slipped the object into the sleeve of her leather jacket and under several bracelets secured at her wrist, before she began to lose consciousness once again.

Season woke from a nightmare about suffocating under a velvet ocean. She lurched forward, coughing and spluttering. Her head ached and thudded with her heartbeat, but the pain was nothing compared to that of her nose. She tried to touch her face, but finding her hands restricted, settled for licking her lip. It confirmed what she thought as she tasted the dried blood there. Her nose had been broken.

'Oh my God.'

'Yes, you broke your own nose.'

Her eyes flicked towards the sound of her best friend, who was restrained on a tree next to her. Season's eyes ran over the rope that started at Paget's wrists and looped through a metal latch drilled into the tree. She cocked her head upwards to find herself secured in an identical manner. Their feet barely touched the ground with Paget – the shorter of the two – straining on her tip toes.

'With the gun?' she asked, after she digested the situation.

'Yup. I warned you about the recoil.'

'Yeah, you did.'

'You did good though.'

'Did I shoot one of them?'

'Yes. You shot their dog.'

'I what?'

'If we weren't about to be fed to a Yowie, I'd find that funny,' said Paget, smirking.

'Fed to a *Yowie*? Paget, can you hear yourself right now?'

'Season, can you look at yourself right now? I've been awake for a whole hour longer than you, so I have the advantage here.'

Season glanced around, realising for the first time that they were bathed in light. An unnatural yellow was illuminating and simultaneously blinding the women as four large spotlights were set up around a circular clearing. They were in the bush – that was obvious – and it was still night. From the sounds of the wildlife around them, it wouldn't be dark for much longer. Sunrise was on the way.

'Where are they?' whispered Season.

'I don't know where *he* is, but *she* said she was going back to the car to get the camera.'

'The what? What do they need a camera for?'

A gush of breath escaped Paget's mouth, followed by another and another until they were coming in quick succession. She appeared to be having some kind of panic attack.

'Paget? Paget you have to breathe, okay? I know it's bad, I know it is. But breathe. I need you. I need you to get through this and you've never failed me before,' Season pleaded, trying to keep her voice calm and authoritative. 'Breathe, think of a way out of this and breathe. You helped me shoot a dog for God's sake, you can breathe through this. Breathe.'

Slowly, Paget's panicked rasps began to settle. With every third breathe she would struggle and shudder over it, but she was calming as Season spoke to her. She kept repeating the words 'breathe' and 'relax', even though she knew they were some of the most impossible things to do in their current situation. After a long while Paget began to settle and she stopped mumbling 'we're about to be fed to a yowie' over and over. Nothing needed to be said as the two friends smiled at each other, albeit sadly. Tears glistened in Paget's eyes as she took in the appearance of Season and her blood-smeared face.

'What's the camera for, Paget?' Season asked.

Paget's smile faltered. 'I think they're going to film it.'

'Film what?'

'Our deaths.'

'As they feed us to a Yowie? I don't believe in that rubbish – surely you don't?'

'They brought us all the way out here.'

'Where is *here*?'

'Bushland somewhere in the Blue Mountains. I woke up while we were still in the boot of their car on the drive here and as far as I could tell we kept driving for about 45 minutes. I tried to count the minutes, but I don't know how long I was asleep for. We can't be that far from town though.'

'That's good, it means we won't have that far to run. Oh! I just–'

'What?'

'He used to work in a movie theatre, is that why he films us?'

'Probably. Although she's the one who films it, I think.'

'What does he do?'

There was a long silence penetrated only by a frog's single croak.

'I don't know,' whispered Paget. 'But I know they've done this before. You were right, with all the skulls you saw. They said they've been doing this for four decades. *They* are the Bushwalker Butcher. Well, butchers. They set Benjamin Lee Britton up to take the fall after the police started paying too much attention. They used to travel the country selecting victims before they got old and their concentrated efforts brought too much heat.'

'How do you know all this?'

Paget looked sharply at Season. 'They were chatty as fuck when you were unconscious.'

'Why would they tell you everything? That's dangerous. What if we escaped? How egoistical are these assholes?'

'Totally. They said no one has ever escaped.'

'Bullshit. In 40 years? Even on bad luck alone someone would have had to have broken free.'

'I dunno, maybe they died in the bush or–'

'What is it?' Season watched as Paget began moving her fingers in an unusual way.

'I forgot! Oh my God!'

'*What?*'

She began to ease the orange tip of the blade out of her jacket, carefully using her fingertips to pull it from under her bracelets.

'Is that the knife I tried to use to cut you free?'

'Ssshh. I don't know where they are. They could be listening.'

'Is it sharp enough to cut through the–'

Twigs snapped under heavy footfalls. Rosanna announced her arrival almost a full minute before she appeared in the clearing with a tripod and a small recording camera under her arm. Her head was barely visible under a blue raincoat with the hood pulled up high. She trudged into the centre of the clearing and kept going until she walked in between the two women and stopped a few inches behind them. Positioning herself directly between the two trees, the women could hear her grunting and huffing as she set up the tripod and rested the camera on top of it. She spent several more long moments getting everything ready, and she even stepped into the light to remove a large stick from the clearing before ducking back behind the camera. Season and Paget were silent, not daring to say a word to each other. Season's eyes followed movement upwards to where Paget wielded the blade at an awkward angle and was attempting to hack at the rope.

'OKAY!' screamed Rosanna, making both girls jump. Paget nearly dropped her utensil with shock, but regained composure at the last minute.

'Okaaay?' came a far-off voice.

'I SAID OKAY!' she repeated, sighing with irritation.

There was an unsettling silence that stretched on for minutes and both women froze. Even Rosanna was quiet, hunched behind the camera and out of their line of sight. A rustling in the bush broke the gloom, followed by a guttural growl from the darkness. The animals of the forest fell silent. Twigs and branches snapped under the weight of something large and lumbering moving through the bush.

'Oh my God,' whispered Season, while Paget's eyes widened in horror. She began frantically cutting at the rope that held her, faster and harder.

The final cluster of shrubbery separated to reveal a monster in every true definition of the word. Season screamed in one piercing, shrill note that seemed to stretch on forever. Paget wanted to, but she couldn't get her mouth to work: her vocal chords were frozen by the sight in front of her. Step after shuddering step, the beast inched closer and closer towards them. Its enormous shadow trailed behind like an ominous second presence. The dirt was being scratched up as the beast moved and at first Paget thought it was claws being pulled along the ground. She winced with the spine-chilling noise. Then she noticed it was dragging a long, thick club that had sharp implements jutting out at odd angles. Old blood had dried on several of the edges until it looked like black rust.

Paget's eyes flicked to the creature and she jumped at the human eyes staring back at her, blinking calmly. Under a thick, leathery suit with chunks of fur scattered randomly across it was a man. This was no Yowie: this was the murder uniform of Peter Lomond. He was focused on Season, walking closer towards her until he hovered in front of her face. His breath came out of a mouth-slit in a steaming cloud of air and she screamed again, louder.

Yet it wasn't the proximity she was fearful of, it was the suit. As he attempted to sniff and grunt around her body, Season couldn't tear her eyes away from the 'material'. Parts of it were animal skin, that was clear, but it was sewed together with another type of skin. Patches of dried and treated flesh had been carefully stitched into others like a twisted quilt straight out of hell. The 'fur' was actually human hair, chunks of scalp and clipped locks that had been added to the suit over the years.

Season shook uncontrollably as his hands ran over her legs.

'Wait, stop!' screamed Rosanna, causing her husband to pause in his torment. 'There's something; God, this blasted thing. It's gone blurry.'

'HNGH TGETPHER!'

'Don't yell at me, you know I can't hear you in that thing.'

Its shoulders slumped as the mangled claw of an arm reached up and yanked off the mask. Peter's frustrated face emerged from beneath it, sweaty and red with anticipation.

'Did you leave the lens cap on *again*?'

'No, I did not leave the lens cap on and I told you not to use that tone with me!'

'God damn it, Rosanna, we were already filming.'

'I don't know what to tell you, it was all fine and then when I tried to focus in on you it became fuzzy.'

'Fuzzy?'

'Yes, fuzzy.'

Paget was using their argument to maximum effect and she glanced up at the rope holding her in place to see there were only a few more strands left. She was determined to cut herself to freedom and began to use her body weight to strain against the bindings. Lifting her feet off the ground, she heard the rope creak under the added pressure.

Season heard it too and saw just how close her friend was to freeing herself. 'Hey, hey! Maybe I can help?' she called, in attempt to give Paget more time.

Peter paused mid-sentence, spinning to stare at her. 'How could you possibly help?'

'Well, I'm younger and I'm very confident with cameras. If you just bring it over here I might be able to take a look?'

Rosanna shuffled forward, nudging Peter out of the way. 'This is the problem,' she said, tapping at the screen.

'Uh, I see what you mean.'

'See how it's blurry?'

Season nodded. 'Yes, I see that.'

'What's the problem?' Peter huffed.

'I'm not sure, can you hold it up closer to my face please?'

'Hurry it up, Rosanna, it's almost light and we need to finish shooting before we can move the bodies. They can't find another one, we've discussed this. It will all be over.'

'I know, I know,' his wife snapped back at him.

'That's the issue, it's out of focus. You need to zoom back,' Season said.

'Zoom back? How do I do that? It's a new camera and the man at the store said it would–'

'If I could just get a better look – can you press that button there?'

'This one? No, that didn't do it.'

'Try the one above?'

'No.'

'Switch it to the auto setting. It must have come on to manual.'

'How do I do that?'

'I think it would probably be easiest if I did it. It would be quicker.'

There was a pause as Peter and Rosanna shared a look.

'You wouldn't have to untie me completely,' pushed Season. 'Just one hand so I could reach the screen.'

Peter stepped forward, pulling the thickest knife Season had ever seen from behind his back. She froze as he brought it towards her, resting the sharp tip on her stomach.

'No funny business,' he growled. 'I use this knife for piggin'. You try something like that again and I'll slice you from your belly button right up to your nose.'

'I'm not t-trying anything,' stuttered Season. 'I just need one hand.'

'Well, you're not getting it.'

'Okay. No funny business. Just bring the camera closer to my face please.'

Peter stepped back, his point proven, as a heavy thud behind him made him turn. 'WHAT THE–'

Paget was finally free, the long rope trailing from her wrists where she had cut it. She attempted to run, pivoting on one foot and making a dash for the bushes,but Peter lunged out and grabbed one of the tendrils of her restraints that was still slithering behind her.

He yanked, hard, and Paget came flying backwards and landed on the dirt. She fell perfectly between his legs whereon he raised the club high above his head to bring it down on her body.

Season acted. She threw her back against the tree and kicked Rosanna with every inch of strength she could muster. The elderly woman flew into her husband, knocking both of them sidewards and to the ground.

Paget leapt to her feet and sprinted to her friend, pausing momentarily to pick up the sinister looking knife Peter had wielded only seconds earlier.

'HURRY!' Season screamed, looking desperately over Paget's shoulder as the couple fumbled to get to up.

'Working. As fast. As I can,' Paget said through gritted teeth as she cut Season's arms free. 'Done!'

The knife was much sharper than the weathered implement she had been using and she risked a few extra seconds to cut the long rope dangling from her wrists. She would not be caught by those again.

'Come on!' she shouted, grabbing Season's arm and tugging her in the direction of freedom.

'Paget, look ou–'

Season pulled her to the ground just as the deadly bat swung over their heads. Peter was on his feet and waving the weapon wildly as he attempted to incapacitate his prey permanently.

'FUCK! YOU!' screamed Paget, throwing her body forward as she sunk the knife deep into his foot until she felt it make contact with the ground on the other side.

'ARGGHH!' Peter screamed in pain, dropped the bat and fell to one knee.

Paget scrambled back from Peter on all fours until she ran into her friend, who did her best to yank her to her feet. Season was so busy trying to help, she didn't notice Rosanna pick up the bat behind her.

Paget did, and as the woman silently swung the bat she threw herself in front of Season. She barely had time to protect herself, but feebly raised her hand in front of her face. The sound of the bat meeting her flesh was sickening, with it slicing and crunching through her bone simultaneously.

'Ffuu–' Paget dropped to the ground, unable to finish the word as the pain overwhelmed her. Spit flew from her mouth and she dribbled, biting hard down on her lip. She clutched her forearm where the bat had wedged itself.

'Enough!' Season shouted. She was a blur as she ran at Rosanna and punched her square in the face. Then she leapt on her, smacking her again and again and again until the woman was scratched and bloody and unconscious.

Season straddled her, breathing heavily until she regained her sense of self; not quite willing to get up off the old wench just yet. She twisted and moved just enough to see Paget yank the club from her limb with an exhausted cry.

Peter was still stuck in place, anchored to the ground by the knife he was unable to pull from his feet.

'Paget,' Season murmured, tripping to a standing position.

'I'm, I'm okay,' she winced, standing as well. Blood was seeping through her fingers where she was clenching her arm.

'Is it–'

'Yeah. I heard the bone snap. It's broken. Did you kill her?'

Season tilted her head.

'Okay, stupid question.'

'I knocked her out.'

'Thatta girl! I'm so proud of you.' Paget stumbled into Season, who hugged her friend as much as she could given her injuries. They stayed like that for several long moments, watching as Peter continually tried and failed to remove the knife.

'Doesn't have much tolerance for pain, does he?' said Paget.

'Ironic, given how much of it he has dealt out over the years.'

'God knows how many have died at his hands.'

Season looked pointedly at her friend and Paget shrugged. 'Hey, if you want to do this, it's all you. I can barely hold a conversation at the moment let alone a bat.'

Season nodded. She walked over to the weapon, nudging it with her toe. 'I'm not a killer.'

'Oh thank God!' Peter panted. 'Listen, we can sor–'

'But that doesn't mean you deserve to *live*,' she hissed.

Season picked up the bat, feeling the weight of it in her hands. She dragged it across the dirt behind her as she walked towards him, slowly. Paget followed closely behind, a sheen of sweat damp on her forehead.

Peter looked up at the young woman who was staring down at him with a look of complete and utter disgust. The look was so strong, it was only topped by that of the dark-skinned woman who joined her.

'I'm going to knock you out,' Season said, finally.

'Mama said knock you out,' nodded Paget.

'Now let's neg–'

Peter's words were cut short as the wooden bat was brought down on his head. His skull made a dull thud sound as the weapon connected and he collapsed on the ground.

'You had to hit him with the smooth, wooden portion of the club? You couldn't slip it up higher from the base? Just one good whack with the broken nail there?' Paget asked, leaning against Season for support.

'It's not in my nature,' she replied. 'Let them rot in prison instead. Forever.'

The women looked between the bodies laying at opposite sides of the clearing. A particularly loud owl hooted above them and they both jumped.

'Let's get out of here,' said Season.

'So very with you on that,' Paget agreed.

'Uh, one problem: which way is *home*?'

'This way,' said Paget, dragging Season in to the darkness of the bushes. 'Rosanna came from that direction.'

They walked blindly into the darkness until the glare of the spotlight was far behind them. There was a vague semblance of a path beneath them, which they could feel every time they wandered slightly off it. In the distance they heard a car honk and it gave them hope: they weren't far away and civilisation was waking up. Every foreign sound, every animal noise, made them jump and huddle closer together, clutching each other. When the growl of what Paget suspected was a feral cat of some sort made her screech, they decided they'd had enough.

'Can you run?' Season said, turning to face where she thought Paget's face was. She could barely make out shape of her eyes in the consuming darkness.

'You read my mind.'

Stumbling, tripping and helping each other up, they could do little more than jog through the black of the night. They were panting heavily when they felt the ground slope upwards beneath their feet. They ran headfirst into the parked car of the Lomonds, but it only gave them further hope as they pushed on. The faint glow of a streetlight in the distance made the friends accelerate until they finally broke through at the top of a steep hill. They crouched over, breathing deeply.

They were just above a suburban street.

Season shook her head. 'I can't believe it. We made it.'

Blue and red lights flooded the usually quiet residential area in the Blue Mountains. Every surface was drowned in the conflicting colours, which were providing some of the only illumination as emergency personnel ran around the scene in the early-morning light.

Season's hands clasped a styrofoam cup of tea that she drank slowly to accommodate her facial injuries. She answered questions from two detectives in between sips. It took her three cups before she was able to relay the whole story and by the end of the telling she decided to ask for coffee instead.

'There's forensic unit going through their residence as we speak,' said the older of the two detectives. 'They've already confirmed that the skulls you spoke about are human.'

Season nodded. 'And the Lomonds?'

'Speak of the devils.'

The barking of police dogs heralded the arrival of the search party, who had been sent out to retrieve the real Bushwalker Butchers. Several men and women emerged from the shrubbery, carrying two stretchers between them.

Season glanced at Peter and Rosanna. They were both conscious and handcuffed firmly to the stretchers that were supporting them. Rosanna was quiet and watching everything with wide, attentive eyes. Peter, on the other hand, was shouting and muttering about monsters.

'It was the Yowie!' he said, attempting to sit up as the words flew from his mouth in a stream of bubbles. 'It had to be fed! You don't understand! The Yowie had to be fed!'

Season grimaced as she noted that he was still wearing his costume, stictched from the skins of his human victims and other animals.

The detective touched her arm to draw her attention from Peter. 'I know you must be exhausted and we will have more questions, but right now the most important thing is getting you two checked out.

'There's been a lot of drugs in your system over the past 24 hours, let alone the trauma you have experienced. And your friend Paget *definitely* needs to see a doctor. That arm is going to require surgery.'

'Yeah, where is she?' Season scanned the crowd.

Paget was sitting in the open doorway of an ambulance, her eyes closed to the humdrum that was happening around her. She was switching between breathing through an oxygen mask, and sucking on the green whistle of no-more-pain. A paramedic was adding the final touches to a temporary cast on her arm and she lifted her hair gently to tie a sling behind her neck while humming a jaunty tune.

'We've done as much as we can here, Miss Stevenson, but your arm does not look good,' said the bubbly blonde.

'Mmm-hmm.'

'I can't say for sure without an X-Ray, but I think it's going to need surgery. The lacerations alone are a problem and I'm guessing you have several major fractures.'

'Yup. Mmm-hmm.'

'I'm going to ask the detectives if we can get you out of here.'

'Uh-huh.'

Seconds or minutes – meh, maybe hours, later – someone else was annoying her by trying to get her to talk.

'*Paget?*'

She picked up on the urgency in the tone. 'Yesss.'

'Can you open your eyes?'

'Ah, nuh-uh. Paget not here right now, leave a message after the–'

'Paget!'

'*Beeeep.*'

A finger underneath her chin titled her head upwards and she finally opened her eyes.

'Season?' she blinked.

The piercing eyes of her best friend stared back at her, full of concern. A small bandage covering the cut on Season's forehead poked out from under her hijab. Paget waved the green pain-relief whistle, but her fingers felt like melting butter.

'Here, let me,' Season said, attempting to help her.

'No, it's okay I've got it.'

'Paget, you're getting tangled in the oxygen cord.'

'I can–'

'Let me help, you only have one functioning arm!'

Paget paused, grinned and let her friend do what she wanted.

Season shook her head. 'You're a wreck, Paget. We–'

'Yowies.'

'What?'

'I was so mad when they wouldn't give me the Bushwalker Butcher story, Season. So mad. And Fredrick did such a shitty job with it, but you know what?'

'What?'

'I ended up getting the story anyway,' she giggled. Her giggles turned into a maniacal kind of laughter and Season soon realised she was crying.

'Oh, girl,' she said, bringing her forward until she was sobbing into her chest. She stroked the back of her neck gently, soothing her but careful not to add any pressure to her arm.

'I hate it when you call me that,' she sniffed, emerging from her arms.

'I know,' she grinned.

'Ergh, I'm so sorry. I cried on your coat; this is a nice coat,' she said, distracted by the fabric of the trenchcoat as she stroked it.

'One of the detectives loaned it to me.'

'Oooh, which one?'

'The cute one,' smirked Season.

The two women grinned at each like idiots before Season climbed into the ambulance, taking one of two available seats in the rear of the vehicle.

The paramedic returned with her partner in tow. They helped Paget onto the stretcher. She was snoring lightly the moment her head hit the pillow.

'We can drive you girls to the hospital now.'

'Good,' said Season. 'And keep her sedated; she's going to need the rest.'

'And why's that?' the paramedic queried.

'Because when she wakes up, she's going to have one hell of a story to write.'

LINDY CAMERON

Feedback

The airboat splashed to a stop outside the dilapidated facade of 223 Collins Street. I hadn't said a word but the pilot had rightly figured this was the place to drop me. Even without the five cops providing crowd control on the dock out front, I knew it was the right place too coz I'd been here before. I also knew I was about to face one of those dreaded moments when the victim at the scene was someone with whom I'd been acquainted.

I powered up my anti-grav pod, hauled myself into the seat and strapped in. The idiots loitering in the drizzle hoping to catch a glimpse of something dead really pissed me off. I made a close calculation and 'just' cleared the heads of the nearest onlookers. I did shout *look out* so it wasn't entirely my fault that half of them ended up face down on the wet promenade.

'Thought they revoked your licence for that thing,' Officer Jordan said.

'Just a wild rumour,' I said over my shoulder, as I hovered towards the lifts.

'Another one?' she smiled. 'Lifts aren't working. Chief said use the fire stairs.'

Oh great. I leant forward to check for downward traffic before I began my ascent. The tightly-angled stairwells in these late 19th century buildings were not designed for anti-grav manoeuvring; in fact they wouldn't be much use in a fire. At least they'd only burn down to water-level these days.

Aggie and I – yeah, my inanimate anti-grav pod *does* have a name – made our way up to what had once been the 19th floor, but was now the 14th above high-tide canal level.

The fire door at the top opened directly into the warehouse space of Napper Trading which overflowed the entire 15,000 squares. Rows of metal shelving stretched in every direction piled with terminals, naru-engine parts, jakka tools, odd pieces of weaponry and satellite components, cranial fittings, vintage hologram projectors, service bots, vid-screens and even antique radio and TV parts. The reception area was an old teflon desk with a metre of clear space around it.

'What's the deal?' I asked the officer who was ferreting in the apparent havoc.

'Place has been ransacked,' she said. 'I'm looking for clues.'

'Wouldn't bother,' I said. 'This place *always* looks like a lunatic looking for a whippet screw went through at warp speed. Where's–'

'Chief's in the back with the Cutter and the deader.' She pointed.

'The Chief? He *never* leaves HQ.'

'Reckon this case has connections that require his physical participation.'

I hovered in the direction of the Chief, the coroner and the body, keeping to the dead centre of the aisles in case I brought a century's worth of recycled tech down on my head.

The sound of Chief Bascome's gravelly voice biting off orders prompted two medtechs to scuttle out of the corner office, as if keeping their skin intact depended only on getting out of his reach. This was strange indeed. In six years I hadn't known him to leave HQ, let alone attend a crime scene.

'You're scaring the children, Chief,' I said from the doorway to the room where Chief Bascome was leaning over the corpse that lay in the crash chair, and Dr Huang Delta Ann was crawling round the floor.

'Where in Hades have you been?' he bellowed.

'Having my toenails buffed.'

The Chief gave me the once over, from my head to where my feet would be, if I had any, and snorted: 'And my cat has joined the space cadets.'

I ignored the dig. The casual observer might think the old man didn't like me, but in truth the Chief loves me like a daughter – okay, like the daughter he never wanted, but he loves me nonetheless.

'Why are *you* so grouchy? After all, that's *my* uncle you're prodding.' I hovered over to take a look.

'Jimmy Strong's long past caring; and I didn't think you'd give a damn,' he stated.

'True,' I looked down at the deceased. Jimmy wasn't really my uncle – that being a scientific impossibility – but he *had* co-habited with my Aunt Juno for five years until last summer. She'd insisted I call him Uncle; a request I avoided by not calling him anything at all. Poor stupid bastard. He hadn't been good for much when he was alive, and now he was good for nothing at all. Judging from the muscle spasm in the face that contained his vacant eyes, even his brain would be rejected by the organ banks.

'Where's he been?' I asked, removing the burnt-out lead from the socket behind his ear.

Delta Anne got to her feet. 'No idea. The external black box is scrambled.' She handed me the matchbox-sized Data Locator Unit that, in situations *not* like this, records a trawler's route and flags the cords of places they wish to return to. 'All I can do now is tell you what killed him.'

'That's obvious,' I remarked. 'The real question is why.'

'Take a guess,' the Chief said. 'Stupid jerk – wrong place – wrong time.'

'That's why we have to ask why,' I said. 'Jimmy didn't go trawling, Chief. The man had a phobia about cyspace. He dealt every kind of tech, but only ever hardware. And look at this jack.' I indicated the dodgy skull socket. 'This is a bad pirate job. It's not even fitted properly. Some backyard tech implanted this in such a hurry it's amazing Jimmy didn't have a stroke on the way home.'

The Chief looked hopeful. 'This might be a stroke?'

'No way,' Delta Anne stated. 'This is murder. Capra is going to have to find out where he's been.'

I smiled joylessly. Capra, that's me. Agent Capra Jane – cybercop, attached to the Southern Indian-Pacific Corps, headquartered in Melbourne City. I trawl the mean streets of Cy-city and the other virtual resorts – the ones that ordinary beat cops fear to tread. And that doesn't mean *they're* gutless and I'm some kind of hero. Far from it. In fact even *I'd* agree that statement says a boat-load about common sense versus foolhardiness. They have it – common sense that is – and I, well I basically don't *give* a shit.

I removed and studied the other end of the lead that had introduced Dr Death to Jimmy's cerebellum. It couldn't have been just inexperience that made him incapable of protecting himself against the surge that effectively desiccated his brain.

I glanced at the vibrating plasma-phone in my forearm. It was my mother's ID; the one with her 'urgent' face. As her idea of imperative differed greatly from mine, I figured she could wait. I opened Aggie's tool kit instead.

Delta Anne was right – the black box was cactus; but at least it hadn't fused to Jimmy's Terminal Interface. Once I cleaned out the charred wiring in the TI's input socket, I'd be able to jack in and use my own sensorpad to search the TI's internal black box. I could trace where Jimmy had gone trawling – or, at least, where he'd last been.

'Capra Jane?' the Chief said.

'Why are you here?' I asked him. 'Since when do you even leave your office?'

The Chief ignored me. 'Just do a prelim scout for now, Agent Capra. You'll have a partner on this case.'

'Oh no, you know that always ends badly, Chief.'

'Part of the exchange deal with the Space League. We *all* get to pull duty with the RSL.'

'*Returned* Spacers?' I said in horror.

Pouting seemed like the best response but I controlled myself. 'There are only ever two reasons for space jockeys to be classified *returned.* Either they've been sectioned-out coz they're psycho from space fever *or* they're old codgers who might not last the next voyage.'

I snapped a surge protector into the socket I'd cleaned. It wouldn't save me from a direct hit but it'd give me a few seconds grace to get out *if* I saw an attack coming. I opened Aggie's deck to reveal the tools of my trade: the left-hand keypad, calibrated precisely to the measured speed and dexterity of my fingers; the cylindrical joystick, connected to my control-deck by a long flex-wire; and, finally, a set of state-of-the-art, three-point tracer leads.

I logged in with my left hand, then removed my hat and fitted the second point of the tracer lead to the skull socket over my right ear. I palmed the joystick, picked up the free end of the tracer lead, leant forward and jacked into the terminal.

Jimmy Strong's office and its occupants dissolved around me as I made contact with the cyber matrix. It's never a good idea to keep your eyes open when the connection is made; coz the shift in perception is kind of like stripping away the reality of your existence.

But if you *do,* the rush out the other side is exhilarating.

The tracer program began its hunt for the entry or exit trail of the previous user, while I swerved bodiless against the precipitous, transparent walls of information that surrounded me and progressed forever outwards in every direction.

Waiting for entry induces a nausea that makes mentally pacing this void unpleasant. None of this is necessary if you know where you're going, or what you want to access, but when you're tracking someone else, this is invariably how you have to start. And the wait depends on the skill of the previous user. An expert who doesn't want to be followed can keep you out for several minutes and then lay false trails all over the matrix. But idiots like Jimmy can keep you at bay for longer simply coz they have no idea what they're doing, so there's no logic to follow.

I received the sensory shove that indicated re-entry and surged up and over – these being relative terms – the splendid purple rim of the DaerinCorp Research Foundation's feeder link; and into the record banks of their research division.

Shit Jimmy, what were you up to? I followed his trail which paused at the towering data stacks of DaerinCorp's Future Projects Division which, not surprisingly, he'd been unable to get into. Even *I* don't have clearance for that level access, despite my badge and closer family ties to Daerin's board of directors.

An odd shimmer below caught my attention. It appeared someone else had piggybacked on Jimmy's poorly-executed hack. I wondered if the hitch had been intentional or the trawler had just been passing and decided to latch on. I slowed my onward motion to try to make out the tag name but couldn't quite…*Whoa!*

A virtual quiver in the matrix at my back sent an orgasmic frisson curling into my brain.

Nice – but, naturally, I span around.

Nothing and no one. Not that I could see anyway.

I could, however, sense someone laughing.

I returned to the original trail but suddenly everything went black. This was followed by a rippling sensation and the realisation that the mid-section of Jimmy's trail had been fried, and his last port of call was about to cross paths with my current position.

Twin moons glowed overhead, the sound of smooth reko-jazz filled my ears and a neon sign ahead blinked: 'Beer, Boys and Babes'.

Downside?

The usual moment of rational dislocation was replaced by the familiar, as the holographic-construct of Cy-city's shanty town folded around me.

What the hell were you doing here, Jimmy Strong?

Back in the real-world my left hand worked the key pad to access one of my avatar cloaks. Form – mine – materialised out of the matrix and I found myself standing in one of the maze of back alleys near the notorious Pit Club.

'About time,' growled a metal-plated Neanderthal who was aiming a Rat Gun at me.

I flung myself sideways, tucked myself into a roll to get my feet under me, then hit the ground running – I *love* running – around the nearest corner and out of immediate harm's way; while my real fingers, in that other reality, flew across the sensorpad searching for an exit. I found it, reached for the terminal connection point and jacked out so suddenly that I flipped backwards across Jimmy's office.

While I waited for the interference in my brain to clear I realised that someone was swearing up a storm. I opened my eyes to find myself upturned and hovering over a sprawled Chief of Police.

'That was a stupid place to stand,' I said, drifting away so I had a clear area in which to turn right-way up. The motion, combined with perception-residue from the trawl, had a hokey affect on my vision. Still upside-down, the shadows in the far corner of the room seemed to be alive with...with deeper shadows.

Ack! I haven't done this flipping nonsense for years. Used to happen all the time when I first acquired Aggie. Caused me a great deal of aggravation – hence, the best reason for her name.

'Why'd you come out so fast?' the Chief asked. 'You were screaming blue murder.'

'A reject from a horror vid tried to take me out with a Rat Gun,' I said. 'Think he was waiting in case Jimmy came back. Or maybe for whoever came in after Jimmy was shot.'

'Your Uncle was shot?'

'Yes and no, Chief,' I said.

'Well there's no sign of a struggle,' he said. 'So he must've known who did this.'

'Why?'

'For the killer to be here and walk right up to him–'

'He wasn't killed here,' Delta Anne said.

'What, so this is a body dump?'

'No. It was feedback.' Delta Anne turned Jimmy's head indelicately to reveal the scorched flashpoint round the socket.

'So his socket blew a fuse?'

'Not exactly,' said Delta Anne. 'This *is* more like a powder-burn from close proximity to a weapon.'

The Chief looked exasperated.

'The Doc means Jimmy was here, when he was killed elsewhere,' I said.

'Feedback,' Delta Anne said again.

'A Rat Gun,' I elaborated.

'Knew I should've retired last month,' the Chief said. 'Now, about your new partner Capra–'

'Not gonna happen, Chief,' I said, distracted again by the weird shift in the shadow that shrouded the back of the room. I shook my head.

'No choice, Capra. This comes from High Command. Five Spacers have been missing for nearly two months and, according to their envoy, *their* case leads to your Uncle.'

I laughed. Jimmy Strong dealt with crooks – it's why the thing with Aunt Juno was doomed – but he wasn't himself a bad guy.

'You find that amusing?' The shade within the darkness spoke for the first time.

'Yep,' I acknowledged, then turned back to the Chief. 'Let me guess. Secret Agent Shadow here is from the League of Space Loons. Chief, you know they have, *had* a gripe with Jimmy coz he whistleblew their smuggling racket.'

'I'm not *with* the Returned Spacers League.'

The Chief looked like he was about to enjoy something way too much. 'Agent Capra Jane,' he said, 'meet Captain Zanzibar Black – of HomeWorld Security'. He indicated the shadow that was stepping out of the inky-dark, still morphing into something tangible. Literally. Not that the Chief saw the transformation. His eyes were on me for some reason; and my eyes clearly needed testing coz I was seeing things…

Oh.

And crap! My world tilted as the darkest of hours-past engulfed my soul with *all* their reality: the nightmares, the peace, and the fabulous imaginings.

I'd long ago chucked the deluding meds that had made me relive the too-real bad, while yearning for the clearly impossible. The constant mind-shift from blood-spattered trenches to an irresistible beguine, from the pits of hell to a dance of sheer reckless joy, had been way too much.

'Capra Jane? You okay?'

Frak'n hell – flashbacks are a bitch! I hadn't had one for seven years; until this slight shift in perception, this trick of the limited light had turned a ghostly shade to a shimmer of such beguiling colour…

Maybe my implant needs realignment.

'Capra Jane!'

'Yes Chief,' I said, blinking to re-focus on the now completely corporeal HomeWorld rep.

Oh my!

Captain Black: eyes – green or blue, or green; hair – short and blood-red; mouth – perfect.

Zanzibar Black: sex on two long, *long* leather-clad legs.

'You sure?' he patted my arm.

'Yes. Chief. I'm sure.'

'That wasn't quite the reaction I was anticipating.'

'*Why* were you expecting anything?' I glared at him and collected my senses, before turning to the Amazonian spook from Espionage HQ. 'Here are you – who. Why?'

'That's more like it,' the Chief said.

I ignored him and raised my eyebrows at Captain Black, waiting; as if I'd made perfect sense.

She had the grace to simply answer, 'The late Mr Strong met with two of the missing Spacers.'

'Returned Spacers came to Jimmy all the time to catch up on the history they'd missed while out beyond the Belt. He's the only merchant in the Free Zones who dealt the old tech.' I explained. 'I assume they were cleanskins.'

'Yes. But only the men came to Mr Strong.'

'Well yes, of course,' I said. 'The women from the Jump Ships have no need. It's only the men who are banned from implants.'

Zanzibar Black shrugged – eloquently.

How was that even possible?

'In between meeting the Spacers and them going missing, Mr Strong also made contact with a Judah Plenty.'

Uh-oh. I always knew that connection was gonna bite Jimmy on the arse. I steered my pod over to the bank of computers, hovered higher, retrieved a framed vid-image and handed it to Black. 'They were in the same unit in the Border War.'

'I'm aware of that.' She glanced at the faded picture of Jimmy and his mates with the low-rider tank they'd liberated from the Raven Brigades. 'But as you know, Agent Capra, *ex*-pilot Judah Plenty is now a known slave trader.'

I looked Zanzibar Black up and down, slowly – mostly because the view was great – before nodding. 'If he's so *known*, Captain Black, why haven't your lot shut him down?'

'Please, call me Zan,' she said – for no good reason at all. 'Plenty's connections have been…'

'Let me guess, Plenty-useful to HomeWorld Security,' I finished for her. I was trying valiantly to *appear* interested in late-Jimmy, bad-Judah, lost-Spacers or anything, while an aural flashback this time – a soft whispering of my name – began liberating my libido from its four-year hibernation.

The Chief cleared his throat. 'Capra, return to HQ and report to Chief Jayla Ellen so she can intro your new partner.'

'What?' I looked from the Chief to… 'Aren't *you* my partner, Captain Black? Zan.'

'No. A Returned Spacer, one Milo Decker, will do the field work with you. He *is* a League member, and a cleanskin, just like those who are missing.'

'Oh.' *Damn.*

The Chief waved his data-strap over my touchscreen and Aggie thrummed to attract my attention. I read, aloud, all about my newest liability. 'Ensign Milo Decker. Stellar cartographer. Born Geelong, January 4, 2040. Shit!'

'What?' he asked.

'This bloke's nearly 90!'

'Technically he's only 87,' Zanzibar Black said.

'Is that a problem?' The Chief flexed his 83-year-old muscles in some kind of strange manly pose – which did not a thing for me.

'No Chief, unless it's combined with a lifetime in those Jump Ships flashing around the galaxy at 50 times the speed of light, exploring new worlds and fighting the Sakaas for the mineral rights to every asteroid they pass.

'Those spacers, especially the old codgers, have big trouble re-assimilating. This I know from personal experience. My Great Aunt Marin drove us batty every time she came home, just on leave, until she discovered the jetcar circuit. And she's only 66. And *this* one,' I protested, 'this one will be old *and* whacko. Sixty-eight years in the Space League and the guy's still an ensign!'

'He might surprise you,' Captain Black said.

'Don't like surprises,' I snarled; but not at her.

I glared at the Chief, who cajoled, 'Hey, he's healthy. There aren't that many of us left. You should be nicer to us.'

'Why? You blokes brought the shit on yourselves.'

I began securing my gear, until two other things occurred to me: Zanzibar Black was also a cleanskin; and therefore, 'Is this Spacer of yours bait?' I asked.

'Of course not, Capra Jane. And yes, I too am tech-free.' As she ran her hands through her hair in demonstration, my skin tingled with way-more than lust. It was almost an erotic prompt or sensual proposal.

Bloody hell – these weren't flashbacks. Well, not all of them.

The damn woman was a telepath.

No, Capra Jane. It's not that simple. Look at me.

Okay. So, although I 'heard' that in my head, and knew without doubt that no one in this room had 'spoken' those words, I did as I was asked. I looked at Zanzibar Black… and marvelled at the truth.

I am Beninzay. A second-generation hybrid.

While Zan was having a quiet little chat with my mind, an oblivious Chief was searching his pockets. That means she … *you, that means you can also turn invisible.*

I felt rather than heard her laugh – and it was a joyous thing.

It's camouflage Capra, not invisibility. But we do have skills that even urban myth hasn't dreamt up yet.

'Agent Capra, go back to work.'

'Right. Yes Chief.'

Later, Capra Jane.

I didn't want to 'think' anything revealing; well, anymore than I already had – *bugger* – so I just left.

It took me 10 minutes to get back to SIP Corps HQ but an hour later I was still hovering around the Chief's 44th floor office. On my own. Bored out of my brain.

Report to the Chief the Chief had said. Problem was, Chief Bascome's new Co-Director of Operations was nowhere to be found. And there's only so much you can do in someone's space without resorting to hacking their Terminal. I'd already gone through her drawers.

Sure, Chief Jayla's office – in one of the causeways built back in 2051 between the Eureka and Southern Cross Towers – had a great panorama; but it was no more spectacular than the view from my apartment. Hers took in the Great Southern Harbour, which comprised old Port Phillip Bay, the tidal flow of the Yarra River – the lower reaches of which still flowed under there somewhere – and the multitude of inner waterways that formed our island city. Mine overlooked the canals that threaded what had long ago been the streets of Melbourne City. Whatever the view, it was a bloody lot of water.

'Ah, Agent Capra.'

Finally! I directed Aggie to face the side door, through which Chief Rho Jayla Ellen, had entered her own office. At 37 she was the youngest SIP agent ever to take the Corps' top job, and therefore one of the Southern Hemisphere's highest command positions. She deserved it; even Chief Bascome admitted she was damn good at 'their' job. The 50-year age gap between the two chiefs was seen as a good thing by all who gave those things any thought. Not that the old man had a choice. All positions of any import held by men across the Southern Indian-Pacific had to be shared by the Alpha-Omegas. The Clan could hold solo positions, but the boys had to share. And there was no use complaining; it was all their own fault.

Chief Jayla tossed me a coffee tube then thwarted any possible complaint on my part. 'Your new partner is a done deal, Agent Capra.'

I sighed and cracked my tube. Instantly-hot coffee fizzed as its perfect aroma jazzed my nostrils. I took a sip. 'But an *old* codger?'

She shrugged. 'HomeWorld Security's choice.'

'So where is he?'

'He entered HQ about 40 minutes ago. Probably sorting gear.'

'He's an 87-year-old ensign; he's probably lost.'

'Go find him then, so he can help you find your uncle's killer.'

'He's *not* my uncle,' I smiled. I got as far as the open main door before she finally stated the bloody obvious. I manoeuvred to face her.

'You realise that HomeWorld Security's interest makes this more than a simple murder.'

'No such thing as a simple murder, Chief. Even a snap domestic homicide carries a shitload of baggage.'

'But this could prove delicate.'

I laughed. 'You realise I don't do delicate, Chief. I don't care about the politics; don't really even give a shit about Jimmy Strong. I just do the job and go home.'

'Denial might be why you're so good at your job.'

Denial? 'You trying to shrink me, Chief?'

'I wouldn't dare. I've read your file, Agent Capra. I know why you are…you.'

I seriously doubt that. 'Yeah? We should compare notes some time.'

'Over dinner?'

Oh great! The new Chief was flirting with me. When I smiled – a yes and no – an uncomfortable prickle scrambled up my spine, as if Aggie had sparked me right through my coccyx. I backed out of the office and into something that shouldn't have impeded my exit.

I turned to find one of the finest specimens of manhood I'd ever seen, sprawled on his back in a silk Jimani suit. Not *my* type at all, in any sense – but definitely beautiful. And despite a strangeness about him, I contemplated taking him home for my mother.

This was the second bloke Aggie had flattened today though; maybe she'd developed a thing against minority groups. Speaking of which, I realised Chief Bascome was also in the passageway; loitering and laughing.

'That better not be directed at me, Chief.'

'I'm laughing at your old codger,' he said, pointing at, 'Milo Decker.'

'What,' I began, and then ran out of ideas.

'To allay your fears about my ability to assimilate, I do not suffer from space fever or any other stress-induced syndrome and I've never been on a Jump Ship,' Decker announced.

'I apprised him of your concerns,' the Chief mocked. I scowled at him.

'But yes, Agent Capra, I *was* born in 2040 and I *have* been in space for 68 years, although for me it was more like five.'

Oh – frakn – no.

'I was part of the original Australian Probe Ship Mission.'

'Give me strength!' I begged. 'How long have you been back?'

It hit me then, that what was stranger than the thing I'd half-noticed earlier – that Handsome had a full head of hair and no implants – was the fact that this cleanskin was so young.

No, take that back. The huge oddity was the fact that he was a *man* so young.

'One month,' he was saying.

I turned on the Chief and snarled, 'You're assigning me a techno-retard as a partner?'

'Calm down. He'll catch on quick.'

'Realise I sound like a walking cliché, Chief,' I began.

'I don't mean to be offensive Agent Capra,' Decker interrupted, 'but I doubt you could be a walking anything.'

Valuable commodity he might be, but Ensign Decker had just demanded an arse-kicking. I pinned him to the wall before he realised I'd moved. 'Your file says you're 87 years old, Decker,' I said quietly. 'What's your calculation?'

'I'm 23,' he stammered.

'Good, so by anyone's calendar, you're old enough to know that it's unacceptable to say what you just said.'

'Yes, Agent. But you called *me* retarded.'

'Technologically-retarded, is what I said. That referred to an educational inadequacy, *not* your physical appearance. Did not call you brainless, did I?'

'No,' he replied.

'Then do not ever point out that I am legless. Got it?'

He nodded.

'Good,' I said, and hovered off down the hall. 'You coming?'

Twenty minutes later I was sitting in my office crash chair, hot-wiring the lead wire from an elderly virtual reality helmet into my TI so I could piggy-back *Ensign* Decker into Cy-city.

'So, we're going inside the computer?' he said.

'No. We're going to use the Terminal Interface to hitch a ride into the matrix of cyberspace and go anywhere we like.'

'Except we don't leave this room.'

'Of course not,' I replied.

'I'm having trouble with this.'

'They must have had some kind of cyber tech 68 years ago.'

'I'm sure *they* did,' Decker replied. 'But my experience was limited to what was relevant to my training. Preparation for my voyage began when I was six. It was a combo of survival skills and firearm drills, plus advanced biology and stellar cartography. My only personal interest at the time was archaeology.' He shrugged. 'I wanted to explore the old San Francisco ruins.'

I raised my eyebrows. 'Gone now.'

'Yeah,' Decker grumbled. 'Guess I'll have to learn to pilot a sub to realise that dream.'

'OK, so that was then,' I said, handing him the helmet. 'What's stopped you since?'

Decker smiled. 'Since? Agent Capra, you forget that by my body clock I was only gone for five years – during which time I mapped the Margolin quadrant and the entire sector between Allyo and Jajaray.'

'That's quite a bit of space.' I was genuinely impressed. 'But I can't process that you're a 23-year-old who's been alive for 87 years. Travelling at light speed always *was* beyond my understanding.'

'Try going offworld for five years and returning to find your little sister's a great-grandmother,' he said. 'I was 18 when the Australian Mission left Earth. Our Light Ship was at the cutting edge of state-of-the-art; we were *so* advanced we were still science fiction.

'By travelling *at* the speed of light, months as you know them passed like days for us. Our voyage lasted five years; but decades went by back here. We thought we'd been contacted by an advanced alien culture when we came across a Jump Ship on our way home. Those things travel at up to six *billion* kilometres a second. They can flip to Titan and be home for dinner. We felt like dinosaurs.'

'Well prepare your dino balls for another future shock, kid,' I said.

Decker looked nervous and pointed at my vid-screen. 'And there's really a city in there.'

'Not in there,' I corrected him. 'And not even – more logically – in the bio-cell vault which is in *there*.' I stroked the translucent purple interface deck that shielded the banks of neural gel-cells and my nano-tech maintenance crew.

'Cyspace is out there; *every*where in *non*-space.' I waved my hands in the general direction of nowhere in particular, trying to find words for a concept that was incomprehensible – until you'd seen it.

'It's an artificial alternate universe. And yes, there are *cities* there. Our beat is Cy-city or, more often, Downside; a sprawling shantytown of cabo halls, blues bars, data saloons and holo-brothels. It's in a hundred back alleys off the old Information Superhighway.'

Decker looked like he was in pain.

'It's like *imagining* information. Parts of cyberspace are still just stacks of data or ribbons of info; at least that's what it looks like when you're trawling. When you access something specific, however, you can actually see it. Although what it *looks* like depends on how it was stored in the first place. Much of the old stuff is just dry, endless reams of figures, words or images – some flat, some 3D, some holo-fabrications. Like what you'd see on your vid-screen or projected via a holo-imager.

'More recent or imaginative info is like a full-on interactive vid. You *can* view it unplugged, but when you jack *into* cyspace, through a Navigation Controller like CC-Fly or ParaWeb, then you see and feel that information as a version of reality.

'For example, the stuff you charted on your voyage would appear, all around you, exactly as *you* saw it, and logged it, in person out there.' I waved in the direction of outer space realising I was giving Decker directions to the same 'nowhere in particular' that I'd called cyberspace.

'You don't see it with your eyes though, right?' Decker said.

'Well *I* don't,' I said, 'coz my skull implant is connected directly to my brain's visual cortex. You, however, will be seeing things the old-fashioned way, coz you have to receive the data via the visor. Assume you've at least used one of these before.'

He rammed the thing on his head. 'For games.'

'Games?'

'We each have our skills,' Decker stated. 'While you've been scragging this inorganic ersatz universe, I've been flipping through the real thing cataloguing star systems and making contact with new species.'

'Okay game boy; this works the same. Images and sound get delivered via the visor and, just as you once believed you were in the crew lounge on Asimov Base, or fighting the Granks in a space battle, now you will *know* you're in Cy-city.

'The cities in cyspace are way more than virtual reality; they are, in a sense, virtually real. It's the ultimate head-trip coz you're not confined by a program that generates a game. You can go anywhere that information is stored, and *everywhere* you go takes you somewhere else, even if it's just back to the *central* matrix, which is a misnomer coz it's not *at* the centre, and there's actually more than one of them. Cyberspace is like real space; it has no centre, no edges, and no top or bottom – *and* it's an expanding universe.'

Decker was still unsure. 'But it's not real.'

I laughed. 'No, it's not real. But *real* is a relative term, just like time and space. You of all people should understand that.'

Decker grunted. 'So how can you *be* a cybercop?'

'Why you'd *want* to be one is a better question,' I said. 'When people started spending half their lives in cyspace, for recreation, knowledge exchange, propaganda or profit, some bright spark came up with the idea of creating virtual spaces where trawlers could meet – anonymously, by using avatars.'

Decker shrugged. 'You mean you could lie.'

'Yes, you could lie. You could *be* anybody or thing you wanted – including yourself. You could reveal the you that had zilch to do with an ugly face or a lack of arms, or *any* real-world signifiers that supposedly *describe* you but really just label you as a mottle-skinned, bi-gendered accountant.

'Then a pair of tech-heads co-named Breckinridge Fink, took the virtual notion, juiced it with imagination and made it tangible. They established ParaWeb, and turned parts of cyberspace into permanent holographic constructs of the landscape of the cyber matrix.

'Breckinridge Fink built Downside, Cy-city and BerinSpace but it was only a dash before competing NavCons and matrix architects went on-line. Suddenly there were trade regions, cities and resorts like CaraBazaar and ParisBo. They're still amazing amalgams of ultra-tech and unfettered creativity; where blissful paradise meets darkest nightmare in the same scape; and where the avenues and edifices are blended fact and fiction. It's a wondrous hybrid of myth and common reality.'

'I'm waiting for the but,' Decker said as I leant over to adjust the audio flaps on his helmet.

'But it is beset, naturally, by that parasitic by-product of all human endeavours.'

'What's that?'

'Crime,' I snarled. 'And more varieties of it than you'd ever think possible. I might be a cybercop but when I enter cyspace I'm going where there is *no law*. My badge, your new badge, no badge, same thing. The *rules*, such as they are, are loosely *guided* by a century-old, free-market code of honour that is just that: an honourable, civilised kind of thinking. And 'thinking' is the only *truly* operative word, concept and act in the whole of cyspace. It's a region that works cleanly and honestly – in its intentions.

'Bad elements, however, turn up wherever there's a buck to be made or a drek to push around; so we are tolerated coz we proved ourselves to be useful. But, until the NavCons ask for an official SIP Corps presence we're merely bounty hunters or secret agents, using cyspace just like everyone else does, to get or pass info. Don't be fooled though; it's as dangerous for cops in cyspace as it is on any streetside posting.'

I jacked Decker's tracer lead into my TI deck to check the calibration. I hadn't used something as hokey as a VR helmet in decades.

'When you enter any cyspace city or resort,' I continued, 'you sling on a Cloak, or adopt an avatar, of anything you like. While there you can eat, drink, talk or listen to a rantan band; you can have mind-blowing sex in a holo-brothel, without risk of disease; you can even pick a fight and have the crap beaten out of you if that's your quirk.

'If you've got an implant, like mine, you'll actually *feel* and taste it all. Your avatar will bleed and bruise but the experience leaves no mark on your real body at home in its crash chair. But, coz your brain *thinks* it's real, your endorphins get triggered, your adrenalin pumps and up goes your blood pressure. If your heart can't take it, your brain will shut it down. If your *mind* can't take it, then there's a tank-load of cybertherapists listed in the Yellow Files.'

Decker shifted uncomfortably in his seat.

'You *should* be nervous, Decker. Life is strange enough out here, but our beat trawls the seriously weird. Have I put you off yet? Or are you going to lower your visor and take a look for yourself? Make up your mind Ensign Decker coz *I'm* going now.'

The noise that followed me into the matrix told me Decker was right behind me. He sounded like he'd been thrown out of a Jump Ship that was still warping through space.

'Fraaakn-ell!'

My left hand keyed in the cords for Downside and, as the public entry point for the town materialised around us, I accessed my Cloak and chose an appropriate avatar for my new partner.

'Turbo*shit,* what a charge!' Decker exclaimed.

The permanently rain-slicked main street reflected the neon-lit, forever night-time world of Downside. Tonight, that being a relative term, the footpaths of Bernezlee Alley were crowded with trawlers of every description, and there was music, conversations, arguments and laughter spilling from every establishment down the strip.

'Close your mouth Decker, you look like an idiot; particularly considering how you're dressed.'

He looked down, then swivelled to catch his reflection in a window. He had to search for himself coz the person who looked back *at* him was not only barely dressed but didn't look a bit *like* him.

'What is this?' he demanded.

'Apollo,' I replied. 'Thought you'd look good in a toga.'

'Yeah?' he snarled. 'Well I like your *legs* Agent Capra, but who are you supposed to be?'

'Incognito! As are you, *Ensign* Apollo,' I responded tartly.

Whatever Cloak I adopt, and this time I'd chosen a fem-punk variation, I *always* grant myself killer legs; so I decided against punching Decker in the mouth for mentioning them again. I headed off down Bernezlee towards The Bender. A sleazy nightclub was always the place to start.

'There's one thing I still don't understand,' Decker trailed after me.

'Just one?' I reacted involuntarily to the vibration of my plasma-phone. I raised my real arm long enough to hear my mother snapping: 'Jane, this really is urgent' then waved the call off.

'If you can get beat up here and there's no mark on your real body, how was Strong killed here?'

'There's a wicked illegal little device called a Rat Gun that gives a badarse electric shock or, if it hits *just* the right spot, a synaptic power surge. If a drek with one of those takes a dislike, you're fried toast in seconds. The last thing you'd ever see, while lying in a Downside gutter, is *these* neon lights. But your body, and a skull full of soup or dust, will be found in your crash chair at home still jacked into your terminal. Just like Jimmy.'

'Do these murders *ever* get solved?' Decker asked.

I thumbed myself. 'Best clean-up rate in the Corps. Hope you're not gonna ruin my record, *Ensign*.'

'Hope you're not gonna spend our entire partnership being patronising,' Decker remarked amiably.

Five minutes later we were sconced in a Bender booth, waiting for a drink and listening to a very bad rantan artiste.

'What *is* he trying to do?' Decker asked.

'*Can't* do it, that's his problem.'

'Is it supposed to be music?'

'You sound like my mother. Yes, this *is* supposed to be music. Not this bloke though; he should be refried.'

A five-note chime announced the return of our bartend Beano, a snake-skinned rogue who growled at Decker, 'Sit back, mavrak.'

'Right*o*,' Decker snarled back.

I glared at Decker then smiled at Beano. 'He's a virgin,' I apologised.

Beano grunted: 'K'n tourists,' and slid back to the bar.

'What's with him or whatever that was?'

'He's a bartend. It's his prerogative to be mean as batshit – if he wants.'

Decker tasted his burly and curled his lip. 'Seems pointless if you can't taste it.'

'Pointless to you, maybe,' I shrugged. 'Tastes vivid to me, like riko juice and deepsouth bourbon.'

I scanned the patrons for the tag-signs of my snitches. The crowd this night was a spicy mix of mean-faced dealers, xotic-limbed hosties looking to score, club ragers, and chronic barflies. The latter were lazy dreks who'd missed the point of trawling and only ever came to drink and ogle.

'Incognito?'

'What?' I asked.

'Sorry. I didn't know what to call you,' Decker said.

'Incognito's good,' I smiled. 'Did you want to call me something for a reason?'

'Yeah. I was wondering *how* you lost your legs. Bascome said it was in the Border War but...' Decker recognised my expression for what it was. He took a breath and pressed on regardless. 'It's just that I don't know anything about that conflict, not having been here and all. It must have been hell to deal with, I mean–'

'The war or the legs?' I squinted at him. I had no intention of letting him off the hook for asking such a personal question so soon in our relationship. It didn't matter that I felt remarkably comfortable with this young man. I rarely took to anyone quickly, but Decker possessed a strangely intimate quality. Either that or I was drunk already.

'Both, I guess,' he muttered. 'I mean how do you deal with a physical loss like that? And, um, what I *did* hear about the northern trenches was...scarifying.'

Poor bastard still had a lot to learn about social etiquette, so I gave him a point for refusing to *pretend* he was sorry about broaching an inappropriate subject.

'The legs thing is *not* a subject for today, Decker. Okay? Spose it *is* a good bar story – how I lost them in a swivel grenade blast – but there's nothing you *need* to know about that. And what you might *want* to know is a matter of public record. Look it up. Also, I've no intention of helping you comprehend a near-decade of bloody warfare by letting you inside my head.'

Decker's Apollo-visage smiled a genuine apology; so I smiled back.

'Besides, my ringside account wouldn't give you an objective view. You'd just get my anger, my gunsight and my nightmares. And believe me you don't want to know about my nightmares.'

Or my escape. That incredible dance on the edge of utter abandon. I took a swig of burly. I hadn't told a soul about that imagined passion with my exotic lover. Weird that it was the second time today, and the first time in years, it had come to mind. The memory felt like a coiled snake of pure elation had shifted in my chest.

'History is never objective,' Decker said. 'It's always written by the–'

'The winners, I know. And we were the winners, so from me you'd get double-subjective, coz personally I think we should've walled the Raven Brigades into their precious enclaves afterwards. They're a scourge, liable for more life damage on this planet than any other group since humans first stood upright and worked out how to whack someone else over the head with a rock.'

'Easy to say with hindsight,' Decker nodded. 'But back before the Raven Corporation was so blatantly manipulative, they–'

I snorted. 'Rackers! You *do* need a history lesson, Decker. Manipulative is how Raven Corp began; genocidal is how its brigades ended up. That we didn't know about it for half a century just shows how deceitful they were. But let's start with the World War, precipitated by the fuel crisis… Oh, but you were here in 2047 weren't you? So you'd remember – bad war, good result; coz it led to the International Power Pact.'

'I was seven.' Decker grinned.

'Oh, reality check,' I groaned. 'I wasn't even born then; and now I'm ten years older than you. Okay, so as a kid you were oblivious to the rumour, later proven, that the fuel crisis was facilitated by the Raven Corporation.

'Then, after you left earth, the United Nations' Eugenics Moratorium was abandoned after a decade of legal stoushes over the 'right to free trade' bankrupted the UN. The resulting Gene Trade Disputes, while an obvious outcome of an economic system with no controls, were just legal money-spinning clashes of ego and marketing between the world's largest gene-makers like the US Genofactory, EuroGene and Raven Corp.

'But, having opened the market to free trade, these egos then tried to control it; but buggered themselves by not noticing the emergence of an international blackmarket, orchestrated by the secret Raven Corp Brigades.

'The once morally-respectable Gene Trade took a back seat to the truly free but illegal street trade. And, in a decline reminiscent of the previous century's drug wars, the gene trade soon degenerated into armed skirmishes, then major border conflicts and finally the full-blown Gene War of 2060.

'The latter made the Gene Traders, especially Raven Corp, rich beyond belief but even their wealth couldn't protect them when one of their own, that lunatic Ferry Barcolin, let loose the Mantaray retrovirus in 2063. And you *do* know the result of that, Decker, coz of what you are now that you're home.

'But,' I continued, making the most of the soapbox I hadn't intended to climb on, 'out of every parcel of man-made shit – and I used the word *man* quite deliberately – comes something good; and in 2067 we got the very best that civilised human beings could come up with: the Alpha-Omega Accord.

'The AOA enabled First Contact, the Interplanetary Exchange, unprecedented techno-progress, world peace until – and again after – the seven-year Border War; which was, of course, initiated by feral remnants of the Raven Brigades.

'These are the bare dry facts, Decker, and all a matter of historical record. You want colour? Go to the holomuseum. Maybe, if you stick around long enough I'll tell you my legs story. Until then it's personal, and it's history – much like my actual legs.'

Decker looked like I'd beaten him around the face with an old-fashioned encyclopaedia; and then he smiled. No idea why that delighted me as much as it did. It was disturbing.

'It was Second Contact,' he said.

'What?'

'Your wonderful Alpha-Omega Accord enabled Second Contact. Our Probe Ship made First Contact. We traded with the Creons, lived with the Benin; hired several Avanirs as pilots.'

'That may well be Ensign – but if the Jump Ships hadn't found your vessel out there beyond the Belt we'd never have known what you did or who you met.'

Decker smiled again. 'Except for the strange stories those other spacefarers would've told about our passage.'

I shrugged. 'True. But right now – apart from warning you that one of my way-weird snitches is about to join us – there's only two stories we need to know about each other in order to bond. And they are that *you* are one of only 4000 human males on this planet with viable sperm; and *I* am Lambda Capra Jane of the Alpha-Omega Clan.'

My snitch was a tech-trader called Zippo Farqar. Tonight his avatar was a scaly humanoid with antlers and piercings. He sat, I ordered him a stinger, he sniffed at Decker.

'Weird one, this.'

'True,' I agreed.

'No. I mean frak'n weird,' Zippo insisted.

'How do you recognise each other if you're always switching avatars?' Decker asked.

Zippo sniffed again. 'Pheromones.'

I grabbed Zippo's antler but addressed Decker. 'Every trawler has a batch of tags; separate people-specific codes we can exchange. I enter Downside with my Farqar-tag switched on. If he's in, and wants to meet, he finds me. Or vice versa. If incognito is preferred, the tags stay off or ignored.'

'Ah, she's a cleanskin,' Zippo said, running a talon across Decker's hand.

The reaction was instant, and bone-crushing. Zippo nursed three fingers.

'Impulse-control not your thing?' I asked my new partner.

'Do I *look* like a she?' Decker asked.

'Don't be ridiculous,' I said. 'Downside is the great lie, remember.'

'Want my intel, or not?' Zippo asked.

'Want,' I nodded.

'Okay. Uncle J came Downside three times. Or three times shared his tags.'

'I gave Zippo the master ID to Jimmy's tags,' I explained to Decker.

'First time, he asked all around for word on stem factories, organ harvests and gene therapy.'

'What the frak for?' That made no sense. Jimmy cared bugger-all for anything but hard-tech.

Zippo shrugged. 'Second, he got took to a Zen-den down Styx Alley.'

'Which one?' I asked, giving Decker the 'later' signal before he asked the obvious.

'*Triple 6*. Run by Charon Marx.'

'What did Jimmy want?'

'Charon wouldn't say. Third visit, Jimmy gets turfed from *Triple 6*, goes troppo on Styx, and is rat-gunned and dies a click away by the flagpole on the Crop. Though no one saw nothin.'

'Of course not.'

'This next is for your ears only.' Zippo waved a dismissive finger.

'Decker, go wait outside while I pay my dues.'

When we were alone Zippo said, 'Didn't think you'd want this shared with your weird frak'n girly-boy-Apollo. Intel threw up a connect to your Juno.' He raised his hand. 'I *know* they had a thing Cap. It was a threat against her.'

I stood. 'Jimmy would never harm Aunt Juno.'

'No; he was Downside doing *whatever* coz of the threat.'

Jimmy playing hero? That didn't gel either.

'What's with the *she* refs to my Apollo?'

'I thought you, of all dykesters, would have sniffed to that one.'

'I was with Decker when *he* cloaked. I chose his avatar.'

Zippo touched his nose. 'I told you, Cap – pheromones.'

'Dream on. The person who masters original-trawler scent will be rich indeed.'

He smiled. 'You know I'm a real-world Pharma. I've nearly perfected it.'

'Nearly is the word, Zippo. Come see me, real-world, when you perfect at least a valid gender id. I might bankroll you.'

I rejoined the buff Milo 'Apollo' Decker outside.

'Secrets?' he said.

'Maybe.'

I led the way to the seamier, nastier realm of Downside; the quarter known as Hangman's Crop. We threaded our way between street vendors – hawking everything from food and microchips to T-shirts and banzai – and entered Crop Plaza. Trawling there – where Bernezlee Drag met Pyramid Way and the five Cracker Alleys – was a circus of freaky avatars trying to outdo each other with visible weirdness or strange behaviour. And Decker, still the dopey tourist, kept bumping into them.

'Watch it jerkman!' snarled a three-foot kewpie doll. With chainsaw teeth.

Decker recoiled, then snorted.

Please don't laugh Decker. I grabbed his arm in the same moment that mine – back in my rack – had been touched; reassuringly.

'The green kewpie,' I said, yanking Apollo Decker from trouble, 'could be an amped-up gym-jock. While lugnuts there,' I pointed to a scarified ogre, 'is probably a schoolgirl.'

'The lie thing again,' Decker smiled.

'Yup.' Despite feeling strangely turned-on by – I've *no idea* what – I clasped Decker's forearm and headed for the flagpole at the centre of Hangman's Crop.

'What are you looking for?' Decker asked as I scoured the area.

'This is where Jimmy bought it.'

There was no such thing as a crime scene in cyspace; no way to collect forensic evidence; and, as Zippo said, *no one saw nothin.*

'And?' Decker said, sussing I was clueless.

'Doesn't make sense that Jimmy died here. The feral with the rat gun was down an alley near the Pit Club.'

'Could he have made it here and then died?'

'Technically no. If a rat gun kills you, which it did Jimmy, then you die where you're hit. Unless where I entered on his trail was the last moments of his life; not the end. I had to run; maybe he did too.'

'You look excited.' Decker sounded surprised.

'Graffiti! Look for a message.' I turned to the closest walls.

'You're joking!' Decker's reaction was understandable given Downside's exterior walls were an ever-evolving canvas of doodles, scribbles and the rare masterpiece.

'Incognito,' Decker called.

'Yeah?' *Whoa!* An unconventional thrill surfed my brain. Decker's fingers – back in my office – were on my arm again.

'Stop that,' I snarled. 'I don't do boys.'

'Sorry. But remember I can't feel stuff in here like you can.'

'Doesn't mean you get to real-world touch me. What do you want?'

He was on his knees, pointing at the flagpole's base. 'Did you say your Alpha-Omega honorific was 'Lambda'?'

I joined him on the ground. 'Oh Jimmy, you clever, stupid bastard.'

My left office-hand took a snapshot of Jimmy's graffiti. It was a small rough circle containing the letters, *λCJ*; the words, *Daerin Juno*; and the scrawl, *37.48 144.57 libr*.

'Damn. Zippo was right.'

'About what?' Decker asked.

'Jimmy's being here was connected to my Aunt. Come on.'

We headed into Chin Sha's Emporium, zigzagged a multitude of tables laden with exotic curios, to the entrances of the five notorious Cracker Alleys. I pointed and named them for Decker: 'Acheron, Erebus and Tartarus; Hades – location of the Pit Club; and Styx – which is where we're going. Welcome to Hell Ensign Apollo; try not to draw attention to yourself.'

Decker gestured at his pecs and barely-there toga.

'It's attitude not avatar that gets you noticed down here,' I said and waded into the ankle-deep fog that forever-curled above the flagstones of the sharply-angled Styx Alley. We followed a centaur along its twists and turns until he slipped into Black Persephone's Tavern. I then calculated the best route to the Zen-den enclave.

'You were going to elaborate about these Zen places,' Decker said.

'Ah, yeah,' I frowned. 'They're like last decade's oxygen, b-boy or porn bars,' I began, then recalled Decker hadn't been on Earth last decade. 'A Zen-den is this century's hookah bar or opium den; where people zone on whatever floats their boat. Some dens have virtual reality pods; others are hands-on S&M joints, fight rings or saunas. Drugs, sport or sex – pretty much covers everything.'

'Isn't VR superfluous in a virtual world?'

'I guess; never really thought about it.' I stopped before a red door bearing a large brass 666, but had to grab Decker by his toga and yank him back to me. I rang the bell, an eye-level door slot slid back and a foul-smelling voice demanded the password.

'Frakn hell,' Decker swore, 'how are we–'

The door opened.

I laughed and pushed my partner into the haze and heavy-metal thump of the *Triple 6* before the door drek changed his mind.

'I can't touch *you*, but obviously you can drag and shove me on a whim,' Decker complained. The hand that Apollo the avatar placed in the small of my back, was matched by Decker's real one.

I glared at him. 'Do that again and I *will* break your fingers.' I scoped for the Boss of 666. The place was kitted out like Valhalla – all stone, shields and animal hides – but with demon heads on pikes and human torsos roasting over braziers. Wenches of indeterminate sexes delivered ale mugs to patrons at pitted log tables in barred booths.

'Popular joint,' Decker shouted.

'His joint,' I said, nodding at the towering mish-mash of scary mythic beings who sat on his skull throne on the dais above Hades Gates.

'Charon Marx?' Decker verified

'Real-world Bruce May,' I said. 'He is such a poser!'

'He's not alone,' Decker said, running to keep up with me.

I knew the trolls and ogres loitering below the dais were Charon's goons, employed to keep the hoi polloi at bay. Also knew the only way to the top of any pile is on the backs of those you step on. So that's the route I took.

I barely touched the first five trolls, but they ended face-first on a beer-soaked floor rug. I felled a gnarly ogre on the second step with a groin kick and another with an elbow to his throat, and then literally used them as stepping stones to the top.

No idea where Decker was in 666, but beside me in my office there were noises suggesting he was being thumped or was choking in disbelief. No one else in the Hall paid much attention – except Charon Marx himself who'd leapt into a defensive squat on his menacing throne.

'Step away from my man!' It was a Cyclops – with huge bare breasts.

I was still laughing after my spinning back kick laid her out at the foot of Charon's high chair. *I love my legs!*

I leapt up beside the God of 666, and whispered, 'Hey Bruce.'

'Oh crap, you bitch!'

'Come on mate,' I cajoled. 'Buy me a drink.'

Moments later Decker and I were sconced in Charon's private suite chatting about old times.

'So tell me why you threw a punter out into the alley about 18 hours ago...'

Charon gave his best Overlord laugh. 'Don't know why the last five scrags were bounced, Capra, let alone yesterday's–'

'...to get chased and ratgunned – to death,' I finished.

'Oh. Him.'

'Yeah him. My Uncle Jimmy.'

'Uh-oh.' Charon's avatar morphed from the Hellgod of Supreme Ugly to a face and figure only a smidge removed from the original Bruce May – or at least the one I'd met in the flesh five years ago. This avatar was bald, thin and ancient; but still oozing his trade-mark androgynous sex-appeal.

Decker must have sensed a bit of reality had arrived in the *Triple 6*, coz he grabbed my real-world arm again. I didn't raz him this time because Bruce really was almost a collector's item.

'Hang on,' Bruce frowned. 'You can't have an uncle. It's genetically–'

'Impossible, I know Bruce. But he and one of my Matriarchs had a thing, so he's almost family.'

'Don't call me Bruce, you know I hate it.'

'Why was he here, yesterday?' Decker was finally doing the cop thing.

I patted his real-hand encouragingly; then stopped immediately as that same damned-exquisite vibration flooded the parts of me that Zanzibar

Black had switched on earlier. A burning urge to track her down and give her a piece of my…*everything* made no sense at all. And then…

Frakn hell; again?

'You okay?' Decker whispered in my real ear, while his Apollo-avatar faced the still-talking Charon. I made mine get up and pace the den.

'First, I didn't know the man,' Charon stated. 'He got ejected from my premises after a scuffle. Second, I investigated after I heard he got fried and – *still* didn't know the man – but Ragnor said he'd been here once before wearing a different Cloak.'

'A scuffle? Really Bruce? Sorry, Charon.'

'Okay. A bloodbath brawl.'

'Jimmy was fighting?'

'Didn't say that, Cap; said there was a brawl. Ragnor reported the now-fried pirate, er your Uncle, was in it; but it more happened around him. And maybe to him.'

'He got beat up in your establishment, so you threw *him* out?' Decker said.

'Threw them both out.'

'Two people had a bloodbath?' I said. 'Was Jimmy cage fighting?'

'Course not. Was obvious to a gnat the bloke was a Startup.'

'A what?' Decker asked.

'Fresh meat,' Charon said. 'Like you. All wooden and such.'

Apollo glanced down at his perfect form and then at me, and acknowledged, 'Attitude not avatar.'

Charon poured three cups of mead and pushed ours over. 'Didn't know he was the same bloke till hours later.'

'What same bloke?' I asked.

'Same bloke as the one asking me about the Liebestraum Institute.'

'You said you didn't know him, *Bruce*.'

'Oh. Right.' Charon downed half his drink. 'I met him the time before; when he was a ninja and asked for an audience. With me, I mean.'

'You personally? Why?' I asked.

'Man wanted to know shit about organs.'

Well, that gelled with Zippo's intel. 'And stem factories?'

'No, just organs. Oh, and juice banks.'

'Why ask you that?' Decker asked.

'Don't he know who I am?' Charon looked hurt.

'People forget, mate,' I shrugged. 'Since you've moved in here, there's a generation never heard of you.'

Decker's hand was back on my arm, as Apollo gave me a quick glance. Charon didn't need to know that my partner was both too young *and* too old to have ever heard of the Liebestraum Institute, let alone Bruce May and his cohorts.

Although, strangely, I got the sense that he had. And that he knew… Decker removed his hand.

Okay. Knew what? I was starting to wonder if I hadn't been tagged by that bloody Rat Gun. Obviously not enough to kill – unless this really was hell – but maybe a blast-residue had followed me out of Jimmy's terminal. It would certainly explain the flashbacks and the inappropriately heightened libido and – *that too, dammit* – that sense that someone was laughing at me.

'Capra? You okay?' I looked up to find that Bruce had resumed a smaller version of his Charon Marx avatar. Probably so he could sulk discreetly about being a long-forgotten rock star.

'What could *you* tell him about the Institute?' Decker asked.

Now, you see… very odd question. I looked at my partner who was clearly avoiding eye contact. Given everything else he hadn't known today, his question should've been: *what* is the Liebestraum Institute?.

'I live there, man,' Charon said, as if the whole world should damn-well remember that.

'I don't understand,' Decker said.

'Charon, or rather Bruce and a motley collection of entertainers–'

'Motley?' Charon objected.

'…pooled their substantial fortunes to fund the Dreamscape Wing of the Liebestraum. It was then opened to anyone – who could afford it – to take up permanent residence; rather than, you know, *die*.'

'Your tone suggests disapproval, Capra,' Bruce said.

'Talk to me when it's available to all on UniCare and I might be less subjective in my opinion about who gets to die or not, *Bruce*.'

Decker tapped the table. 'Dreamscape Wing; organ harvests?'

I looked at my partner again. Ensign Clueless had suddenly become Detective Impatient. What's more he continued to avoid eye contact.

'We have 1341 Dreamers residing in the Dreamscape Wing,' Charon began.

'Who exist on life-support, in induced comas, while living permanently in Cy-city,' I finished.

That made Decker look at me. 'Living in here.'

'Will you show him, mate?' I asked the Undead Host of the *Triple 6*.

Without a word, Bruce May allowed his Charon Marx avatar to morph from the achingly-handsome Rock God who'd been lead singer of *Scattered Heads* 60 years ago, then on through the gracefully-aging legendary lead of *Fraught*, to the avatar he'd shown us moments before, to – and I felt Decker's shock, beside me in my office – the total reality of the wizened and barely-recognisable comatose shell that he was now.

Although this avatar was looking at us with Bruce's eyes, I knew that back in the Dreamscape Wing, his eyes – like those of the other 1340 Dreamers – were closed; permanently.

'Remember I said some of the Zen-dens had virtual reality pods?'

Decker nodded.

'Well, one good use for them would be for Dreamers like Bruce.'

'Except *I* don't use the pods.' A scowling Charon was back with us.

'I know, mate. Explain to Decker how the Dreamers get a different reality from the average Pod people.'

Charon got to his feet and beckoned. 'Come with, I'll show him.'

Decker and I fell in behind a regular-human sized Charon Marx and wended our way through the dance crowd in his great hall, to Hades Gates beneath his throne. The music dwindled to silence the moment we descended the nine steps to Charon's suite of Zen-dens.

I'd been down here many times and knew the *Triple 6* layout, so kept half my attention on my partner's reaction to his newest frontier.

'So, Startup,' Charon addressed Decker, 'Bruce May exists at the Liebestraum but I, Charon Marx, live here. Close to 500 other Dreamers live in Downside or other parts of Cy-City; the remainder live in CaraBazaar, SanFran or Hawksnest; and a great many of them all circulate throughout the zones.

'*Triple 6* is my joint. I am the architect, builder and Lord of all I survey. I frakn love this place. And coz I choose to recognise *this* as my world, I've never felt the need for extra virtual reality. Although I often relax in my Zen-dens, like this one.' Charon opened a set of double doors to a sandy arena with a martial arts deck where a bloody fight was in progress.

We continued down the hall. 'And this one,' Charon brushed his hand over a panel that turned the stone wall translucent, to reveal a Roman orgy in full swing.

'A thousand of my regular clientele – tourists I mean, not residents – take The Plunge, that extra trip into deeper VR, maybe a couple of times a year. But some of the Liebestraum Dreamers do it weekly, or even daily, because by doing so and then returning to their Downside homes, they reckon life in here feels more real.'

Charon had stopped again, this time at the balcony that overlooked the 400 VR pods – rows and rows of arm-chair or bed booths, stretching into the distance. He peered at the panel of stats he'd conjured on the wall beside him.

'Got 123 Dreamers and 73 tourists in at the moment.'

'What has all this got to do with our dead man and organ harvests? Decker said.

'And the juice banks remember,' Charon said. 'That's what he took most interest in after he'd seen my Abandon Pods.'

'What?' Decker and I said in unison. I added, 'So you brought Jimmy Strong down here too?'

'If Capra Jane, you're asking did I personally bring a ninja calling himself Dweedack down here, then, yes. He wanted to know if any clients other than Dreamers stayed for extra-long periods.'

I poked Charon in his oversized bronze chest. 'Please don't tell me you call them Abandon Pods coz they forget to leave; or you abandon them coz they don't pay?'

'I am deeply offended, Capra. Leaving non-paying customers in situ is not good business. I can't rent out occupied space. I use Ragnor's bone-breaking skills for that.'

'Who the hell is Ragnor?' Decker was either playing bad cop to my good, or he was genuinely aggravated.

'She's my wife, Startup,' Charon's snarled, as 'Bruce' added a fleeting doubling of his avatar's size to tower over 'Apollo'. 'She was on the dais with me earlier.'

Apollo-Decker stood his ground. 'You mean the one-eyed, triple-breasted leviathan that Agent Capra knocked out with one kick?'

'Yes, her,' Charon laughed heartily. 'I told Ninja Dweedack that only the Abandon Pods were addictive enough to hook people into protracted sessions. Why? They're called Abandon Pods coz most feature hard-core sex programs; or other adrenalin-endorphin raising adventures. Either way they're designed to get your juices flowing.'

'Ah, hence the juice banks reference,' Decker said.

This time I joined Charon in the exaggerated laughing.

'What?' Decker asked.

'Juice banks are sperm banks,' I managed to say. 'Their contemporary existence is the stuff of urban myth of course. But until mid-last century they were nearly as common as blood and stem-cell banks.'

Decker's real-hand, clasping my forearm, this time conveyed an unmistakable sense of foreboding. It was shaking.

'What is it?' I asked him.

'Charon,' he said, 'what exactly did Jimmy see down here and, specifically, what did he ask you?'

'He saw everything you've seen, plus the Abandon Pods. Come with.' Charon took the wide circular staircase down to the Pod Deck.

'And you just showed him, Charon?' I asked.

'Capra when will you learn, I don't do favours. Except for you. The ninja paid for a personally-guided tour. Paid well enough for me to let him scope some of the Plungers.'

'So much for privacy,' I noted. '*What* did he ask about organ harvests?'

Charon tapped at the plasma screen on his left palm. The VR Pods began moving around the cavernous space, jostling gently for position.

'Ninja Dweedack asked if the black market in cloned organs still existed. I said of course it did. Dumb frakn question really.'

'Cloned organs, not harvests?' I said.

Charon rolled his shoulders. 'I *now* surmise he wasn't interested in organs at all. After I explained the nature of most of the Abandon Pods, his quizzing became precise, and turned quite earnestly to the subject of juice banks. You with us on that subject now, Startup?'

'Yes,' Decker sighed.

'When we got to this very spot here, he wanted to know if any new Plungers, say in the last two months, had been introduced to Hades Gates *by* someone. Especially if the *same* someone intro'd more than one.'

'And?' I asked as Charon suddenly seemed distracted by the tango his pods were doing. 'Sorry, I'm calculating. Step back a bit please.'

Decker and I did as we were told.

'And when I checked,' Charon consulted his plasma again, 'I found that 33 Trawlers had been 'treated' to first-time Plunges by friends; but only five had been intro'd by the same friend. But not all together. Each of their first visits were a few days apart. After a week, the same-someone – a drek Ragnor later ID'd as Belbo Armitage – escorted them in together; like there were regular old-world bucks. The five have since been here, like clockwork: three-days in Abandon, two days gone, back again for three, etc., for a total ranging 52 to 59 days.'

'And Jimmy's juice bank questions?' I asked.

'Your 'ninja uncle' seemed convinced the banks were a reality; and that I *must* know their real-world location.'

'Why?' Decker asked.

'Because of the five Plungers, I think,' Charon said. 'But as I told him, over and over, there's no point in juice banks when the produce is 45 years beyond its use-by date.'

Oh frak. I glanced at Apollo-Decker who'd clearly seen the same light.

'Here they are,' Charon announced as a group of pods pulled to a stop before us.

Decker and I stepped in to take a look at 'the five Plungers' as the realisation of what was most likely happening to the missing Spacers hit home.

I was swamped by a tsunami of anguish and distress; of almost… *oh help, unbearable grief.*

But not mine.

Not my grief. What the hell?

I grabbed hold of Apollo's arm to see if the misery emanating from the pods was affecting him too. In the same nanosec that he resisted my attempt to make him face me, I remembered he couldn't *feel* anything in here.

Real-world Decker then snatched his hand from my arm; and Apollo… disappeared.

'That,' Charon pointed to the empty space, 'is exactly what your Uncle Ninja Dweedack did.'

'I don't get it,' I said – to both Charon in Downside and Decker in my office.

Only Charon bothered to answer. 'Ragnor said that when your uncle came back as *Pirate* Dweedack he met with Belbo Armitage, the Plunger's escort. Then the brawl started and they were thrown out.'

I inspected the Plungers again. They were all wearing simple masquerade masks – the most-basic of avatar cloaks – which meant they really looked just like the blokes in the Pods. I took a better look at the one Apollo had been checking…out.

It was, it looked like…

I reached out, removed the mask then shook my head. It didn't help. For the second time today I was gazing down at one of the finest specimens of manhood I'd ever seen.

The young man in this particular Abandon Pod was Ensign Milo Decker.

As my office-hands performed vital logging-out procedures, my fem-punk avatar waved goodbye to Charon Marx. The real-world materialised around me and I swung Aggie around to find out how the hell anyone could be in two – *no, who knew how many* – places at once.

My freshly-minted partner was lying on the floor. Again. Only this time he seemed to be out cold. Probably hadn't accounted for the lack of space between my terminal and the wall behind, when he backed out of Downside so fast. Obviously yanked the VR helmet off and smacked his head into the wall.

None of which explained the fact that Milo Decker and his spiffy Jumani suit were shimmering – I squinted – no, phasing in and out of focus.

I stared at my own hands then the wall.

Not shimmering.

I directed Aggie down to the floor but still couldn't reach him coz my anti-grav unit was in the way. I unbuckled and heaved myself over the edge to lie on the floor beside the definitely-phasing Decker.

I poked him. The shimmering stopped. Then started again.

I patted Decker's cheek. He grabbed my hand *and* stopped shimmering.

'Who the frak *are* you?' I asked.

He blinked. 'Who do I look like?'

'You look like the bloke in the Pod back there.'

'Really?' he frowned, then hauled me across his body and held me there.

I struggled for three seconds until I registered that the person below me was now morphing like a changing avatar. Decker became Bruce May became – *bloody hell, me* – then Decker again.

This was simply not possible in the real world.

'It's coz I hit my head,' whoever-it-was beneath me said.

No, clearly I had died earlier today. And this was my hell, forever caught nowhere at all.

Capra Jane.

Ooh peace. Oh that's nice.

Look at me, Capra Jane.

I did as I was told because now the morpher looked like that delicious Captain Zanzibar Black; and she was doing that talking in my head thing again.

Jane, remember. It's time to come back to me.

Well! With an invitation like that, how could I *not* let this brilliant hallucination kiss me like her life depended on it.

The sound of distant gunfire, exploding shells and screeching Atter-jets filled my mind. No not my mind; it was outside, scragging the air around me and tainting it with noxious fumes.

Where was I again?

I shifted on the makeshift hospital bed and my blood chilled me to the core.

'Major Capra, wake up.' I did, so Dr Black kindly held my hand.

Not again.

It's okay my love. You're not really there.

Fresh air, music. A deep throbbing tango; just like sex on legs. Don't have legs.

Jane, concentrate. On me.

I was now kissing Zanzibar Black like *my* life depended on it. And clearly it did, coz nothing could feel this good and not be intrinsic to my very existence.

Her tongue was in my mouth. Mine was in hers. I was never going to let her go; ever again.

And then I did.

Just to check which part of my fractured existence I was in at the moment.

Yes, I am real.

Zanzibar Black was lying on my office floor; under me. We had been kissing each other.

And now I felt *completely foolish.*

I rolled away from her and sat up, shaking my head in an effort to say: *I. am. so. sorry.*

What for?

'Speak,' I said. 'Who the frak are you?'

She smiled and – *my insides melted* – said, 'Zanzibar Black, just as your Chief introduced us earlier.'

I scowled at her. 'My other Chief intro'd my new partner as Ensign Milo Decker. But he was in Downside and, and now it seems I've–'

'Been with me all along. Sorry.' Captain Black got to her feet. 'I'm going to check out Jimmy's lead.'

She walked out my office.

Just like that.

What? Did you forget I can't just follow you? I mind-shouted, in the hope she'd hear me. She did.

I'm sure you'll catch up, Jane.

Jane? What's with the Jane nonsense?

I rolled over and into Aggie; hovered back up to my terminal and began an intel-hunt on Captain Zanzibar Black. Only family called me Jane, dammit. Family and lovers. And actual 'lovers' *not* two-minute stands.

Why on earth, while kissing a woman I'd met today, had my strongest feeling been not to let her leave me again? Actually, that was the strongest *emotion*, in my chest and mind; the earth-shattering feeling was in a whole other place.

Concentrate.

I brought up the image I'd taken of Jimmy's graffiti and stared at it, while my terminal did its own analysis.

λCJ

Daerin Juno

37.48 144.57 libr

Okay. λCJ equals Lambda Capra Jane; easy. Daerin Juno? Was that simply a ref to Aunt Juno being on the Board of the DaerinCorp Research Foundation, or an actual clue? Jimmy's final route into Downside had been via Daerin's data stacks; specifically their Future Projects Division.

But what could any of this have to do with Juno herself? What would be enough to prompt Jimmy Strong to turn into the most-unlikely of heroes to protect her?

And why would Captain Black, a spook from HomeWorld Security, impersonate a missing Spacer? Coz it was obvious – well *now* it was – that Milo Decker and the other four of Charon's five Plungers were indeed the missing Spacers.

If Jimmy had also been searching for them *and* asking about juice bars, then Charon's off-hand remark about use-by dates was the crux of this whole mystery. My 'partner' obviously had the same revelation about the value of 'viable' juice in an age when the expiry-date of genetically-useful men was nearly half-a-century gone.

Dammit. I'd even reminded Decker – or Zanzibar – myself that he was one of only 4000 humans in existence with functioning sperm.

My terminal chimed so I glanced down at Aggie's screen.

Zanzibar Black: Beninzay, female, born Benin, 2068; father Benin, mother Beninzay. Ranks/designations: current – Captain, HomeWorld Security; previous – Medical Officer-Surgeon, Benin MedCentre, Battalion Field Hospitals on Western Front, Sydney and Auckland, North Border.

Bloody hell. Captain Black. Dr Black. North Border Field Hospital. I checked the date of her deployment there.

2116. Eleven years ago. The year I lost my legs in the northern trenches.

No evac for three months from that stinking on-border field hospital. Stranded, in a mostly drug-induced fog, dancing a beguine with the imaginary love of my life. Or so I thought.

I headed out of my office to find out if Chief Bascome had thought to pin the usual visitor's trackerbot on our mysterious bloody HomeWorld spook, so I could track her down and...

My plasma-phone vibrated with my mother's urgent ID again. I'd put her off too many times, so I forced a smile and raised my wrist so we could see each other. I also took the lift to the next floor.

'Finally! I've been calling for hours.'

'I'm kinda busy Mum.'

'I know, Jane. You're investigating your Uncle's murder.'

'He's *not* my uncle.'

'He most surely is today, Jane. He was helping your Aunt.'

'You knew about this?' I snapped.

'No. I just knew he was helping.' My mother – the queen of deniability. 'Not that his endeavours actually helped. She's been kidnapped.'

'What?' I hovered out of the lift and headed for the Chiefs' wing.

'Juno – my sister, your aunt – has been kidnapped.'

'Why didn't you call the cops, Mum?'

'I did. You didn't answer,' she snapped, scowling like *all of this* was my fault.

'There *are* other cops…forget it. How do you know? Is there a ransom demand?'

'I was with her when they snatched her from the Daimaru Flywalk. Three men in masks pushed me over, dragged her into a scootercab and made off with her.'

'Okay Mum. I'm on it, now.' I waved the call off and opened the Chief's door without knocking. He and Chief Jayla Ellen were sharing a meal.

'Sorry Chiefs, but I hope you pinned Captain Black. I need to know her current location; now.'

Chief Bascome knew when urgent meant yesterday. He turned to his terminal. 'Sending you the cords,' he said.

'Have you found the missing men, Agent Capra?'

'Almost, Chief Jayla. I think they're being… Actually I'm not sure what you'd call it. I suspect they're being held captive, probably together, while as avatars they're regularly taken to a hardcore porn suite in Downside for the purposes of arousal. So they can be milked.'

The Chiefs blinked at me and then stared at each other.

'I'll leave you to think about that then, shall I?'

I reverse-hovered to the door. 'Oh yes. One other thing: the President has been kidnapped.'

I was already in the lift by the time both Chiefs rushed in the hall demanding more info.

'Later,' I waved. Aggie was screening the results of my analysis requests. It seemed *37.48 144.57 libr"* was the latitude and longitude of Melbourne's old, very old, Library; which explained why Zan Black's trackerbot placed her on Swanston Canal heading north.

I emerged from SIP HQ, zipped onto the nearest police airboat and asked the pilot to take Russell Canal to La Trobe. The only part of the Victorian Library building that was still above water at high tide was its massive copper-green dome and one upper level; which constituted nearly half its original above-street-level height.

It was 6.20 pm, Melbourne's nightlights were on, a storm was brewing south-west of the city, and the tide was about to come back in. I knew this coz, as the airboat approached one of our few almost-remaining truly historic city landmarks, I could see the extra floor that was exposed every low tide.

I directed my pilot to the pedestrian Skywalk that ran around the dome and off in several directions to connect with the others that spider-webbed the city. The statuesque Beninzay who stood at the apex seemed to be waiting for me.

I joined Captain Zanzibar Black on the high deck that overlooked the dome's oculus. The five-metre wide skylight provided an eerie glimpse into the partially-illuminated interior: 35 metres down to the dry top-most gallery level that ran around the octagonal space.

'It's quite incredible,' Zan noted.

'Yeah,' I agreed. 'When the tide returns that second level down will be back under water though. At the moment it's a good 10 metres deep over the dome room's floor; which is another level above the old street.'

'Bloody weather,' Zan said then turned to me. 'What took you so long?'

'You left me on my arse on the office floor. Then I had to report to the Chiefs.'

'Right,' Zan noted, as if we always talked this way. 'Do you think my boys are in there?'

'Probably; and I think whoever's got them also kidnapped my Aunt Juno today.'

'The President? Damn. What is her connection to all this?'

'Something to do with DaerinCorp's future projects I think. I hope she'll be able to tell us. Shall we suss this joint?

'After you Capra Jane.'

Call me Jane.

Okay, my love.

There was no time to sort our history out now. I pointed Zan to the ladder and hovered beside her as we descended to the concealed service entrance at the base of the dome. My SIP universal passcode gave us immediate access and we slipped into the upper gallery.

There were arguing voices echoing across the 35-metre diameter which made it hard to pinpoint their exact location but, as one, Zan and I pointed to the same spot.

'Why did you camouflage, if that's the right word, yourself as Milo Decker?' I whispered.

'So you would give a damn about what happened to him.'

'What made you think I wouldn't care about these Spacers?'

And, yes, I am offended.

Zan smiled at me. 'You haven't cared about anything much for a decade, Jane.' She headed clockwise through the annulus, the walkway between the concentric walls of the gallery levels, with me right behind her.

'That's not true,' I said.

She turned and raised an eyebrow.

'Okay. So what? You're right. I don't give a shit about anything much.'

'Are you worried about Milo now?'

I squinted at her. 'Maybe. It depends how much of that performance you gave was even him.'

'Oh it was him,' Zan said. 'That's the gift of the Beninzay. With basic information, we can camouflage as anyone. If we've met them, it's even easier. I was as much Milo Decker as he is. It's not sustainable of course; and it *is* only a superficial personality reproduction.'

The argument we'd been approaching stopped suddenly – as if the two men had perhaps heard us. It was a momentary hiatus, followed by the sound of smashing furniture.

Captain Black and I drew our weapons and covered the remaining distance at speed; she ran the 80 metres or so around the annulus, I dropped over the nearest balcony and hovered across the gap. We entered what turned out to be the scene of the crime at the same moment.

Two men were having a full-on fist fight; pushing, shoving and smacking each other senseless. Another bloke was watching them go at it. No one paid us any attention.

The man spectating is Belbo Armitage.

To the right was a row of maybe 40 hospital beds, each with people hooked up to the most basic life-support equipment. To the left, tied by the waist to a chair but drinking a beer, was Aunt Juno.

One of the fighters sent the other sliding face-first across the floor. He came to an unconscious stop at Zan's feet.

'Shit, where'd you two come from?' Armitage fumbled around the table next to him.

'Move again and I *will* shoot you,' I said.

Zan crossed the room, grabbed and threw his semi-auto against the wall and punched him in face.

'Jane darling, how nice of you to come rescue me.'

I shook my head. 'I didn't know I even had to do that until half an hour ago, Juno.' I hovered over, took a laserknife from Aggie's toolkit and cut her free.

When I turned back Zan was going patient to patient, looking for her Spacers. No, it was more than that: she was looking for a certain Spacer.

'Juno, what the hell is this really about? I mean apart from the produce collection that's going on.'

Aunt Juno held my hand as we walked the line of hospital beds. 'All of these men number among the 4000,' she said.

'That much we figured.'

'Judging by their ages, most are original Earthers resistant to the *Mj21 Virus*;' Juno said.

That made sense. The first 20 beds, according to info scrawled on the wall behind, held men aged from 62 to 80. They were all so emaciated though it was hard to tell. None looked half as good as Bruce May and the comatose Dreamers I'd seen at the Liebestraum; only 13 of whom were resistant.

'They're not gonna survive this, *whatever* it is, are they Juno?' I said.

'No, my dear. Maintaining their lives was unimportant to that villainous-excuse for a scientist over there,' she pointed at the bleeding Belbo Armitage. 'Not even the younger ones further down the room will recover enough for their lives to have meaning. This procedure is killing, has, effectively killed them.'

'But…why?' I asked.

'DaerinCorp have been trying for decades to find a cure for the Mantaray retrovirus. Armitage, who I may well execute before we leave this room, worked in our labs until six months ago. He thought he could get Jimmy to break into the Daerin banks to steal the latest breakthroughs to use in his own cloning research.

'Jimmy tried once, because he believed Belbo would assassinate me he didn't, but realised it was beyond him. So he came to me and we set about finding out exactly what Belbo was up to. It's just terrible that it got Jimmy killed.'

I squeezed Juno's hand, but the wash of sorrow that suddenly flooded my senses came not from her, but from Zan at the far end of the room. I went straight to her.

Milo Decker, or what was left of him, was holding Zan's hand. She wiped at the tears trickling down his sunken cheeks, and he opened his eyes.

Again I felt an anguish and heartache that – this time – also brought to mind a day long gone. The day, now real to me, that Zan left me in that field hospital. Left me to the care of others; to return home to the troubles brewing on her own world.

I knew she wouldn't leave this young man. But I also knew he was not going to live to know that.

Are you sure?

The question my mind heard, was for Decker. He blinked, licked his lips and blinked again.

Zan glanced at me. 'Yes, that's her,' she said aloud.

Decker smiled, barely.

Zan leant forward, kissed his forehead and – before I could do anything to stop her – put her gun to Decker's head and pulled the trigger.

'What the frak?' I dragged her away from the bedside. She let me do it and then crumpled to the floor.

For the second time today I set Aggie down on the floor and threw myself out.

Zan allowed me to hold her and we sat rocking for a moment.

'I don't understand,' I whispered. 'Why camouflage as him and then do that?'

Zan held me at arm's length as her blue-green-blue eyes searched mine. 'Do you care that he's dead?'

Stupid question!

'Yes, Zan. I liked him; you, him a lot. I really do care.'

'I needed to reach you. Make you care again.' She smiled wanly. 'He was my grandfather.'

'Oh dear,' said Juno.

Zan glanced at her then back at me. 'It was three years ago, for him, on that Probe Ship; 58 years ago for my grandmother. Milo Decker and Zanzi Aru were famous in the history of everything as the first Benin-Human coupling.

'I came back to Earth for him,' she said. 'And for you.'

Zan got to her feet, then bent and lifted me back into Aggie.

And I let her; which was something I'd never allowed anyone else to do.

Clan Destine Press would like to thank
our fabulous editors, **Ruth Wykes** & **Kylie Fox**;
artist **Vicky Pratt** for the wonderful title page illustrations; **Ron Gallagher** for the illustration on page 379, & artist **Sarah Pain** for the amazing cover art and design.

When we sent out the coded message to the cohort of Aussie and a few Kiwi genre writers to come and play in our sandpit, we were thrilled by the response.

We thank the 32 authors who dared to take up the challenge, causing us to extend the ***And Then...*** project to two volumes.

We salute their willingness to gird the loins of their heroes, don their many-coloured hats, lock-and-load their explodey things and set off on adventures galorious.

In many cases our authors – for now they are *ours* – not only bent but tripped out of their usual genres to seek action elsewhere.

And Then... was partly funded by fellow writers and two Indiegogo campaigns.
We would like to thank the following people for their generous support.

Tor Roxburgh	Angela Lorrigan	Moraig Kisler	L.J. Owen
Amra Pajalic	Yael Bornstein	Ann Davies	Anne Burgi
Aramanth Dawe	Bec Stafford	Bookfrivolity	Bronwennq
Catherine Heloise	Cathy Green	Cheryl Rush	Chris Bongers
Christmas Press	Claudia Colin	Danielle Kovacic	Fiona
Demet Divaroren	Diana Mumme	Diane McWhirter	Julie Bozza
Jodi Lazarou	Joelle Parrott	Julia Scott	Kath Harper
Katharine Stubbs	Kathryn Ledson	Kbmail	Kerrie Duff
Kym Poxon	Leslie Falkiner-Rose	Laurai	Lindymb
Lohma003	LynC	Marcus Liddle	Tim Marsh
Mary Borsellino	Terry O'Connell	Narrelle Harris	Olivia
Natalie Conyer	Sandra Dusconi	Paul May	R Perry
Rachel Smith	Robin Storey	Sally Koetsveld	Pamela
Samuel Spettigue	Therese M Noble	Susanne Munro	silentdan2017
Sandra Wigzell	Tsana Dolichva	Read Cafe Surfers Paradise	

And Then...
the Authors

Cameron Ashley

Cam was chief editor of *Crime Factory* magazine and co-publisher of its book publishing arm. Cam's articles and fiction have appeared both online and in print; and includes stories in the Aussie noir collection, *Hard Labour*, and the Lee-Marvin-inspired collection *Lee.* He writes a weekly column for Eisner award winning retailer, *All Star Comics* , and is at work on several fiction projects.

Mary Borsellino

Mary lives in Melbourne, has lots of tattoos and writes dark YA and adult supernatural/fantasy. She's author of the YA *Thrive*; the five-book *The Wolf House; The Devil's Mixtape;* and the shorts, *Loveless* &*Table for Three.*

Jack Dann & Steven Paulsen

Jack is a multiple-award-winning author and editor of over 75 books, including the international bestsellers *The Memory Cathedral* and *The Silent.* Other collections include: *Promised Land, Timetipping, Visitations* and *The Fiction Factory*. He is co-editor, with Janeen Webb, of *Dreaming Down-Under,* which won a World Fantasy Award; editor of its sequel *Dreaming Again*; and editor of *Dreaming in the Dark,* which won a 2017 World Fantasy Award.

Steven's bestselling dark fantasy children's book, *The Stray Cat* – illustrated by Hugo and Oscar award-winning artist Shaun Tan – has seen publication in several English and foreign language editions. His short stories, which Isobelle Carmody describes as beautifully written and subtle, have appeared in magazines and in anthologies around the world. His short story collection, *Shadows on the Wall* (IFWG Publishing Australia, 2018) contains the best of Paulsen's dark and weird tales plus new fiction written expressly for the book.

Lindy Cameron

Lindy, President of Sisters in Crime Australia and Publisher of Clan Destine Press, authored the Kit O'Malley PI novels – *Blood Guilt, Bleeding Hearts* and *Thicker Than Water*; the action thriller *Redback;* the mystery *Golden Relic;* and co-wrote the true crime anthologies *Killer in the Family*, *Murder in the Family*, and *Women Who Kill.* She's currently writing historical fiction featuring time-travelling archaeologists and Amazons.

Sarah Evans

Sarah writes crime, romance, horror and fantasy. She's published novels, short stories (some broadcast on ABC Radio), songs, poetry, and a lifestyle-recipe book. With Clan Destine Fictions, she has *Call of the Wild, Killing Kindness* and *New Blood*. Sarah teaches creative writing and edits children's books. She's won several category prizes in the annual Scarlet Stiletto Awards, with stories published in *Scarlet Stiletto: the First Cut,* and the *Second Cut*; and is author of the comic crime novel *Operation Paradise.*

Kelly Gardiner

Kelly's YA novels *Act of Faith* and *The Sultan's Eyes* were listed for the NSW Premier's Literary Awards. Books for younger readers include the three-book *Swashbuckler* pirate adventures, and the picture book, *Billabong Bill's Bushfire Christmas*. Her first novel for adults, *Goddess*, is based on 17th-century French swordswoman, Mademoiselle de Maupin; and her latest book, *1917*, is set during the Great War for readers aged nine and up.

Alison Goodman

Alison's award-winning novel *The Dark Days Club* – first in the Lady Helen trilogy of supernatural Regency adventures – was followed by *The Dark Days Pact*, which won the 2016 Aurealis Award for Best YA novel; and 2018's *The Dark Days Deceit*. Alison is a repeat offender when it comes to the Aurealis Awards: *Eon*, the first of her *New York Times* bestselling fantasy duology (*Eon* and *Eona*) won the 2008 Best Fantasy Novel; and *Singing the Dogstar Blues* won Best YA novel in 1998. She is also the author of the crime novel, *A New Kind of Death*.

David Greagg & **Kerry Greenwood**

Kerry and **David** are a gestalt entity who read each other's minds and cover each other's linguistic and musical omissions. She does romance languages while he does Germanic and weird tongues. And she sings soprano so he doesn't have to. She costumes and makes stuff, while he wears armour and hits people with sticks. They were raised in the forest by benevolent wood-elves and are co-curators of a Found Cats' Home. They both write, and finish each other's sentences. Kerry is the author of both the Phryne Fisher and the Corinna Chapman series. With Clan Destine Press she has her ancient history novels: *Out of the Black Land; The Delphic Women* trilogy of *Medea, Cassandra* and *Electra*; and *Herotica*. David writes about gentlemen cats in *Dougal's Diary and When We Were Kittens*, and Vikings.

James Hopwood

James (aka David J Foster) is author of retro-spy thrillers, *The Librio Defection* , *The Danakil Deception*, and *The Ambrosia Kill*. His short fiction has appeared in several publications. As Jack Tunney, he's also scribed the Fight Card series: *King of the Outback, Rumble in the Jungle* & *The Iron Fists of Ned Kelly*.

Maria Lewis

Maria's supernatural action novels – *Who's Afraid?* and *Who's Afraid Too?* – are currently being adapted for television. A journalist and scriptwriter, Maria's articles have appeared in *The New York Post, The Daily Mail, Empire Magazine*, and more. She's a presenter on SBS Viceland's news program, and producer of the *Eff Yeah Film & Feminism* podcast. Her latest novel, *It Came from the Deep*, is her first foray in YA science fiction.

Andrew Nette

Andrew is a Melbourne crime writer, journalist and pulp scholar, whose short fiction has appeared in print and on-line. He's the author of two crime novels: *Ghost Money*, set in Cambodia; and *Gunshine State*, set in Queenaland. Andrew is co-editor of *Beat Girls, Love Tribes and Real Cool Cats: Pulp Fiction and Youth Culture, 1950 - 1980*.

Amanda Pillar

Amanda, an archaeologist by day, is the author of the Graced series of books and stories; the Moonlit Hills series (with K.V. Adair); and several other short stories and novellas. She lives in Victoria with her husband and cats Saxon and Lilith.

Michael Pryor

Michael writes fantasy and science fiction, mostly for teenagers. With more than 30 novels and 50-something short stories published, he's been shortlisted six times for the Aurealis Awards, and seven of his books have been CBCA Notable books. His series fiction includes: and *The Quentaris Chronicles*, co-written with Paul Collins; *The Extraordinaires* (*The Extinction Gambit* & *The Subterranean Stratagem*); the six-book, *Laws of Magic*. Michael has a sequel to his latest book, *Gap Year in Ghost Town,* due in 2019.

Fin J Ross

Fin is a journalist and creative writing teacher who also runs a cattery and breeds cats. She co-wrote (with Lindy Cameron) the True Crime anthologies: *Killer in the Family* and *Murder in the Family*. She's the author of *AKA Fudgepuddle*, the 'true-life' adventures of a cat called Juno; and the forthcoming historical novel, *Billings Better Bookstore and Brasserie*. Recently side-tracked into writing crime fiction, she has won several category prizes in the annual Sisters in Crime Australia Scarlet Stiletto Awards, and has stories in three *Scarlet Stiletto 'cuts', (anthologies): the 6th , 7th* and *8th Cuts.*

www.ingramcontent.com/pod-product-compliance
Lightning Source LLC
Chambersburg PA
CBHW060633310726
48982CB00003B/756